The door to Katie's room stood open. A glance reassured Britt that she was sleeping soundly. Katie lay on her side, her long hair spread out over the pink pillowcase, the covers tossed aside in the unseasonably warm air that had followed the rain.

Silently, she groped her way down the stairs. Reaching the kitchen, she stopped in her tracks. The room was black; no light shone through the window from the patio.

Check the switch, she told herself. She inched her way toward the sliding glass door, knowing where to step, what to touch to avoid bumping into something. About to open the drapes, she hesitated, peeking out from between the folds. She leaned closer to the door and pressed her nose against the glass.

A dark shape moved.

Britt jumped back. Shock took her breath. Her knees bent like folding table legs, and she grabbed the counter to steady herself. She resisted an urge to scream. . . .

Books by Donna Anders:

The Flower Man
Another Life
Dead Silence
In All the Wrong Places

Published by POCKET BOOKS

For information regarding special discounts for bulk purchases, please contact Simon & Schuster Special Sales at 1-800-456-6798 or business@simonandschuster.com

THE
FLOWER
MAN

DONNA ANDERS

POCKET BOOKS
New York   London   Toronto   Sydney   Tokyo   Singapore

An *Original* Publication of POCKET BOOKS

POCKET BOOKS, a division of Simon & Schuster Inc.
1230 Avenue of the Americas, New York, NY 10020

ISBN 978-1-5011-8225-9

First Pocket Books printing November 1995

10 9 8 7 6 5 4 3 2 1

POCKET and colophon are registered trademarks of Simon & Schuster Inc.

Cover art by Paul Barton/The Stock Market

Printed in the U.S.A.

For my sisters and brothers
Diane and Erik Ronnegard, Glenn and Nancy
Anderson, with love always

ACKNOWLEDGMENTS

For their friendship, expert advice, encouragement, and support, I am deeply grateful to Ann Rule, Leslie Rule, Jeanie Okimoto, Anne Jaeger, and Cheri Luxa. Special thanks to my daughters: Tina Abeel who scaled the fly system with me to take my research photos, Ruth Aeschliman who stayed up all night with the doors locked reading my first draft, and Lisa Pearce, a world-class brainstormer of story plots. Last, but certainly not least, my thanks to Michael Rule for his expertise on competitive sports.

I would like to thank Bill Grose, Julie Rubenstein, my editor, and everyone at Pocket Books.

FOREWORD

There are in our society, in frighteningly increasing numbers, adults who view children as *love objects,* or even more terrifying, as *prey.* Each predator, usually a man, is as obsessive, compulsive, and fixated on his chosen child as the stalker who relentlessly pursues his adult female "lovee," even unto death.

The stalking pedophile is often a loner with a convoluted and compartmentalized life. His job, his friendships, any relationships with adult females, are all kept safely separate from one another. A pedophile often has been abused, humiliated and stripped of self-confidence during childhood. As an adult he may be afraid to participate in a sexual relationship with a grown woman. She is too threatening, too liable to recognize his inadequacy. He may even have experienced ridicule from a woman about his sexual performance or the size of his genitals. He himself may perceive, wrongly, that his genitals are undersized and that he is not the man other men are.

A pedophile may regard women as whores, and see only a child as pure. His own motivation is not pure. The child he fixates on is usually just at the budding phase of puberty—a child at the edge of womanhood—her breasts barely discernible—perhaps nine to twelve. There is no way to be certain about what went wrong in the psyche of a pedophile. It may have been his child-hood environment; it may be genetic. It may have been one single traumatic incident in his past. The whys are hard to pin down, but his objectives are crystal clear: power, dominance, and control. Inside, he has no power; he is as empty as a paper bag, although his facade may be one of brute strength.

The man who focuses on a single child as a sex object is not the typical serial pedophile who victimizes one youngster after another; his concentration on his "lover" excludes everything else. He will not be dissuaded, nor will he transfer his "affection." With cunning dedication, he will be a ghostly presence on the periphery of the child's life, always watching, waiting his chance. He will persevere for years if necessary.

A child stalker is a manipulative sociopath, an eroto-maniac, as well as a pedophile. His tunnel vision makes him ultimately dangerous, fully capable of killing those people who stand in his way. His innocent victim will become dehumanized by a terror she is incapable of coping with, or even understanding. The adults in her world will eventually be as vulnerable—and as scarred —as the victim.

Child stalking is epidemic in America today. As this is written, there are new cases being reported almost daily in the wire services across the country. *The Flower Man* is a composite of these cases, and, tragically, of cases yet to come.

THE
FLOWER
MAN

PROLOGUE

September 1992

SHE LAY IN A PATCH OF WILD FORGET-ME-NOTS, HER BLOND hair shining like a halo around her head. She was so still, as perfect as a photograph, her blue eyes wide open. Only the blood on her naked body told the real story: she had died violently.

The man behind the wheel slammed on the brakes and brought the van to a skidding stop. He shook his head to clear the image from his mind, forcing himself to concentrate on the school yard below the hill where he had stopped.

He had timed his arrival just right. The recess bell rang. A moment later the grade school doors burst open and children ran from the building, their voices filling the clear September afternoon. The man pulled off his dark glasses to study the youngsters who played their games, unaware of his presence.

He didn't see *her*.

She would have blond hair and blue eyes, and she would remember him. They had been together during many past lifetimes. His thoughts raced ahead. Once he found her again, he would take care of her better than ever before. She belonged to him, and she would understand that intuitively.

I'm up here. He concentrated on speaking to her

1

telepathically. *Give me a sign, so I will know you.* He repeated the message over and over, like a mantra.

No one glanced in his direction. His hands tightened on the wheel; sudden heat blistered his forehead with sweat. He felt as if he were invisible, as if he hadn't yet been reborn . . . as if he were a nonperson.

Like being locked in the closet when he was little, becoming one with the darkness so it wouldn't hurt him. He could still hear his mother's voice: "You stay in there, Buddy, you hear?" And her coarse laugh, and the man's —*and the other sounds.*

His heart fluttered, and he began to wheeze. He clawed through the glove compartment, dumping the contents on the floor until he found his nebulizer. He sucked the spray from the mouthpiece, then gulped deep breaths.

The school bell rang again to signal the end of recess. The children lined up, and he could see them clearly as they marched through the door. By the time the last child disappeared into the building, his frustration had begun to suffocate him.

She hadn't been there.

He forced himself to stay calm. Why couldn't he find her? His hands tightened into fists, as if by sheer willpower he could suspend time, hold back the darkness that always came unbidden, the memories that confused and terrified him.

Concentrate, he told himself. Focus on something.

His gaze fastened on a stand of Douglas fir trees beyond the school. Gradually the mental images receded from the space he controlled. He was the eye of the hurricane; he would not be sucked into the swirling madness that surrounded him.

The boughs look so green against the faded blue sky, he thought, and concentrated harder, aware that the darkness still hovered on the edge of his awareness. How wispy and seductive the trees were when the wind danced through their branches. Do female trees seduce male trees? he wondered.

The inane question spiraled upward to overpower his

control, to free the demons locked in his brain until his mind became a light show of flashing perceptions. He knew what was coming. It had come many times over the years since that day when he was fourteen.

Fight it. Fight it. Don't look.

He grabbed his nebulizer and gulped in more vapor. Frantically he started the engine, twisted the wheel, and floorboarded the accelerator. He had to find his beloved soon. Only she could banish his terror, make everything all right.

His tires blew gravel, and dust boiled up from under the wheels. Desperation was a bitter bile in his throat. Just before the van reached the freeway, he leaned close to the open window and spit it out.

Next time, he thought.

She will be there next time.

PART ONE

Fall 1992

1

Hidden in the darkness, the man watched through slits in his mask. The room had been diminished to a small circle of lamplight by the encroachment of night. Ceiling-high shadows threw eerie patterns out of the corners and across the Oriental rug to the feet of Britt Hinson, who sat reading.

Absorbed, Britt was unaware of the subtle shift of shadow on shadow, of a sound no louder than the whisper of a page being turned. She didn't see the form of a man separate itself from the darker hues of the room, nor did she hear his stealthy approach from behind her. His black gloved hand on her throat came as a shock.

"No! Please, no!"

Her startled cry was cut off by leather-clad fingers jammed into her mouth, gagging her. Her head was pressed into the cushioned chairback, and the book clattered to the floor. Desperate for air, she clawed at the gloved hands. Her assailant's grip only tightened, his arms lowering to trap hers against the sides of her body. She kicked, her legs thrashing to no avail, because their target was behind her.

She couldn't breathe. Tiny flashing lights danced over her vision, and she felt as if she were floating away, as if she were dying. Panic surged as she made one last effort to free herself.

Squirming lower in the overstuffed chair, Britt twisted away when her attacker momentarily adjusted his grip in an attempt to stop her struggle. Briefly, her eyes were caught by his. Lamplight blazed in his black pupils. She was jolted by an instant of absolute terror. It was as though something evil looked back at her.

"Stop—stop!" she cried hoarsely, breaking the scene. "You're hurting me, Jeb. That's not in the script."

"Huh?" Jeb jerked his hands away from her, as though he'd been scorched by her flesh. He straightened to his full six feet, shaking his head as if to clear it. "Britt, I'm sorry. I was really into it." He pulled off his gloves, then yanked off his ski mask so that his brown hair tumbled over his forehead. "I swear, it was like I had a fix on the killer's thoughts."

"I noticed." Britt's voice shook. She stood up, massaging her neck. The struggle had pulled her shirt tail out of her jeans, and she tucked it back in. "You scared me. For a second I thought you *were* the killer."

His eyes widened in surprise. "I was only trying to make the bastard come to life."

"But you don't have to kill me to do it," Britt said, combing back her long blond hair with her fingernails.

"Kill you? You've got to be kidding. I'm an actor, not a murderer."

"I know that, Jeb," she said, regaining her composure. "But it still feels like you sprained my neck."

Britt stooped to pick up the book. Playing Cozy, a brassy but classy prostitute who lured the wrong man to her bed and became his murder victim, was depressing. She wondered if it was worth the psychological effect it had on her. This play, *The Man Who Loved Dead Women*, was a downer—and a challenge to her acting skills.

She straightened up. Jeb Walker could deny it, but he was adversely affected by the story, too. Who wouldn't be? Toni Bucci had actually interviewed serial killers before she wrote the play, and her research showed. It was too close to the bone. Britt wondered if Portland,

Oregon, was ready for such a gruesome slice of reality. Had they not already started rehearsing off-book, she would have let someone else take over her role.

The house lights came on, and the director strode down the middle aisle to the stage. "Damn it, Britt! Jeb was on top of the scene. What in hell's eating you?"

Britt held his gaze, determined not to back down. Art Sills sometimes lost his formidable temper when a scene didn't go his way. Despite his diminutive size, wild hair, and unpretentious way of dressing in jeans, T-shirts, and Birkenstocks, he could outshout anyone at rehearsal.

"Nothing that living and breathing won't cure, Art," she said. "Jeb was suffocating me."

"This is the story of a fucking psycho." Art's tone was deceptively calm. "Have you forgotten? We're striving for realism."

"I know, but—"

"No fucking buts about it. You can either act the part or you can't."

"Acting is not the issue."

"What the hell is, then?" Art scowled at her.

"Jeb can portray the killer without jamming his fist down my throat and squeezing my neck so I can't breathe."

"Now wait a minute, Britt," Jeb said, interrupting. "You don't think I was really trying to hurt you?" He hesitated. "I'm an actor, not a psycho."

She chewed on her bottom lip, feeling frustrated. Maybe she had overreacted. The scene was difficult and they'd both flubbed it, only Jeb's ego wouldn't allow him to admit it.

"Look, let's do the scene again," she said finally. "Just fake the violence, Jeb. I know you didn't mean to kill me, but that's what it felt like." She was about to plop back into the chair when Art's voice stopped her.

"Hell, that's it for tonight. The mood's gone and it's getting late." His voice grated with irritation. "Think you can stay in character tomorrow night, Britt?"

"You know I can," she retorted, "but this time the scene got too real. I'd appreciate it if you'd direct Jeb to lighten up next time."

Britt shivered, feeling the dampness of the September night. She hated being on the defensive, but if she didn't stick up for herself, Art would shout her down. Jeb's portrayal of the killer had scared her: it was that simple.

"This discussion can wait. Everyone's tired, including me." Art inclined his head toward the stage manager and Angie Moore, the costume designer, who was gathering up her notes. "Tomorrow night, everyone. Seven sharp." He left them without a good-bye.

"I'm sorry if I hurt you," Jeb said. "I didn't mean to."

She smiled. "I'm sorry if I sounded bitchy."

He grinned back. "We'll get it right tomorrow."

Britt nodded and headed backstage to pick up her handbag and jacket. She wanted to get home anyway. Sam, her two-year-old, had the croup. And her husband, Mark, had to leave for work earlier than usual in the morning, which meant she'd have to get up at sunrise if she were to do her five-mile jog before he left.

"Hey. Don't go yet," Angie called behind her. "I have something to show you. I'll be there in a minute."

Britt waited in the hall by the dressing room, her mind replaying the scene with Jeb. Her glance moved over the dark-paneled walls. Somehow a play about a serial killer didn't fit the turn-of-the-century ambience of City Theater.

She loved the drafty old building with its crimson carpeting and drapes, its crystal chandeliers and the huge stained-glass dome over the auditorium. It was ornate and still elegant—when the lights were low. Although the theater lacked state-of-the-art lighting and a modern fly system, Britt felt that its age only added to its charm.

"What's with the smile? I thought you were upset."

She hadn't seen Angie's approach. "I was thinking about how much I love this theater."

"That figures." Angie grinned. "You love old houses and antiques."

Britt stepped into the dressing room, then held the mahogany door open for Angie. "And I wasn't really upset, just scared."

"What happened?" Angie's dark eyes registered concern. "I wasn't watching the scene."

Britt explained. "I'm really having doubts about this part, Angie. It's not right for me."

"But you're doing a great job. I think the play is just, uh . . . different."

"It's more than that. It's ugly. But I'm stuck with it now." She managed a grin. "Hey, you need a ride home?"

She often dropped Angie off after rehearsal. Angie and her husband, Bill, lived at the foot of the West Hills, only minutes from Britt's house a couple miles farther up the hill. Bill, a reporter for the *Oregonian,* and Mark were friends; they shared a passion for sports.

"Thanks, but not tonight. Bill's picking me up for a late supper." Her curly black hair, always unruly, stood out in all directions where she'd run her hand through it while she worked. "This is *the night.* Bill even agreed to miss Monday night football with Mark and the guys, so you know how anxious he is to have a kid. We're setting the stage—you know, candlelight and wine. Maybe we'll get lucky and I'll get pregnant."

"It'll happen."

"Before I'm forty, I hope."

Britt knew better than to joke about Angie having a baby. Like Britt, Angie was thirty-seven. She'd seen specialists, followed a healthy diet, and taken her temperature daily to determine the time in the month when she was the most fertile. Bill's sperm count was low, and artificial insemination would be their next step if she didn't get pregnant soon. Bill was thin, high-strung, and concerned about being over forty, and Britt secretly thought he put too much pressure on Angie to conceive.

They moved to the long makeup table and picked up their handbags. A row of bar lights above the mirror illuminated them in a stark brilliance that revealed every

11

line, wrinkle, and imperfection. Thirty-seven wasn't twenty-one.

Angie and I don't look our age—except in this light, Britt thought. Angie was small, dark, and serious while she was tall, slender, and blond. Angie was a free spirit, an only child whose parents had once been hippies. She dressed in gauzy skirts and oversized sweaters and often wore hiking boots. Her fringed suede shoulder purse was a bag lady's dream. Britt waited while she rummaged through its rattling contents.

"Here it is." Angie handed a newspaper clipping to Britt. "Read the ad in the bottom left corner. The one about the competition to find child models. They're using this theater."

"Why would that interest me?" Britt shook her head. "These groups aren't legitimate as far as I'm concerned."

"Go on, Britt. Just read it."

Angie doted on Britt's daughter, Katie, often giving her old clothes and makeup to play dress-up. She meant well, so Britt resisted the urge to toss the ad away. After scanning it, she glanced up.

"It's a bunch of crap, Angie. A moneymaking scheme for the promoters. Only starstruck moms fall for this hype—and everyone knows I'm not one of those."

"But you love acting, and so does Katie."

"This isn't acting. When Katie is older, she can take classes, if she still wants to. She's only nine. She has plenty of time." Britt dropped the ad into her purse. "The promoter is probably sleazy. I know his type. I wouldn't dream of allowing Katie to do this."

"Come on, Britt. Lighten up." Angie's grin took the bite from her words. "I wasn't suggesting Katie run off to Hollywood. Only have a little fun strutting her stuff, like she does in those backyard productions she puts on for the neighbor kids. You know what a ham she is." She hesitated. "Takes after her mom."

Britt forced a smile. "I'm still feeling a bit unsettled. I guess the scene with Jeb shook me up more than I realized." She caught a glimpse of herself in the mirror.

Her eyes, usually a bright blue, seemed to have lost their sparkle. "I've never been that scared onstage before."

"You've never had a role like this before."

"You're right." Britt nodded. "And I'm tired. I was up most of the night because of Sam's coughing."

Angie grabbed her things. "So give the ad a second glance when you're not tired. It would be fun for Katie. And who knows? Maybe she'll win. Think of that. Katie Hinson, the Shirley Temple of the nineties."

"Heaven forbid. She's pretty dramatic already."

"She's also a very well adjusted kid. It wouldn't hurt her."

"Kids grow up too fast these days," Britt said, frowning. "I want mine to enjoy their childhood. That's why I quit my job when Sam was born—to be home when they needed me. Reality hits them soon enough." Britt pulled out her car keys. "You know what I mean, Angie. You and I were both acting by the time we were ten." She shook her head. "I don't want that monkey on Katie's back."

"We loved it—don't forget that. And we didn't lose our childhood."

"No, but we got our hearts broken, remember? We believed we were destined for Broadway." Britt held the door again and they headed for the back entrance. "It was a hell of an adjustment when we had to settle for local productions because there were so many other actresses with more talent."

"It wasn't that bad, Britt."

"It was for me. I don't want Katie on that merry-go-round."

They stepped outside into the rain. Impulsively, Britt hugged Angie. "See you tomorrow," she said. "And— break a leg tonight!"

Angie gave her the thumbs-up sign, then darted toward the waiting car. Britt sprinted across the street, dodging puddles, to her aging Volvo which she'd parked in a lot. She started the engine and switched on the wipers.

Britt headed over to Jefferson, then took Vista to wind

up into the West Hills. In only minutes she was out of the downtown area, following the wet, tree-lined road that curled and twisted through the peaceful ambience of Portland Heights. The Old World charm of turn-of-the-century houses set behind retaining walls lush with flowers and shrubs came as a welcome relief. The higher she climbed, the calmer she felt. This was her part of town, and she loved it.

She was ready to relax, maybe have a glass of wine. Let Sam have a good night, she told herself. And let the Monday night football game be over and Mark's TV-watching buddies already be gone when I get home.

2

DAMN, BRITT THOUGHT. THE GAME MUST NOT BE OVER. THERE was still a car parked in front of the house. Mark's football cronies hadn't left yet.

The garage doors whispered shut behind the Volvo. Britt unsnapped her seat belt and got out of the car. She reached back for her handbag and made sure that her playbook was still tucked inside. She wanted to read through the first act again, get a better fix on the stalking scene. She had no intention of losing her concentration tomorrow night.

Britt was almost around Mark's Honda when the automatic light connected to the garage door mechanism went out. Oh, shit, she thought, disoriented for a second by the absolute blackness. She was never quick enough to make it to the door. A prickle of fear rippled down her spine.

Silly ninny, she told herself, still jumpy from rehearsal. For Pete's sake, get a grip.

With outstretched hands, she groped for the house entrance. She tried not to think of her mother's claim that an unexpected case of the heebie-jeebies was a precognition that something was about to happen. I'm just tired and worried about Sam's croup, she reminded herself.

Her hand found the doorknob but before she could turn it, the door opened. Light spilled from the laundry room into the garage. She jumped, startled.

"Mark! You scared me." Her laugh sounded shaky.

"So I see." His quizzical expression was the same one he gave a ledger that didn't balance. "Who did you think would open the door, the Phantom of the Opera? I live here, remember? I was in the kitchen and heard the garage door."

He stood in the doorway, looking taller than his six feet two. His burgundy velour shirt was open at the neck, and his dark curly hair looked disheveled from repeated fingering, a testimony to his passion for football. He peered at her from behind his dark-rimmed glasses.

Britt bent down to pet the tan cocker spaniel who'd run out from the kitchen to greet her. "Hello, Tippy, you good, good boy," she said, rubbing the dog's long, soft ears. "Inside, fella," she told him, patting his rear end to send him back into the kitchen. Then she straightened up and stepped closer to Mark, dropping her handbag on the dryer. "Come here, Mr. Bogeyman." She pulled his face down, removed his glasses, and planted a kiss on his mouth. "There, I feel better now, not scared at all."

"Mmmm," he murmured against her lips. "The guys are just leaving, and the kids are asleep." He pulled her into his arms and held her close. "So you and I are going to have a glass of wine in the den, once we're alone."

"Are you trying to seduce me?"

"What do you think?"

She bit playfully at his mouth. He was a great lover—when he wasn't preoccupied with work. Since being promoted to chief financial officer at Carver's, Inc., a

15

high-tech industrial firm, he often worked evenings at home. Watching football with his friends once a week was a way for him to relax.

"Come on, let's say good-night to my buddies."

Mark reached around her and pulled the door closed. He took back his glasses and put them on as they moved into the kitchen, interrupting the conversation between two men who were putting freshly washed dishes back in the cupboards.

"Hi, Jim." Britt grinned at the tall, muscular blond man, Mark's best friend since childhood. "What did I do to deserve such preferential treatment? Mark usually leaves the dirty dishes for me."

Jim indicated the tall, lean man next to him. "Len is the one to thank. He twisted our arms, and insisted we clean up after ourselves."

Britt's eyes shifted to the sandy-haired man who'd turned from the sink. "We haven't met, but your reputation has preceded you," she said. "Angie says as long as Len Holmes is with the guys the place will always be cleaned up." She stepped forward and offered her hand. "I'm Britt, in case you haven't already guessed."

His return smile started slow, as though her words had embarrassed him. "I've heard about you, too, Britt— and I'm pleased to finally meet you." His voice was deep but soft, and his grasp was firm. "There's only one thing I hate more than dirty dishes, and that's waking up to them in the morning."

"Len is single," Mark said, as though that explained everything.

"Not because I want to be." Len put up his hands in mock horror, his pale blue eyes twinkling with humor. "You guys just don't know how lucky you are to have wives who clean up after you."

"Hey, man, you can always get married." Jim flashed his crooked teeth in a wicked grin. "Don't let him kid you, Britt. Len's a freelance photographer. He has a dozen women lined up—models, starlets, even a lawyer and a doctor—all waiting for him to settle down. Trouble is, it's an embarrassment of riches. He can't choose."

Len grimaced. "I'm not a Don Juan. There aren't as many available women as you think. The good ones, like Angie and Deb and Britt, are already taken. But I'm still hoping—and looking. I've been married once, so next time has to be for keeps."

"We'll keep our eyes open," Britt said, liking him. For all the ribbing, he seemed a little shy. Mark had told her that his ex-wife had cleaned him out in the divorce and immediately married another man. He'd been left with only his photography equipment.

"Thanks for the use of your house, Britt," Len said as the two men stepped outside and headed for Jim's car. "Next time I hope I get to meet the kids."

Mark closed the door behind them. "Great guys—but I'm glad they're gone. I'll pour us some wine and meet you in the den."

His expectant smile reminded Britt of the Mark she'd met when they were both students at the University of Washington up in Seattle. It had been a case of opposites attracting. Someone had brought him to a cast party, introduced her, and in a matter of weeks they were a couple. Later he'd confessed she was his reason for crashing the party.

She grinned, remembering how persistent he'd been. Tenacity was one of his stronger character traits, she'd learned later. He went after what he wanted—earning his CPA license and master's degree in one year and then setting up college funds and ensuring a comfortable life for his family.

"I'll peek in on Katie and Sam while you get the wine. Okay?"

He gave her a push. "Just don't wake them. And hurry back. Some things can't wait."

They separated in the vaulted hall that divided the house. Mark moved toward the kitchen, and Britt headed for the wide staircase and the upstairs bedrooms.

"Oh, I almost forgot." Mark turned back. "Dick Burnham called, your computer company client. Said he needed to talk to you about the employee policy and procedure manual. He wants you to call him in the morning."

"Gotcha. Thanks."

She was pleased. Despite Mark's doubts, she was getting her freelance human resource consulting business off the ground. Her timing had been good. With the poor economy, many corporations had eliminated their human resource departments and were relying on contract services. Her goal was to be a full-time mother with a part-time consulting business she could manage from home.

Britt went to Sam's room first. He was sprawled sideways, his covers kicked away. One chubby arm was flung over his curly black hair, the other clutched Mr. Mort, his teddy bear, against his chest. My precious baby, she thought. Mommy wants you to get over that bad croup. He looked like Mark, same dark eyes and hair and incredibly long eyelashes. "The men always have the lashes," her mother often said with feigned disgust.

Bending down, Britt brushed Sam's forehead with her lips. He still sounded stuffed up, but he felt cool. Thank goodness, she thought.

Gently she pulled up the quilt, then propped a pillow to keep him from falling on the floor. My little Sam is growing up, she told him under her breath. So proud of his big-boy bed since we took the crib away.

She left his door ajar so she could hear him if he started coughing, then went to Katie's room at the back corner of the house. Katie had chosen the room because there was a robin's nest in the tree outside her window. When a baby bird had fallen from the nest in a windstorm, she'd nursed it, cried when it died, and then held a funeral for it in the backyard. Katie was a neighborhood Good Samaritan who always found homes for stray cats and dogs.

A tree branch scraped against the window, drawing

Britt's gaze to the night beyond the pink Priscilla curtains. Katie liked her drapes open at night. It was a habit she'd picked up from Harriet and Paul, Mark's mother and stepfather who lived downtown in a condominium on the Willamette River. "No one can see in once the lights are out, Mom," Katie would explain, parroting her grandmother.

Britt stood beside Katie's bed, marveling at the difference in her children. Katie's hair was as white-blond as hers had once been, and she had Britt's blue eyes. She was fair, and Sam was dark like Mark. Britt tucked the blanket around her neck. She'd hoped for a son like Mark, and Mark had wanted a daughter who looked like her. They'd both gotten their wish.

Katie's eyelids opened briefly. "I love you, Mom."

"Love you too, sweetheart," Britt whispered. "See you in the morning."

Back in the hall, Britt hurried to the master bedroom at the end of the hall and quickly slipped into a navy silk nightgown, a recent birthday present from Mark's parents. She brushed her teeth and hair, and after a quick glance at the mirror, headed downstairs, her bare feet silent on the steps.

The curved staircase, lighted by a crystal chandelier, was her favorite part of the 1920s house. Although the plumbing and wiring had been updated, the original woodwork and fixtures had been left intact. It had taken her and Mark's joint salaries to qualify for financing, but the house was worth it. The quiet neighborhood was a safe place to raise children.

A sudden burst of windblown rain sprayed the stained glass windows beside the front door, startling her. She quickened her step and joined Mark in the den in the back corner of the house. The small room was their retreat, comfortably furnished with an old tweed sofa and an overstuffed chair, hand-me-downs from Harriet and Paul when they'd moved from a house to a condominium.

"I was beginning to think you'd gone to bed."

Mark patted the cushion next to him. Two glasses of white wine sat on the little table at his elbow. He handed her one after she sat down.

"A toast. To us," he said softly. "To our future. May we always make the right decisions."

"We usually do, don't you think?" Britt stretched her legs toward the warmth of the fire in the fireplace.

"Uh-huh, most of the time." They clinked their glasses and took a sip. Then Mark brushed a kiss across her cheek. "But lately, Britt, I've been giving serious thought to some things."

"What things?" Britt sipped her wine. She waited, knowing the signs. Mark was leading up to something.

A draft blew down the chimney, pushing a puff of smoke into the room. Mark quickly adjusted the flue, then sat down in the overstuffed chair facing Britt.

"We have to think about the course of our lives—our future."

"What do you mean, Mark? Our lives are on track. We're doing more than okay." She waved a hand at their surroundings. "We have a great house, wonderful kids, even a seaside cabin, such as it is."

He nodded, his expression guarded, as though he was mentally forming his argument.

"Just tell me what's up, Mark," she said softly. "Trying to guess makes me nervous."

The rain intensified, hitting the windows like fine spray from a hose. A few drops even made it down the chimney to sizzle on the burning logs. Suddenly cold, Britt pulled her robe closer around her.

"I'd like you to give some thought to the possibility of going back to work full-time, Britt."

"Is that what this is all about . . . me working?" His words totally destroyed the warm glow of the wine and the fire.

His forefinger traced a pattern on the arm of the chair. "I went over our college fund projections, and we aren't saving enough to keep up with inflation."

"We're not doing so bad, either. I'm making a little

profit from my freelance business, and once I get rolling, I'll make more than if I went out to work and paid for day care."

"Britt honey, I'm not trying to upset you." His jaw muscles twitched. "And I'm not suggesting you go to work now, only that you give yourself a deadline for your business. If it doesn't work out, then we'll need more income just to keep afloat."

"Why did you pick now to discuss this?" She stood up. "I feel as if you built the fire and plied me with wine just so I'd agree to go back to work."

"That's not true." He got to his feet, looking upset and misunderstood. "I'm just trying to plan ahead for Katie's and Sam's education." He glanced away. "But you're right. My timing was bad."

She nodded, suddenly tired. "I'm going to bed." She knew he wanted her business to succeed, and he liked her being home with the kids. He just worried too much about money.

"I'll lock up." His voice was stilted, as though he regretted having brought up a touchy subject.

At the stairs she hesitated, remembering her playbook, and went to get it. She grabbed her handbag and took the back stairs from the kitchen, dropping the bag on the carpet next to the night table when she reached the bedroom. Then she got ready for bed.

"I'm sorry, Britt," Mark said, when he joined her a moment later. "I didn't mean to ruin the evening."

"Let's not talk about it, okay?"

"Am I forgiven?" His lips quirked in a lopsided grin. "I love you, Britt."

"I love you, Mark, and I understand. There's nothing to forgive. You worry too much, and I'm oversensitive." She grinned. "We're quite a pair."

She rummaged in her bag for her playbook. The newspaper ad fluttered to the floor, and Mark stooped to pick it up, glancing at the section Angie had circled in red ink.

"What's this?"

She snapped on the bedside lamp and climbed into bed. "Angie gave it to me, thought it might be something for Katie to do. I told her no."

Mark didn't answer, scanning the ad. He looked up. "Why did you say no?"

"Because I believe those modeling competitions are only moneymaking schemes for the promoters." She glanced at him. "I don't want Katie involved with people like that."

"Britt, some of them are legitimate." He tapped the newspaper with a finger. "Remember Elmer Wyberg, my first boss after I graduated? His daughter was a child model, had an agent and everything. She made enough money in a couple of years to pay for college and law school."

"She was an exception, I'm sure."

"No. Elmer said modeling was a moneymaker, so long as the kid was supervised by the parents." He tipped his head. "I think Angie's right. There's no harm in this."

Britt put down her book, still out of sorts. "If you think Katie's going to model to build up her college fund for you, forget it."

His face went white. "That was a low blow."

"Mom? Daddy!" Katie's voice from the doorway startled both of them. "Are you having a fight?"

"Your daddy and I were just talking," Britt said. "We're sorry if we woke you up."

"We were having a friendly disagreement," Mark added when Katie looked unconvinced. "Parents sometimes have different opinions."

Katie sized up the situation at once. "You were arguing," she said. "Don't treat me like a two-year-old. I'm not a baby."

"Of course you're not," Mark said, soothing her with words and a hug. Over her head he winked at Britt, his anger put aside. He loved his kids.

"I heard what you were talking about," Katie said. "The model competition. My friend Jennifer gets to do it." She glanced between them. "I was going to ask you if

I could, Mom, but you weren't home, so I was waiting until morning."

Mark held back a smile.

Britt got out of bed and led Katie out of the room. "We'll discuss it tomorrow, honey. For now you need to go back to sleep." She didn't even glance at Mark, sensing his grin.

She tucked Katie in, fielding her questions about play practice. That was the problem. Katie loved the stage as much as she did. Modeling would appeal to her, just as Angie had said.

When Britt went back to her own bed, Mark was under the covers, his back turned to her. She got in beside him, picked up her playbook, and then thought better of going over the scene. On occasion she'd sensed that Mark resented her acting because she spent so many evenings at rehearsals. She wouldn't push her luck.

Britt switched off the light, then lay in the dark watching tree shadows do a witch dance on the ceiling until Mark's even breathing told her he was asleep.

She sighed and plumped up her pillow. She hated it when they disagreed. He was a good father and husband. And she loved him.

Thoughts swirled in her head. Maybe she was being stubborn about the modeling thing. Maybe Angie and Mark were right. Could it hurt to let Katie compete in a harmless little contest?

He loved the night when he was out-of-doors. It was only when he and the night were trapped together within four walls, when its currents were stagnant, that Buddy felt the terror of being alone. He'd known the feeling always, but this time it would be different. He would find safety with his eternal soul mate.

Buddy huddled in a doorway out of the rain, his collar up against the damp breeze. He stared at the theater across the street. Giant columns beside the wide steps marked the entrance, and ornate terra-cotta sculptures of a bygone era embellished the cornice around the roof.

He smiled, suddenly exhilarated. Déjà-vu. It was as though he'd once known this place, had driven up to it in a fancy buggy to watch his sweetheart perform, the soul mate he would meet here again soon.

The rain whispered against the pavement, holding the city in gentle hands. The air was redolent with the sharp river smell of the Willamette, which flowed through Portland, dividing the city, splitting it into two oddly different sections, before emptying into the Columbia.

Buddy breathed deeply, then crossed the street, his eyes on the play poster for *The Man Who Loved Dead Women*. Most actresses were whores, he thought. And most females were whores once they grew up . . . like his mother.

His chosen one would be different. She would be pure and would cherish only him. She would forsake everyone else for him. And he would not allow anyone to change that.

He tucked the newspaper into his pocket. He'd *known* when he saw the ad. She'd been coming to him in his dreams every night lately, preparing him for their meeting. She was so real. He could see her in his mind, hear her voice speaking to him. He would recognize her beauty and her innocence.

Buddy didn't approve of modeling, but he forgave her. She was searching for him, just as he had been searching all of this life for her. His skin pimpled with anticipation. He could not wait to make her his.

A bus pulled up to the stop nearby, waited, then accelerated in a burst of diesel exhaust when Buddy didn't move. It was time to go.

Yet he lingered a moment longer, feeling her presence, allowing the rain to cool his hot face. Then he ran to the van he'd left parked on the next block. By the time he drove east over the Steel Street Bridge he was calmer, his mind on his preparations.

He must be ready for her.

3

"WHY DID I EVER AGREE TO IT?" BRITT MUTTERED. KATIE'S participation in the modeling competition was stretching her time past the limit. She'd been manipulated by her kid. Steamrollered by her husband.

She raced around the kitchen, wiped the counter, emptied the dishwasher, and tried not to hurry Sam, who was still picking at his breakfast and passing bits of toast to Tippy, who rarely left his side. She felt grumpy, tired. She'd been up late the night before, preparing an employee manual of company policies and procedures for Dick Burnham, her computer client.

Whoever said housewives had it easy? she asked herself. She'd never worked harder in her life. She tossed the sponge into the sink, splashing water.

"Damn it!"

Britt jumped back and dabbed a wet spot off her suit skirt. She'd gotten up at six, jogged, fixed breakfast for Mark, who'd left at seven, then managed to get herself ready for her ten o'clock meeting downtown. Wearing a suit and heels rather than jeans or sweats cramped her style these days.

A glance at the wall clock reminded her it was getting late. She hurried to the back steps that went from the kitchen to the landing of the main staircase.

"Katie!" she called. "You're going to be late for school. Get down here. You're not leaving the house without breakfast!"

"I'll be right down, Mom!" Katie's high-pitched voice echoed down the stairwell.

Britt sighed, resigned to the morning routine. Katie

25

took so long deciding what to wear to school that she often had to gulp her food. To avoid fights, Britt allowed her to choose any outfit except those reserved for special occasions.

Heaven help me when she's a teenager, Britt thought, remembering her own conflicts with her mother. Girls seemed concerned about their appearances earlier these days.

Since they'd signed Katie up for the modeling competition, Britt hardly had time for rehearsals. She scheduled her few business meetings during school hours, depending on Mark's mother, Harriet, or her own mother, Alice, to baby-sit for Sam.

A burst of knocking on the back door signaled her mother's arrival. Relieved she was on time, Britt opened the door.

Alice stepped into the house, and before she could say more than hello, Sam flew into her arms. She planted a kiss on his round jam-smudged cheek, leaving a bright red print of her lips.

"You stay, Nana?" He looked up at her with big dark eyes.

"That's right, sweeters." Alice had a Bette Davis voice and, like Harriet, she doted on the kids. "You and Nana are going to play while your mommy's gone."

"Tippy, too?" Sam asked seriously.

Britt sighed in resignation. Her mother loved the cocker spaniel almost as much as Sam did, and Britt suspected that once she was gone, Tippy would be allowed in rooms that were usually off-limits to him. Oh, well, she told herself. Indulging the grandchildren was a grandparent's privilege.

Britt watched Sam and Alice fuss over Tippy. Her mother had a Peter Pan quality that appealed to children. Her permed hair was long and wild; she looked like a bohemian from the 1950s in her nubby wool skirt, black turtleneck, and ballerina slippers. Because she was also short and slender, Alice and Britt were often mistaken for sisters.

THE FLOWER MAN

Alice had hoped to be an actress, a dream she'd transferred to Britt, taking her to local auditions from an early age. Just so she doesn't impose that dream onto Katie, Britt thought as she cleaned up the remnants of Sam's breakfast. Now Alice did volunteer work in the theater community, another reason Britt wouldn't quit her prostitute role: Alice would be embarrassed.

At least I've overcome the glitches in the stalking scene with Jeb Walker, Britt told herself. But she'd be relieved when the play ended its run.

Too bad her mother couldn't have had more children, Britt thought, glancing at the pair by the patio door. Then Britt's decision to not pursue an acting career wouldn't have been so disappointing to Alice. Her father's insistence that Britt have another profession to fall back on had blunted her own sense of loss. That, and falling in love with Mark.

As an adult, Britt had realized how much her father loved her mother to put up with Alice's dreams. Her dad, a self-educated man, was tall and blue-eyed, kind and courtly.

"How can a mailman be courtly?" he'd ask her with a laugh.

"You are courtly, Fred," her mother would reply. "You could have been a Shakespearean actor."

And then her father would hunch his shoulders and duck his head, embarrassed.

Katie bounded down the back steps, drawing Britt's attention from her introspection. Her eyes widened. Katie had waited until the last minute to come down, gambling that her mother wouldn't make her change clothes and be late for school.

"Good morning, Grandma Alice," Katie said. "What do you think of my new outfit?" She pivoted slowly in the middle of the room, showing off her red knit shorts and matching jacket trimmed with blue piping. "Don't you think the blue tights and ballerina shoes give it a complete look?"

Britt and Alice exchanged glances.

"It's . . . very chic," Alice said, hugging her. "You look like a real model. You're going to win, honey, I just know it."

"Thanks, Grandma," Katie said. "But I know I might not. My friend Jennifer says there are lots of pretty girls competing."

"Then we'll just have to practice harder," Alice said.

"But not now," Britt said. "Katie, you know that outfit is inappropriate for school." She pointed to the steps. "Hurry and change."

Katie hesitated. "Mom, you don't understand. Jennifer and I are trying to look like models so we'll do better when we compete. Jennifer's mother is letting her wear her new green skirt and blouse today, so please, Mom. She'll think I'm a liar if you don't let me."

"What would it hurt, just this once," Alice said, siding with Katie.

Katie's wide blue eyes filled with hope. "Please, Mom."

Britt didn't like the way things were going. Katie was too smitten with the whole modeling idea. Why hadn't she burned the lousy ad?

"Okay . . . this once, Katie," she said. "But next time ask me first."

Katie grinned at her grandmother, then ate her cereal and even finished her orange juice without an argument when Britt insisted. Donny, the neighbor boy, called to her from the front sidewalk. Katie grabbed her books, kissed them all, and headed outside to join her friend for the walk to school.

"She's a very sweet child," Alice said, standing next to Britt in the open doorway. "Even though she has a genetic predisposition for dramatics."

"Inherited from you," Britt said dryly.

They watched the kids disappear around the corner. Britt's final glimpse of Katie's long blond hair against her red outfit lingered in her mind. She shivered suddenly and closed the door. It was bright outside, but chilly.

THE FLOWER MAN

She needed to hurry. It was important to be on time. Dick Burnham was a client who wanted everything done yesterday. Britt went to put on her suit jacket and pumps. She despised heels. She'd rather wear thongs. For that matter, she'd rather be weeding her herb garden than driving into the city.

I'll weed it this afternoon, she told herself. If I have time.

"Hey. Look this way, Katie."

Len Holmes's voice, deliberately squeaky and high-pitched, came from beyond the footlights. He stood behind a tripod that held his camera, the shutter-release button in one hand, a puppet in the other.

"Come on, precious. Smile for Mr. Wiggly, or Mr. Wiggly will cry." The clown puppet danced on the edge of the light while the man holding him remained in silhouette.

Katie smiled stiffly and looked self-conscious. The photographer's assistant, a sullen man with a full beard and long hair, had repositioned her bench twice. The photo session, scheduled prior to the evening modeling competition, had taken all afternoon.

"Boo-hoo! Boo-hoo!" The hand puppet now appeared to sit on the camera, his white hands over black-jeweled eyes. "Katie doesn't like Mr. Wiggly. Boo-hoo. Katie doesn't believe Mr. Wiggly has feelings."

"Clowns don't cry," Katie said, and giggled. Instantly Len snapped the picture, and Katie moved off the bench to make room for the next child.

"Can you believe it? Len Holmes is a ventriloquist," Britt whispered to Angie who'd come early to help dress Katie. They stood with the other mothers in the orchestra, watching the photo session on-stage.

"And a pretty damn good one," Angie replied. "It doesn't surprise me. He likes everyone."

"What *is* surprising is that he's the photographer."

"Not really. Len does all types of photography—

family portraits, magazine assignments, swimwear shoots in Hawaii and Mexico, photos for catalogs, and he covers beauty pageants for the tabloids. He's even done night work with night-vision goggles."

"What are night-vision goggles?"

Angie shrugged. "They have some kind of a night-scope lens that allows the photographer to take pictures in the dark."

"I'm impressed. Len Holmes is almost too good to be true."

"Yeah, he'll make some woman a great husband." Angie grinned. "Len has more jobs than he can handle, and he doesn't come cheap. Jay Fisher Productions was lucky to get him. I bet this extravaganza *is* connected with legitimate modeling agencies."

"No wonder it cost so much."

"How much was it?"

"Registration was two hundred fifty dollars, plus Len's photo fee. And that doesn't include the two-dollar-a-head admission tickets, Katie's outfit, or the candid shots once the competition starts."

"I think the cost is pretty typical, Britt."

"I suppose so," Britt said, her eyes on Len, fascinated by his smooth technique. He was so good with the kids.

After the last sitting, everyone was directed backstage by a red-haired woman in her early forties. Wearing heavy eye makeup and a tight black sheath, she reminded Britt of an overweight raccoon.

"Just call me Pearl," she told them crisply. "You might want to touch up the kiddies' hair and makeup. Curtain goes up in forty-five minutes."

"What a bitch," Angie whispered as the woman walked away.

"I don't like her either," Britt whispered back. "Too self-important."

Angie looked around at an aggressive stage mother. "Doesn't it make you sick the way some of these mothers try to push their daughters ahead of everyone else?"

"It's child abuse," Britt said. "Those girls will go home devastated because their mothers set them up to win."

Angie nodded. "I'd forgotten how awful it is to see a stage mother in action."

Britt glanced at her watch. Mark and Sam and both sets of grandparents would be arriving soon. Thank goodness the competition was almost over, she thought. Although it was less than two weeks since Katie registered, it felt like a month.

The dressing room was stuffy and crowded. Britt fingered stray hairs back into the roll at the nape of her neck. Her floral silk pants and blouse were lightweight, but she still felt hot.

"Mom, do you think my outfit is as good as Jennifer's?" Katie stepped in front of Britt, her expression anxious.

"Honey, I think it's prettier." Britt smiled reassuringly. Katie had lost some of her confidence since seeing her competition. Britt remembered the feeling. She'd had it often as a child. "Angie did a good job on your makeup. Did you thank her?"

"Uh-huh." She flashed Angie a smile.

Angie had brushed Katie's long lashes with mascara, her cheeks and lips with pink blush. Britt had pinned up her hair so that it hung down her back in layers of curls. Wispy ringlets outlined her face, emphasizing her delicate features.

"Maybe I should have saved the red outfit. Maybe—" Katie's voice faded away as her eyes darted over the other girls.

"Honey, you're perfect, except for opening-night jitters." Britt dabbed the powder puff over Katie's forehead. "Angie and I know how that feels, don't we, Angie?"

Angie nodded. "The blue velvet looks great, kiddo. It enhances your blue eyes." She put an arm around Katie's slender shoulders. "You're a sure winner."

Britt shook her head at Angie behind Katie's back. She

didn't want Katie getting too pumped up to win. She'd already talked to her about losing. The fun of competing should be more important than winning, she'd said.

Across the room Jennifer was dressed in a brilliant scarlet dress, a brown-eyed young Elizabeth Taylor. In Britt's opinion the competition was between Jennifer and Katie, whether the judges preferred blondes or brunettes. Jennifer had the advantage of having attended charm school during the summer, but Katie had Angie and Britt and Alice, who'd taught her how to walk, how to act to the audience.

"Time for the mothers to leave," Pearl announced, sounding like a school principal.

Britt kissed Katie. "Remember, you're the prettiest girl here." She smiled encouragement. "I love you, and so do Daddy and Sam and Nana. We'll all be rooting for you."

Katie swallowed, looking scared. "I know, Mom."

Britt hated to leave her, and realized she was acting just like her mother used to. She wanted Katie to win, because she knew how it felt to lose.

"Come on, Britt. They're blinking the house lights. Let's go so Katie can get out there and knock 'em dead. Right, Katie?"

Angie's words had the desired effect. Katie straightened, tilting her head exactly as her grandmother had taught her. Britt suppressed a grin. Katie would be all right, whatever the outcome. She wasn't Alice's granddaughter for nothing.

Katie gave them the thumbs-up sign, a gesture she'd copied from Angie.

Britt was smiling by the time she took her seat next to Mark. The music started, and the first set of children stood on the stage behind gauzy drapes that opened with a dramatic flourish. As the commentator described their apparel, each would-be model strolled down the lighted runway, pivoted, and returned to the stage. Then the music changed, the curtain closed, and the next group went through the same routine.

"This Jay Fisher puts on a pretty professional show," Mark said between sets. "The music suits the clothes the kids are wearing, and I like the way the lights change color. The special effects are great."

"Shhh." Britt gestured to the stage as the gauzy drapes billowed open to music from the movie *Beauty and the Beast*. Katie and Jennifer were in the final set of models wearing party dresses. Jennifer was first to walk the runway. Her poise and timing were excellent, her long black hair dramatic against her scarlet taffeta dress. Katie followed.

"She's something else," Mark whispered proudly. "Can you believe that little beauty is our kid?"

"Hi, Katie!" Sam hollered suddenly.

"Hush, Sam," Britt whispered. The interruption distracted Katie, but she quickly regained her poise, giving an extra pivot at the end of the runway. Len captured the move on film, and Katie paused to smile into the camera for a second shot.

She strutted back to the stage, swinging her hips as her grandmother Alice had taught her, to join the others in her set. The spotlight silvered her hair, and for a moment she looked ethereal, like the angel in a Christmas pageant.

The music changed into the grand finale, and the curtains closed to end the competition. The announcer said there would be a ten-minute intermission so the judges could make their final determinations.

"I think Katie has it sewed up," Angie said.

"So do I." Mark leaned across Britt to talk. "And I wouldn't be surprised if she got some modeling assignments."

Britt bit her tongue. Now was not the time to get into a disagreement with Mark. It remained to be seen if the winners became models because of Jay Fisher Productions. She hadn't received a straight answer when she asked which agencies they represented. She suspected they operated on a freelance basis, found possible mod els, and marketed them for a fee. But win or lose, Katie wasn't going to forfeit her childhood. Not if Britt had anything to say about it.

Jay Fisher, a florid, overweight man in his forties, walked onstage with Pearl. Without preamble, he announced the top three winners, Katie among them. There was a drumroll, and the three girls came from the wings as the audience clapped.

He named the third-place winner—a girl she didn't know—and Britt held her breath. Her prediction had been right. First place was between Katie and Jennifer. Mark grabbed her hand.

In seconds it was over: Jennifer won first place, Katie second. Pearl handed out plaques and gave Jennifer a bouquet of roses. Jennifer walked onto the runway, followed by Katie and the other girl. Len took more pictures; then the girls left the stage and the house lights came on.

While Mark waited with the others, Britt went to find Katie. Len Holmes stopped her as she approached the dressing room.

"Hey, Britt, I was so darn surprised to realize you and Mark were Katie's parents."

"Not as surprised as I was to see you were the photographer. You're very good with kids, Len."

His smile broadened, crinkling the corners of his eyes. "Kids are good photo subjects. Unfortunately they aren't my specialty."

She raised her eyebrows.

He looked embarrassed for a second. "I hate to sound mercenary, but my other work pays a lot more."

"I can understand that. We all need to make a living."

"I've got to run," he said. "Bobby and I have to get my equipment out of here."

"Bobby?"

"My assistant, Bobby Lee." He indicated the bearded man who waited about ten feet behind him. "He's the one the kids saw. I was the one in the shadows."

"I won't keep you, but I'm looking forward to seeing the photos. Angie says you're really good."

"Glad to hear it." He sounded pleased. "Listen, I'll give you and Mark a call when they're developed. You can be the first to see them."

"Is that legal?" She grinned, liking him even more.

"Sure, why not?"

"Katie will be thrilled."

They said good-bye and Britt went to find Katie. Pearl's authoritative voice jarred her the second she stepped into the dressing room. The woman was answering questions from disgruntled mothers.

"As I said, we keep the winning names on file. When assignments come up, and if one of our girls fits the requirements, we call the parents to see if she's available."

"Oh, sure!" someone shouted. "I think we've all been ripped off."

"Not everyone wins," Pearl snapped. "And we aren't in business to rip anyone off."

There was a subdued murmur in the dressing room. Several girls were crying, and some of the mothers were tight-lipped with disappointment. Britt was disgusted. This was not a healthy environment for a child. Katie was lucky; she'd won this time. But Britt vowed never to subject her to this again. A steady diet of modeling would be destructive to a child's sense of self-worth.

She glanced at Jennifer's mother. The woman seemed oblivious to everything but the fact that her daughter was number one. Britt separated Katie from the crowd by reminding her that her grandparents and Angie and Bill were coming to the house for ice cream and cake.

"You did great, honey," she said, giving her a bear hug. "We're all so proud of you."

"Thanks, Mom," Katie said, glancing at one of the upset losers. "But winning doesn't feel so good when everyone else feels so bad."

Britt pulled her close. "I know, honey. And I'm happy that you realize that."

She hurried Katie out of the theater, glad that the competition was over. There was no need to worry about Katie becoming a model. After listening to Pearl she was convinced Jay Fisher Productions was a flimflam outfit that operated just inside the law.

They could put all of this behind them.

The Honda swung out into the traffic. Buddy waited until it turned the corner, headed toward the West Hills. Only then did he put his van in gear and follow, staying a discreet distance behind the car. He rolled his window down to let the evening breeze cool his face.

She had come. *She had finally come to him.*

It was as he'd dreamed it would be. He'd known her at once. She was exactly as he'd pictured her, his life-mate. His foot itched to press the gas pedal to the floor, catch up with the car, claim her now.

He curbed the impulse; it was too soon. She would need time to realize she belonged to him. It was better that way. He must be patient.

The road twisted higher into the residential district of turn-of-the-century houses. The same vintage as the theater—*where he'd found her.* It was another sign. He'd been here before, too. In another life . . . with her.

He tamped down his excitement. When the Honda turned into a narrow street with a dead-end sign, he drove on past and stopped farther up the road. He waited five minutes, then turned around, drove to the dead end, stopped again, and studied the big houses. Those on the upper slope of the hill were separated from the tree-lined lane by high banks reinforced with rock walls. There was no car access to those properties. The homes across the street had drive-in garages. He could see the Honda in the open garage of the house with three extra cars parked in front.

Unexpectedly, his mother's words freed themselves from a hated childhood memory. "Rich people call us white trash, Buddy. No rich girl will ever love you."

You're wrong, whore! he screamed in his mind. I've found her. She'll change everything. It's not too late.

Slowly he drove out of the street. But he would come back.

4

OVER THE NEXT FEW DAYS THE COMPETITION OFTEN POPPED into Britt's mind and reminded her of the attractive photographer. She found herself contemplating the single women she knew, wondering if any of them would be interested in Len. Mark had told her that Len was so busy he had little time to cultivate a permanent relationship with a woman, even though he met many through his work. Britt suspected it was an excuse. Len seemed shy to her, and he'd been deeply hurt by his ex-wife.

Her hands stilled on the dry herbs she was sorting into bottles. Britt Hinson, stop it, she told herself. You know how much you once hated matchmaking.

She concentrated on the herbs. She would use some of them for spices, some for tea, and the fragrant ones, like myrtle and mint, for potpourri. Each Christmas she gave herb wreaths, dried bouquets, and tea assortments for gifts. It was a holiday project she and Katie worked on together.

Britt stood up to stretch, sniffing the air in the garden room, where drying herbs and flowers hung above the workbench from thin bamboo poles Mark had put up for her. The scent was reminiscent of dried roses in a Victorian trunk. The sudden shrill of the phone made her jump. She dropped the herbs and started running. The garden room was at the back of the garage, its doorway near the laundry room door which stood open.

Please don't wake Sam up from his nap, she chanted

silently. Leaping up the step into the house, she darted around the half-asleep spaniel and grabbed the phone.

"Hello." Britt propped the receiver between her ear and her shoulder, then wiped her dirty hands on her jeans.

"Hi, Britt. It's Len. I hope I'm not disturbing you."

"Of course you're not. We've been waiting to hear from you." She switched the receiver to her other ear.

"I have Katie's pictures ready. Do you guys still want to take a peek at them before I turn them over to Jay Fisher?"

"You bet we do."

"Great. I think you're going to like them."

"Katie will love them. This has been a big deal for her."

"Yeah, it's exciting for a kid. But it can be tough on the losers."

"I agree. That's exactly why Katie won't be doing it again. I don't really approve of these kinds of competitions."

"You're a good mom, Britt."

"Thanks. I try."

"Anyway I shouldn't knock it. My fees are high and the promoters are willing to pay them. I just feel bad when a kid gets hurt." He hesitated. "So when can I bring the prints over?"

"I have rehearsal tonight. How about Saturday evening?"

"Can't. I have a date. I'd bring her, but we have game tickets." He paused. "Would Saturday afternoon work?"

"Sure. Name the time."

"Two?"

"We'll see you then."

"Oh, Britt. One more thing—off the record. I've made up a set for you. It's a gift."

"Len, we can't let you do that."

"It's my pleasure. Mark is my friend. I wouldn't dream of charging you." He laughed. "Just don't tell Fisher."

"Of course we won't. And thanks. That's really nice of you."

"Like I said, my pleasure. Bye for now."

The dial tone buzzed in her ear. Slowly Britt hung up, feeling good about everything. The best thing about the competition was Len. She had a feeling that he was one of those special people who became valued friends. Smiling, she went back to her herbs.

Katie ran into the kitchen through the back door, her cheeks flushed, her curls snarled by the wind. She held a bouquet of wilting forget-me-nots in one hand.

"Mom, can I use the little white vase?" she asked, dropping her backpack on the kitchen table. "The one Grandma Harriet gave us?"

"What on earth made you pick wildflowers, Katie? They're covered with bugs." Britt wrinkled her nose. "They'll infect the houseplants."

She glanced out the sliding glass door to check on Sam who was playing with Tippy on the lawn. The backyard was securely fenced, but Britt kept a close eye on him. He had a way of getting into mischief.

"I didn't pick them." Katie was rummaging in the cupboard under the sink. "A man gave them to me on my way home from school. He said they matched my eyes."

"What?" Britt's eyes narrowed on her daughter. "Katie, you know we've told you not to talk to strangers. What did he want?"

"Gee, Mom, he didn't want anything. He was just being nice. And all I said was thank you. It was no big deal." She stood up with the vase in her hand. "Donny and the other kids thought it was cool. No one ever gives *them* flowers."

"The man wasn't from Pinecrest, was he?"

Katie shook her head impatiently. "No, and you're wrong about Pinecrest, Mom. Those people wouldn't hurt anyone. My teacher told us all about them. She says their bodies grew up all the way, but their minds didn't, so they're like great big children."

Britt gave Katie a hug. "I'm so proud of you, honey, for being so kind and so understanding, but I'm upset with you for accepting flowers from a stranger. What did this man look like?"

Katie made a face and sighed. "Oh, *Mom . . .*"

"Describe him, Katie."

"He just looked like any ordinary nice man."

"Well, he had no business talking to a little girl, and you are not to speak to strangers ever again, no matter what they offer you. Do you understand, Katie?"

"I understand, and I won't do it again . . . but I'm not a little girl."

The phone rang, and Britt sighed. "We'll discuss this further when I get off the phone."

She picked up the handset. "Yes?"

"It's Len. Sorry to bother you again, but I need to change the time. Something's come up. Would one o'clock on Saturday be okay instead of two?"

"Of course."

"Great. I'll let you go, then. You're probably fixing supper."

"It's already in the oven—we eat early on rehearsal nights. But I am having an important conversation with Katie."

"Nothing serious, I hope."

"I don't think so. I was just reminding her not to talk to strangers."

"That *is* important. I'll let you get back to it."

"Thanks, Len." She said good-bye and hung up.

"Who's Len?" Katie asked.

"One of Daddy's football buddies. He was the photographer at the modeling competition. Remember?"

"Was he the one who told me where to stand?"

"No, that was his assistant." Britt handed Katie dinner plates, her cue to set the table. "Len was the man with the hand puppet, the one who took the pictures."

"I remember Mr. Wiggly, the puppet," Katie said, "but I couldn't see the photographer, 'cause the lights

40

were in my eyes. I didn't like his assistant, though. No one liked him. He was mean."

"Well, Len is very nice. He's even offered to bring your pictures here on Saturday."

"Maybe he'll take my picture when they call me to be a real model," Katie said.

About to remind Katie that Jay Fisher Productions might not call, Britt was interrupted by Sam and the dog running into the kitchen.

"Fowers, Mommy." He handed Britt a stalk of parsley.

Somehow he'd managed to reach into the box garden, but he looked so pleased and his expression was so much like Mark's that Britt couldn't take away his pleasure with a scolding.

"Thank you, Sam," she said. "We'll put it in the salad for dinner, and then you can help me feed Tippy, and . . ." She glanced at the clock and wondered where the afternoon had flown to. "Let's take Tippy out to his special doghouse for a while, shall we? Come along."

Britt operated on automatic pilot, mentally listing the tasks that remained to be done before she left for rehearsal. There hadn't been time to continue the discussion about the man who'd given Katie flowers, but she hadn't forgotten. There'd be time later.

Mark arrived home to supper on the table, Sam in his sleepers, Katie's homework completed, and Britt ready to leave for rehearsal once they'd eaten. Just because I don't work for a big corporation doesn't mean I'm not a supermom, Britt told herself, as she drove into the city.

Rehearsals had gone well since the night she'd lost the stalking scene. Art Sills had taken her seriously, and shown Jeb how to make the killer real without going too far. Since then the play had progressed without many glitches. Once practice started the hours melted away. It seemed she'd barely arrived when she was on her way home again.

The house was quiet when she stepped from the garage

into the kitchen. She tiptoed through the house, checking door locks and switching off lights. When she finally crawled into bed Mark pulled her next to him.

"How'd it go?" he whispered, his mouth in her hair.

"Smooth. We're ready for dress rehearsal." She snuggled closer. He was so warm and her hands and feet were cold. "Thanks for taking care of the kids, Mark." She lifted her head and kissed him. "I know things have been hectic lately."

She was relieved he hadn't mentioned her going back to work lately. Adding another client to her freelance consulting business had impressed him. Mark, like Katie, still believed there could be a modeling assignment. "Did Sam go right to sleep?" Britt asked.

"Out like a light," he said. "And Katie showed me her flowers."

"Did she tell you a strange man gave them to her?"

"Yes, and she also told me you were very upset about that." He looked concerned. "You worry too much about strangers, Britt. This is nothing but a spontaneous gesture to a pretty little girl. All strangers aren't child molesters."

She sighed. "I know. You think I'm overprotective."

"No, but I think maybe you overreacted a little, don't you?" His arm tightened around her, and Britt tried to put the incident out of her mind.

Mark was probably right. It was nothing. The flowers were a simple gesture of kindness. But still . . .

"Mom, guess what? Someone left forget-me-nots on my desk at school." Katie glanced up from the homework she'd spread around her on the living room carpet.

It was Monday night, four days since Katie had been given the wildflowers by the stranger. Sam was asleep, Mark was watching Monday night football with his friends at Bill's house, there was no rehearsal tonight, and Britt was enjoying a cozy evening at home, daydreaming as she watched the flames in the fireplace, a book in her lap.

A perfect ending to a nice day, she told herself. Her new client had given her a lead for another account, she'd completed two wreaths, and she'd called Len and ordered prints for the grandparents. Len couldn't stop talking about Sam, who'd charmed him on Saturday.

"He's a terrific kid," Len had raved. "Another reason why I've got to settle down again. It's the greatest thing in the world for a man to have a son like Sam."

"Little girls are nice too," Britt had remarked.

"Oh, I didn't mean—Katie's great."

"I understand," she'd said with a laugh. "All men want a son to follow in their footsteps."

Katie's words suddenly sank in. *"What* did you say?" Britt asked, a feeling of unease creeping over her.

"I said someone gave me more forget-me-nots."

"Where are they?" Britt straightened and put her book aside, staring at Katie in her long flannel nightgown, her cheeks flushed from the heat of the fire.

"I threw them in the wastebasket at school." Katie chewed on the eraser end of her pencil. "And there was a note on my lunch box at noon. It said, 'You should have won first place.'" She rummaged in her backpack and pulled out a rumpled piece of lined paper, the kind used for grade school penmanship lessons. "See?" She handed it to Britt. "It's signed, 'Forget-Me-Not.'"

The printing was large and uneven, as if it had been written by a child. Britt felt the tension seep out of her muscles. One of the kids at school was teasing Katie about the man who'd given her the forget-me-nots, she decided. Nothing to worry about this time.

"I think one of the boys at school has a crush on you, Katie," she said.

"Mom!" Katie looked embarrassed. "I don't like boys."

That ended the conversation. Katie went back to her homework, and Britt tried to read her book. But an unsettling thought kept nagging at her mind: Katie had been talking more and more about wanting to become a model, trying to convince Britt. She hoped the note

43

wasn't part of a plan to do that. She knew Katie was being influenced by her friend Jennifer.

I'll have a talk with Jennifer's mother, she thought, and then immediately dismissed the idea. The woman had more stars in her eyes than the girls did. She was probably the instigator.

Her tranquillity had been replaced by disturbing thoughts. The room was quiet but for the sound of the fire. Britt separated the night sounds beyond the windows like herbs on a drying rod: a car passed slowly on the street; a light wind swayed the cedar and fir branches against the siding; a dog barked several houses away— had a raccoon ventured into someone's yard in search of food scraps?

Britt was still unsettled when she tucked Katie into bed. She waited up for Mark, and told him about the latest incident.

"I agree with you," he said. "Either some boy has a crush on her, or Katie has gotten a little carried away with modeling. And Jennifer and her mother aren't helping matters."

"What should we do about it? I'm a little concerned, Mark."

He shook his head. "Don't be. The whole thing will blow over. The girls may never be contacted to model." He shrugged sheepishly. "I hate to admit it, but I think you were right, Britt. The competition was only a money-making scheme for the promoters. Len filled me in tonight on how some of these promoters operate."

She sighed. At least he'd admitted that. She resisted rubbing it in. It was enough that they were united on the modeling issue. She hoped Katie would get over this phase soon.

But Britt's concern grew the next day when Katie came home with another story. "The man who gave me the flowers was watching me at recess, Mom."

"For heaven's sake, Katie. What does this man look like?"

"I don't know."

"Of course you do," Britt said. "If you saw him, then you can describe him."

"Mom, I told you. I can't remember!"

Britt and Mark attended Back-to-School Night that evening, and she asked Katie's teacher about playground surveillance, explaining what had happened.

"The teachers take turns with playground duty," Mrs. Young assured her. "Anyone who seems even vaguely suspicious is reported." She smiled. "But I will mention this at the next faculty meeting. We can't be too careful these days."

Britt felt better—until the following afternoon. She'd left Sam with her mother, and Alice had taken both children to the park after school while Britt was at her aerobics class.

"The flower man was there at the park," Katie announced when they returned home. She lowered her lashes, not meeting Britt's eyes. "I don't like him watching me all the time."

"Did you tell Grandma?"

She nodded. "But Grandma didn't see him. He was gone when she looked."

Britt was at a loss. No one ever saw this "flower man" . . . except Katie.

"Break a leg." Mark blew her a kiss from the dressing room door.

He'd come backstage, as he always did before curtain time on opening night. He'd left Katie to save their seats; Sam was home with Mark's parents, Harriet and Paul. Both sets of grandparents had tickets for other nights.

"Mommy! Daddy!" Katie ran down the hall, pushed her way around Mark, and stepped into the brightness of the dressing room where Angie was helping Britt get ready. Katie gulped a deep breath. "The flower man smiled at me. He walked up the aisle and kept looking at me."

Britt and Mark exchanged startled glances.

"Honey, did you really see him?" Britt placed her arm around Katie's shoulders and held her close. "Maybe you only thought you did. There's a big crowd of people out there—a full house."

"I really did." Katie tugged at Mark's sleeve, her expression strained and pale. "I'll show you, Daddy. He has a beard now but I know it's him. He's sitting three rows down from us. He got up and turned around and looked right at me. You'll see him this time, I promise."

"Okay, sweetie. I'm coming. Let's have a look at this guy." Mark spoke gently and took her hand. Above Katie's head he met Britt's gaze, as if to say he'd take care of it.

Britt watched them go, then turned to Angie. "This flower man stuff is really upsetting." She hesitated. "Katie has never been a kid to make up stories."

She dabbed more rouge on her cheeks. She had a terrible case of opening night jitters. Please, God, don't let me blow that first scene again.

"You know Katie," Angie said behind her. "She can be dramatic."

"I know." She faced Angie. "I'm worried that she might be making up stories."

"Why on earth would she do that?"

Britt shrugged. "I don't know—but I *do* know it started when she became convinced that she should pursue modeling, like her friend Jennifer."

"Maybe she's just going through a phase." Angie grinned. "Come on, Britt. Try not to worry. You have to go out there and knock them dead—no pun intended."

Angie walked her to the wings and gave her a thumbs-up sign as Britt took her place to await her cue. Her anxiety lingered. Children who needed attention sometimes told lies. Maybe Katie was insecure and she and Mark just hadn't realized it. Maybe the flower man was a variation on the imaginary playmate, created to fulfill some need.

"Your cue is coming up," the stage manager whispered next to her.

She nodded and tried to concentrate. When she was given her cue she stepped onto the stage. Seconds later she was caught up in her role. Her worries didn't surface again until after the final curtain.

Someone opened champagne backstage and the cast and crew raised a toast to a successful run. The final applause had told them that *The Man Who Loved Dead Women* was a hit.

No one lingered; there was tomorrow night's performance to think about. Britt joined Mark and Katie, and they drove home, Katie dozing in the backseat. The conversation was limited to the play and Mark's praise of her performance.

"Did you see the flower man?" she asked Mark later, after Katie was in bed.

He shook his head, and Britt saw that he was trying to play down his concern. "The seat where she said he was sitting was occupied by a woman. I don't think there is a flower man, Britt." He saw her anxiety and patted her arm. "We'll talk to Katie in the morning. Reassure her about how much we love her."

Her stomach felt hollow. "Mark, do you think this is a serious problem?"

"Shhh." He kissed her gently. "You're beat, Britt. You need to go to bed. We can deal with this in the morning."

Exhausted as she was, one thought circled in her mind: what if there really was a flower man?

5

THE WEEKEND PASSED IN A BLUR OF CHORES AND PERFORMANCES. Katie and Sam spent Sunday with Britt's parents, and by Monday morning Britt and Mark still had not found time to talk with Katie. Although Mark was anxious to get to work, Britt insisted on discussing the problem.

He laid his briefcase on the kitchen table and tossed his jacket on a chair as she called Katie downstairs.

"Katie, you know Mom and Daddy love you," Britt said. "We're worried about these flower man stories, and we're trying to understand what's going on."

"I *know* you love me," Katie said. "But I'm not making up stories. There really is a flower man."

"We know you don't invent things, honey." Britt hesitated. "It's just that no one else has seen him, and you can't seem to tell us what he looks like. We're confused, that's all."

"You don't believe me." Tears glistened in Katie's eyes. "I can tell."

"We want to." Mark's tone was edged with impatience. "You know, Katie, parents understand that kids fib sometimes, and—"

"I'm telling the truth!" Katie looked stricken. She whirled around and ran up the back steps. Seconds later her bedroom door slammed.

Britt started after her, but Mark grabbed her arm.

"Let her cool down. We can't buy into the histrionics. It'll only make matters worse."

She jerked free. "But what if there is a flower man, Mark? What if she's telling the truth?"

"Britt . . . God!" He yanked his suit jacket off the chair and put it on. "I can't listen to this shit. I'll be late for work."

"Shit? That's what you call Katie's problem?" She snatched up his briefcase and flung it at him. "Go to work, damn it. Being on time is more important than your daughter!"

"Britt, I'm sorry." He shook his head, looking contrite. "I don't have any answers. I guess all we can do is wait and see what happens. Maybe this will just go away."

She expelled her breath, still angry.

"Don't think I'm not taking this seriously," Mark said.

"I am. If we can't cope with this phase, or whatever it is, we might need to consider counseling for Katie."

Britt nodded and made an effort to calm herself. Mark looked so serious, so professional in his dark suit and white shirt. No wonder he'd been tapped for one of the top positions in the firm.

He kissed Sam, who sat in his high chair, then gave Tippy an affectionate pat and started for the door. "I'll be home early tonight. I have a meeting out by the airport this afternoon, so I'll come directly here after that."

"Maybe a quiet night at home is just what this family needs. I don't have another performance until Thursday night." Britt walked to the garage door with him and watched him back the Honda onto the driveway. His mind was already on his meeting, she realized. Maybe fathers weren't as emotional about their children as mothers were. She went back to the kitchen, wondering if she'd given her mother such fits. She couldn't remember anything to compare with the flower man stories.

Katie came downstairs a short time later, trying to act as if nothing had happened. "Would you pin my hair up, Mom?" she asked. "I can't get it right."

"Sure." Britt forced a cheery tone. She hated friction between them. She and Katie had always been close. She'd hoped their open communication would continue through the teenage years.

When Britt finished fixing her hair, Katie faced her.

"Mom, are you still mad at me?"

"Of course not. I was never mad, only concerned."

"Is Daddy mad?"

"No, he's not mad either." Britt hesitated, wondering how much she could say without upsetting her again. "Katie, if you see that man again, you will tell me, won't you?"

Katie's blue eyes widened. "Then you do believe me, Mom?"

"You've never lied to us, have you?"

She shook her head. "And maybe the flower man won't

Donna Anders

come back anymore. Maybe he'll like someone else pretty soon."

Was Katie evading the question? Britt wondered. But she let the subject drop, for now. And she reminded herself that Katie had never been inclined to make up stories about imaginary people.

She watched Katie put on her jacket and check her backpack for homework. She kissed Sam, and their curls met in a contrast of black and white. She's so beautiful, Britt told herself. Surely my sweet daughter can't have changed so much just because she was in a modeling competition.

Maybe I'm to blame. Britt's sudden thought was disturbing. Katie had been exposed to the theater since babyhood. Had make-believe blended into her reality after winning the competition?

Katie opened the door when her friend Donny called to her from the sidewalk.

"Come straight home from school, Katie," Britt said. "And don't speak to strangers."

"I won't—I promise." Katie hesitated in the doorway, facing Britt. "I almost forgot. Jennifer's mom is letting her go to charm school on Saturday mornings, even though she already took some of the courses last summer. And Jennifer wants me to go, too, so I can learn to be a better model." She gave a wide, pleading grin. "Can I, Mom? Please?"

"Your father and I think you've had enough modeling for now, Katie."

"But Jennifer and I are going to put on a talent show and charge admission and then use that money to pay for charm school ourselves, okay?"

"Katie, don't plan on this."

But Katie was already out the door.

"What does this mean?"

Mark strode into the kitchen after his run the next morning, the newspaper under his arm and a white lily in

50

his hand. He dropped the lily on the counter and held out a folded sheet of lined paper to her.

Britt put down the toast she'd been buttering and took the folded note.

"Where did you find the lily?" she asked curiously.

His jogging shorts and shirt were molded to his skin with sweat. He went to the sink for a glass of water. "It was in our mailbox. Read the note, Britt. Someone is playing a sick joke on us."

She unfolded the smudged tablet paper and read aloud. "'Your beauty is pure and lovely like the lily. Think of me when you look at it. I'll be thinking of you. We'll meet soon.'" Britt glanced up, dumbfounded. "It's signed 'Forget-Me-Not.'"

"The printing looks like a kid wrote it." Mark shifted his weight from one foot to the other, giving away his uneasiness. "But I don't know. Do kids use words like 'pure' and 'lovely'?"

Britt shook her head. "Not any kid I've ever met."

"And who the hell is Forget-Me-Not?"

She dropped the note as if it had fangs. "Mark, you don't think this is connected with the man who gave Katie the forget-me-nots? And there was that note on her lunch box at school. That was signed 'Forget-Me-Not,' too. Remember?"

Mark examined the note again. "Same kind of paper, and it looks like the same printing."

Britt tried to envision the other note. Where had she put it? Did Katie still have it? She took a deep breath, and made an effort to control her rising apprehension. She'd find it later. "Mark, do you think this note was written by Katie's flower man?"

He wiped his face with the sleeve of his sweatshirt and looked away, fixing his eyes on the wall behind her, as though he was putting all the known facts together. "No, I don't think so," he said a few seconds later. "Because I don't believe there is a flower man."

"How can you say that?"

"I think one of the kids who was with her when the man gave her forget-me-nots is playing a joke on her. It could be Donny. His parents have a greenhouse. Maybe they grow lilies."

"They don't. I've seen what they grow."

"Then it's one of the other kids." He took off his smudged glasses and cleaned them with a paper towel.

"I don't believe that," she said. "Katie's friends all like her. I can't think of one of them who'd play such a mean trick on her."

"Don't forget how much Katie loves her status as a budding model."

"What does that mean?"

"Only that the flower man stories started after Katie won the contest." He tapped his foot on the floor, clearly agitated. "We have to consider that Katie might have taken the first forget-me-not incident and expanded it into a childish fantasy to convince us that she should be a model."

She glanced away. That possibility had already occurred to her.

Mark opened the cupboard door under the sink and tossed the lily into the garbage. The door snapped shut with a hollow sound. "I wish to hell I'd listened to your advice about that competition. You were right, Britt. She was too young to handle it."

"Do you think Katie put the lily in our mailbox herself?"

"I'm just taking a realistic look at all the possibilities," he said. A vein pulsated in his temple.

"Where would Katie get a lily?"

"At Steward's. She passes that store every day on her way to school." He hesitated. "I've seen lilies in their florist department. Katie could have bought one with her allowance."

Britt sank into a chair. This was preposterous. Katie was a normal child. She wasn't capable of such an elaborate deception.

"We'll see how it goes," Mark said. "I don't think we should mention the lily."

She nodded. At least she agreed with him on that point. It was best not to draw attention to the lily. Whoever was behind the incidents wanted attention—whether it was Katie or one of her schoolmates or a stranger.

Mark glanced at his watch, then headed upstairs to shower and dress for work. "If this continues, we'll have to seek professional help. Nip this behavior in the bud before it becomes a real problem."

Britt was silent. There was no use arguing. Mark was displaying the very trait that had gotten them into the modeling predicament in the first place. Tunnel vision. That always happened when he thought he knew best.

He was wrong this time. Britt knew it in her bones. They already had a real problem.

"Why can't I go to charm school with Jennifer?"

"I've been telling you no all week, Katie. And my no is final."

"But her mom will take us. You don't even have to drive. And if you had let us hold the talent show, we could have paid the fees ourselves. All the kids wanted to come."

Katie stepped farther into her parents' bedroom. She was already dressed, and Britt knew she'd been waiting for them to get up. Mark was shaving in the adjoining bathroom, and Sam was still asleep.

"Please let me." Her blue eyes pleaded.

Britt tied her robe around her. She would shower after she fixed breakfast. That was the beauty of a Saturday morning after a performance. She didn't have to rush.

Sam's voice rang out from down the hall, saving them from an argument.

"Come on, Katie." Britt moved to the door. "We can talk downstairs." She didn't want Mark involved in this discussion. No need to spoil their weekend with a fight.

"I'll run outside and get the paper." Katie ran ahead of her. "There's something I want to show you."

Katie bounded down the steps to the front door while Britt went to get Sam. She was coming down the stairs, slowly leading Sam, who was still in his sleepers, when Katie raced back into the house. She slammed and locked the door behind her.

Britt was brought up short at the bottom of the stairs. "Katie? What's wrong, honey? You're so pale!"

"Mom, he was here!" Katie's eyes were round with fear. "I know it was him." She held up a sprig of sage, and Britt's heart constricted. The note in Katie's other hand propelled her forward, and she grabbed the lined paper. It had been a couple of days since the last note arrived, and Britt had almost convinced herself that it had meant nothing.

"What does he want, Mom? Why is the flower man doing this?" Katie's voice broke.

Mark came down the steps behind Britt and read the note aloud over her shoulder: "'You haven't forgotten me, have you? Make some tea to strengthen your memory. Nothing matters except your memories. And our future together. I've been with you always. Forget-Me-Not.'"

"This has gone too far." Mark pinned Katie with his gaze. "You never bring in the newspaper. Why did you run outside to get it this morning? I heard you tell your mother that you wanted to show her something." He grabbed the note from Britt and waved it in the air. "Is this what you wanted to show us?"

"No, Daddy." Katie's voice quavered. "I wanted to show Mom the ad about the charm school. Jennifer's mom said it would be in today's paper." She glanced at her parents, not completely understanding the meaning behind her father's questions.

"That's enough, Mark." Britt shot him a warning glance. "We'll have breakfast, and then we'll talk about this—without tears and raised voices."

Mark waved her to silence, his attention on his daughter. "Katie, you cannot go to charm school."

Katie's face crumpled. "But Jennifer's going, Daddy, even though she already took a course there. Her mother said—"

"I don't care what Jennifer's mother says. The woman's a space cadet—an airhead," he snapped. "You are not going to charm school. Is that clear?"

"Why can't I?" she cried. "You act like I've done something wrong, and I haven't!"

"No charm school," Mark retorted angrily. "I forbid you to mention it again."

Katie gulped, unable to reply. Then she ran past them, up the steps, and into her room.

Sam started to cry, frightened by the raised voices.

"Are you satisfied, Mark?" Britt asked sharply. "You've scared the daylights out of your kids."

He drew his mouth into a narrow line. "We'll discuss this later. Something has gone wrong here, and I think I know what it is."

He strode down the hall to the den, tossing his words behind him like darts aimed at a bull's-eye. "You're too caught up with the theater to stay on top of your own kids." He turned in the doorway. "Don't bother to fix any breakfast for me. I'm not hungry."

Then he slammed the door, leaving Britt to cope with Sam whose frightened wail drowned out everything else.

The weekend was ruined.

That night Britt's performance was weak. Her mind was on Mark and the kids. Nothing had been settled between them, and she'd felt Mark's resentment when she left for the theater. She wondered if he was using Katie's situation as an excuse to air his own resentment of her passion for the stage. She sighed. She refused to feel guilty, but it would be a relief when the run of this play ended.

Everyone was in bed when she returned home from the

theater. As she undressed and crawled under the covers Mark didn't move. She knew he was feigning sleep. It was the first time in their marriage that he hadn't pulled her into his arms.

Britt lay awake most of the night, trying to figure out what was going wrong with their perfect life. At six the next morning she finally got up, put on her robe, and went downstairs. After starting coffee she opened the front door to get the Sunday paper.

Her gaze fell on the green sprig of rosemary that lay on top of another folded note tucked under the rubber band that held the newspaper in a roll.

A chill ran along her spine, and she glanced out at the quiet street. *Someone was watching.* She could feel his eyes.

Low clouds dripped a steady drizzle, and night still lingered in the woods. Nothing moved except the rain. Even the wind was still.

Britt was struck by the isolation of the houses on their street despite its proximity to the city. Anything could happen here and none of their neighbors would know. The slope of the terrain, the high banks and retaining walls, and the shrubs and trees concealed the houses from one another.

She had to force herself to move normally, to grab the paper, step back, and close and bolt the heavy door. Even that barrier between herself and the porch failed to restore her composure. Don't be silly, she told herself. But she couldn't stop thinking that someone—a flower man?—was out there . . . watching.

Someone was out there. Someone had left another note—and a sprig of rosemary.

The hand on her shoulder almost brought her out of her slippers. Her heart jolted, as if she'd touched an electric wire.

"Britt?" Mark turned her to him. "What's wrong? You're shaking."

Wordlessly, she handed him the note. Their eyes met

and she saw a flicker of alarm in his before he looked down.

Who was doing this to them? she asked herself. Who?

Mark opened the note and read it to her: " 'I know you remember me. Don't fight fate, my love. It's inevitable. Drink your tea and you will remember.' " Mark glanced up. "It's signed like the others. 'Forget-Me-Not.' "

The words hung in the damp silence of the hall.

"We have to face facts," Mark said after they'd gone over everything that had happened. "These incidents always seem to be connected to Katie's dream of modeling. Yesterday we didn't let her go to charm school."

"Maybe you were right in the first place," Britt said. "Maybe one of the neighbor kids is behind the flowers and notes."

Mark got up to refill his coffee cup. "We can't close our eyes to the facts, Britt. The sage and rosemary came from your herb garden. I'd stake my life on that."

As Britt watched him head for the den, she felt as if she'd been punched in the stomach. Mark sounded so matter-of-fact, so unconcerned. And yet she couldn't believe that Katie was playacting. That would simply be too unlike the little girl she knew. Britt rubbed her scalp with her fingers, trying to ignore a headache. The worry and upset, combined with no sleep, felt like a hangover.

It was early, barely light, and the children were still in bed. She opened a can of dog food, scooped it into Tippy's dish, and set it down for him on the patio. Tippy ran to her wagging his tail, then sniffed the food and turned away.

"Not hungry, Tippy?"

She patted Tippy's head and left the food there in case he changed his mind, but her eyes were on her box garden of herbs. Pulling her robe tighter, she moved from the shelter of the patio and made her way across the wet grass. Her slippers were soaked through after the first couple of steps, but she had to know if sage and rosemary had been snipped from her garden.

The rain intensified, a low humming whisper in the leaves and evergreen boughs beyond their back fence. She stood perfectly still, her eyes fixed on the herbs. One rosemary plant was uprooted, part of its stalk broken off. A third of a tricolor sage plant was gone.

"Oh, God, don't let Mark be right," she whispered. "Don't let it be Katie."

Britt stood in the rain, shivering. Her robe and nightgown clung to her. She tried to hold back the suspicions that were circling through her thoughts. If a stranger had been in the backyard Tippy would have barked. Anyway a stranger wouldn't know she even had an herb garden. And a stranger would be afraid of being seen, because they kept the patio light on all night long for Tippy.

A slow creeping sensation itched at her spine, lifting the hairs on the back of her neck. A gust of wind jingled the chains on the swing that hung from the big maple tree. Britt told herself to stay put. This was her backyard; she knew every blade of grass. She resisted an urge to call out to Mark.

Damn, she thought. She was too old to be spooked in broad daylight in her own yard. She started to turn toward the patio and stopped, her eyes drawn to the playhouse in the back corner of the lawn. The fence behind it separated the small gingerbread building from the wooded hill that sloped away from the yard.

The door of the playhouse was ajar.

Had Katie forgotten to shut it? Or had the wind blown it open? Britt forced her apprehension aside and dashed through the drizzle toward the building. Her hand was on the doorknob when she hesitated. Should she check inside or just close the door? The curtains she'd made were drawn and she couldn't see inside.

Her spine prickled another warning. She sensed a presence in the playhouse, someone poised for her next move. Everything in her screamed danger, warning her to get out of there. She pulled the door shut with a loud thud.

She lost her balance, tripped on the little step, and sat

down hard on the wet grass. She scrambled up and, without looking back, ran to the patio. Tippy came out of his doghouse, wagging his tail in greeting.

"Tippy, come inside now, good boy." Britt's teeth were chattering and she was wet to the skin. "Come in, Tip." She looked down and saw that the dog still hadn't touched his food.

Then she saw why: he'd been gnawing on a big raw soup bone.

Who gave him the bone?

And why?

To keep him quiet?

Without even glancing back into the yard, she let the cocker spaniel into the kitchen, then followed him inside and locked the door.

6

"THE MORE I WONDER ABOUT THIS," MARK SAID, "THE MORE I think Katie may not be responsible for what's going on."

He sat on the sofa next to Britt in the den, his stocking feet resting on the coffee table. The kids were in bed, and he and Britt had taken the opportunity to talk in private. They hadn't mentioned Tippy's mysterious bone to Katie.

"I've wondered that all along," Britt said. The implication of his statement was frightening. If Katie hadn't written the notes, who had? She'd flatly denied leaving the playhouse door open. "My stuff would get all wet if I did that, Mom," she'd explained patiently.

"Oh, I believe she took the first incident of the man giving her forget-me-nots and elaborated on it," Mark said. "Probably made up the stories of seeing him later, even wrote that first note on her lunch box." He massaged his eyes with his fingers. "But I think the later incidents were the work of someone else."

"Katie's flower man?"

"Of course not." He couldn't keep the annoyance out of his eyes when he looked at her. "Listen to what I'm saying, Britt: *there is no flower man.*"

"Then who is doing these things?"

He removed his feet from their perch so he could face her. "Did you mention this—uh, our problem at the theater?"

"Well, yes. Why?"

"This could be important." He squinted at her. "Who did you tell?"

"I told Angie, and several others might have overheard us talking." She hesitated, suddenly defensive. Mark held his feelings closer to the chest than she did, and he believed their concerns shouldn't be discussed outside the family. "I was worried about Katie, and Angie is my best friend."

"Suppose . . ." he said. "Just suppose for a moment that one of your actor friends has a crush on you, Britt."

She recoiled, astonished. "That's absurd."

His sigh was impatient. "Someone could have seized this opportunity to let you know how he feels."

"Are you saying the notes were written to me, not Katie?"

He nodded. "I'm saying it's another possibility."

"That's really far-fetched," she said, annoyed. "For goodness sake, Mark, *try* to be objective."

"*You* be objective, Britt. The other actors know your schedule, your kids, your husband, your hobbies—including herb gardening." He drew in a breath. "Think about it. Remember how Jeb lost it at play practice, thought he was the real killer? Maybe *he's* behind these incidents."

"That's crazy!"

"The hell it is!" His resentment surfaced. "You don't

know what goes on in a man's mind, who he wants to fuck."

"Don't be crude, Mark," she snapped. She put more space between them on the sofa. "In case you've forgotten, Jeb's gay. And he has a lover."

"What about that hotheaded director?" he asked. "Don't close your eyes, Britt. Your theater pals aren't saints."

She jumped up. "I'm going to bed. I refuse to let you use Katie's problem as a weapon to attack my friends. Your suggestion is preposterous, Mark. It's *nuts!*"

He got to his feet slowly, his features stiff with anger. "What's the matter, Britt? Did I strike a nerve?"

"Damn you, Mark!" She strode to the doorway and faced him again. "Has the thought occurred to you that it was *you* who encouraged Katie to enter the modeling competition? If you hadn't, we might not be in this predicament."

"That's a low blow."

"And so is what you said about my friends."

They stared at each other, neither giving ground. Britt was the first to look away. She hated fights. Why couldn't she and Mark simply talk without getting mad? She went into the hall. "Make sure the porch and patio lights are on and the doors are locked before you come up," she told him. "We don't want some crazy actor sneaking in during the night."

She ran upstairs before he could respond.

Tippy's bark brought her straight up in bed, listening. Mark didn't stir beside her.

Straining her ears, Britt heard a squeak this time, different from normal night sounds, but vaguely familiar. Tippy would keep barking if there was an intruder, she told herself. *Unless the intruder gave him a bone.*

The sound came again. She thought of the gate to the backyard, with its squeaky hinges. The urge to check her children and the house was too strong to resist. She hadn't locked up before going to bed. She'd left that to Mark. What if he'd forgotten?

Britt slipped out of bed and tiptoed into the hall. She paused. The house was quiet. A night-light glowed reassuringly from the bathroom between Katie's room and the staircase.

The door to Katie's room stood open, and she moved toward it. A glance assured Britt that she was sleeping soundly. Katie lay on her side, her long hair spread out over the pink pillowcase, the covers tossed aside in the unseasonably warm air that had followed the rain.

Across the hall, Sam was sprawled on top of his dinosaur-print sheet, his legs twisted in the blankets. Britt tucked him in gently, careful not to awaken him.

Silently, she groped her way down the stairs to the front door. It was locked. She turned and headed toward the back of the house.

Reaching the kitchen, she stopped in her tracks. The room was black; no light shone through the window from the patio. Had the bulb burned out?

Check the switch, she told herself. Maybe Mark hadn't turned it on. She inched her way toward the sliding glass door, knowing where to step, what to touch to avoid bumping into something. Her hand found the switch. It was in the on position. The bulb *was* burned out. About to open the drapes, she hesitated.

Don't be dumb. Stay concealed, she told herself, and peeked out from between the folds. The night was dark, but she could make out the dog house and playhouse. She leaned closer to the door and pressed her nose against the glass.

A dark shape moved.

Britt jumped back. Shock took her breath. She stared wide-eyed at the draped door. Was someone outside it? Her knees bent like folding table legs, and she grabbed the counter to steady herself. She resisted an urge to scream.

She gulped in deep breaths, and reason began to reassert itself. The house was still quiet. There were no sounds from the patio. There's no one out there, she told herself firmly. The door was made of glass. Glass reflected images, even in the dark. She'd seen her own reflection.

She forced herself back to the door. She had to satisfy herself that a phantom didn't lurk in her backyard. Cautiously she looked out, making herself stay there until she was able to distinguish everything in the yard. Then she saw Tippy. He was sleeping on the mat just outside the patio door as he often did.

Relief whistled from her mouth on a long breath. No one could have stood where Tippy lay sleeping.

Light bulbs, she reminded herself. Mark kept them on a shelf in the laundry room. If she changed the bulb she'd conquer her fear. The socket was next to the door; it would take only seconds. Still she hesitated. Maybe she should wait for morning.

No! Before the notes had begun arriving she wouldn't have hesitated to go outside at night. This is my house, my yard, she told herself. Let the prowler be warned. She would not be frightened by scare tactics.

She fed her anger. It propelled her to find the bulb. Her hand was on the patio door before she hesitated again. She instructed herself to carry on. Ignoring a prickly sensation of fear, she slid the door open and stepped outside. Tippy jumped up, his tail thumping her leg, excited by her unexpected visit.

Britt stood ready to leap back into the house. The night sounds raised goose bumps on her arms and a breeze whipped her nightgown around her legs like a straitjacket. She tucked her tangled hair behind her ears and resisted an urge to run back inside.

Her eyes began to adjust, and familiar objects took shape. She felt better; this *was* her backyard, after all. A faint noise, like the rustle of dry leaves, made her head jerk toward the playhouse. It had sounded like a forest creature scampering through the salal and wild huckleberry bushes beyond the back fence. Nothing human, she reassured herself.

She unscrewed the burned-out bulb and replaced it with the new one. Instant light was an arc of brilliance that pushed back the shadows. But the darkness beyond seemed even blacker.

Shivering, Britt felt naked in her skimpy nightgown. Her apprehension returned with a feeling of being watched.

Tippy jumped up, ready to play. She scratched his back and spoke softly to him, her eyes on the yard. Then she backed into the house, slid the door shut, and locked it.

Fear prickled at the very roots of her hair, and she raked her nails through it, as though she could scratch away the feeling. She still felt the eyes on her through the closed drapes. It was as if someone had her in the cross-hairs of a high-power rifle. She dropped the burned-out bulb on the counter, then whirled and ran.

The hardwood floor felt cold beneath her bare feet as she hurried through the kitchen and up the steps. The dark currents of her house, usually so friendly, swirled around her. Britt pulled herself up short at the top of the stairs, aware of her sleeping family. She tiptoed into the bedroom and crawled back into bed beside Mark.

She couldn't shake her apprehension, even when she reminded herself that Tippy would have continued to bark if a prowler had come into the yard. As she lay listening to each strange sound, her mind switched to a story she'd heard on the evening news about gun control. Maybe they should buy a gun. Britt cringed at the thought. She hated guns. Guns killed people.

Slipping out from under the sheet, she went to the bathroom and switched on the light. The miniature crystal chandelier beside the mirror cast a fractured brilliance on the blue floral wallpaper. As she drank some water, her eyes met their reflected image in the glass. She recognized a new expression in them.

Fear.

* * *

THE FLOWER MAN

Had she seen him?

Buddy stood among the trees, going over what had happened in his mind. He'd been at the glass door when she looked out, but by the time she stepped outside onto the patio he'd melted into the darkness and snapped open his switchblade.

She'd had something in her hand, and he'd thought it might be a flashlight. He'd jumped back even farther, his jeans scraping the waxy leaves of a rhododendron shrub, and he'd seen her look in his direction. He'd crouched low in the grass and watched her from ground level. When the patio light came on, he'd been concealed.

Slut, he thought, remembering how she'd stood in the pool of light, reminding him of his mother. She'd worn nightgowns like that—for the men.

The rage surged again as he thought about her standing on the patio, about her long neck and half-exposed breasts. He fingered the switchblade in his pocket.

He wanted to punish her.

After she'd stepped back inside and locked the door, he'd stayed put. He'd known she could look out a window and see him. She was sly. She'd surprised him at the patio door by not turning on a light. He'd believed they were all asleep.

That stupid mutt had awakened her, he told himself. Buddy hated dogs. They made him wheeze.

An upstairs light had come on, startling him again. Then it had gone out, and he'd decided it was in the bedroom she shared with her husband. Buddy stared at the dark windows and imagined them fucking. The muscles in his throat constricted. He pulled out his nebulizer and gulped the spray.

He hadn't known until now who slept in which bedroom, except for the little boy's room in the front of the house. Once he'd stood on the rock wall across the street and watched her put the kid to bed. The light was never on in the room next to the kid.

That left the bedroom on the back corner above the

playhouse and garden room roof. It had to belong to the girl.

Buddy grinned, pleased. He wasn't even mad at the mutt anymore. If the dog hadn't barked, she wouldn't have gotten up. And he would still be wondering which bedroom was which.

Now he knew. Everything was falling into place.

"No, sir, I never see anyone this early in the morning," the paperboy told Mark. "Everyone is still asleep. I'm lucky if I see a car, other than my mother's."

"How about parked cars on the street that don't belong in the neighborhood?" Mark asked.

The boy shook his head, then hurried back to the street where his mother waited with the car engine running, the headlights illuminating the predawn street. In seconds the car disappeared, leaving Mark with the newspaper in his hand.

"Do you believe him?"

Britt stood behind Mark in the open doorway. They had both gotten up early enough to catch the paperboy.

"Yeah, I do." Mark flattened one palm against his forehead and looked down at the note in his other hand as they stepped into the hall and closed the door. "This note and these forget-me-nots were already on the porch when the paperboy got here." He held them between two fingers as though they were garbage. "Shall we see what this one says?"

Britt nodded.

"'Do you remember me yet?'" he read. "'Do you long for me as I long for you? Be patient. It won't be long now.'" Mark hesitated, his facial muscles constricting. He glanced up. "It's signed 'Forget-Me-Not.'"

"I'm calling the police." Britt grabbed the note and started down the hall. "This has gone far enough."

"Wait a minute, Britt. What if they find out that Katie is involved?"

"You said you didn't think it was Katie." She whirled around to face him, feeling as frustrated as he looked.

"Hell, Britt," he said blankly, "we don't really know what's going on here. I keep going back to the printing on the notes. It looks like a kid's handwriting."

"But we agreed that the content is too adult for Katie."

"So that brings us back to square one—your theater friends."

"Oh, for Pete's sake! I refuse to argue about that again. I'm calling the police. Let them sort it out."

Britt strode directly to the phone in the kitchen. "Whoever is involved," she told Mark, who was right behind her, "it's time to get to the bottom of it."

"If you're determined to call, then I think you should wait until a decent hour. Have you forgotten it's only five o'clock?"

"People typically call the police at the time of the crime," she snapped. "I'm calling now."

"Crime? I doubt they'll think these notes are a crime." Mark drummed his fingers nervously on the counter.

"Whatever they are, I'm scared." She picked up the handset, then hesitated, her eyes caught by the uncertainty in his.

"Go ahead, call them."

He turned away to pour coffee beans into the grinder, and she dialed 911. While Britt talked to the dispatcher, Mark started the drip coffeemaker. A few minutes later she hung up, exasperated and even more frustrated.

"He was rude," she said. "Aren't the police paid to protect the public?"

"That's what we're told." Mark watched the coffee drip into the carafe. "What did he say?"

"He kept asking me if I had a suspect. That *if* someone was really leaving notes, then it was probably nothing more than a prank, or a neighbor with a grudge."

"Didn't you tell him there have been several notes? That we suspect we've had a prowler in the backyard?"

"Of course I did, you heard me," Britt said, annoyed. She flung the note on the counter.

The man's voice on the phone had been patronizing, as if he thought she was a neurotic housewife with nothing better to do than call the police. When she'd insisted on an investigation he'd sounded doubtful and reminded her that the police had their hands full with more serious crimes.

She slumped into a chair and propped her elbows on the table. "I don't think the dispatcher believed a word I said. He thought I was a wacko. He asked questions, and I didn't give the right answers."

"Like what?"

"Like which neighbor was I fighting with, and which kids had a grudge against Katie." She pursed her lips and mimicked the officer in a singsong voice. " 'Lady, I suggest you call back when you have something concrete. In the meantime, make peace with your neighbors, have a talk with your daughter's friends, whatever. I guarantee your problem will disappear.' "

"In other words, the police won't get involved." Mark took mugs from the cupboard, poured coffee, and slid a cup across the table to her.

"He said they'd send someone out to talk to me this afternoon. Procedure, I guess. He made it clear that there's nothing he can do."

"Shit." He sat across from her and tried to look objective. "Try not to worry, Britt. Maybe the cop is right. Maybe the problem will disappear. Especially if Katie—"

"Don't start in on Katie again, Mark. I don't want to hear it."

"Okay, okay," he said, and went to put cold water in his coffee. His sleeve brushed the burned-out light bulb she'd left on the counter. "Where did this come from?"

"The patio. Tippy woke me up last night. I came down here and found the light out. So I changed it."

"In the middle of the night? What in hell did you do that for? What if—"

"Someone was out there?" She finished his question. "That's exactly why I did it. I heard a sound, and because of our current paranoia I figured I needed to prove I was letting my imagination run wild."

His jaw went slack. "Have you lost your mind? Someone has been on our property, leaving notes."

"So you do believe it wasn't Katie." She seized the opportunity, turning his words on him.

"I don't know who it is," he said, almost shouting. "Maybe it's Katie and maybe it's someone else." He bent toward her. "Until we know what's going on around here let's not act stupid. Okay?"

"You don't have to raise your voice, Mark. I knew what I was doing. Tippy was sleeping on the doormat. If someone had been in the yard he would have barked."

"Like he did when he got the bone?"

Sighing, she squeezed her eyes shut. "Mark, can't you understand? I need to put this into perspective. Normal sounds have me looking over my shoulder."

He examined the burned-out bulb more closely. "I just changed that bulb a few weeks ago, but I put in a *sixty*-watt bulb."

"What are you saying?"

He tapped the blackened glass. "This is a hundred-watt bulb. It's not the one I screwed into that socket. The fixtures won't tolerate higher wattage."

"Couldn't you have put in the wrong bulb by mistake? Maybe that's why it burned out so fast."

"No way." He shook his head. "Somebody changed the bulb so the yard would be dark." Mark strode to the glass patio door and whipped back the drapes. Light was seeping over the eastern horizon, pushing back the darkness of the woods behind their house. Tippy barked, begging to be let in, and Mark slid the door open for him, then turned to face Britt.

"If someone was out there he watched you change that damnable bulb." He drew in a ragged breath. "Don't *ever* do such a stupid thing again."

She clasped her coffee mug with both hands and remembered the flash of movement she'd seen outside the glass door. And that rustling sound—had it been a little animal, or someone trying to hide from the light?

* * *

Buddy moved swiftly through the trees to his van. He walked with the surefooted grace of an Indian guide, as he'd learned to do when he was a kid and his mother took him to that timber town up in Washington State. That was the best year of his life. He was ten then, and while his mother tended bar he'd roamed the woods behind their rented cabin.

He breathed the fresh dawn air deeply, his senses attuned to the rhythm of the forest. The wet smell of the evergreen boughs gave him a euphoric high. There was no constant scrutiny here; the prying eyes couldn't see him in the woods. This was his refuge.

When he lived in the logging town he'd often spent the night in the woods. The darkness among the trees had felt safe, unlike the impenetrable blackness of a closed room. Once, though, his mother had caught him sneaking out, and she'd locked him in the root cellar. At first he'd screamed and pleaded, but later he'd sat perfectly still, oblivious to the rats and the spiders, leaving his mind free to wander in the forest.

The gray sky was brightening as dawn gave way to a new day. A stillness surrounded him, broken only by an occasional twig snapping under his feet. Nature was poised in momentary silence, girding itself for the next onslaught of rain.

Buddy pulled his hood up and quickened his step.

7

THE FRONT DOORBELL WAS SUDDEN AND INSISTENT, STARTLING Britt. She jumped up from her desk so fast that her hand came down on the corner of her file folders, tipping them onto the floor with her notes.

"Damn it!" She stared at the mess with dismay; it would take a half hour to sort it all out again. And she needed all of the facts and figures on paper for her meeting tomorrow. The doorbell rang even longer the second time.

She left the clutter of paperwork in the den and hurried into the hall, her sweat socks silent on the polished hardwood floor. About to open the door, she hesitated. A draft raised goose bumps on her arms. She leaned forward and peeked from behind the lace curtain that covered the door's oval window. At first she saw only black shoes and dark trousers. Then she realized it was a uniformed policeman. His patrol car was parked in the driveway. She released the bolt lock and opened the door.

"Is this the Hinson residence?"

"Yes, it is. I'm Britt Hinson."

"I'm Officer Wallace. You called in a complaint this morning?"

"Yes. Please come in."

She opened the door wide, noting that he was middle-aged and ordinary looking, if somewhat stern. He stepped into the hall. The leather holster on his hip creaked against his pistol as he moved, and his police radio gave short bursts of static each time there was a transmission. He turned the volume down.

"Uh, would you mind coming into the kitchen, Officer Wallace?" she asked, closing the door. "My little boy is napping and I don't want to awaken him." She hesitated, feeling awkward. Damn it, policemen in uniforms always made her nervous, as if she were guilty of something.

"That'll be fine," he said.

Britt led the way to the kitchen, and they sat down at the table. Then he glanced up, his blue eyes direct under bushy brows.

"I understand you might have a prowler, Mrs. Hinson?"

She nodded. "Actually we've had a number of strange incidents lately."

"Uh-huh." He scribbled something down on a notepad he'd placed on the table. "Why don't you start with the first one."

She drew in her breath and plunged into the story, starting with Katie bringing home the first bouquet of forget-me-nots, ending with the light bulb incident. "I know someone was in the backyard last night, Officer."

"But you didn't actually see anyone?"

"Well—no. And we don't know if the prowler is the same person who left the notes and who gave Katie the flowers. But if it *is* the same man, then our daughter has seen him."

"Is she the only one who saw this, uh, flower man?"

"No. The first time she was with a couple of her friends. They saw him, too."

"But after that, no one was around when she says she saw him again?" His pen tapped the pad.

"That's right."

She felt a prickle of annoyance. She should have known he'd be just like the dispatcher she'd spoken with earlier. He thought she was exaggerating.

"Why don't you show me the backyard, where you think you saw someone last night." He stood, taking his pad and pen with him.

She led him to the patio door, demonstrated how she'd pulled back the drapes, and told him that she'd thought the movement was her reflection.

He nodded and stepped outside. He walked around the yard, talked to Tippy, looked in the playhouse, checked the fence gate, then examined the windows and doors. He noted his findings on his pad. When he finished they went back inside.

"No evidence that anyone tried to pry open the windows or doors," he said. "No footprints in the flower beds, and no loose boards on the fence."

His tone seemed to say it all: there was no prowler.

Don't get mad, she told herself. It's not the officer's fault. Her story sounded far-fetched even to her ears. She breathed deeply, then told him about the mysterious hundred-watt bulb and about the incident when Tippy had been given a raw soup bone.

"I'd like to see the notes, Mrs. Hinson." Officer Wallace paused. "If you still have them."

"Certainly," she said, ignoring the feeling that he doubted her. She took the notes from a drawer and handed them to him. "They're clipped together in chronological order."

He scanned each one and gave them back. "I'd say they were all written by a kid," he said.

"I'm surprised you don't find the content too mature for a child to have written."

He shook his head. "You'd be shocked if you knew how much some kids know these days. I've known a few eight- and ten-year-olds whose language would make a convict blush."

"I wasn't referring to profanity, Officer. I was talking about the choice of words. They don't seem typical to a child. My husband agrees with me," she added for emphasis.

He squinted at her and nudged the bill of his cap higher up his forehead. "Mrs. Hinson, I'd stake my badge on it being a kid. Probably someone from the neighborhood who has a crush on your little girl. These things are pretty common."

"Leaving notes on the door in the middle of the night is common? I don't believe it."

"Yeah, this kid's gone too far, and he's gonna be in trouble if he's caught." He tucked his pad under his arm and picked up his radio. "I suggest you let folks in the neighborhood know the police have been called. When the note writer hears that, I think your trouble will be over."

"What about the light bulb? How do you explain that?" Her frustration leaked into her tone. "I don't think a kid would change the bulb on my patio in the middle of the night."

"I agree, Mrs. Hinson." He started walking to the hall. "I think your husband probably put in that hundred-watt bulb and didn't realize it, and what you saw at the patio door was your own reflection." His smile was condescending. "In the middle of the night the imagination can work overtime."

His radio suddenly came alive with a transmission as they reached the front door. He cocked his head to listen. "This is my call," he said.

She opened the door and he stepped onto the porch. "I have everything I need here for my report." His eyes met hers briefly. "I think you can relax, Mrs. Hinson. The notes will stop as abruptly as they started. And you and the family will get back to normal."

"I hope you're right," she said bleakly. She could tell that he believed she was overreacting to a neighborhood prank.

"But give us a call if there are further incidents." He stepped into his patrol car, shut the door, and took his call, his mind already on the next case.

She went back into the house, feeling worried. Mark and his friends were meeting for beer and pizza at a local tavern this evening to watch Monday night football on a big-screen TV. Britt was apprehensive about being alone, but she hated to ask him to stay home.

Her apprehension lingered throughout the afternoon and into the evening as she waited up for Mark. But when there was no note the next morning she began to think the officer had been right.

Maybe the scary episodes were over.

Steward's parking lot was crowded, but Britt found a space near the front doors. The market-deli was unique to Portland; it stocked everything from exotic flowers and imported delicacies and wines to unusual gifts and groceries. Shopping at the spacious store was always a pleasant experience.

"Your parking karma strikes again, Mom," Katie said, unsnapping her seat belt.

"Kerrrma," Sam parroted from his car seat behind

them. He lunged against the restraining straps. "Sam out!"

Britt grinned as she got out of the Volvo and opened the back door and lifted Sam out of the car. "You're right. When I assume I'll find a parking place up front, I always do."

"I know. Daddy says your parking karma really works."

"The karma part is just a joke, Katie. Daddy thinks it's funny that I always find a parking spot up front, but the reason I do is because everyone else assumes there won't be one. Daddy and I don't believe in karma, Katie."

Britt locked the car, and the three of them walked toward the low brick building. Crimson geraniums still bloomed along the walkway, and the miniature maples behind them were just beginning to turn color. Across the street the elms and oaks among the tall evergreens in Hilly Park were still green. Always that way in late September and early October, Britt thought. The leaves would change overnight after the first frost.

"I don't believe in karma," Katie said. "Only the parking kind."

As they entered the crowded store, Britt noticed a man using the pay phone near the door. Another man was bent over the newspaper dispenser, and a third was placing flyers on car windshields in the parking lot.

"Oh dear, all the carts are taken." Britt sighed. It was no easy task to walk Sam through store aisles; he tended to grab anything within reach. She had Katie pick up two shopping baskets, one for herself and one for Britt.

"Sam ride!" he demanded, and thrust his lower lip out defiantly.

"We'll have to make this quick," she told Katie. "Sam is in a cranky mood."

The baskets were filled before Britt was finished with her shopping, and Sam kept trying to squirm out of her grasp. She dropped the bread on the floor, then spilled the little red potatoes when she lunged for him. She wore her purse around her neck like a necklace; she didn't have enough hands to hold everything. Even Katie complained about being overloaded.

"Hurting Sam's hand!" he whined pitifully when Britt tightened her grip on him.

An elderly couple gave Britt a dirty look, as though she were a child abuser. Shit! she thought, feeling the sweat roll down her back under her shirt. She was tempted to put the baskets down and walk out. She wondered how she'd manage to write a check for the groceries. Sam was so wound up he'd dart away from her the second he was free.

"Katie, go see if there's a cart available now. Put down your basket and we'll wait right here for you."

Katie sighed dramatically, a gesture like her grandmother Alice. Her expression was pained. "This is embarrassing, Mom. Everyone's looking at us."

"No, they aren't. People know how toddlers are in stores. Just go see if there's a cart."

"Sam go toooo!"

He began to wail. Britt put everything down and picked him up. He cried louder as Katie disappeared around the end of the aisle. Nothing pacified Sam until Katie returned with a cart and Britt lifted him into the seat and gave him a cookie from a package she was buying. The crying stopped.

Katie and Britt exchanged glances, relieved. She gave him another cookie for good measure, and Katie took two for herself. Britt even ate one—she needed a sugar hit. After that, she was able to finish her shopping in peace.

"Have a good day, Mrs. Hinson. The little fellow, too." The checker handed her the receipt as the bag boy put the last sack into the cart.

"Thanks, we will." Britt smiled and started toward the door, pushing the cart with the bagged groceries and Sam still in his seat. The rigors of motherhood, she thought.

"I have homework," Katie announced when they reached the Volvo. Her forehead creased with worry.

THE FLOWER MAN

"We have a geography test tomorrow." She hesitated. "Do I still have to set the table, Mom?"

Britt sighed. Kids and chores—they always tried to get out of them. She was too tired to argue. She'd worked on her accounts all morning, gone into the city for a meeting, and managed to get home before Katie arrived from school. Her mother had watched Sam—that was Sam's problem; he hadn't napped. Much as she loved acting, it was a relief to know the play would close on Saturday night. Fitting everything into her schedule had become impossible.

"I'll set the table if you'll help me carry the groceries into the house," Britt said. She lifted Sam out of the cart and buckled him into his car seat.

"Thanks, Mom." Katie brightened enough to help load the car without being asked.

Britt climbed in behind the wheel. She really didn't blame Katie for begging off on setting the table. Their routine had changed lately. A few weeks ago she would have let Katie stay home and study while she went to the store, but since the notes had begun arriving, Britt was afraid to leave her alone.

As she was about to start the engine, Britt noticed a flyer stuck under her wiper obstructing her view. "Damn," she muttered under her breath and unrolled her window. Decorating cars with advertising flyers should be against the law.

Stretching her arm out the window, she couldn't quite reach it. Still grumbling, her day's energy about gone, she got out of the car and yanked the flyer off her windshield with hardly a glance at the printed ad. Crumpling it, she strode to a litter can to toss it away. Then she hesitated. Something was printed in pencil on the back of it.

Her head jerked in the direction of the Volvo only a few feet away. Both of her children sat waiting, eating cookies. They'll spoil their supper, she thought inanely. Katie must have dipped into the grocery bags.

Don't look at the note. Throw it away, an inner voice instructed.

She glanced furtively around the parking lot. She saw no one. Across the street, kids were playing ball in the park. Above the trees cumulus clouds, like swelling domes of alabaster, filled the sky. She smoothed out the crinkled flyer and felt her heart convulse. "Don't eat cookies, my lily. You'll get fat." Her eyes scanned the awkward printing, recognizing it. "Karma is real, you know that. Remember?" As always it was signed "Forget-Me-Not."

Britt's legs moved of their own volition toward the car. I must stay calm, she told herself. I must not panic. Katie doesn't need to know about this.

Her eyes missed nothing as she returned to the Volvo. She noted the cars passing on the main road, customers leaving the store, others arriving. In the few seconds it took her to reach the car she'd pinpointed all visible activity.

It was him. He was out there somewhere, watching. She could *feel* him. She stopped short, about to get into the car. He'd overheard their conversation about karma, seen them eat cookies in the store. Dear God. He'd been so close—and they hadn't known.

"What's wrong, Mom? You look funny." Katie leaned across the seat, her expression anxious. "Are you sick?"

"Oh, no—no." Britt pulled herself together. "I, uh, was just wondering if we were out of ketchup." She managed a squeaky laugh. "You know how much you love ketchup."

"We just opened a bottle." Katie's frown deepened.

"You're right. I forgot." Britt started the engine, then remembered the flyer in her hand and stuffed it into her jeans pocket.

"Why didn't you throw it away?" Katie asked.

"Uh . . . because it's an ad for—for a car wash." Britt improvised as she spoke, her mind only a word ahead of her voice. "I decided to keep it. Daddy and I don't always have time to wash our cars."

"I could do it," Katie said. "If I washed the cars, you

could pay me." Her voice rose with enthusiasm. "I could use the money to pay for charm school. Jennifer says there are new sessions four times a year."

Britt suddenly felt annoyed. "Katie, remember what your father said? No charm school!"

"Why won't you and Daddy let me go? Daddy acts like he doesn't trust me anymore." Katie sounded defiant, but her chin quivered.

Britt didn't bother to answer. Her nerves were shot. She slammed the Volvo into reverse and backed out of the parking space, her eyes narrowed against the glare of the sun, which had escaped from behind the clouds. She drove out of the lot, then headed up the hill, her gaze darting to the rearview mirror. No one was following.

She knew he was too cautious to be seen. But how had he managed to overhear her and Katie talking about karma without her seeing him? It was uncanny.

Katie sniffled, and Britt had a terrible thought. Katie had gone to the front of the store for the cart. Could *she* have printed the note on the flyer? Was it a ploy to convince her parents about charm school?

She glanced at Katie, who was staring straight ahead, tears streaming down her face. Could she be that good an actress? No! It's impossible, Britt told herself. Katie was just upset because she couldn't go to those stupid charm classes. Besides, it was normal for a little girl to dream of being a model or actress, especially a girl whose mother was an actress.

And Katie couldn't be the prowler, either—if there was a prowler. Maybe a neighbor had given Tippy the bone. Maybe Mark only thought he'd put in a sixty-watt bulb. And maybe the notes *were* intended for her and not for Katie. After all, Britt had also talked about karma and eaten a cookie.

Questions spun in Britt's mind, and she pressed her foot down on the gas pedal. She slowed at once, but her disturbing thoughts accelerated. Was it possible that Mark was right—that there were two things going on?

Maybe Katie and her imaginary flower man were separate from the prowler and the later notes.

By the time they drove into the garage Britt's head was pounding. It didn't make matters any better when Katie ran upstairs without helping her unload the car, but Britt was too spent to argue. She'd talk to Katie after she got the groceries and Sam safely inside the house.

Britt was about to start supper when she stopped in her tracks, staring at Sam, who sat on the floor playing with Tippy. It was *after* Katie got the cart that she'd opened the bag of cookies, so Katie couldn't have written the note that mentioned the cookies.

She scooped Sam up and headed for Katie's room. "Please, God, help us understand what's happening," she murmured.

The next afternoon Britt's thoughts about the flower man shifted again. The phone rang just as her mother was about to leave. It was the principal's secretary, who informed her there had been an incident at school concerning Katie, and that the police had been called.

"Is Katie okay?" she cried into the receiver.

"Katie is fine, Mrs. Hinson. But we do request you come and get her. She's pretty upset."

Britt went outside, still wearing the gray sweats she'd changed into after her meeting, grateful that her mother could stay with Sam.

"This note business has gone on long enough," Alice said, looking worried. She followed Britt to the garage door. "Someone has to do something about it!"

Britt only nodded and got into the car. There was no time for speculation; she and Mark had gone over everything with their parents. No one had any answers.

Let this nightmare end, she told herself. How much longer can we stand it? She was soon out on the main street headed downhill toward Fenton Heights Grade School.

The old two-story brick school, built at the top of a rise, was edged on one side by woods and flanked by playgrounds. There was a little store across the street where the children bought candy after school.

A safe neighborhood, Britt thought as she parked on the street under a big-leaf maple. She was on the downward slope of the grade, separated from the back of the school yard by a twenty-foot retaining wall. She ran toward the corner and headed uphill, past the smaller playground, and around to the other side of the building.

"Let Katie be okay," she chanted over and over, startling a blue jay.

Britt didn't break stride until she was inside the building. The oiled wooden floor squeaked under her Nikes as she hurried to the principal's office. Classes were in session, and the halls were empty. She didn't see a secretary, so she continued to the door with a brass nameplate that said "Mr. Lotze, Principal." When no one answered her knock, she walked in, interrupting two men who were deep in conversation.

"Mrs. Hinson, please come in and sit down," Mr. Lotze said, his brown eyes concerned. His chair creaked under him when he lifted his massive weight and stood up, his starched white shirt straining at the buttons.

"Where's Katie? Is she all right?" Britt sounded breathless, her voice edged with dread. She didn't feel like sitting. She wanted answers.

"She's just fine." He came around his desk and led her to a chair next to the other man. "She's in the teachers' room with my secretary. She was upset, but she's okay now. You can take her home in a few minutes."

"Please tell me what has happened." Britt sat on the edge of the offered chair.

Mr. Lotze went back around his desk and sat down. Although his flushed face suggested high blood pressure, he never seemed stressed or rushed. He would explain in his own time. She barely glanced at the other man who was hardly more than a teenager.

Mr. Lotze adjusted his black-rimmed glasses on the slope of his wide nose. "I informed the police about the incident. Katie's teacher said you'd mentioned a previous occurrence to her, and Katie said someone has been watching her." He nodded toward the other man. "Before we proceed, I'd like you to meet Detective Charlie Simon."

He was a detective? As Britt glanced at him her eyes were caught by a vivid green gaze. He was long and lean, wore his brown hair longer than any policeman she'd ever met, and looked young enough to be wearing a high school letterman's jacket.

He unfolded his legs and leaned forward to offer his hand. "How do you do, Mrs. Hinson." His voice was deep and his grip was firm, but his habit of jerking his head to flip his hair off his face seemed immature.

"Detective Simon," Britt said. Her eyes darted back to the principal. "I'd like to know exactly what happened to Katie."

The principal pushed a piece of paper across his desk to her. "Read this, Mrs. Hinson. It was left on your daughter's jacket, together with this carnation, while the jacket was hanging on Katie's coat hook out in the hall." He indicated the long-stemmed flower on his desk.

The muscles in her throat constricted when she saw the familiar lined paper, the same childlike printing. Her eyes scanned the words on the sheet: "It's time. I want to run away with you. I want to marry you. I love you. Forget-Me-Not."

She glanced up. "Did anyone see who left this?"

"Unfortunately, no." The principal's swivel chair creaked again as he leaned back. "The printing indicates that it was probably one of the kids, maybe a fifth or sixth grader."

"I don't think so." She shook her head and handed the note back to Mr. Lotze. "There have been other notes— left on our front porch, on our car, here at school."

"Please start at the beginning, Mrs. Hinson. I want to hear everything that's happened from start to finish." Charlie Simon sat back, crossed his legs, and took a notepad and pen from the inside pocket of his suit jacket.

He flipped his hair back again, then narrowed his eyes and waited for her to start.

She expelled her breath in a deep sigh. The skin on her face felt tight, as if it might crack each time she began to speak. She glanced at the principal.

Mr. Lotze stood up. "I'll go see about Katie while you explain things to Detective Simon."

Once the door closed behind him, Britt started talking to the detective. The incidents poured out, from the progression of notes to the light bulb mix-up and someone giving Tippy a bone. "We think we have a prowler," she said, "and we don't know if the prowler and note writer are the same person."

"Uh-huh." The detective was noncommittal.

"Mark, my husband, even thought the notes might be intended for me." She did not mention their conflict over her theater friends or their suspicion that Katie might have written some of the notes herself. "But this one is obviously meant for Katie."

"Uh-huh," he said again. "Is that it?"

"Yes, I think so," she replied.

An awkward silence dropped between them. The detective tapped his fingers on his knee, his eyes fixed on his notepad.

He seems so detached, Britt thought, and wished the police had sent someone older and more experienced. Charlie Simon was a kid barely out of college. This was probably his first case.

"Can you help us?" she asked, breaking the silence. "This has been very upsetting to my family and me."

The detective replied with a question of his own. "Has anyone ever seen the prowler? Or the note writer?"

"No one except Katie. She calls him the flower man."

He glanced up from his notes. "When I got this call," he said, "I made a routine check to see if there had been other complaints, and I learned that Officer Wallace had already visited you. What did he tell you?"

"He suggested it was someone who knew Katie, maybe

had a crush on her. Or someone who was mad at her, or at Mark and me. He said it wasn't a police matter at this point." She hesitated. "I don't agree with him."

"Uh-huh," he said again.

Britt's heart sank at his casual reply. He didn't seem to be taking any of this seriously. Did he think she was exaggerating?

"At the time of the first incident was anything unusual going on in Katie's life?"

"It happened soon after Katie won second place in the modeling competition, shortly after school started."

"And the first note, the one she found on her lunch box. That note mentioned the modeling competition, didn't it?"

Britt nodded, worried about the direction of his questions. Like the principal, he seemed to think the note writer was a child.

"Is Katie having any problems right now?" the detective asked. "Either at home or school?"

"No, not anything serious." Britt thought about the charm school conflict and glanced away from the hot intensity of his vivid green eyes. "Just normal things."

"So you're pretty sure that your daughter wouldn't have made up the story about a flower man?"

"I'm positive," she said. "My daughter doesn't lie."

The door opened and Mr. Lotze stepped into the room in time to hear Britt's statement. "According to her teachers, Katie is a well-adjusted, responsible girl," he told the detective. Then he smiled at Britt. "Your daughter is fine now, Mrs. Hinson."

Charlie Simon stood up, stretching his length to a full six feet three or four inches. "Let's get Katie in here. Maybe she can shed more light on this."

Mr. Lotze picked up his phone and asked his secretary to bring Katie into his office.

Charlie Simon half slouched on the corner of the desk and picked up the carnation. "This came from a bouquet in the teachers' lounge," he said. "There was a party for one of the teachers at lunchtime." He straightened and put the flower back on the desk. "Mrs. Hinson, do you know that Katie's coat hook in the hall is next to the teachers' lounge?"

She was taken aback. What was that supposed to mean? Was he implying that it was Katie who took the carnation from the teachers' lounge? That it was Katie who wrote the note? She stared at him, determined to hold his gaze.

The door opened, and Katie ran to her mother, tears brimming her eyes. "Mom, the flower man was here. Oh, Mom, why is he doing this?"

"I don't know, honey, but we've found someone who will help us. Katie, this is Detective Charlie Simon." She brushed Katie's tears away and made room for her on the chair. "He wants to ask you some questions. Is that okay?"

Katie looked uncertain, but she nodded slowly.

"Hi, Katie," Charlie Simon said, smiling. "You don't mind talking about what's happened, do you?"

Her lashes fluttered. "No."

"Good. Let's start with a description, Katie. What does this flower man look like?"

"He—he—" She broke off, uncertain, and moved closer to her mother. "He looks sort of like you."

Britt caught an exchange of glances between the two men.

"What color is his hair?"

"It's dark."

"Black or brown?"

"I don't know, maybe black." Katie twisted a curl around her finger. "It's just real dark—and long."

"How long?"

"Over his ears. Maybe as long as yours."

"Is he an older boy? Or is he a man?"

"He's a grown-up." Her voice faded. "I don't know—old like you, but not as old as Mr. Lotze. He has a mustache."

"Doesn't he have a beard, too?" Britt prompted.

Katie looked startled. "He didn't have a beard this time."

"He had a beard on another occasion?" the detective asked.

"I—I thought so." Katie hesitated. "But maybe he really didn't."

By the time the detective finished, Katie's lips were quivering and tears were threatening again. The description she'd given was so vague that it could have fit almost anyone.

"Tell you what I'm going to do, Mrs. Hinson," the detective said. "I'll ask the custodians and the teachers if they saw anyone loitering in the school." He hesitated, as though going over everything in his mind. "And I'll talk to Katie's friend Donny, who was with her when the man gave her the forget-me-nots on the way home from school."

Britt nodded. "I'd appreciate that." Then she decided to be honest. "Detective Simon, I sense that you don't think this is a serious matter."

"On the contrary, Mrs. Hinson. We consider all calls serious, and we investigate them."

"And our school staff is always watchful of strangers," Mr. Lotze added. "We like to think we protect our students."

"Give me a call if there's another incident." Charlie Simon was already shaking hands with the principal. "You too, Mrs. Hinson. I'll make a report and it'll be on file." He handed her his card. "My number, at work and at home."

After reassurances from the principal, Britt and Katie were on their way to the car. Damn! she thought, frustrated. Her lack of confidence in the young detective equaled the apprehension she saw in Katie's eyes.

As they walked along the sidewalk, Katie held her mother's hand, something she hadn't done in a long time. She faced straight ahead, but her eyes moved back and forth, from the woods to the street and back again.

Britt realized she'd been wrong. There was more than apprehension in Katie's eyes. The child was terrified.

8

"MOM, I ALREADY TOLD DETECTIVE SIMON ALL ABOUT THE flower man."

"I know, honey, but Daddy wants to hear, too."

They were in the den watching television, and when the program ended, Mark had mouthed the word "now" behind Katie's back and turned the volume down. Sam was in bed for the night and Katie had finished her homework.

Britt had brought the subject up carefully before asking Katie to describe the flower man. When they'd left the school she'd kept the conversation light, hoping to allay Katie's fear.

Mark moved next to Katie on the sofa and placed his arm around her. "Your mom and I want to stop this, but we need your help. If you can give us more information about this man, then maybe we can find him and make him stop this foolishness."

Katie swallowed hard. She was trying not to cry. "I want him to stop too, Daddy. I don't like him. He makes me feel creepy."

"We know, honey." Britt sat on the other side of Katie. "He gives us the creeps, too."

Katie's eyes were round with fear. "Are you scared of him, too, Mom?"

"I'm more mad than scared." She smiled reassuringly. "He has no business doing things to frighten you."

Britt didn't want Katie to know just how scared she

was. Others could shrug the incidents off, but she knew there was someone out there, and it seemed to her that he was after Katie.

"Start with what happened today," Mark said. He squeezed her hand. "Your mom hasn't filled me in yet."

"It was afternoon recess," Katie began slowly, "and I went to get my jacket. That's when I found the carnation and the note tucked into the collar." Katie's voice broke on a sob.

"Go on," Britt prompted gently.

"It scared me, Daddy." Katie twisted her hair around her finger, exactly as she'd done earlier when Charlie Simon questioned her. "Because I just knew it was from *him.*"

"And then what did you do?" Mark smiled encouragement.

"I looked around—and I saw the flower man. He was at the end of the hall going out the door."

"Did you see his face?"

"Just for a tiny second, from the side, sort of. But I know it was him."

Mark met Britt's eyes momentarily. "How did you know it was him?"

Katie drew her knees up to hug them. "I just knew." She hesitated, then spoke in halting sentences. "He was wearing jeans, and he has dark hair that waves a little, and a bushy mustache. His hair is longer than yours, Daddy, and he's as tall, but I don't know how old." She paused again, frowning. "He looks like a nice man, because he always smiles." She glanced between them. "He reminds me of someone I saw on TV once." Her arms tightened around her knees. "But I don't like him."

"Did any of your friends see him today?" Mark asked softly.

"I told Jennifer, but when she looked he was already gone."

"Then none of the other kids saw him." Mark's words sounded flat.

Katie shook her head. "And the carnation and note weren't on my jacket when I went to the bathroom before recess."

Mark kept his gaze on Katie, but Britt sensed his body tense.

"So when you went to the bathroom you walked past your coat?" Mark asked.

"Uh-huh. I had to pass my hook on my way to the girls' room."

"You didn't tell Detective Simon that you went to the bathroom before recess," Britt said softly. "How come?"

"I forgot, that's all." She lowered her head to stare at her lap.

There was a pause. "Katie, did you know that the teachers were having a party in the teachers' room?" Mark asked.

Katie shook her head. "No, but us kids saw the florist bring the flowers."

"I see." Mark withdrew his arm, his expression troubled.

Britt knew he was bothered by the fact that Katie knew the carnations were in the teachers' room. "Is there anything more you can tell Daddy and me?" she asked. "Anything you might have forgotten?"

Katie shook her head again, glancing up at her dad. "You do believe me, don't you, Daddy?" Her eyes shifted to Britt. "Don't you, Mom?"

"I think you believe there's a flower man, honey." Mark managed a smile, but Britt saw his doubt. "Do you think it might be possible that you only thought you saw him? Of all the kids in the hall at recess, don't you think it's odd that no one else noticed him?"

Katie jumped up, looking hurt and angry. "You don't believe me! Neither of you do! You've never believed me!" Tears welled up in her eyes.

Britt stood up, too, and shot Mark a warning glance before he said more. It was upsetting to realize that Katie knew about the flowers and that she had been in the hall just before recess. Too many details pointed to Katie herself. But some things did suggest a stranger, Britt reminded herself—like the note on the car windshield. Katie hadn't put it there, and all of the notes had obviously been written by the same person. Didn't that mean that Katie hadn't written any of them?

"We know you wouldn't lie to us," Britt said finally. "Daddy and I need to ask questions so we'll know everything you know." She dabbed at Katie's tears with a Kleenex. "We want to find this flower man and tell him to stop bothering our little girl. Okay?"

Katie took a shuddering breath, but the tears stopped. "All right, Mom." She managed a smile, and for a second she looked more like a four-year-old.

"That's better," Britt said.

"I just want you and Daddy to know I'm telling the truth." Katie wiped her wet face with the hem of her nightgown. "No one else believes me, but the flower man is real, and I'm scared of him."

Britt took Katie's hand. "Come on, honey. It's time for bed. I'll go upstairs with you and hear your prayers." She gave her a little nudge toward Mark. "Give Daddy a good-night kiss."

Katie kissed Mark, then impulsively hugged him close. "I'm glad you believe me, Daddy." Her eyes were wide, and she gleamed with innocence. "I love you—and Mom and Sam." Then she went upstairs with Britt.

Mark was waiting when Britt came back down. "I can't accept her story," he said. "The way Katie described the flower man you'd think she was describing a television actor." He sighed and pressed his fingertips against his forehead, as though he had a migraine.

"I don't think Katie is lying, Mark," she said. His head jerked up, and she went on quickly. "Oh, I know how it looks, but how do you explain the note I found on my car at Steward's? That was one time we know she wasn't involved."

"She could have picked up a flyer when she went to get the cart, Britt. She could have written on it in the store, then put it on the windshield while you were busy settling Sam in his car seat."

She drew in her breath sharply. "If she's that devious, then she must really be sick. I don't believe it!"

"I don't know what to believe anymore." He hesitated. "I think you'd better have a talk with Dr. Peters, Britt. Get his advice. Maybe he'll recommend a child psychologist."

Britt dropped her head into her hands, her thoughts spinning. Maybe everything Katie said was true, but what if it wasn't? She would talk to their family doctor. He'd known Katie all her life and would know what to do.

She lifted her head. "I'll call him tomorrow," she told Mark.

Five days after her decision to call Dr. Peters, Britt sat in the office of Dr. Hyatt, a child psychologist. She'd left Sam with her mother, picked Katie up after school, and driven downtown just ahead of the rush-hour traffic for the four o'clock appointment. Alone in the mauve and gray waiting room, she killed time by watching the boats on the Willamette River beyond the window.

She sighed. It had been a busy few days. She was just glad her play had closed on Saturday night.

Britt leaned back against the leather cushion, fidgeting with her purse strap. Let him be a good doctor, she thought. She closed her eyes, remembering her brief conversation with Dr. Hyatt. He'd seemed so opinionated about what she'd told him, so sure about his conclusions.

The thought was disturbing. Katie was in his hands right this minute. Dr. Hyatt comes highly recommended, she reminded herself. His manner with Katie might be very different from the tone he'd taken with Britt on the phone. She tried to reassure herself, but it was no use. The doctor had turned her off. If Mark hadn't insisted she go through with the appointment, she would have canceled.

The wallpaper's mauve and gray swirls were depressing. Whirlpools of the mind? she wondered. The image seemed appropriate. When Dr. Hyatt had come out of his inner sanctum to greet Katie, Britt had been even less impressed. He was a tall, thin man with a high voice and baggy trousers, his brown eyes peered owlishly from behind silver dollar–size wire-rimmed glasses, and his attitude was condescending.

Restless, Britt got up and went to the window. Don't let this be a mistake, she told herself. He was messing with her daughter's mind. What if he made things worse?

Dr. Hyatt had no receptionist. He answered his own phone, made his own appointments, and greeted his patients himself; during sessions his answering service took messages. Everything was discreet, and the doctor charged accordingly.

His office door opened finally, and he came out smiling, leading a somber Katie. "You just sit there like a little lady while I chat with your mommy." His round eyes shifted to focus on Britt.

Katie nodded and sat down, her long lashes lowered, her hands clasped in her lap. She didn't even glance at her mother.

"Are you all right, honey?" Britt was concerned. Katie seemed intimidated.

Katie looked up. "I told the truth, Mom. I didn't lie."

Britt glanced at the doctor. What had he done to her child? Ignoring him, she sat down next to Katie. "I know you told the truth." She took her hand. "Are you sure you'll be all right while I talk to Dr. Hyatt? I won't be long and then we'll go home."

Katie swallowed hard, then nodded again.

Britt still hesitated. Her impulse was to take Katie and leave, but reason asserted itself. She gave Katie's hand a squeeze, kissed her on the cheek, and followed the doctor into his office.

He closed the door, indicated she sit in another leather chair, then hoisted his trousers and sat down on the other side of the coffee table. A gas fire burned in the fireplace, books lined one wall, and plants grew under the picture window, but nothing softened the austerity of the room. Britt felt chilled as she sat down and placed her purse at her feet.

"Coffee?" He indicated the silver carafe on the table and gave a slow, owlish blink behind the magnifying lenses.

"No, thank you."

He poured himself a cup, stirred in a sugar lump, and took a sip. Time stretched the silence. She wondered if the coffee was a deliberate delaying tactic. She instructed herself to remain composed until he spoke.

"Well, Mrs. Hinson." He paused for another sip. "I'll be direct. Katie has some problems. They aren't serious yet, but they will be if they're not addressed."

Goose bumps rose on Britt's body. "Surely Katie does *not* have a serious problem, Dr. Hyatt." She sounded argumentative. "She was a perfectly normal child until the advent of the so-called flower man."

"I'm sure you realize that this man might be a figment of her imagination."

She leaned forward. "You can't be suggesting that a normal child has suddenly become a liar."

He smiled patiently. "It might help you to know that many parents go through denial." He sobered abruptly. "But let me assure you, Mrs. Hinson, burying your head in the sand won't help Katie."

She took a deep breath. "I was seeking perspective from you, Dr. Hyatt, not accusations."

"It's not my intent to accuse, Mrs. Hinson," he said with infuriating calm. "Helping Katie cope with her problem is."

She stiffened. "What are you suggesting is Katie's problem?"

"Mrs. Hinson, please bear with me for a moment." He rubbed his palms together and stared at her. "I've heard the whole story from Katie's viewpoint, and it's my belief that she invented this flower man. It's likely she wrote the notes. It's even possible one of her friends is in on it; that would explain the discrepancies."

She started to protest, but he lifted a hand for silence. "Let me finish, please. Katie appears to have an excessive need for attention. You yourself explained that she was carried away by the modeling competition, that she keeps insisting on attending charm school."

Britt could hardly be civil. Her first impression had been right: this man was a pompous ass. "My daughter was dazzled by the attention, yes, but she's not a liar. Her fear is real, Dr. Hyatt. You haven't witnessed her terror."

"Mrs. Hinson, I agree with you that Katie is fearful." He paused. "But I believe she may have transferred a suppressed fear to a situation she made up."

"Why would she do that?"

"To give herself a vehicle through which to express her fear." His eyelids came down in a slow blink, and he took a sip of his coffee, prolonging the moment. "I believe Katie may feel upstaged by the birth of her brother. She may fear that he is loved more than she is."

Britt laughed. "Dr. Hyatt, you can't be serious. Sam is two years old. Katie was thrilled when he was born. She was seven then, not a preschooler."

"I'm quite serious, Mrs. Hinson."

She blushed angrily. "Why would Katie wait until now to express the fears you suggest?" she demanded.

"I don't know. That's what we'll try to find out in therapy." He hesitated. "Once I've peeled away the top layers, I'll be able to give you a clearer answer. Of course it's possible that the problem stems from something else entirely."

"Such as?"

"Low self-esteem resulting from physical, mental, or sexual abuse." He spread his hands. "As I said, it's too early to make a determination."

"You can eliminate abuse right now," she said indignantly.

He stood, ending their conversation. "I want you to

94

talk to your husband about what we've discussed. I know it's a lot to take in." He smiled stiffly and extended his hand. "I recommend that Katie have one therapy session a week."

"My husband and I will discuss that possibility and let you know what we decide," Britt said, but her mind was already made up: she wouldn't let Katie go anywhere near this man, ever again.

He led her back to the waiting room, wiggled his fingers at Katie, then stepped back into his office and closed the door.

Katie's eyes were red-rimmed but dry. Britt put her arm around her as they rode the elevator down to the parking garage.

On the way home Katie started to cry in earnest. Britt reached out and squeezed her hand.

"No one believes me, not even Dr. Hyatt," Katie said, brokenly. "Everyone thinks I'm lying about the flower man."

"I believe you, honey," Britt said, and meant it.

"I hate Dr. Hyatt," Katie said with a flash of anger. "Please don't make me go back to him. He asked me if my grandmas and grandpas loved Sam more than me. He even asked if you and Daddy loved Sam more than me." She stared wide-eyed at Britt. "You don't, do you?"

"You know we don't, Katie. Daddy and I love you and Sam the same, but you and Sam have different needs. Sometimes you get something and Sam doesn't—and vice versa. We love you both very much, and so do your grandparents."

Katie managed a smile. "That's what I told Dr. Hyatt, but he acted like he thought I was making up stories. Do I have to see him again?"

"No. You aren't going back to him, Katie." Britt glanced at her and caught her grim expression. "If you'll give me a smile, I'll tell you a secret."

Katie managed a lopsided grin, and Britt whispered, "I didn't much like Dr. Hyatt either."

Katie's forced grin turned into a genuine smile, and

soon they were laughing out loud. By the time Britt pulled into the driveway they both felt better. Britt knew the psychologist was wrong about Katie. She hoped she wasn't.

"She's not going back to see that awful man, Mark, and that's final."

"I can't believe you rejected the doctor because of a gut-level response. You've lost your perspective, Britt. We need professional assistance with this problem. You aren't helping matters by swallowing this flower man story whole." He lowered his eyes. "That is, I believe Katie, too—up to a point."

Britt sighed, her gaze on Katie and Sam in the backyard. Katie was teaching him how to bat a ball. She was far more patient than most big sisters. *She didn't resent Sam.*

"Supper is almost ready," she said. "Let's not talk about this now and ruin our meal. Believe me, if you'd met that sanctimonious doctor you would have felt the same way. He had everything figured out in fifty minutes —no, forty minutes. He spent ten with me. He wouldn't consider any opinions except his own."

"Don't forget, Britt. He *is* the doctor."

"And I'm the mother. No one wants this mess straightened out more than I do." She put on an oven mitt and pulled the roaster of chicken breasts out of the oven. "Katie *will not* see Dr. Hyatt again."

"Then at least agree to let her see someone else. We can't just sit here and do nothing."

"What about Katie's feelings?" Britt tossed the mitt on the counter. "What if—just what if she's telling the truth, Mark? I won't have some idiot screwing up her head."

He poked at his black curls until they stood out like a Halloween wig. "So what do you suggest, Britt? That we continue to live under siege, waiting for the next note, fearful in our own home?" He pounded a fist on the counter. "Maybe we should sell the house and move."

"Come on, Mark. I don't need your dramatics. I'm not saying we don't have a problem. Only that I don't believe Katie caused it. She isn't a liar, and she is *not* emotionally disturbed."

"Mom! Daddy!" Katie tapped on the glass door, interrupting them. "Watch Sam hit the ball."

They stood by the window and watched Katie make sure the ball hit Sam's little plastic bat. Sam yelped with pleasure, and Katie beamed with pride.

"She's so patient," Mark said, as the game resumed.

"Because she loves him," Britt said softly. "She's not jealous of him, Mark. Dr. Hyatt is wrong."

He shook his head. "I don't know what to believe. I'm just glad your play is over. At least you'll be home more now."

Britt let the comment pass. She felt like reminding him that it wasn't the play that started it all; it was the modeling competition—Mark's bright idea.

Katie woke up with a sore throat and fever the next morning and was home from school for several days. Then Sam came down with the virus that immediately turned into the croup. Britt didn't bother going to bed that night.

As she refilled the vaporizer in Sam's room she thought he seemed better. He wasn't coughing at the moment, and his fever was down. He lay sprawled with only the dinosaur-print sheet over him, his dark curls moist with sweat. She resisted pulling up his blanket; the doctor had said to keep him cool.

She checked on Katie next, standing for a moment beside her bed as she slept. No notes had arrived since Katie got sick, and Britt had mixed feelings about that—relief and dread. Dr. Hyatt's words came back to haunt her.

Turning away, Britt went down to the den and picked up her book. It was four in the morning, she hadn't even catnapped, and her body ached with fatigue. After a while, despite her resolve not to sleep, she dozed off.

A sound brought her upright in her chair a few minutes later. A small scraping noise, like tree branches grazing a window. She put the book aside, stood up quietly, and crept into the hall, her eyes on the front door. The glow from the porch light shone in through the window, casting a patch of light over the Oriental runner on the floor. She stayed in the shadows, waiting for the sound to come again. The doors and windows were all locked. She'd checked. It was her nightly ritual these days.

There it was again.

The sound came from the front of the house. It could be a stray dog, she thought. Or raccoons.

Or it could be the prowler.

Britt stepped out of her tennis shoes, tiptoed to a window, and peeked out from behind the curtain. Nothing moved outside. She went through the dining room to the kitchen and checked the backyard. The patio light was on, Tippy was curled up on the doorstep. The house creaked above her, settling as it always did during the night.

She had an urge to check on the children. Maybe she'd only thought the sound came from the front; perhaps it was really above her. Her heart jolted.

She ran up the back steps to the second floor and hurried to one room, then the other. Sam was breathing better with the cool vapor, and Katie was in a deep sleep. Her children were safe.

Still the apprehension clung to her like the predawn chill. She went back to her book in the den, but she couldn't read, nor could she doze off. Fear does that to you, she thought, wide awake, her ears straining to hear the smallest sound. At first light Mark came downstairs.

"You look as if you could use some coffee," he said, then gave her a closer look. "Weren't you able to sleep at all?"

"I dozed off once for a few minutes."

She raised her lips for his kiss, then followed him into the kitchen. Tired or not, she enjoyed their early morning coffee together. We'll be doing this when we're in our rocking chairs, she thought.

Mark went to get the newspaper and came back a minute later, the paper in one hand—a note in the other.

"It's like the others. Says the same things and is signed 'Forget-Me-Not.'" He slammed the note down on the table. "When will it stop!"

"Mark, I heard him. I was dozing, and a sound woke me up. It was sometime after four." Slowly she got up from her chair. Her words sounded breathy and disjointed. "I checked on the kids, and they were both sound asleep. *Katie was sound asleep.*"

He stared as if she were a raving madwoman.

"Don't you get it?" She grabbed the sleeve of his sweatshirt. "The person who left the note wasn't Katie."

"The doctor said it could be a friend."

"Fuck the doctor!" She didn't care how crude she sounded. "None of Katie's friends would be out at four in the morning, and you know it!"

"If it wasn't Katie," Mark said, looking dazed, "then who was it?"

"It was Forget-me-not. The flower man."

9

"I CAN'T BELIEVE IT'S STILL GOING ON." ANGIE FROWNED IN disbelief. "What's it been—about a month since you first mentioned it?" She put down her wineglass. "It sounds serious, Britt."

Angie had listened all through lunch while Britt brought her up to date on what had happened. She hadn't meant to talk about the notes, but when Angie mentioned the tryouts for *The Mousetrap*, she'd explained why she couldn't accept another part. The reasons had spilled out nonstop.

"It is serious, Angie." Britt traced the rim of her glass with her finger. "Even though it's obvious to me that Katie is this guy's target, Mark thinks the notes might be meant for me, that someone connected to the theater might have a crush on me."

"No offense, Britt, but I haven't noticed anyone with a romantic interest in you. Most of the guys are either happily married or gay."

"I know. It's ridiculous." She spread her hands. "We're shell-shocked, grabbing at straws. We don't know what to believe. Mark even insisted I stop jogging early in the morning and just stick to aerobics for now, because we're so spooked."

"I think that's a good idea." Angie hesitated. "And I agree that the psychologist is a world-class asshole."

Britt grinned. "I almost told him that, he made me so mad."

Angie sobered. "How do you and Mark plan to handle this?"

Britt drank the last of her wine, and Angie motioned the waiter to bring them each another glass. They had a window table, and she glanced out at the ducks floating on the water. The restaurant was built over the Willamette River, its entrance reached by a catwalk. The serene setting made their crazy situation even harder to credit.

"We're open to suggestions." Britt's voice cracked, and she cleared her throat. "Do you have one?"

Angie shook her head. "I wish I did." She hesitated, her dark eyes concerned. "You have no idea who's doing this?"

"None."

The waiter brought their wine, and they waited until he'd moved away before resuming their conversation.

"If the police can't do anything, then what about the postal inspector's office?" Angie tapped a red fingernail on the tablecloth. "Isn't it against the law for this guy to use your mailbox?"

"I called them a couple of days ago. They're sending a form for me to fill out. And there's nothing they can do, anyway. They're mostly interested in major disasters, like letter bombs and fraudulent advertisers."

"Did you tell them someone was using your mailbox illegally?"

"Of course. But the notes didn't actually come through the mail, so they're out of the postal inspector's jurisdiction."

"I've got it." Angie leaned forward. "What if you call our representative to the state assembly. I recently read in the newspaper that he's lobbying for a state law against stalking."

"I did talk to someone in his office. She listened to my story, confirmed that it could be a stalker, and said that time would tell." She clasped her hand around the stem of her wineglass.

"But the representative can't help you?"

She shook her head. "Other than to give me the profile of a typical stalker—his modus operandi."

"And does this guy fit the profile?"

"Unfortunately, he does." She glanced out the window again. "They said this type of stalker is usually a stranger. He finds someone to fit his fantasy, and then he never gives up."

"Good God!"

"If it is a stalker, we may never see him until he strikes. And even if we do spot him, there's no law to protect us unless he actually gets caught doing something illegal. Stalking alone isn't a crime."

"They can't do *anything?*"

"Not until a law is passed. That's what the representative is lobbying for. But it takes time." Her voice broke. "And what if we don't have time? What if some horrible pervert is after Katie?"

Angie reached out to pat Britt's hand. "Let's hope the whole thing goes away like the cop said, that it's a kid with a crush on her."

Britt managed a smile. Her mother's instinct told her

that Katie was the target of someone far more dangerous than a kid.

The conversation switched to the tryouts, and when the check came, they paid and left the restaurant, crossed the catwalk to shore, and walked to the garage. As they separated, Angie hugged her.

"Let me know if there's anything I can do to help."

"Thanks, Angie."

"And keep me posted, okay?"

"Sure." Britt glanced at her watch. "I've got to run."

Angie gave a quick nod. They both knew why Britt had to hurry—to make sure Katie got home from school safely.

On Saturday morning the patio light was burned out again. Mark came into the kitchen carrying the bulb.

"I wonder if there's an electrical problem. This is a sixty-watt bulb."

Britt shook her head. "It's not an electrical problem," she said. "There was another note outside the door. It's over there, on the table."

Mark picked up the note, scanned it, and put it back down. "Same old crap," he said.

"Aren't we getting blasé?"

He ignored her gibe. "I'm calling the electrician anyway. It would explain a lot if this turns out to be a simple wiring problem."

"What would it explain?" Britt crossed her arms and stared at him.

"That some of the shit we think happened might only have been our imagination."

His sharp tone discouraged her from voicing her argument to the contrary. "I think you're wrong, but go ahead. Get the electrician's opinion."

He sighed loudly. "Everything that goes wrong around here isn't because of this—this note writer." He swept the note off the table onto the floor.

"Don't take your fear out on me, Mark!"

"I'm not the one who's afraid of my own shadow." He

grabbed the telephone book and thumbed through it. "You're making a big deal out of everything, including burned-out light bulbs."

"A big deal?" Her tone was incredulous. "And you're trying to find excuses so you can deny the problem!"

He picked up the telephone. His finger hesitated on the push buttons. "No, Britt. Unlike you, I'm trying not to magnify the problem beyond what it is."

"Don't twist my words, Mark. You know what I'm saying. And you know I'm right."

His retort was cut off by Katie running down the back stairs. "What's wrong, Daddy?"

Mark set his jaw, turned away, and called the electrician. While he talked, Britt started breakfast, diverting Katie from whatever she might have overheard. When Mark put down the phone he was calmer.

"Bob Wright is coming out this afternoon."

"On a Saturday?" Britt was surprised.

"I agreed to pay his Saturday rate." He started toward the steps. "It'll be worth it," he said over his shoulder, and went upstairs to shave and shower.

The electrician reported that the wiring was fine. Britt didn't comment, but she knew what had happened. The prowler had replaced the good bulb with a bad one again. She was relieved when Mark asked Bob Wright to install a light at every corner of the house. Britt came out to watch while Katie and Sam played with Tippy in the backyard.

"They'll be automatic," Mark said, joining her outside, but not meeting her eyes. "Come on at dusk, go off when it's light."

"That's a good idea."

A silence dropped between them. "I'm sorry, Britt," he said, and hesitated.

She waited, giving him time. It was hard for Mark to apologize.

"I was wrong . . . about the wiring."

He was dressed in Levi's and a red sweatshirt; both

were smudged with dirt from helping the electrician. His hair hung down over his forehead, and he looked virile and sexy . . . and ashamed of himself.

"I love you, Britt. I don't know what got into me. Having another burned-out bulb threw me for a loop, and I lashed out at you."

"The bulb and the note upset me, too." She paused. "And I love you, Mark. I'm sorry I got mad."

He glanced away. "I get so frustrated. Sometimes I don't know what in the hell to think anymore." His tone hardened. "That bastard out there better take warning. He's messing with my family."

She took his hand and squeezed it. "And mine."

Britt took advantage of Sam's nap time to winterize her box garden of herbs, a task she'd put off while the kids were sick.

She stood up to stretch, brushed the dirt off her old blue sweats, and rubbed a crick out of her back. Mark was watching a football game on television in the den, and Katie was writing a book report in her room.

Glancing at the patio door, she wondered if she should check on Sam before getting started again. The sunlight shone directly on the glass door, highlighting smudges and rain spots. She stepped closer. Some of the smears were higher than either Sam or Tippy could reach. She touched the highest mark, which was about six inches above the top of her head. It felt greasy. A couple of inches below the grease stain was a small oval mark, as if something soft had been pressed against the glass.

"Oh, my God!"

She jerked her hand away, as if she'd touched snake venom. The window above the kitchen sink and the garden room window were smudged in exactly the same way, at the height of an average man. Her eyes darted to the sun-dappled woods behind the fence, where the changing leaves were like an artist's palette of earth tones among the towering evergreens.

THE FLOWER MAN

What if he's watching?

Stay calm, she told herself. Don't panic. Make sure of your suspicion before you alarm Mark.

Britt put down her trowel, ran to the garage, and went straight to the tool drawer in the workbench. "Where's the damn tape measure?" she muttered. In frustration, she dumped the contents onto the top of the bench.

"What's all the commotion?" Mark said from the doorway that connected the garage and the laundry room. "What are you doing, Britt? You're making a mess of my tools."

"I need the tape measure." She didn't look up. "Where did you put it?"

"It's where I always keep it." He stepped behind her and pulled it from a hook above the bench.

She grabbed the tape and took off for the kitchen.

"Britt, what's going on?" He trailed her through the kitchen to the patio door, where she hesitated.

"I need to measure something. I think he's been looking in our windows."

"What?" He glanced past her to the woods.

Exactly my first reaction, she thought.

"What are you up to?" he asked sharply. He stopped her hand before she opened the sliding glass door. "Britt, please tell me what you're doing."

"I'll show you."

She led him outside. "See those smudges." She indicated the windows. "I'm going to measure the height, see if they're all the same." She didn't have to say more.

Mark took the tape and measured them himself. Each smudge was exactly the same distance from the ground. "Let's check the other windows while we're at it," he said grimly.

She nodded. They walked around the entire house in silence, not bothering to measure the other smudges.

"The marks are on all the ground-floor windows." Britt's voice was a shaky whisper. "He followed us from room to room."

105

"Looks that way." He stooped suddenly to examine the flower bed under the kitchen window. Seconds later he glanced at her. "Take a look, Britt."

She moved closer, her eyes on where he pointed. "A footprint."

"Uh-huh."

She bent closer. The indentation was clearly defined in the mix of bark and moist dirt. "Could it be yours?"

He shook his head, pointing to the footprints next to it. "Those are mine. They're smaller, with different markings on the soles." He hesitated. "And mine are fresh, the other one has been there awhile."

Her hands clenched into fists. "What are we going to do? He's out there. And no one believes us."

"Believe me, I'll do something. That fucker isn't getting away with this." He moved to the patio door and carefully touched the smudge with his index finger. Then he smelled it. "Some type of hair product, I think."

"Then the lower smudge would be where his nose was pressed against the glass."

"Or an ear."

"Heaven help us, Mark. I'm scared to be in my own backyard."

"Let's get inside." Mark took her arm. "I've got goose bumps right now too."

"Like we're being watched?"

He didn't answer. They went inside, and he closed and locked the door.

"Do you still have that detective's card—the one who came to the school?"

"Yes. Good idea."

Britt called Charlie Simon's office number, left a message, and was told that he would call her back as soon as possible. Then Mark upended a wooden box over the footprint to preserve it, placing a heavy rock on top of the box to prevent Tippy or Sam from displacing it.

They ate supper, watched television with Katie and Sam, and managed to keep a normal atmosphere. Each time the phone rang Mark left the room to answer it. They didn't want to frighten Katie.

The detective hadn't called by ten the next morning so Britt took the children to church alone. Mark insisted on staying home. "I don't want to miss Simon's call," he told her.

When Britt returned with the children Mark called her into the den and said he had talked to the detective. "Charlie Simon was out on another case. That's why it took him so long to return your call. I gave him a rundown of what's been going on, and I told him about the footprint and the smudges. He's coming here tomorrow morning at ten o'clock."

Shortly before dawn the next morning Britt sat straight up in bed, fully alert, listening. The wind gusted against the house, shook the shrubbery, and rattled the window screens. Rain whispered and shuffled against the roof shakes.

She went to look in on the children, moving down the shadowy hall like a wraith. Both slept soundly. She hesitated in Katie's doorway, suddenly apprehensive.

Silly ninny. Fraidycat, she chided herself. You're programmed to be scared these days. Every time the autumn wind blows, you imagine someone's out there.

Her eyes were drawn to the corner windows. No light shone through the drapes.

She crossed the room on tiptoe. A peek from the side of the drapes confirmed her fear: the new automatic light was out.

Her knees buckled and she sat down on the carpet. She took deep gulps of air. Get a grip, she told herself. Seconds passed and she stood up, forcing herself to look outside again. Reason told her that no one could be lurking outside the second-story window.

The side window of Katie's room looked down onto the roof of the garage and garden room; the rear windows into the backyard. Nothing moved. Britt expelled an uneven breath; she hadn't realized she'd been holding it.

Sleep was out of the question now. She felt compelled to make sure that no one was in the house. Leaving Katie's room took all the courage she could muster. She thought about waking Mark but decided against it. She would not allow fear to control her life.

But fear did dominate her emotions for the next few minutes while she crept downstairs to inspect the locks, confirming that her house was safe.

She went back to bed finally, to wait until it was light.

Breakfast was almost ready when Mark came downstairs shortly before seven, grumbling about the rain, which had subsided to a dreary gray drizzle.

Britt poured some coffee for him, and then told him about the light.

For a second, disbelief was reflected on his face. Then he said, "I'll check that out right now."

She watched him turn off the automatic light switch so he could test the bulb manually, set up the ladder, climb it, and examine the bulb.

"Flip the switch for me, Britt," he said. "The bulb wasn't screwed in all the way. I tightened it."

She nodded, and flipped the switch. The light came on.

"That's a relief," he said, climbing down the ladder. "For once there's a logical reason for a light being out."

A short time later Mark left for work. "Good luck with Simon," he said as he got into the Honda. "I'll call you this afternoon."

"I'll be here."

Britt blew him a kiss and watched him back out of the garage. She was relieved to know Charlie Simon would be there at ten. Still her apprehension lingered, and she decided to drive Katie to school.

"It's still raining and you'll get wet if you walk," she said when Katie protested. "You just got over a cold virus, and we don't want it coming back."

She had no sooner returned home than Charlie Simon rang the front doorbell. She opened the door to find the detective looking even more youthful than she remembered, in a tweed jacket and sharply creased brown trousers.

"Mrs. Hinson, I'd like to look around your yard before we talk, okay?"

"Of course. Go right ahead."

His manner seemed more professional than it had before, Britt noticed, and that was a good sign. And she liked the way he looked her straight in the eye when he spoke. Maybe he was better at his job than she'd suspected.

He put his collar up and started toward the back.

"When you finish, come on into the kitchen," Britt told him.

"Right."

Britt had barely settled Sam on the kitchen floor with Tippy when Charlie Simon tapped on the patio door, then stepped inside with a gust of damp wind that billowed the drapes. The detective looked at her strangely, his eyes noncommittal. There was a brief silence. A chill rippled over Britt.

"What in hell's going on here?"

"Pardon me?"

"Mrs. Hinson, there are no smudges on the windows, and there's no footprint in the flower bed."

Britt stared wide-eyed.

10

It took several seconds for Charlie Simon's words to register. "That's impossible!" she said. "The rain couldn't have washed the smudges away. The windows are under the overhang, and unless the wind is blowing just right, they don't get wet. And the footprint can't have been washed away. My husband put a box over it to protect it. Come with me, I'll show you." She stepped out onto the patio, and the detective followed.

As they walked through the drizzle to the flower bed, Britt's eyes narrowed on the spot where she'd found the footprint. She couldn't believe it: the box was gone, and the dirt was absolutely smooth, as though it had been raked.

Her gaze darted to the window. The greasy smudge was gone, as was the smaller mark beneath it. Britt ran to the patio door, then to the garden room window. No smudges. She was about to continue on around the house, when the detective's words stopped her.

"Don't bother. All of the windows are clean."

She whirled around to face him. "I don't understand. How could the marks be gone?"

He spread his hands, as though he couldn't figure it out either, but his green eyes were intense as they met hers.

"Mark and I both saw them!"

Britt glanced at the shadowy woods beneath the dreary sky. How had he known? Had he watched her find the spots? Had he seen Mark measure the smudges on the windows? *Was he watching right now?*

She hugged herself to stop shivering. "It was the prowler." Her voice was hardly more than a whisper. "He wiped away the evidence so you wouldn't see it . . . so you wouldn't believe us."

Simon's expression didn't change. The wind caught his hair, blowing long strands into his face. He brushed them away as he considered her words. "That's possible, of course." He hesitated. "But it's a little far-fetched."

"You don't believe me, do you? You think the prowler is a figment of my imagination."

"I didn't say that, Mrs. Hinson, but I am having difficulty with this." His smile didn't quite reach his eyes. "Let's get out of the rain and talk about it. I'll take it from there once I've heard everything."

For a second longer she hesitated. "I only ask that you keep an open mind, Detective Simon. Something is going on here. We don't know who is doing it, or why. Maybe it's some kind of a sick joke." She managed to sound calmer. "We only know someone is scaring the hell out of us, and we're beginning to feel like prisoners in our own home."

They went back inside, and the detective closed the sliding glass door behind them.

"Nice kid," Charlie Simon said, indicating Sam who sat playing on the floor. "Well behaved for a— How old is he?"

"Sam is two."

"Any other kids beside Sam and Katie?" He took a leatherbound notebook and ballpoint pen from an inside pocket of his jacket.

"No." She felt soggy from the rain and wiped her hands on a dish towel. "Please, sit down."

He pulled out one of the oak chairs, then folded his long legs under the kitchen table as he sat. "Easier to write," he said, with a brief grin and a flash of dimples that reminded her of how young he was.

"Mind if I ask you a question?" She took the chair across from him, near Sam.

He was writing and glanced up. "Go ahead."

"You seem . . . young to be a detective. I was wondering—"

"I'm thirty-two." His expression tightened. "I assure you, Mrs. Hinson, I'm an experienced investigator, if that's what you're getting at." He drummed his pen on the notebook. "My degree is in police science; I graduated cum laude. I've been with the department for seven years, even got sent to Quantico to study profiling and forensics."

"Quantico?"

"The FBI Academy in Virginia."

"Oh. Sounds impressive," she said, her voice stiff with embarrassment. She felt stupid.

His dimples came and went so fast she didn't know if he'd smiled or not. "Why don't you fill me in on everything that's happened since the incident at Katie's school? Your husband told me on the telephone that you had received quite a stack of notes."

Britt got the notes out and gave them to him. "They're in chronological order."

He didn't comment as he read through them. When he finished, he set the pages aside and made a notation.

"Go ahead," he said, looking up. "Start with the first incident."

She licked her lips. Why did she feel that this was an exercise in futility? Because he hadn't commented on the notes? She remembered her impression at school—that he suspected Katie had written the notes. She wondered what he thought now.

"The first incident occurred shortly after Katie was in the modeling competition," she began. "She came home with a bouquet of forget-me-nots a strange man had given her." She went through the whole chain of events, hesitated, then decided to get everything out on the table. "Because the whole thing was so puzzling at first, we wondered if Katie was a little stagestruck, fibbing about seeing the, uh, flower man." She leaned toward him. "But we know now that Katie didn't fib about anything. And she's never been one to exaggerate, either."

He lifted his impenetrable gaze to her. "Tell me more about the modeling competition."

She explained how it had worked and how Katie had happened to take part. Then, as she went on to the more recent incidents, Britt found herself talking faster, over-emphasizing small points when Charlie Simon didn't comment. Her final words fell into another silence. He continued to scribble in his notebook. She tried to see what he'd written, but his arm obstructed her line of vision.

"Is that all?" he asked when his pen paused on the paper.

She nodded, waiting.

He tucked his notebook and pen back into his pocket. She couldn't stand the suspense. "Can you help us?"

THE FLOWER MAN

"I'm afraid we don't have any real evidence here, Mrs. Hinson." He unwound his legs from under the table and stood up. "It's too bad the smudges are gone. If they'd been at the same height on each window it might have indicated you had a peeper."

"*If?* Detective Simon, there *were* smudges, they *were* at the same height, and there *is* a prowler." She got to her feet.

He nodded noncommittally. "I'm afraid we need hard evidence."

"You've read the notes, and you have our statement of what's happened." Her voice rose. "And I want to assure you again that Mark and I do not exaggerate. What I've told you is completely true."

"I have no reason to doubt your honesty, Mrs. Hinson," he said. "The problem is that we have no suspect, no real threat, no evidence, and no clear description of the so-called flower man. No one's ever seen him, except your little girl and her friends. I talked with her friend Donny, and he couldn't add anything to what Katie said. In fact, he hardly remembered the guy who gave her the forget-me-nots."

"But Mark and I both saw the smudges and the footprint, and—" Frustration choked off the rest of Britt's protest.

"Mrs. Hinson, I can't arrest a phantom who may or may not have been hovering around your property."

"The man is not a phantom. This is my family. Our lives are being threatened."

"Has someone threatened you? You didn't tell me about that."

"Not directly, but we *feel* threatened." Her gaze was direct. "I want you to be honest with me, Detective Simon. Can you help us?"

He let out a long whistling breath. "To be frank, I can't do much, aside from alerting local patrol cars to keep an eye on your house, swing through your street a couple of extra times at night."

"That's it?"

"At this point, yes."

"I guess that answers my question." She couldn't hide her disappointment.

"Have your neighbors seen anything?" he asked. "Have you discussed your prowler with them?"

"Mark asked the close neighbors and the paperboy if they'd noticed any strangers on our street. No one had. We haven't mentioned the recent incidents."

"I see." He nodded. "Then I suggest that you and your husband talk to all of your neighbors and let me know what you find out." He moved toward the door, ruffling Sam's curls and patting Tippy as he passed them.

Britt led the detective to the front door. She met his eyes. "Please take this seriously, Detective Simon."

"As I told you at school, we treat all calls seriously. Believe me, we take each case as far as the law allows us."

Britt pressed her point, so frustrated she was on the verge of tears. "What if there is someone out there watching us? What if he's just waiting for a chance to—to do whatever he's going to do?"

For an instant he looked concerned. Then he glanced at the wall near the front door. "You don't have a burglar alarm?"

"We never thought we needed one," she said.

"The new high-tech systems are pretty sophisticated. Once the alarm is set, it'll go off if someone presses against a window. Maybe you and your husband should think about getting one."

Then the door was open, and he stepped onto the porch. He made a dash to his unmarked police car in the driveway. In seconds he'd backed into the street and disappeared around the curve.

The rain intensified during the afternoon, offering Britt an excuse to pick up Katie at school. She left early to swing by the cleaner's and the supermarket. When they returned home the phone was ringing. She picked up the receiver to hear Dick Burnham, her computer company client, on the line.

"I thought you were a nineties person, Britt." His words came over the wires like bursts from an automatic rifle. "Your answering machine wasn't on. I couldn't leave a message, and it was important."

His meaning was clear: if she didn't measure up, he'd find another human resource consultant. He was a demanding client, but he paid her sixty-dollar-an-hour fee. She apologized, assured him the machine would be on next time, then hung up after making an appointment to go over the employee stats with him in his office the next day. At least he hadn't fired her. That would have been a disastrous finish to a bad day, she thought. She could not allow the prowler situation to affect her business.

Katie had gone upstairs, and Sam had gotten into the cupboards while she talked on the phone. He sat on the floor among the kitchen gadgets he'd taken from the no-no drawers. Britt sighed and let him play while she called Katie to come down and set the table. At least Mark had decided to forgo the Monday night football get-together at Bill's house. Her nerves couldn't stand him being gone tonight.

As she pulled the roast from the oven, Mark came in, anxious to hear about Charlie Simon's visit; she'd been gone when Mark called, too.

"You didn't have the answering machine on," he told her on his way upstairs to change his clothes.

"It won't happen again," she snapped.

He raised his hands in mock surrender. "Did I say something wrong?"

She glanced at him. "I'm sorry. I didn't mean to take your head off." She shot him a knowing look. "I'll explain later."

About to say something, he nodded instead and continued up the back steps.

By the time the nightly chores were done and the kids were asleep, Britt wanted to go to bed herself. She compromised by slipping into her nightgown and robe before joining Mark in the den. He'd drawn the drapes and started a fire in the fireplace, and when he saw her, he patted the sofa cushion next to him.

"Have a bad day?"

"That's an understatement." She tucked her feet under her robe and snuggled close to him.

"I assume it has to do with Simon? What happened?"

"That's the problem, Mark. Nothing happened."

"Didn't he show up?"

"He came, all right." Her voice wobbled. "And found —nothing."

He squinted at her. "What does that mean?"

Her hands clenched on her lap. "There were no smudges on the windows—and no footprint in the flower bed. The windows had been wiped clean, Mark—every single one. The flower bed looked as if no one had ever stepped in it, and the box had vanished."

He yanked off his glasses and cleaned them on his shirttail, as if seeing better would help him understand. "You showed him the notes, told him everything?"

Britt nodded. "I don't know if he believed me or not." She took a deep breath. "He wrote a report and said he'd alert local patrol cars to keep an eye on our house."

"That's it?"

She shook her head. "He suggested we inform the neighbors and think about installing an alarm system." She paused. "And he wants us to let him know if any of the neighbors have seen the prowler."

Mark slid forward on the cushion. "He can't help us, then?"

"He says he can't arrest a phantom."

He jumped up to pace back and forth in front of the fireplace. "Damn it, if the police won't help us, who will?" He stopped suddenly, socking his palm with his fist. "I'd like to get my hands on this maniac. I'd stop his crazy game."

"It's not a game, Mark. I think he's dead serious." She glanced at the draped window and lowered her voice. "He knew we'd found the smudges, and he wiped them off so no one would believe us."

116

"I realize that, Britt." His eyes, reflecting the firelight, looked feverish. "The son of a bitch must have seen us measuring the prints. He figured out what we were doing and assumed we'd call the police."

"Mark, I have such a crawly feeling. Why are *we* his target? Why *us?*"

He came back to her and pulled her close. "Don't worry, honey. We're not going to lie down and die. We'll do something—even if the cops can't help. The jerk won't get away with this for much longer."

"We don't even know what he looks like. Where do we start?"

"By talking to the neighbors, setting up a neighborhood watch." He paused, thinking. "I can get home early tomorrow. Let's do it before supper . . . if you can arrange it."

"I'll try." She went over her schedule in her mind. "I have a meeting with Dick Burnham, but I'll be finished in time to pick Katie up from school. My mother is watching Sam, so I'll ask her to stay while we visit the neighbors. Dad can come over after work and join us for supper."

He nodded.

The room seemed charged with uncertainty. She felt drained from worry and tried changing the subject. A brief discussion about Katie's resistance to being driven to and from school ended in silence.

"Just keep doing it," Mark said finally. "She has to be safe." He paused. "I confess I haven't gotten completely off the fence, Britt. The man's overtures to Katie could be a smoke screen. He could really be after you."

"I don't agree—but I've thought of another possibility. What if it's someone with a grudge against *you?*"

"Britt, that's reaching." Mark shook his head, dismissing her words. He picked up the fireplace poker and pushed the embers to the back of the firebox. "I don't know about you, but I'm bushed. I'm going to bed."

She waited while he adjusted the fireplace screen and switched out the lamp. They walked into the hall together, then went through the ritual of checking door locks and exterior lights before going upstairs.

Mark was asleep in minutes. Britt tossed and turned, her ears tuned to the night sounds. She checked the house and children two more times before she finally started to doze. So much for Charlie Simon's promise, she thought. Not once had she seen or heard a patrol car on their street.

I've lost my peace of mind, she thought. And I don't know how to find it again.

Britt was ready when Mark arrived home at four the next afternoon. She'd managed to arrange a brief meeting at the house next door with some of the neighbors, and to sidestep Katie's questions by telling her that all neighborhoods had a block watch. She had a casserole in the oven, her mother was in the den with Katie and Sam, and her father would be there soon. Britt made sure the doors were locked, then followed Mark out through the garage.

"Who's going to be there?" Mark asked as they headed down the sidewalk to the Gilliam house next door.

"Well, Donny Gilliam's parents, the Helms, and Mrs. Wilson. Mr. Wilson is out of town."

He nodded. "I don't know about the Helms; they're old and pretty reclusive."

"I chose the houses closest to us," she said. She'd been lucky to get anyone on such short notice. "It's a start."

Britt had reservations about the meeting. Their own house was the last one on the street before it curved through the woods to the main road. She would be surprised if anyone had seen their prowler.

The Gilliams' house was the same vintage as theirs, but larger and more ornate, with impressive columns in front and polished brass door fixtures. Mark rang the bell, and Ann Gilliam opened the door at once.

"Britt, Mark, come in," she said. "The Helms and Mrs. Wilson are already here."

She was a gracious woman in her early fifties, too

angular to be pretty. Her husband, Walt, stood behind her, a semiretired corporate lawyer with snappy dark eyes and a bushy mustache that overcompensated for his lack of hair. Donny had been a change-of-life baby; their other children were grown and married. Although friendly, the Gilliams, like the Helms and the Wilsons, didn't socialize with their neighbors. It was only because Donny and Katie were friends that Britt knew the Gilliams at all.

She and Mark were ushered into a living room furnished with pricey antiques. After exchanging greetings and small talk, Britt realized everyone was curious about the meeting. She hadn't explained on the phone other than it concerned the neighborhood. She nudged Mark to begin.

He got right to the point. Mrs. Wilson, a heavyset woman in her sixties, raised her eyebrows when Mark spoke about the notes. The Helms exchanged glances when Mark explained about the prowler. The Gilliams listened politely.

"We've had the police out. Detective Charlie Simon suggested we inform our neighbors about this, ask if you've noticed anything unusual." Mark glanced at Britt. "That's why Britt called you."

"Heavens, nothing like this has ever happened on our street before." Mrs. Helm's words rang with disbelief.

"Frankly I find it hard to believe." Mrs. Wilson's nasal tone grated like a fingernail on an emery board.

Britt felt her face flush. Was Mrs. Wilson calling Mark a liar?

"Let's get this straight." Walt Gilliam sounded as if he were cross-examining a witness. "You haven't actually seen anyone. Even the smudges disappeared from the windows."

"That's right," Mark replied, tight-lipped.

"Only Katie has seen this man, aside from that day on the way home from school." Walt's glance darted to Britt. "And you don't really know if the man she saw is your prowler, whom you've never seen."

119

They're in denial, Britt realized, astounded by their reaction. The suggestion that a prowler had encroached on their upscale neighborhood was unacceptable.

The conversation went back and forth. They weren't getting anywhere. When Mark glanced at her, Britt stood up and managed a thank-you that included everyone.

"I appreciate your hearing us out," she said stiffly, as the Gilliams walked them to the front door.

Walt shook hands with Mark. "Let me know if this turns out to be a real prowler. Maybe I can help." He lowered his voice. "I could turn up the heat on the police department."

"Don't worry, my dear," Mrs. Gilliam told Britt. "I'm sure everything will be just fine."

Outside the house, Mark took her hand. "Count to ten, Britt," he said. "I just did."

"I can't believe their reaction. It wasn't that they didn't believe us. *They didn't want to.*"

"It was Looney Tunes." Mark kicked a pebble into the street.

They reached their front porch as her mother flung open the door. Alice appeared to have been waiting for them. One look at her stricken face and the air went out of Britt's lungs.

"What's wrong?" Britt pushed past her. "Are the children all right?"

Alice grabbed her arm, stopping her. "Your father's with them—they're fine. Katie's setting the table and Sam's in his high chair."

"Something's happened," Mark said, as they went inside and closed the door. "What?"

"Just come in here." Alice led them into the den. "When Fred got here Katie wanted to show him how Sam could hit the ball. We were outside for only five minutes. The phone must have rung just before I came back in, but I heard the voice on the answering machine." She hesitated. "And it scared the hell out of me."

"Did Katie hear it?"

Alice shook her head. "I came in before Fred and the kids—to check on the casserole."

For a second neither Mark nor Britt moved. Then Mark rewound the tape on the answering machine.

A hollow voice spoke in a rap cadence. "She belongs to me. Why won't you see? She belongs to me." There was a pause. "She is mine. I won't leave her behind. Because she is mine."

There was a click and the tape stopped. Britt's whisper broke the silence as she voiced what they all thought.

"It *does* sound like a phantom."

11

"THAT VOICE DOESN'T SOUND HUMAN." CHARLIE SIMON pushed the stop button with his forefinger. "I feel as if a rabbit has just run over my grave." He shook his head, as if to rid himself of the voice that had spilled out of the answering machine to fill the room with dread. "Either he's using a voice synthesizer . . . or you've got a phantom." He hesitated. "I'm not even sure it's a he."

"This is serious, Simon." Mark's eyes were bloodshot from lack of sleep and he needed a shave. He looked beat. "Let's skip the phantom bullshit."

Britt's hand on Mark's arm brought his pacing in front of the desk to a stop. She'd never seen him so tense; he was like a marathon runner high on nervous energy. He glowered at Charlie Simon as though the detective were an ill-behaved teenager.

"You have to understand, Detective Simon," Britt said. "We're scared."

Charlie Simon had arrived at nine that morning wearing jeans, a bright orange windbreaker, and a baseball cap. She wondered when the police department had relaxed their dress code.

He nodded, his eyes suddenly solemn. "I realize that."

"This . . . voice is the last straw," she went on. "We're worried sick, feel literally under siege, and no one takes us seriously."

The detective straightened. "I never thought you weren't serious, Mrs. Hinson." His eyes narrowed. "But this type of situation is difficult to call. It's hard to separate fact from fiction. As I said before, we can't make an arrest without a suspect."

"We have a suspect." Britt pointed to the answering machine. "You just heard him."

"But our suspect is only a voice altered by a synthesizer," he explained patiently.

"What do you want?" Mark asked. "A damned body? Does someone have to get hurt before you do something?"

"I've got to go by how the law defines the situation." Charlie Simon spread his hands. "Even if we had a suspect we'd have to prove he'd broken the law before we could arrest him." He hesitated. "Without those laws the jails would be filled with innocent people, put there by hearsay and false evidence."

"We only want someone to do something." Britt moved closer to Mark. Outside the window the October morning was overcast and blustery, as it had been earlier when she'd driven Katie to school and taken Sam out to her parents' house. "Could you explain what a voice synthesizer is? And why the voice on the phone isn't evidence?"

"I've heard of voice synthesizers, but I didn't know they were accessible for personal use," Mark said.

"They are now, at specialty stores that sell electronic gadgets." The detective glanced down, but not before Britt glimpsed concern in his expression. "And they can be purchased through mail-order catalogs."

"And it's not against the law to use them?" Britt asked.

"No, unfortunately," Charlie Simon said. "But it is

against the law to use them to harass another person—if someone's lucky enough to catch the user."

"How exactly do they work?" Mark asked, pushing for technical information. "Maybe knowing that will tell us something about this guy."

"The synthesizer is an electronic device that produces a computerized version of your voice," the detective said. "The catalog version usually looks like a telephone, but it has extra buttons you can push to choose the voice you want. An old person can choose a young voice, a man can sound like a woman, and so on."

"Detective Simon, tell me truthfully: do you believe the flower man, prowler, is real?" Britt asked, changing the subject.

As Charlie Simon considered the question, Britt held her breath. He *had* to believe them.

After hearing the taped message the night before, Mark had gone straight to the phone and caught the detective at his desk. He'd told Charlie Simon about the phone message, and the detective had agreed to come to the house in the morning.

"Of course I believe he's real," Charlie Simon said finally. "I've always taken what you said seriously, Mrs. Hinson." The detective sighed, revealing his own frustration for the first time. "Look, at this point I'm as helpless as you are to do anything about the situation."

He pushed the message button and listened to the voice again, writing down the words. Then he glanced up. "In the beginning I hesitated to suggest what I'm about to say now, but I did mention it to Katie's principal." He paused. "This guy fits the profile of a stalker. He's probably after Katie, but we can't rule out Mrs. Hinson."

A stalker. The hollow feeling in Britt's stomach tightened into a knot and she sat down in the nearest chair. She'd discussed the possibility of a stalker with Angie and with the state legislator's office, but hearing Detective Simon say it terrified her. Oh, dear God, let him be after me, not Katie, she thought. The idea of her child being in that kind of danger was unthinkable. But she knew.

He was after Katie.

"Are you okay, Britt?" Mark took hold of her, doing a deep knee bend beside her chair so his face was even with hers. His dark eyes reflected her fears.

She managed a nod.

Charlie Simon cleared his throat. "If I'm right, you need to know what you're up against."

Mark straightened to look the detective in the eye. "Just what *are* we dealing with?"

"A stalker is obsessed, probably a sociopath." He hesitated, frowning. "He never stops going after what he wants."

"If you catch him, can you arrest him?" Britt's voice was unsteady. Something about the detective's controlled expression suggested that he was worried.

He glanced at his notes, then at Britt. "Maybe we could all sit down and discuss this." He stuffed his notebook and pen into the pocket of his windbreaker.

"I'll make some coffee."

Britt strode into the kitchen ahead of them, fully aware that Charlie Simon had avoided answering her questions. A new dread took root and began to grow.

When the coffee was ready she poured it into mugs and sat down with the two men.

The detective took a sip. "You make good coffee, Mrs. Hinson." His dimples flashed when he smiled, for the moment disregarding their impatience to resume the conversation. "Why don't you both skip the 'detective' stuff and call me Charlie?" he suggested. "Being on a first name basis always makes things a little friendlier."

"Sure," Mark said. "Call us Britt and Mark."

Britt nodded, but her mind clung to his suggestion. Why was he suddenly so friendly? she asked herself. Because he knew they'd be seeing a lot of him? Did he suspect something far worse than he'd said? Britt went back to the earlier question he'd sidestepped. "Will you arrest this stalker if you catch him watching us?"

THE FLOWER MAN

"That depends." His mug scraped the table as he put it down.

"On what?" Britt leaned toward him.

"On whether he breaks the law or not."

"But—"

He waved her to silence. "Even if this man *is* a stalker, he hasn't yet broken the law, except by trespassing on your property. Until he does, we can't stop him legally under current Oregon law. In this state the crime of menacing requires a definite threat of bodily harm. We can't arrest someone just because he's scaring you."

Mark opened the drawer where Britt kept the flower man's notes. He tossed them on the table. "Isn't leaving these notes against the law?"

Charlie shook his head. "He didn't send them through the mail, and the threat implied in the notes is too subtle to satisfy a judge."

"What about the prowler?" Mark demanded. "And the light bulb? Tippy's bone? The smudges on the windows and the strange sounds we've heard at all hours of the night?"

"As I said, if we catch him trespassing on your property, we can take him in." He shook his head. "But he'll probably be released right away unless we can prove he's a burglar or that he's threatening you."

"Katie has seen him on her way home from school, at school, at the theater, in the park." Britt pushed her coffee away. It tasted like acid. "It's obvious he's following her. As far as we're concerned, he *has* broken the law."

Charlie's gaze didn't waver. "Unfortunately, we don't have an anti-stalking law in this state, although there's a movement afoot to introduce a bill in the legislature." He tapped the mug with his finger. "It'll take time to pass the measure in both the state assembly and the state senate, but we're hoping it'll be in place within a year."

"A year?" Mark's eyes narrowed. "In the meantime who will protect my wife and daughter from this wacko?"

"We can't do much without a suspect," Charlie said.

"The law doesn't recognize what you *think* is happening, only what you can prove."

"It sounds like you're telling us we're on our own," Mark said. "When—if this guy comes out of the woodwork, and I believe he will, he'll hurt someone." He stiffened against the wooden chair. "I'll tell you one thing. I won't let him harm my family. I'll shoot the bastard first!"

"If you do, Mark," Charlie said, "then you'll be the one to go to prison."

"You mean we have *no* legal recourse?" Britt shook her head, dazed. "Are you saying the law is on a stalker's side?"

"I don't like this any better than you do." Charlie paused. "And I want you both to know that I don't intend to just let this drop. Even now there are a few things we can do."

"What things?" Britt had never been so scared. She'd always believed in law enforcement, thought it would be there if she needed it. Dear God, what was happening?

Charlie drained his mug and pushed it aside. "I'd like you to keep a diary of what happens. Be specific. Write down the times and dates. Save anything that could be evidence. Next time you see a footprint call me immediately. If there are more messages on the answering machine, save the tape." He frowned. "If you receive more than three calls from him in a week, I can authorize the phone company to put a trap on the line to trace the calls."

"Why not request the trap now?" Mark asked.

"No. One call isn't enough to warrant such a move."

Mark knocked on the table to punctuate his words. "That figures."

"Also," Charlie said, unruffled, "think back to what was going on in your lives when this started. Who were you in contact with? Who might have acted odd or overly interested in either Britt or Katie?"

Britt shook her head. "He's after Katie, not me."

"We don't know for sure," Charlie said. "He could be using Katie to get at you."

"I doubt it," she said, swirling the coffee in her mug. "The stalking started right after Katie appeared in the modeling competition. I told you that before."

"And Britt was in a play at City Theater at that time," Mark said dryly. "Her leading man, Jeb Walker, was really into his serial-killer role."

"Mark, you know he's gay," Britt said, annoyed that he had brought Jeb up again.

The detective had been scribbling on his pad and glanced up. "You're an actress, Britt?"

"Couldn't you tell by my dramatics?" She smiled wryly at her own joke, then told him about *The Man Who Loved Dead Women,* and her role as a prostitute.

"You're kidding. I saw that play," Charlie said. "I didn't recognize you. Sorry."

He glanced at his watch suddenly, whistled softly, and stood up. "I've got to run." He put his pad and pen away agaein. "It's still possible this guy will go away," he said. "Keep me posted."

Britt and Mark walked him to the front door. He shook hands with Mark and nodded at Britt. "Thanks for the coffee."

He put on his cap and grinned. "This is my day off, and I'm late to pick up my girlfriend. Nothing new, but she'll be annoyed. We're driving down to Seaside."

"Thanks for coming," Mark said. "We're sorry if we spoiled your day off."

"No problem. You didn't know."

Britt smiled. That explained his clothes, she thought. She couldn't even muster up guilt for misjudging him. She was too worried.

"One last thing." Charlie hesitated on the porch, his eyes on Britt. "Katie shouldn't go anywhere alone until we get a better fix on what's going on."

"I've been driving her to school."

"Good." He hesitated. "And I don't think you should be out alone in dark places at night either."

The wind swirled through the big maple across the street, sending dried leaves scuttling over the blacktop. Britt felt the chill and wrapped her arms over her chest.

Charlie gave a final salute and ran to his car. Mark closed the door, then attached the chain lock and slipped the bolt into place.

The calls came in clusters. The first four came within one hour of one another in the middle of that same night. Each time, the caller breathed the same hollow words, "She belongs to me," repeating the statement several times in the cadence of rap music.

When Britt returned from driving Katie to school the next day, she found another series of four calls on the answering machine. The messages were followed instantly by a click, as though a finger had been poised over the disconnect button. She logged the calls and rang Charlie's office.

"I'll get a case number to the phone company," he told her. "The trap will be on your line by tonight, so they'll be able to trace any future calls. But, Britt, you still need to keep a log of every call you receive. Be accurate about recording the time, because after each call you'll have to inform the phone company, so they can separate his calls from any others." There was a silence. "You know it's possible we'll find he's someone you and Mark already know. Be prepared for that, Britt."

She pressed the phone to her ear. She didn't want to think about that possibility. She forced herself to respond calmly. "Will you be able to identify the caller if he's using a voice synthesizer?"

"You bet. We'll get a voiceprint."

"A voiceprint?"

"Yeah. Even if a voice is disguised we can make a match, so long as we have a suspect. Once we trace the calls back to the source, we should have a name. Then, synthesizer or not, we'll be able to find out if the voice on your answering machine matches his."

"And if it does, you can arrest him?"

"That depends on what we've got in the way of evidence."

"But you just said—"

"Whoa! Slow down, Britt. One thing at a time. First we trace the call, narrow down the possibilities with a voiceprint." He paused. "At that point we'll at least know who this guy is. Then we can concentrate on how to put him away for good."

"What if he's calling from a phone booth?"

His long sigh came over the line. "Let's wait and see what we get. No use asking for trouble, all right?"

"I'm just trying to understand." She switched the receiver to her other ear. Somehow it all sounded like a pat solution to a third-rate mystery movie. She wanted to feel hopeful, but she had to ask another question. "If he's someone we don't know and he's calling from a pay phone, then we won't know who to compare his voice to. Isn't that right?"

"If our man is using a synthesizer, he's probably calling from his own place, because an over-the-counter electronic device might not be easy to use at a pay phone. If he's not calling from his house, then we're looking at other options. He could have access to another person's phone and synthesizer, or he might be disguising his own voice." He paused. "But you're right. If the calls originate from a booth he may be hard to trace."

"And we'll be back to square one."

"As I said, let's wait and see what happens."

"If voiceprints are so accurate, why didn't you request a phone trap after that first call?"

"I explained that. There are privacy issues. We have to go by the book."

"We have rights too, Charlie. We aren't hurting anyone. Someone is hurting us."

"Look, I sympathize, okay?" His sigh was as loud as his words. "I'll get back to you when I know something."

"Thanks, Charlie."

"Oh, Britt?"

She'd been about to hang up. "Yes?"

"Have you and Mark thought any more about installing an alarm system?"

"We've discussed it." She hesitated. "They're pretty expensive."

"It might prove to be a good investment."

He said good-bye and Britt replaced the receiver, then sat staring at it. The house was still. The grandfather clock in the hall gonged the hour, and she wondered what the rest of this day would bring.

When the phone rang she was startled out of her chair. She picked it up, fearful of what she'd hear. When she heard Mark's voice, she went boneless with relief and dropped back into the chair.

"What's wrong, Britt? You sound upset."

She explained her conversation with Charlie.

"Just a minute, Britt." She heard him speak to someone in his office, then his voice was back in her ear. "Honey, I can't talk long. I just called to check out a date for having the Slaters over for dinner."

Not now, Mark, she thought. We're too stressed. That morning he'd mentioned entertaining his business associate, and when she protested, Mark had only frowned and said that he would not allow fear to rule their lives.

"Phil is in my office right now. This Saturday is fine with them. Are we free?"

"I guess so. But what about—"

"Good." Mark cut her off. "We'll ink it in on the calendar, then." His pleasant tone sounded contrived. He was trying so hard to keep their lives normal. "Phil and Susan are looking forward to this almost as much as we are. Listen, honey, I have to run now." He lowered his voice. "And take care." A moment later the connection was broken.

Britt went into the hall and was about to go upstairs to check on Sam when the phone rang again. She ran back into the den thinking Mark had forgotten something, catching it on the second ring.

"Hello."

At first there was no response. Then the sounds came

all at once. A whispery background chant of "Belongs to me, belongs to me" was almost overpowered by the hollow voice.

"Don't try to stop me. You can't."

He switched off the recorder and hung up the phone simultaneously. Then he removed the tape and tossed it into a garbage bag. The black telephone synthesizer followed the cassette after he'd unplugged it. He wouldn't need either of them again.

Buddy put on his jacket, tied up the bag, and headed out the door to his van. There was a Dumpster at a retirement home several blocks away. He would dispose of it there. The garbagemen would come in the morning.

He sucked in a quick spray from his nebulizer, then pulled out onto the street.

"You can't outsmart me, whore!" he said aloud. "And you can't win. You can only die."

12

THERE WERE NO MORE CALLS. THE LAST ONE HAD COME IN before the tracer was installed, but Charlie had assured Britt the trap would remain in place.

The silence was unnerving. The stalker tried to keep them off-balance. Even the notes had stopped. She wondered if that was part of his plan—waiting until they let down their guard in one area so he could strike unexpectedly in another.

That thought was sudden and terrifying. She'd been mixing a crab dip, and her hand stilled on the wooden spoon. How would he strike? By hurting someone? By kidnapping Katie because he thought they belonged together?

"Mom, what's wrong?" Katie put down the bag of potato chips she'd just opened.

"I . . . uh, nothing, honey." Britt managed a smile.

"I can tell there's something wrong, Mom. Are you mad about Daddy inviting Mr. and Mrs. Slater for dinner?"

"Of course not, Katie. I'm sure that Phil and Susan are nice people. Daddy and Phil work together, and they want their families to get to know each other." She dropped a kiss on Katie's head and tried to erase the flat tone from her voice. "They have a boy two years older than you and a girl your age."

Katie poured the chips into a bowl, but when she looked up again, Britt saw that she still wasn't convinced.

"You're worried about *him*. I can tell." Katie paused. "Did Detective Simon tell you something bad about the flower man?"

"No, he didn't." Britt's denial lacked conviction. She tried again. "I told him that the calls and notes had stopped—that we hope the man is gone for good."

"Oh, Mom, if only he is. The flower man scares me. He makes me feel like I need to take a bath. He's . . . awful!"

"I know, honey. He's a bad man to scare us, but he's sick and we have to pity him." She hesitated. How could she put the situation into perspective for a nine-year-old? She didn't want Katie to live in fear, but she had to keep her safe. She could not make light of a man who was probably a dangerous stalker.

"You mean I should feel sorry for him?" Katie looked incredulous. "After what he's done?"

Please, God, Britt thought, help me find the right words to explain a sexual pervert to an innocent child. She gave the dip a final mix, then placed plastic film over it and put it in the refrigerator.

"Katie, I'm going to be honest." She took Katie's hands and looked down at her face, flushed as pink as her corduroy jumper from helping in the kitchen. "The flower man is sick in his mind, and although we can feel

132

sorry for him, we can never trust him. He isn't like us, or like anyone we know. He doesn't know right from wrong, and because he doesn't, he could be dangerous."

"He'd hurt us?"

My little innocent, Britt thought. He's hurt us already. He's taken the joy and safety from our lives. She wouldn't say that, though. Children healed faster than adults. If the flower man could be stopped, Katie would soon forget him. *If* he could be stopped before he did something worse to them. She ran her tongue over her lips and plunged into the discussion. She hated it, but Katie must not let down her guard.

"Yes, that's possible. He's not predictable."

"And you're scared too, aren't you, Mom?" Katie's voice trembled.

"A little," Britt said, "but mostly I'm furious with him." The lie is justified, she told herself. Katie has a right to her childhood.

"Will he kill us?" Katie's voice was lower.

"Oh, Katie." Britt hugged her. "No one would let that happen. We just have to be careful for now."

"Do you still have to drive me to school?"

"Yes, but that's not so bad, is it?" Britt struggled to maintain an even tone.

"No, but I'd rather walk. The kids think I'm being a snob. They accuse me of being too good to walk with them anymore."

"Maybe they're jealous." Britt squeezed her tighter and prayed that the nightmare would be over soon. "Besides. You'll be walking to school again before you know it. Then you'll wish you were still riding." She managed a smile. "Don't forget that you can stay in bed an extra fifteen minutes when I drive you."

Katie pulled away. "I'll probably have to ride until the police arrest him."

She was hard to fool, Britt thought. Katie was in tune with the changing moods in the household lately. Although she didn't understand the full significance of being stalked, she was afraid. She slept with her bedroom door open, she was nervous if one of her parents was gone at night, and she was watchful in public places.

Britt was relieved when the front doorbell ended their conversation . . . for now.

"That must be Mr. and Mrs. Slater," Katie said. "And their kids."

Britt glanced at the clock. "Good heavens! It is them." She looked at her reflection in the glass door of the microwave and smoothed her hair. "Do I need to freshen up, Katie? I don't feel put together."

"You look fine, Mom. Daddy already said your blue sweater was great with the denim skirt." A smile relaxed Katie's features. "Mom, you're acting silly. Remember what Grandma Alice says: 'They're only people.'" Her mimicry of her grandmother was perfect.

Britt grinned back. It was good to see Katie's humor restored. She was suddenly glad the Slaters were there. The Hinsons needed some good company for a change.

The steaks were marinating in the refrigerator, the salad waited to be tossed, the dining room table was set, and Sam was still napping. Britt was ready. Together she and Katie went to the front hall where Mark was already greeting their guests.

Britt smiled and hid her surprise. The Slaters were an unlikely couple. Phil was short, slight, and looked uncomfortable in his baggy khaki slacks and plaid shirt. Susan was taller and heavier than her husband, a dark-haired woman with a florid complexion and nervous movements. The girl and boy waited quietly. Both were dark like their mother and bore no resemblance to their father.

Mark made the introductions, and in seconds everyone was talking. Katie invited Matt and Debbie, the Slater kids, to play computer games, and Phil offered Britt a bouquet of flowers wrapped in tissue paper.

"For the hostess," he said in a surprisingly deep voice.

"Thank you." She shifted her glance to Susan, uncomfortable with the admiring look in Phil's hazel eyes.

134

"How sweet of you both. Mark must have mentioned that I love flowers."

Susan's answering smile didn't soften her permanent frown lines. "Phil says Mark is always talking about you," she said. "Your herbs and flowers, how talented you are, with acting and all." Her words were spoken in puffs and pauses. She didn't glance at her husband. *"Some* husbands are proud of their wives."

"That's uncalled-for, Susan," Phil said sharply, shuffling his small feet under the sweep of his trouser cuffs.

Britt's startled glance flew to Mark, who rushed into the vacuum before she could think of a way to break the awkward silence.

"Why don't you put the flowers in water, Britt?" Mark smiled, the perfect host. "Susan might like to join you while Phil and I mix the drinks."

She nodded and pulled the tissue free from the flowers, conscious that everyone was watching.

"Phil picked them out." Susan's nervous laugh sounded like the bark of a dog. "He plants all the flowers in our yard, so he knows more about them than I do." She laughed again. "He thought I'd spend too much or pick out something dumb like daisies, instead of *Myosotis sylvatica* and carnations."

"Oh, my goodness!" The bouquet dropped out of Britt's hand, falling with the tissue paper to the floor in a shower of blue and white and green.

"Mom!" Katie rushed forward to bend over the flowers. "They're *forget-me-nots!*"

The silence throbbed with tension. Britt's eyes darted to Phil Slater, then to Susan who'd moved close to her husband. They stared at Britt as if she'd lost her mind.

"What's wrong with forget-me-nots?" Susan asked, suspiciously. "Are you allergic? Boy, I understand that. I'm allergic to almost everything—dogs, cats, dust. I can tell you have a dog—my sinuses are already acting up. I—"

"Shut up, Susan!" Phil cut her off. He swallowed hard, working the little bones in his neck. He was blinking nervously. "Britt, I'm sorry about the flowers. They aren't wild forget-me-nots, they're hybrid . . . and costly. I'm not a cheapskate, even if you've gotten that impression from Susan."

"Mom, Mr. Slater isn't the flower man," Katie said. "The flower man is bigger with lots more hair."

It took a second for the words to sink in. When they did, Britt was the one who was embarrassed. She'd forgotten that Katie had seen the flower man and would have recognized him. She bit her lip. When had she become such a basket case?

"Who's the flower man?" Matt spoke for his parents, who looked about ready to leave.

"Listen, we'll explain," Mark said, stooping to pick up the flowers. He glanced at Katie. "Honey, let's forget about this for now, okay? Why don't you get some chips and Cokes and take Matt and Debbie into the den to play some of your games?"

Katie nodded, but she didn't move. "Are you all right, Mom?"

Britt ruffled her hair. "I'm fine, honey. Just a little embarrassed." She glanced at their guests. What must they be thinking? "Why don't you do as Daddy says?" she told Katie.

"All right," Katie said, still sounding reluctant. But she led the Slater kids to the den.

"I'm really sorry about this," Britt began. "I hope you'll let me explain." She managed a smile. "I don't believe you're a cheapskate, Phil. On the contrary, I knew the flowers were from the florist and not wild." She was babbling. Why didn't they say something? Flower man or not, the Slaters were odd.

Phil nodded somberly.

"I trust you won't mind going into the kitchen," she said when they didn't speak. "I need to check on my cooking while Mark and I explain."

"I'll make us drinks." Mark sounded anxious to make amends. "We could all do with a shot of something alcoholic."

That broke the ice, and the conversation moved to the topic of choosing drinks. They walked to the kitchen, where Susan found her tongue again.

"Make mine scotch on the rocks." Susan rolled her eyes skyward. "I can't take vodka or gin. I'm allergic." She noticed Tippy on the patio. "I'm allergic to animal dander. He's not allowed in the house, is he?"

"No, never," Britt lied.

Mark was careful not to meet her eyes. She knew what he was thinking: they were in for a long, exhausting visit with the Slaters. Once drinks were in hand, Britt launched into the flower man story. She had to mend fences, for Mark's sake.

When the Slaters finally left around nine, Britt's jaws ached from the smiles she'd forced onto her face while listening to Susan's endless prattle. She was convinced that the woman was manic. How could Phil stand it? she asked herself as she tidied up.

But then, how could Susan stand Phil? The man's stare had become repulsive to her. He acted like a sex-starved teenager who was too much of a nerd to get a date.

By the time Katie and Sam were tucked in for the night, Britt was ready for bed herself. Mark agreed, and they locked up and went upstairs.

"We redeemed ourselves, thank God," Mark said, undressing. "You know, Britt, Phil isn't a bad guy. He's odd as hell, but he means well." He climbed into bed. "The poor bastard has a hard row to hoe, being married to that woman. He's her second husband; the kids are from her first marriage."

Britt was already in bed. "She's unique, I'll say that for her. I finally had to tell her that I considered her sex life her own private affair."

"Thanks for being a sport, Britt." He kissed her. "They are pretty grim company."

"Susan told me that raising kids as a single mom was tough. I think she was looking for a meal ticket, and Phil was looking for anyone he could get." She hesitated, then propped herself up on an elbow. "Mark, I know you like Phil, but . . . I think he's more than just odd."

"How so?"

"The way he acts and the way he stares, and from what Susan told me, I think he's all screwed up sexually." She bit her lip, forming her thoughts before she said them aloud. "You beat him out for the position of chief financial officer, right?"

Mark nodded.

"Do you think he could be playing cruel little flower games with us—to get even with you?"

"Now, wait a minute, Britt. You're reaching."

"Give me a chance to explain my reasoning on this."

"Go on."

"He has probable cause, as Charlie Simon would say. You were awarded the promotion he believed would go to him."

"How do you know that?"

"Susan told me." She traced a finger over his forehead, smoothing the lines that had deepened while she spoke. "Didn't you notice how he stared at me? It was like he was anticipating my reaction to his flowers."

Mark sat up, and the covers dropped down around his waist. "Phil didn't lose that promotion because he wasn't smart enough. He lost it because of his odd mannerisms. He stares, he blinks, he doesn't have good social skills, he stutters on occasion—"

"And he resents you."

"Britt, you're getting paranoid. Phil gave you a thoughtful gift and you reacted as if he'd given you a rattlesnake. We're damned lucky he was understanding."

"I'm not imagining his creepy way of staring."

"Everyone who stares or has a preference for forget-me-nots or has wife problems is not the flower man. Katie was right. It isn't Phil."

"I'll ask you the same question you once asked me." She dropped her voice so she wouldn't disturb the children, but she was annoyed. "Did you ever tell Phil that Katie was given forget-me-nots on her way home from school?"

"I might have mentioned it a long time ago."

"So your oddball friend could have taken it from there. It would be his speed. I doubt if he's up to confronting you about his resentment."

"Britt, that's preposterous."

"I think it's worth mentioning to Charlie Simon."

"If you do that, I could lose my job. Is that what you want?" he asked sharply. "Our firm is about as conventional and proper as they come. Believe me, they wouldn't understand if I caused even a minor scandal."

"But what if Phil is the stalker?"

"He's not," he snapped. "Maybe Phil didn't get my position, but he has a damn good job that pays a great salary. He's a smart man despite his obvious personality problems. I know him. He's different, but he's no pervert." Mark tossed the covers aside and got out of bed. "I forbid you to tell Charlie Simon about Phil." He hesitated. "I hope you're listening, Britt. I would lose my job."

He went into the bathroom; she heard him take a drink of water. Tears ran down Britt's face. She couldn't stop them.

By Monday morning Britt was more rational about the Slaters and somewhat optimistic that the stalker might be gone for good. It was a glorious October day: bright sunshine, pure air off the Pacific Ocean eighty miles to the west, and crunchy leaves underfoot. Days like this exist only in the Northwest, she thought as she pulled into the garage after driving Katie to school. She let Sam play with Tippy in the backyard where she could watch him while she made some business calls. When Angie stopped by, she welcomed the break.

"I haven't heard from you lately and I wondered how things were going." Angie plunked her purse down in the kitchen next to her chair. "I've been worried."

Britt shrugged. "Nothing is happening, thank goodness. It's been quiet for almost a week. We've got our fingers crossed."

Angie squinted at her. "Why do I sense a certain reservation in all this positive talk?"

Britt poured coffee, then sat down across from Angie, her eyes on Sam beyond the glass patio doors. "You know me pretty well. Guess I can't fool you." She swirled the coffee in her mug. "I have this feeling—don't ask me to explain it, because I can't—that the flower man, whoever he is, is out there watching, just biding his time, waiting for us to lower our guard."

"Whew! That's heavy stuff."

"I know." Britt's gaze was suddenly direct. "At least you didn't say I'm imagining things."

"I've known you for a long time. I may think you have artistic quirks, but I *know* you aren't crazy."

Britt smiled. "That's the value of old friends. They believe you regardless of how something looks, because they know you so well." She patted Angie's hand. "Thanks. I needed that."

"You're welcome." Angie raised her eyebrows. "Just don't forget that when I do something unbelievable."

"Like what?"

"Like killing Bill," Angie answered, a note too seriously.

"You're joking."

Angie lowered her lashes, screening her eyes. "Of course. I'm just upset with him at the moment." She hesitated. "He can't understand why I don't get pregnant. His ego won't recognize that the problem is his sperm count. He wants a son so bad that he's a little crazy, and he blames me." She glanced up. "You know, Britt, life is sometimes a bitch."

"Just a minute." Britt jumped up and ran into her garden room, returning with a plastic packet of dried herbs. She handed it to Angie.

"This is a tea made from dittany-of-Crete, a medicinal herb I grew in my garden. I was told it enhances fertility, among other things, and I thought of you." Britt spread her hands. "It tastes pretty good, and maybe it'll help you get pregnant."

"It can't hurt. Thanks. I'm willing to try anything at this point, even herb folklore." Angie poked at her unruly hair. "Good thing Bill likes tea."

Britt felt sorry for her, even though she couldn't identify with a woman not getting pregnant. She would have had a baby every year if she hadn't taken precautions.

"Britt! I just thought of something!" Angie leaned forward. "Has it occurred to you that the flowers left with the notes might have a symbolic meaning—a hidden message from this flower man?"

About to sip her coffee, Britt put her cup down. "No—no, it hadn't. Angie, you could be right."

She got her gardening books and spread them on the table for them both to thumb through. A book on herbs revealed that rosemary meant remembrance and sage strengthened memory. But it stopped short of giving the folklore behind flowers. She closed the last book.

"I think we're on to something." Britt shoved the books aside. "I can't believe it didn't occur to me that the type of flower might have some significance. I'll have to go to the library."

"I'll stay here and keep an eye on Sam," Angie offered. "You go ahead. I'm dying to hear what you find out."

"The name 'forget-me-not' comes from a tragic legend about lovers who were parted by death," Britt told Angie a couple of hours later, when she returned from the library. She glanced through the photocopies she'd made. "We were right about rosemary meaning remembrance and sage strengthening memory. Now we know that forget-me-nots stand for true love, carnations mean first love, and the white lily is the symbol of virginity."

"The bastard!" Angie's words came out like a long hiss.

"It's obvious, isn't it?"

Angie nodded, looking as shocked as Britt felt. "He's definitely after Katie."

Britt's throat constricted so that it was hard to swallow. "But why the remembrance and the memory thing? What does that mean?"

"Strengthening her memory so she will remember him? I don't know. Who can analyze a deranged mind? Maybe he believes in reincarnation, that they were lovers in another life."

"Angie, no! You're talking about my little girl."

"Sorry. I was just trying to help."

They moved to the door, and Angie turned to face Britt.

"Did you know that Bill and the guys have discussed staking out this creep, setting a trap to catch him? Len said he could borrow a pair of night-vision goggles so they could see him the instant he sets foot on your property."

Britt shook her head. "Mark didn't tell me."

"I'm sure he will, if they decide to do it. In the meantime, maybe you should call Charlie. Tell him what you've found out."

She nodded, then watched as Angie got into her car and backed out to the street. The sun still shone brightly, but the wind was brisk. She quickly closed the door and called Charlie. She was unable to curb her excitement as she told him about the meanings of the flowers. Her final sentence dropped into silence.

"Look, Britt," he said at last, "it's not wise to seek meanings where they might not exist."

"But it all fits. Can't you see that?" She told herself to stay cool. It wouldn't help to sound hysterical. "Do me a favor, Charlie. Think about what I said. Okay?"

"All right, Britt." His sigh came over the wires. "We'll talk soon." He hung up.

She slammed the receiver onto the wall phone. *Damn you, Charlie Simon!* I'm not the certified loon; the stalker is!"

Sam woke up from his nap and they went to pick up Katie. Later she told Mark about the symbolism of the flowers.

"Honey, I have to agree with Charlie on this one." He sounded annoyed. "Your flower theory is too far-fetched for me."

"That figures." She flung the words at him. "You're too literal-minded to think creatively."

"Britt, I won't argue about this."

"You and Charlie are wrong. I just know I'm on to something."

The next morning Britt opened the front door to pick up the paper.

"Mark, come quick!"

They stood together in the open doorway, their eyes on the doormat. One long-stemmed black rose in full bloom was wound around a wire that had been coiled like a snake, so that the flower stood upright.

"A *black* rose?" Mark stooped to pick it up. "It's been spray-painted."

"A black rose means *death.*" Britt could hardly get the words out of her throat. "I learned that yesterday."

"That fucking bastard!" Mark slammed the door. "He's probably out there watching."

Britt suddenly knew the symbolism of the coiled wire. *He was ready to strike.*

13

BRITT FELT THEIR WORLD WAS BECOMING SMALLER, SHRINKING to the safety zone within the four walls of their home. Mark had a state-of-the-art alarm system installed. The windows and doors on the main floor were wired and motion detectors were set up to monitor the main traffic areas. Mark had decided against installing roof sensors and wiring the second-story windows. "The extra protection wouldn't justify the cost," he'd said. "The technician thinks the upstairs is pretty safe."

"The installer said the alarm is noise-sensitive," Britt told Mark on the phone once the servicemen left. "If anyone presses on a window or tries to use a glass cutter, the alarm will go off."

"You sound impressed."

"Intimidated is more like it," Britt admitted. "The only simple thing about this system is the code—press 'pound' then 'stay' to activate it, and '5601 off' to turn it off." She moved the receiver to her other ear. "Guess what I chose for the password?"

"Britt, you can tell me the rest when I get home." He sounded rushed. "Sorry, honey, but I'm late for a meeting."

"Oh, okay." She tried not to sound annoyed. "I just thought you'd want to know."

"I do. But I have to tend to business, too. Someone has to pay for all these extra expenses." She heard his tired sigh. "Look, I'm glad the system is finally in place and that it's sophisticated." There was another pause. "It ought to be. Cost us over four thousand bucks."

Britt hung up, feeling unsettled. Most of their conversations these days were about safety precautions, what had happened to their lives, why it had happened to them, and who was behind it. Their lives were being orchestrated by the perverted mind of their stalker.

The alarm system wasn't the only new safety precaution they instituted in the days that followed. Britt made sure that Katie was never alone; she was positive that invisible eyes watched her all the time. Even Charlie Simon had been giving her flower theory more credence since the black rose incident.

"Keep Katie close to home, Britt," he'd told her on the phone. "Best if she could play in the backyard for now.

We'll keep the security going from this end." There was a pause. "And watch out for yourself."

By Saturday, Britt was a bundle of nerves. She glanced out the window to check on Katie and Sam. How long could she keep Katie interested in backyard projects? she wondered. How many little-girl pleasures must she skip? Like her Girl Scout meetings. She sighed. For now she'd convinced her that Tippy needed to be trained—a task that was overdue—but Katie was upset because she'd been forbidden to join the neighborhood kids for the Saturday baseball game in the park. Britt shuddered at the thought of it.

Katie noticed her at the window. She gestured toward Tippy and then came to the back door. Sam followed her, his round face pink from the wind, his jacket and pants already soiled.

"Mom, Tippy needs obedience school. He wants to play, not mind me."

"You have to be patient, Katie." Britt smiled encouragement. "Remember, he's still only a year old. Follow the steps in the training manual."

"Donny said he's old enough to go." Frowning, Katie cleared her tangled hair from her face and tucked it behind her ears. Her windbreaker and jeans had long dirt lines from Tippy's paws. "Why can't we take Tippy to obedience school?"

"We just can't right now."

"Donny's parents let him take his dog."

Britt thought fast. They'd planned to take their dog to obedience school, and they still would, she told herself, once the flower man was out of their lives. But for now Tippy was her best excuse to keep Katie at home.

"Maybe Donny would like to come over and help you train Tippy."

Britt's suggestion brought another frown. "Donny probably went to the park. At least he can still have fun."

"Why don't you find out?"

"Okay, Mom." Katie started toward the front gate, obviously glad for the reprieve from the backyard.

"No! Stop, Katie!" Britt called after her. "You can call him."

"Gee whiz." Katie turned back, her blue eyes wide. "You don't have to holler at me! It's not my fault that Tippy won't mind."

Britt took a deep breath. "I'm sorry if I sounded gruff. I have lots of work today, and I guess my mind was on that."

Katie stepped into the house and paused. "Are you and Daddy making me stay in the backyard because of the flower man?" Her long lashes lowered and she looked ready to cry.

"Daddy and I think it's important that Tippy be trained, that's all. We're too busy to do it, and we thought you'd like to." She tipped Katie's chin up. "We wouldn't want Tippy to run off or get hurt, would we?"

Katie shook her head.

"Go on, call Donny."

"All right, but I know he'll be gone."

Britt hated the way Katie's shoulders drooped, the way the enthusiasm was being drained out of her. A child had a right to be carefree.

They hadn't told her about the black rose. She was scared enough already.

"Donny's home," Katie said, turning from the phone. "There weren't enough kids for a ball game." She brightened. "He says he knows all about training dogs. He's coming over to help."

Donny, a slim boy with dark snappy eyes and a quick mind, arrived five minutes later with his own training book and some dog treats.

He held up the treats. "These are the rewards for Tippy when he obeys," he announced like an expert. "Is it okay if we give him some, Mrs. Hinson?"

Britt nodded, keeping a straight face. What a relief. Donny was the answer to her prayers.

She served lunch on the patio, and Katie and Donny continued their training program during the afternoon while Sam napped. The bursts of laughter followed by stern commands were pleasant sounds to Britt's ears. But she was watchful, her eyes on the woods.

Donny came back on Sunday after church. That afternoon Britt and Mark were invited to see the dog's progress. Tippy sat down, lay down, rolled over, and shook hands.

"We're going to teach him to speak next," Donny told them seriously.

"That means bark," Katie added. "Tippy is really smart, isn't he, Donny?"

Donny nodded, patting Tippy's head while the dog's tail beat a tattoo against his leg.

The day ended on an upbeat note. If there hadn't been a black rose, Britt might have believed their lives were settling back to normal. The automatic lights came on at dark, reminding her that their life might not be normal for a long time.

"Where's Tippy?" Katie said as she bounded down the back stairs the next morning.

Britt glanced at the glass doors where Tippy always sat watching them while they ate breakfast. He wasn't there, and Britt realized she hadn't seen him this morning. "He must be in his house," she told Katie.

Mark looked up, his eyes meeting Britt's before shifting to the windows. He pushed back his chair and joined Katie at the door.

"He's not there, Daddy." Katie pressed her face against the glass so she could see down the sides of the house.

"He's there somewhere, honey." Mark sounded calm, but Britt caught the edge to his words. "Eat your breakfast, Katie, or you'll be late for school. I'll find our wayward pup, okay?"

Katie hesitated, her face stricken with doubt. "Oh, Daddy, what if he got out? What if Donny didn't shut the gate tight?" Her voice caught. "We haven't trained him yet about cars. If he got out, he might be hurt!"

"I'll find him. You go eat."

Mark and Britt went outside, and before they could stop her, Katie followed. They saw the note hanging from the doghouse at the same time.

"Daddy!" Katie ran to Mark, hugging his waist. "It's another note!"

The print covered the whole page, and there was no way to hide what it said from Katie. "Dogs are troublesome."

"The flower man took Tippy!" Katie's face crumpled, and she burst into tears. "He's going to hurt Tippy! I know he is!"

They led her back inside the house.

"I'll call the animal shelter and the Humane Society," Britt said. "We'll find him. I promise."

"We have to, Mom." She sounded stuffed up from crying, and her voice quavered. "He'll be so scared if we don't find him."

"Shhh. We'll find him." Britt wiped her tears away and kissed her. "He might be here when you get home from school."

Maybe the flower man only let him out of the yard, Britt thought. Fear clutched at the pit of her stomach. She had a bad feeling about it. She remembered the black rose . . . and what it meant.

Britt's worst fears came true the next morning. There had been no sign of Tippy, and he hadn't been picked up by the dog catcher. She'd walked the roads and scanned the ditches near their house, but she'd stopped short of going into the woods. Charlie had gone instead, and found nothing.

Charlie couldn't hide his concern. He'd left with more warnings. Britt knew a detective wouldn't normally come out on a lost dog call. Both she and Charlie knew it was more than that. But they were still punching air.

"Where Tippy?" Sam had repeated over and over.

Britt only felt worse. Katie and Sam had gone to sleep with tears still wet on their cheeks. She and Mark had gone to bed fighting their growing panic. In the morning the backyard was still empty, even though Katie had left the gate open, "Just in case."

"I'm going to look in the yard," Katie told her parents when she came downstairs Tuesday morning.

"He's not there," Mark said gently.

"I have to look, Daddy. Please."

He nodded and Katie slipped out the sliding door. Mark stood watching, as though he was afraid she would disappear just like their dog.

"Damn it, Britt." He shook his head. "What next?"

Katie's shrill scream stopped Britt's answer. She dropped Sam's juice on the floor and ran outside behind Mark. Katie's hand was clamped over her mouth, her chest heaved, and her horror-stricken eyes were on the opening of the doghouse.

"The bastard's crazy!" Mark's voice registered shock.

Two golden dog ears lay on the board floor, the severed ends caked with dried blood.

Bile rose up in Britt's throat. She grabbed Katie and rushed her back inside the house. Katie broke free and darted to the bathroom, where she threw up. It took all of Britt's willpower to keep from doing the same. She concentrated on calming Sam while Mark disposed of the ears.

"It's my fault," Katie said when she was finally coaxed from the bathroom. "I didn't train Tippy good enough, and now he's dead!" Hysteria threatened again. Her voice rose, a broken cadence of horror. "I just know he's dead!"

Britt couldn't deny the truth.

"Why would anyone hurt our dog? He—" Katie's voice broke.

"We don't know, Katie." Britt held her and they rocked together crying. "But it's not your fault. You mustn't think that. A bad person did this, not you." She talked fast. Guilt was a natural reaction to death, and Katie didn't need that added to her fear. Somehow Britt managed to soothe her, holding back her own revulsion and her own overwhelming feeling of guilt—it had been at her insistence that Tippy sleep outside, to protect the house. She shook away the thought—no time for self-recrimination now—and glanced at Mark over the top of Katie's head. "We'll call Detective Simon. He'll help us."

"But he can't bring Tippy back, Mom."

Mark's mouth worked, but no words came out. He nodded at Britt and went to call Charlie Simon.

Britt canceled her business appointment, Mark didn't go to work until after lunch, and Katie stayed home from school. Charlie came and solemnly took down the facts in his notebook.

"I'm glad you installed the alarm system," he told her. "I want you to know that I'm following up on anything that even resembles a lead, Britt. I'm going to get this pervert." He left with a promise to beef up surveillance.

The black rose symbol had come true. Death.

"The note on the drawing said, 'My true love, Forget-Me-Not.'"

The phone felt cold against Britt's ear as she listened to the principal. "Mr. Lotze, where is Katie right now?"

"She's in the nurse's room, resting. She's quite all right, Mrs. Hinson."

"Did she see anyone? Was she threatened?"

"No, not that we know of, but the big drawing of forget-me-nots was taped on the window, and that upset her. No one noticed it at first because the windows are covered with drawings by the kids." There was a pause. "Only that drawing was taped to the outside, not the inside, of the glass. And no one at this school put it there."

"And Katie—"

"Was the one who noticed it first, and she got hysterical. She kept saying, 'It's him! It's the flower man! He's out there!'"

"Oh, my poor Katie!" Britt took a deep breath and switched the phone to her other ear. "Mr. Lotze, I know you're aware of, uh, our situation."

150

"Detective Simon has been keeping me up to date on it, Mrs. Hinson."

"Then you know that we—that is, Katie's father and I and Detective Simon—believe someone is stalking Katie."

There was a pause, as though he was considering his next words. "Yes, I do," he said, concern obvious in his voice. "I intend to call the detective next, Mrs. Hinson. We won't tolerate this happening on school property." He cleared his throat. "If we catch him here he'll be arrested and prosecuted."

"Thank you."

She glanced out the glass patio door at the cloudy day, typical for late October. The woods beyond the backyard were dark and dreary, the fir and pine boughs drooping from the last heavy rain. *He could be out there— watching.* She tried to get ahold of herself. She had to think about Katie.

"Hold on a second," Mr. Lotze said. She heard muffled voices, and his voice came back a moment later. "The nurse just came in. She thinks Katie should go home. She's still pretty shaken."

"I'll leave right now."

A moment later she hung up and ran to get Sam and her car keys. The dark shadow in their lives was steadily moving closer.

"You'll have to take him back. I don't want a dog that might attack the children. That's final, Mark."

Britt couldn't believe he'd brought a trained attack dog home without consulting her. He'd taken her out to the garage to show it to her. She didn't trust the dog. It was a powerfully built animal with a wary look in his eyes and a tail that didn't wag. Her approach brought a low growl and bared teeth.

"His name is Max," Mark said, ignoring her protests. "We'll keep him on a chain during the day, only let him loose in the backyard at night." The dog allowed Mark to stroke its head. "See. He knows me already. He can go in the garage when the kids are outside."

"I say he goes—right now."

Mark wiped his hands on his trousers. "Britt, don't make this any harder than it is. I don't like having a mean dog any more than you do. But we've got to protect ourselves." He expelled a long breath. "When—if—the wacko disappears from our lives, I'll give the dog back to the kennel. And remember, he's trained to attack intruders, not the people who live in the house."

"How will he know the good guys from the bad guys?"

He sighed again. "Britt, the dog has been well trained. The trainer assured me that he'll know. He'll see that the kids belong here. But just in case, we'll take precautions, keep him away from them, like I said."

"I can't believe this. Our life is going to hell." She buried her face in her hands.

He peeled her hands away from her face. "Sweetheart, don't. We have to defend ourselves."

"We have the automatic lights and the security system. Do we really need this dog?"

Mark nodded grimly. "Max will scare that bastard away. Keep him out of the backyard."

"What about the front?"

He lifted his shoulders in a resigned shrug. "We'll have to depend on the security system there, and the police patrol. The stalker is more vulnerable in the front, and we can't let this dog run free." He paused. "For now, this is the best we can do."

"I hope you won't be sorry, Mark. A dog like this is dangerous."

"As dangerous as the flower man?"

She had no answer.

Buddy watched the Honda back out of the garage, wait while the automatic garage door slid closed, then head down the street toward the main road. He knew they were going to the parent-teacher-student association meeting at school, that Katie's Girl Scout troop was presenting the flag and leading the salute.

He waited, as still as the night around him. He needed to be sure they didn't come back and surprise him. Down the street, a dog yipped, followed by an answering bark from the Hinsons' backyard.

The new dog. He hadn't forgotten.

The black sky was low, heavy with the threat of rain. He could smell it. He must hurry. His shoes must not be wet. But first, the dog.

His secret way into the backyard wasn't necessary. They weren't home. He could use the gate. Stepping from the shrubbery, Buddy moved cautiously, aware of not alerting the animal to his presence. He hugged the shadows, ready to duck if a patrol car turned into the street.

He reached out with a leather-gloved hand to unhook the lock, but the gate squeaked when he opened it. He heard the low growl, saw the flash of fur as the dog started for him. Buddy reached for the plastic sack inside his jacket.

"Come here, Max," he whispered gruffly. "See what I have for a good dog."

Max hesitated, poised to leap, his teeth bared in a deep throat growl.

"Good boy." Buddy soothed the dog, reassuring him. In slow motion he extended his hand to offer the large chunk of raw beef he'd taken from the sack.

The dog was obviously torn between his training and his instinct. He wanted the meat.

Buddy dropped it between his front paws. Then he wadded up the plastic and stuffed it into his pocket, backed up to the gate, stepped through, and closed it with a soft click.

He smiled. That had been easy. No barking. No alerting the neighbors to his presence. A piece of cake. So much for vicious dogs. You just had to know how to handle them.

Careful not to step in the flower beds, he moved to the front of the house and up onto the porch. He withdrew the key from his jeans pocket.

Master keys. The only good thing he'd learned about in the joint. There was a master key somewhere to open any lock. The problem was to find that key. Each time he'd left a note he'd tried several keys, until one fit. He'd been lucky to find it before the alarm was installed. After that there was only one catch: they had to be gone for him to get inside. When they were home the chain lock was in place.

He inserted the key and unlocked the front door, slipped inside, and closed it. He had only seconds before the alarm would sound, here and at the monitoring station.

The burglar alarm made him laugh. They were such stupid people. The woman had actually *given* him the code over the telephone.

His penlight cut through the dark, finding the alarm pad. He punched in the code—5601, then the "off" key. The red light instantly changed to green. The muscles in his loins constricted.

He was in her house.

Silence. The quiet was unnerving. A lamp had been left on at the back of the hall, and he flicked off his light. Although the shades were drawn, a flickering glow might be seen from the street. He must do what he'd come to do. And nothing else. This time.

The house had a faint smell of dried roses. He sniffed the air. He liked the scent. Somehow it reminded him of the Washington forest when he was young. An everlasting fragrance. A good omen.

Buddy moved quickly through the house, touching one thing, then another, knowing she had touched them too, saving the best for last. Sharp sensations built within him. He'd known it would be like this. He'd dreamed about it. One day soon it would be perfect. Because she would be his.

His arousal exploded when he opened her door and saw her bed. For seconds he could only hang on the door and gasp. When it was over, he went about his business quickly. What if they came right home after the flag ceremony?

His penlight was his guide. He snipped a length of yarn from the carpet and took a strip of wallpaper from the bottom corner in the closet. He placed them in a small plastic bag and put it in his jacket pocket. After momentarily switching on the light, he used a small flash camera to take pictures of the room. Then he turned to go.

Everything was just as he had found it. He retraced his steps to the front door and pressed his eye to the peephole. The street was quiet.

He pressed "pound," then "stay," reactivating the alarm. In seconds he was out the door and enfolded by the night. Circling to the backyard, he was no longer cautious about the dog.

"Good boy, Max," he whispered hoarsely. *"Now* you're a real good boy. Sleeping like a baby."

He patted the dog's head with one hand and pulled the plastic bag from under his jacket with the other. The chunk of meat was still between the dog's front paws. Buddy stooped and put it back into its container. He straightened, his nostrils flared, his senses alert.

He glanced upward—to her room.

The jolt to his groin was painful. And it was a promise of fulfillment to come. He headed to his secret entrance. Soon. Very soon she would be with him.

He quickened his stride. They would never know he'd been in their house. He was omnipotent. He was guided by the most powerful force of all—finding his one true love.

By the time he reached the woods he felt like shouting, "I'm here! I'm waiting for you! Come to me!" But he didn't.

He could wait.

* * *

Britt saw the dog when she opened the drapes in the morning. He lay stiff, his eyes open, his jaw slack. She knew Max was dead.

Her scream for Mark brought him running down the back stairs, his face lathered with shaving cream. She could only point at the window. He took one look and yanked the drapes closed.

14

"MARK, WE HAVE TO TELL CHARLIE ABOUT PHIL SLATER."

Britt paced the den. They'd been talking since the children went to bed. It was late, and she was tired.

"Phil isn't the flower man, Britt." Mark rested his elbow on the arm of the chair, his chin in the palm of his hand. He looked exhausted. "If nothing else, he's too much of a wimp."

"It doesn't take a Superman to kill dogs."

Each time she thought about Tippy, Britt's stomach flip-flopped. Charlie had come at once after Mark called him about Max's death. He'd loaded the dog into his car and left after promising to try to determine the cause of death. He'd explained the difficulty of testing for poisons but had said the lab would scan for several of the most likely toxins.

"Phil works during the day," Mark said finally. "He couldn't have been at Katie's school when that drawing appeared on the window—or at those other places either."

She stopped pacing and faced him. "You once told me he's often out of the office meeting clients. I think Charlie needs to check if those meetings coincide with the times Katie saw the stalker."

"Katie *did* see Phil. Right here in this house." He

hesitated. "Aren't you forgetting she said he wasn't the flower man?"

"I'm not forgetting anything," she said. "We don't know . . . he could have disguised himself."

"I suppose anything's possible." He shook his head. "But it's hard for me to believe Phil has anything to do with this."

Britt knelt in front of his chair and took his hands in hers. "I know it is, Mark," she said softly. "But we can't afford to ignore any possibility. The future of our family depends on it."

"Okay, Britt." There was a defeated look in his dark eyes. "You're right. We have to follow up on even the slightest suspicion. Tell Simon. I just hope he'll be discreet. I'll lose my job if he's not . . . and Phil is innocent."

"I'll tell him that." She kissed his hands and got to her feet.

Mark reached out to switch off the lamp, then stood up. They went through the routine: locks, lights, and alarm. Mark dropped an arm around her shoulders as they started up the stairs. Katie's scream raised the hair on the back of Britt's neck.

"What the hell—" Mark was already running.

Britt rushed up the steps after him. He reached the bedroom ahead of her and switched on the light. Katie sat wide-eyed in the bed, the covers wrapped around her.

"Mom! Daddy!" Tears ran down her cheeks. "Someone was trying to look in my window."

Britt sat on the bed and pulled Katie into her arms. "Hush now," she soothed. "It was just a bad dream. No one could be out there. That window is too far off the ground."

"It was the side window, Mom. He was on the garage roof." Her glance darted to Mark. "Daddy, I heard him on the shingles." Her teeth chattered as she spoke, and Britt held her closer.

Mark caught Britt's glance and shook his head. He'd already looked outside. No one was on the roof or in the backyard, the exterior lights were still on. It was only a nightmare.

Britt stayed with Katie until she'd gone back to sleep. In the glow of the night-light her delicate face looked so young, so vulnerable. My little angel, she thought, why can't you stay an innocent child for a little while longer? She brushed her lips over Katie's cheek and stood up.

She moved to the back windows, pushed the drape aside, and looked down into the yard. Above the woods, stars sprinkled the charcoal sky. When she was a child her father had told her the stars were fairy dust, that she could make a wish and it would come true.

"I wish my child to always be safe," she whispered into the quiet room. "Make the flower man go away."

The next morning, while Katie was at school, Britt called Charlie and left a message on his voice mail for him to call. Shortly before noon he turned up at the front door. Over coffee, she told him about Phil Slater and his hostess gift of forget-me-nots.

His eyes narrowed. "Why didn't you mention this before?"

She resisted the urge to fidget. His tone was as penetrating as his stare. "Because he works in Mark's firm. Mark doesn't think Phil has anything to do with this."

"So—why do you?"

"Mark won the CFO promotion over Phil."

"I see." He took out his notebook and pen. "Go on."

"He's an odd little man with poor social skills, which is the main reason he was passed over for promotion." She bit her lip. Bad-mouthing wasn't her style. And siccing the police on Mark's colleague wasn't a pleasant prospect.

"Don't worry about this, Britt." He reached out to pat her hand. "I'll be discreet. Mark's job won't be jeopardized." He hesitated, his expression tightening. "We have no choice at this point. We have to check out anyone who might have a motive."

Britt liked knowing he was moving full speed ahead on

their case now. "At least he's a suspect, however improbable. That's more than we've had before."

"We've had a few other improbable suspects," he said, surprising her.

"Who?"

"For starters, your theater friends."

"You're kidding." She didn't know whether to be mad or not. "And?"

"Some of them might march to a different drummer, but as far as I can tell, they're clean."

"You said 'for starters.' Who else?"

"What do you know about the school custodian? His name is Milt Graber."

"I don't think I've ever seen the janitor."

"He's in his fifties. Once arrested for—get this—child molestation." He noted her surprise. "The charge was dropped, and legally he's clean."

"But how could the school district keep him after that?"

"His rap sheet only has the one entry and, as I said, he was cleared." He chewed on the end of his pen. "The thing that interests me is his irregular work habits. He's gone more than he's at school, collecting wages for hours he doesn't work."

"But wouldn't Katie have recognized him? She sees him at school."

"That's the big catch." His eyes were suddenly direct. "I'd like you to feel Katie out about him."

She nodded, but her hope died. Katie would have told them if the janitor was the stalker."

"I've gone out on a limb to tell you this, Britt." He hesitated. "The guy'll have my badge if you mention that molestation charge to anyone. He's never been convicted of anything."

"I wouldn't do that," she said. "I'm not interested in ruining an innocent person's reputation, only in finding the stalker."

"Good. We're on the same wavelength. We'll see what turns up." He glanced at his notebook. After a few seconds he looked up. "What do you know about the patients at Pinecrest?"

"Nothing much. They're developmentally disabled and supposed to be harmless, even though they look scary in those hooded green sweatshirts." She leaned toward him. "Is there someone there who might—"

"I'm checking Pinecrest out because of its close proximity to Katie's school," he said, anticipating her question. "Although none of the patients really fit the profile I'm working up."

"Profile? You mean the stalker's pattern, his modus operandi?"

"More than that." He paused. "There's a general profile that applies to all stalkers. My profile goes further; it's based on what we know so far about *this* stalker."

"How can you come up with a profile of somebody you've never even seen?"

"I know I've told you that detectives deal in absolutes —in things we can see or touch or smell. But profiling is a combination of deduction and instinct. It's not a definite science. It's seat-of-the-pants, the way old cops used to do it before there were computers and fingerprint scanners."

"I still don't see how—"

"Okay. Take what we know about this guy."

"We don't know anything about him."

"That's where you're wrong. We know he walks on his own two legs, and he doesn't limp. Right?"

She nodded.

"And we know he's a male Caucasian. We know he's probably older than a teenager. Kids get mixed up about age, but Katie wouldn't confuse a boy with an adult man. So let's say he's a white male between twenty-five and forty. He's agile, moves fast. He either works for himself or has a job that's flexible. We know that, because his notes and flowers have been left at all different times."

"I see." She was fascinated.

"He knows flowers. He knows what they mean. Maybe he works for a florist, or maybe that's too easy. Maybe he

160

grows his own, or maybe he just likes flowers. If he's into flower symbolism, that might indicate—because of the flowers he's left—that he also believes in reincarnation."

"How tall is he, genius?" She couldn't help the grin.

"Well, he's not short and he's not really tall—Katie would have mentioned that. He's probably five-ten to six feet. The trouble is, Britt, he's probably average. These guys get away with things because they blend in with a crowd—there's nothing unusual about them. So I think this guy is a nice normal-appearing average American man. I think he's fast and strong, and he knows Portland like the back of his hand—because he disappears so fast. He's not afraid of dogs."

"I don't think he's afraid of anything."

"He drives a vehicle, hangs around grade schools, and I don't think he's married."

"Why?"

"Wives get suspicious if their husbands come and go at all hours. If he does have a wife, she's under his thumb and doesn't dare ask questions. Or maybe he has a legitimate reason for being gone so much and that's why she doesn't suspect him." He hesitated. "He probably doesn't have many friends. If he does, they're people he can control, who don't ask too many questions. We know he's a pedophile. He may have a record, or he may have been clever enough to get away scot-free. I'm betting he works around kids, either as a volunteer or in a profession."

"I'm impressed, Charlie."

"Good." He shrugged. "Course, I could be wrong about some of these details, but as we go along, we'll learn more and more about this guy." He stood to go. "By the way, I don't have the lab report on Max yet."

He flipped his hair back, tucking it behind his ears. She wished he hadn't reminded her of a college kid just when she was gaining confidence in him.

Insomnia became a nightly ordeal for Britt, and when she did sleep, it was fitful. Her eyes popped open each time the grandfather clock gonged downstairs or the house creaked or the wind rattled the shingles. Katie often woke up calling for her parents, and Britt would sit with her until she went back to sleep. Even Sam was affected by the tension; he'd become Britt's shadow, upset whenever she was out of his sight.

"I'm staying up tonight," Mark announced a couple nights later. He pulled Britt into his arms. "You need sleep, sweetheart. You can't go on like this or you'll be sick."

"How'll you work tomorrow?"

He kissed her, nuzzling her neck. "I'll manage. I can't have you collapsing from fatigue. The kids and I need you."

"But—"

"No buts. I want to catch that bastard. I know he's out there, watching." He gave a wry laugh. "Unless I'm the one who's crazy."

"What'll you do if you see him?" She stepped back, meeting his eyes. "Promise me, Mark, that you won't run outside and confront him. He's dangerous."

"Don't worry, I'm not stupid. I'll call the police. He won't even know I've seen him."

Unable to talk him out of it, she went to bed. But knowing Mark was prowling the dark house kept her awake, fearful of what would happen if he did see the stalker. She lay in bed wide-eyed, separating the night sounds into mental compartments: the furnace turning on, Sam rolling against his bed's side supports, a dripping faucet in the bathroom. It was her house. She knew the sounds by heart.

By morning she could hardly drag herself out of bed. She'd finally fallen asleep shortly before dawn. Mark, his eyes red-rimmed from fatigue, was shaving when she went downstairs to make coffee. He barely acknowledged her.

Mark went to work, but that night she couldn't talk him out of staying up again. Britt was up and down herself, worried that he was becoming disoriented from lack of sleep. What if he opened a door and the stalker got into the house? Katie wasn't the only one with nightmares. Britt was having them while she was wide awake.

"Enough is enough," she told Mark when he stepped into the kitchen the next morning. "You can't go on like this. You look awful."

He poured coffee into a mug. "What in hell do you suggest? Letting that bastard get away with this?"

"Mark, you're acting irrational. You've lost your perspective from lack of sleep."

"Fuck perspective!" He swung away from her and strode to the patio doors, dripping coffee after him. "I've got to protect my family, and you know it."

She squatted to sponge up the coffee and tossed the sponge into the sink. She joined Mark at the window.

"You're asleep on your feet, Mark," she said gently. "After this we'll take turns watching. But for now I think you'd better call the office and go to bed."

"Leave me alone, Britt!"

"I can't sit back and watch our lives disintegrate even more." She grabbed his sleeve and shook it. "If you behave like a zombie at the office you'll lose your job. Is that what you want?"

He opened his mouth to defend himself, then closed it. Wordlessly he pulled her into his arms and they rocked together. "You're right, Britt," he whispered, shaking his head like a punch-drunk boxer. "I'll call the office, tell them I'll be in this afternoon." He brushed her lips with a kiss and turned to go upstairs.

"Just a sec, Mark. I know you're dead on your feet but I need your opinion before Katie comes down."

He leaned against the wall, waiting.

"Saturday's Halloween and Katie's friends are trick-or-treating around the neighborhood, then going to Donny's for a party." She hesitated. "I don't want Katie out there, even with a group."

"No way! He's just waiting for us to make that kind of stupid mistake."

163

"I know." She sighed, and tried not to dwell on how completely the stalker had altered their lives. "But Katie was looking forward to going, and she'll feel left out and depressed when she can't. I'd like to have something that seems like more fun lined up before I tell her she has to skip Halloween."

"What would seem like more fun to her? That's the question."

"Suppose we go down to the beach cabin on Saturday morning. Make it our own party. We could stay overnight and come home on Sunday afternoon."

"That might work—if we can get out of here without fanfare."

She knew what he meant—without the stalker knowing. She shooed him up the steps. "Get some sleep. We'll figure out the details later."

Angie stopped by later that morning, and over coffee Britt brought her up to date.

"It's ridiculous for you and Mark to lose sleep like that," Angie said. "I'll talk with Bill. I know he and the guys would be willing to come over and try to catch the creep."

Britt only nodded. She and Mark would try anything at this point.

After Angie left, Britt called Charlie. He promised to alert the police patrols that they would be gone.

"So everything's been quiet?" he asked.

She explained about Mark staying up for two nights. "It's amazing—uncanny. How does the stalker always know when to stay away?"

"I've given that some thought." There was a pause. "He might be using a sophisticated listening device."

Her hand tightened on the receiver. "Are you suggesting he's been listening to us when we're in the house?"

"Or on the phone."

"You think he could have tapped our phone? Charlie, can you check that out?"

"I did check it out. There is no drain on your line. It's okay, or we wouldn't be having this conversation on your phone." Another pause. "I should say your line is intact as far as the telephone company equipment is concerned."

"What does that mean?"

"Only that there are portable surveillance devices. One gizmo can be connected to your line from a phone pole, from a van on the street, or from your backyard. It's also possible to direct a little pencil microphone toward an open window. These mikes can pick up voices in the house, including your half of a phone conversation." He paused. "But look, it's unlikely this guy is a high-tech genius."

They hung up, but Charlie's words lingered. Listening devices were something else to worry about.

Mark packed the car trunk in the garage, out of view of anyone who might be watching. By noon, dressed in jeans, sweatshirts, and windbreakers, they were ready to go. Britt settled the kids into the Honda while Mark set the house alarm. They drove out of the garage as though they were leaving only for the afternoon. Within minutes they were out of the West Hills and on the highway headed northwest toward the Pacific Ocean, an hour and a half away. It was only after they were miles beyond the city that Britt stopped watching the road behind them. No one was following.

"Do we get to roast marshmallows in the fireplace?" Katie asked from the backseat.

"As many as you can eat." Mark glanced at her in the rearview mirror. "We'll have your mother cook her famous hamburgers to go with the pop and potato chips."

"And we'll make hot fudge sundaes for dessert." Britt twisted around to grin at Katie, who sat under a clutter of Sam's books and toys. "How does that sound?"

Katie giggled. "Yum-yum. I'm hungry already."

Sam began to chant, "Eat soon, eat soon."

Britt grinned and exchanged a glance with Mark. Their little family was back to normal . . . for the time being.

This was a good idea, she thought, listening to the hypnotic hum of the tires on the blacktop as they ate up the miles. They'd all needed a lift to their spirits.

"I put the VCR and the small television set in the trunk," Mark said later as he downshifted on the outskirts of Seaside. "We can rent movies at Cannon Beach when we shop for groceries."

"Can I pick?" Katie asked.

"Sure." Mark glanced at her in the mirror again. "You and Mom can pick for Sam and me."

Katie leaned forward. "Mom?" Her tone flattened. "Just because it's Halloween we don't have to have spooky movies, do we?"

Britt didn't even glance at Mark, but she sensed his body tense. "We all agree," she said. "No spooky movies."

When they passed Seaside and headed south along the ocean toward Cannon Beach, Britt cracked her window, allowing the cool fragrance of salt air into the car. She breathed deeply, already feeling its renewing effect. Her view of the ocean was often blocked by the rugged headlands, but the western sky stretched to the horizon, a magnificent stage for cloud pageants and gathering storms.

"We're almost there," Mark said, grinning at Britt. "I can't tell you how good this feels. No phones, no work, no . . . problems."

"Don't forget the car phone," she replied. "Your work buddies won't hesitate to call if they need something."

"It's the weekend, Britt." He slowed for the first stoplight in Cannon Beach, then glanced at the backseat. "We're going to have fun. Right, kids?"

Minutes later he pulled into the supermarket parking lot, and they got out and went into the store. The cart filled up quickly with more junk food than Britt had ever bought before.

"What the hell." Mark grinned, reading her thoughts. "It's Halloween. Think of how much candy Katie ate last year—and survived."

"We forgot potato chips," Katie said, looking through the items in the cart.

"So we did." Britt took a jar of hamburger relish from the shelf. "Why don't you get us a big bag? The chips are in the next aisle. We'll meet you at the checkout line."

They were almost to the front of the store when Katie screamed their names.

"Mom! Daddy!" She ran around the end of the aisle toward them, the potato chips in one hand, a long-stemmed white lily in the other. Her eyes were wide with fear. "He's here! The flower man is here!"

"Where?" Mark demanded.

Britt tightened her hold on Sam's hand and grabbed Katie, pulling her children close.

Katie pointed to a startled bag boy who'd followed her down the aisle. "He gave me the lily—said it was from a man by the door."

"That's right, sir." The red-haired boy, no more than sixteen, blanched. "A man asked me to give her the flower. He pointed her out, said he was related." He hesitated, uncertain. "I didn't think I was doing anything wrong."

"You didn't. Don't worry, you're not in trouble. Just help us, okay?"

The boy nodded.

"Come with me," Mark told him, and ran toward the store entrance.

Britt tried to calm Katie as she pushed the cart toward the checkout counter. She forced herself not to reveal her panic and managed to sound reassuring when she spoke. "We don't know that it was the flower man, Katie. Maybe it was someone playing a Halloween trick on you."

Katie glanced up, her expression hopeful. She brushed the tears from her eyes, then wiped her fingers on her jeans. "People *do* play tricks on Halloween."

Mark met them at the checkout counter, and Britt tossed the lily in a trash can.

"The guy isn't in the store or the parking lot, according

to the kid," Mark whispered to Britt. "But I got the boy's name and phone number for Charlie."

She filled him in on her Halloween theory, winking at him behind Katie's back. He got the message: don't frighten Katie.

They paid for the groceries and went back to the car. Apprehension was a cold finger on Britt's spine. *She felt him watching.*

"We're still having our party, aren't we?" Katie asked anxiously. "Mom could be right. It might not have been the real flower man."

Katie looked down to buckle her seat belt and Britt glanced at Mark. Everything in her screamed to turn around, drive back to Portland, lock themselves in their house with their automatic lights and security system. He looked as uncertain as she felt. Going home presented more problems. They'd signal their fear to Katie and then have to say no to Donny's Halloween party.

"Sure, honey," Mark said, and only Britt realized that his casual tone was contrived. "We came for a party and we'll have one." He grinned at Katie. "Still want to rent movies?"

"Yeah!"

They drove to the video store, and Mark parked by the entrance. While he waited with Sam, Britt and Katie went inside, returning ten minutes later with four movies. As they took the highway south out of town, Britt noticed that Mark's eyes were on the rearview mirror almost as often as they were on the road. No one was following them.

"Daddy! You missed the turnoff," Katie said.

"Oh, so I did." Mark tapped his head, pretending preoccupation. "I was thinking about the movies instead of paying attention to the road."

He turned around and headed back to the dirt road that led to their cabin. He had missed the turn on purpose, Britt realized, to make sure no one followed. She sighed. It would be a long night.

Their cabin was hardly more than a two-room shack,

but it had a big stone fireplace, a front porch, and a bathroom. She remembered how happy they'd been to find a beach cottage they could afford. It hadn't mattered that a dune separated them from the water. She just hoped they still loved the place by the time they went home tomorrow.

She noted that Mark brought the car phone into the cabin along with their things. He started a fire in the fireplace, then brought in enough wood for the night. Britt settled Katie and Sam down to watch television while she prepared the party food. Both she and Mark kept up their cheerful chatter, determined to divert Katie's thoughts from the flower man.

They watched the first movie while they ate. Sam was asleep before it was quite dark, and Britt put him to bed in the next room, leaving the door open. Katie lasted through the third movie and then joined Sam in their parents' double bed. Britt and Mark stayed up all night. By noon the next day they were ready to head home. A storm had rolled in at dawn, making beach-walking out of the question.

Thank you, God, Britt thought. The weather had provided a good excuse to go home early. As they drove away, she wondered if they would ever come back. She hoped they wouldn't have to sell their cabin—because of him.

He watched from the coffee shop across the street while they returned the movies. When they pulled out of the parking space, he dropped several dollar bills on the table and went outside. As they headed out of town he stepped into the phone booth and inserted a coin, then punched in the number; he knew it by heart.

His eyes were on the back of the Honda as it stopped for one last red light, then moved forward when the signal turned green. It was just out of sight when he heard the hello in his ear.

He switched the receiver to his other hand, savoring the moment.

"You know, don't you?" He spoke in his lowest tone, filtering his voice through his fingers. "I'm going to get her."

He hung up slowly, smiling.

The ring of the car phone had startled all of them.

Mark shook his head and reached for it. "You're right, Britt. I can't escape that damned office."

When he darted her a shocked glance, and then hung up, Britt knew.

It was him.

15

BRITT STOOD AT THE HALL WINDOW AND WATCHED HER PARents drive off with Katie and Sam, headed for Mark's parents' condo. She didn't like sending them away. She hadn't wanted to let her children out of her sight, but she'd been overruled by her mother and Mark.

She let the curtain drop and turned to face him. "I have a bad feeling. They shouldn't have gone."

Mark sighed wearily. "Britt, they'll be okay. They were looking forward to Halloween treats from their grandparents. They'll only be gone for a couple hours."

"I just want them safe, that's all."

"They've got to live a normal life. If we don't let Katie have some freedom she'll end up neurotic—damaged for life. And our parents know the situation. The kids are safe with them. Believe me, they won't let anyone near them."

"I know that, but—"

"But nothing. Katie and Sam need some space, Britt." He met her eyes. "You can't keep them with you every minute, Britt."

Mark looked tired; the lines on his face seemed more pronounced. He's aged lately, she thought.

"I just want to keep them alive until this lunatic is caught and put away permanently."

She spoke more softly, suddenly thinking about listening devices. What a nightmare, she thought. She found herself checking the yard and street every fifteen minutes.

Mark dropped his head into his hands. "Britt," he began patiently, "you know he won't be put away permanently even if he is caught." He glanced up. "There is no law against stalking."

She fought an urge to cry from sheer frustration. "We have to call Charlie. My parents are bringing the kids back before dark."

"Yeah, I know." He stood up. "Isn't that the only reason you let them go? So Katie wouldn't be here when we called Simon to tell him about what happened at the beach?"

Britt nodded, and found she could still smile. "You know me pretty well, don't you?"

His answering grin was more like a grimace. "Uh-huh. I'll let you in on a secret. It was also the reason I let them go."

He went to call Charlie Simon.

The scream brought both Britt and Mark upright in their bed. It was a wild animal sound, a high-pitched screech that ascended the scale to hysteria and struck a chord of absolute terror within Britt.

"Katie!" she cried, throwing off the blankets. She ran out of their bedroom, Mark right behind her, as Sam set up a frightened howl from his room.

"Go get Sam!" Mark said, heading for Katie's room farther down the hall.

When Katie kept screaming, Sam cried louder. Britt didn't break stride as she veered into his room, swept him out of his bed, and ran on to Katie's room. Mark was already sitting on the edge of her bed, soothing his sobbing daughter.

As she calmed down, Sam stopped crying, too, and Britt realized Katie had awakened from another nightmare. She put Sam down and he promptly climbed onto Katie's bed and snuggled up next to her, patting her back just as Britt patted his when he was upset.

"He was outside my window," Katie said. "I know he was this time. I heard scraping, and then I saw him."

Mark pointed to the drawn drapes. "Honey, you couldn't have seen anyone. It was only a bad dream."

Britt sat in Mark's place when he got up. She stroked Katie's forehead while he opened the drapes and looked out the window. A swath of light from the backyard fell across the floor at her feet.

"I saw a shadow through the drapes—and it moved." Katie squirmed higher in the bed. "I know I saw him—I *know* I did!" Her round frightened eyes looked from her father to her mother. "When I screamed, the shadow went away."

She's on the verge of hysteria, Britt thought, not feeling very calm herself. "Why don't we have a slumber party? You and Sam can sleep with Daddy and me. Would that make you feel better?"

Katie nodded. Wordlessly she got out of bed, took Sam's hand, and led him toward their parents' room. Britt was about to follow when Mark patted her arm.

"You go ahead, Britt." His expression was troubled. "I'm going to make sure the house is secure."

The hollow sensation in the pit of her stomach coiled into a lump of fear. "What's wrong? Did you see something outside the window?"

He hesitated, as though reluctant to frighten her more. He cleared the sleep-tangled hair from his eyes and peered at her with feverish intensity. "There's a loose shake on the garage roof under Katie's window that I hadn't noticed before. It could have been dislodged by the wind or by a fallen branch from the tree. Maybe that's what she heard."

THE FLOWER MAN

"But the tree is by her back windows, not the side window."

"I know. That's why I want to check the house." He moved to the doorway. "You get into bed with the kids. And don't forget the alarm system is on. If someone tried to get in the house it would go off."

She hurried after Katie and Sam. Knowing the alarm was armed didn't calm her fears. She tried not to think about the shadowy corners and dark rooms of the house.

No! You cannot be scared, she told herself. That's what *he* wanted. *To terrify them.*

Mark crawled into bed a few minutes later and indicated that everything was fine. She was telling Sam a story she had made up about a little boy whose big sister had awakened from a bad dream to learn that everything was all right.

Within a few minutes Sam fell asleep, followed by Katie, who was snuggled under the blankets next to her brother. For now she felt safe. After a while Britt heard Mark's even breathing, but she spent the rest of the night wide awake, wondering. The house was secure. But how had the shake come loose?

At daylight she slipped out of bed, careful not to disturb the children and Mark. She grabbed her fleecy robe, put it on in the hall, and went downstairs to make coffee, almost forgetting to turn off the alarm system first. Deep in contemplation of the woods beyond their yard, she didn't hear Mark come into the kitchen. Poor Tippy, she thought. What had happened to their spaniel? They would probably never know.

"Coffee smells good," Mark said, startling her. "I'll look forward to some when I come in."

"Where you going?"

"I just want to look at something. Satisfy myself that the shake came loose naturally."

Mark looked pale in comparison to his navy robe, and absolutely exhausted. She wondered if he'd really slept after all.

She put down her cup. "I'll go with you."

"No," he said at once. "I'd like you to wait by the door." He didn't have to say, "just in case . . ."

She watched him stride across the patio to the back wall of the garage—her garden room. He stood on the damp lawn, his back to the playhouse, and stared at the thick network of rose vines that had climbed all the way to the garage roof, their stems so tightly intertwined that they completely obscured the siding and overflowed the flower bed onto the grass. She sighed. Her roses had run wild. Pruning them was one of her garden jobs that had gone by the wayside.

Turning, Mark glanced around the yard, then scanned the woods behind their property, his body rigid as he focused on the back fence. He moved forward to inspect it, slowly walking the length of it, pulling at the slats, pushing against the support posts. Near the playhouse two of the boards swung outward from the bottom to create an opening in the fence.

Britt's breath caught in her throat. She bit down hard on her lower lip and resisted calling out to him.

She watched Mark pull the bottom of the two loose boards out together, saw him crouch down to judge the size of the opening, then look for the missing nails in the grass. Finally he dropped the slats back into place and stood up, his hands empty. From where Britt stood, the fence now looked secure. The two boards, still fastened at the top, had swung open just far enough to create a crawl hole.

How long had it been there?

Mark's expression was grim as he strode back to the garage and parted the rose vines to examine the ground. His hands stilled suddenly. His glance darted to Britt.

"Bring me the pliers and a plastic bag."

For seconds she only stared back, her thoughts still on the fence, feeling the cold touch of winter in the November air. She clutched her robe tighter.

"Britt. Now!"

At the urgency in his tone, she spun around to find the

174

pliers and plastic bag. When she returned to the doorway Mark was there waiting and she handed them to him. He hurried back to the rose vines, stooped, and picked something up with the pliers and placed it in the plastic bag. Then he came in the house, closed and locked the door.

"What's Simon's number?"

"Mark, it's too early to call Charlie. What's happened?"

He didn't bother to answer her. "Don't we have his home number?"

"Yes, but—"

"But nothing. Take a look at this." He placed the plastic bag on the counter, and Britt bent over it.

"What is it?"

"Looks like a nebulizer. I found it under the rose vines." His tone was low and hoarse. "And remember the rose trellis slats that I made extra strong to withstand the wind? The ones that rise almost to the roof like a ladder?"

Realization dawned with growing horror. She'd forgotten about the trellis because it was hidden behind the overgrown rosebush. Britt nodded and grabbed the counter for support.

"One of the slats is broken, and some of the vines are bent away from the trellis."

Without a word Britt pointed to Charlie's card, which she'd pinned to the bulletin board next to the phone.

He *had* been at Katie's window!

Charlie Simon swung by later that morning after Mark had gone to his office. Britt filled Charlie in on what had happened and watched him go outside to look at the trellis and the loose fence boards. He stood in a steady drizzle scribbling in his notebook. Then he slipped out through the fence opening into the woods. After a few minutes he reappeared, replaced the loose boards, and came back to the house.

"It's wet out there." The shoulders of his sport jacket looked soggy, and there were dirt smudges on his trousers.

She handed him a clean towel and waited while he dried himself.

"I didn't realize there was a trellis under the roses," he said. "I would have told you to take it down."

She glanced away. "We completely forgot about it. Probably because it was so well hidden by the overgrown vines."

"But not well enough. This guy finds any weak link in your security."

"I know. It was a stupid thing to forget." She met his eyes. "But at least he left something behind this time. That's the nebulizer Mark found beneath the rose trellis." Britt indicated the plastic bag on the counter. "Mark didn't touch it. He used pliers to put it in the bag."

"Good." Charlie picked the bag up and studied the nebulizer. "No prescription label." His green eyes narrowed. "You sure it doesn't belong to anyone in your family—aunts, uncles, grandparents? One of Katie's friends?"

She shook her head. "All I know is that I didn't see it last week when I raked leaves."

"It could be medication for an allergy. Whoever lost it might have a breathing problem, maybe asthma, even emphysema." He slipped it into the pocket of his sport jacket. "We'll see what the lab guys can tell us. In the meantime I'd like to take a look at the window layout in Katie's room."

Britt led him up to Katie's room and showed him the dislodged shake on the garage roof under the side window.

"Someone could have been out there all right," Charlie said as they went back downstairs. He hesitated by the front door, his hand on the knob. "This kook is getting serious, Britt. I can't overemphasize the importance of making sure Katie is with a reliable person at all times—until we nail this guy."

Her frustration nearly overcame her good manners. "How much evidence do you need before you can arrest this man?"

"We have to catch him harassing Katie with the intent to do bodily harm."

"At least you know he's out there," she said. "You even questioned the boy at the supermarket in Cannon Beach." She thanked him for driving to the beach the day before on his own time. "Didn't he give you enough of a description to start narrowing our choices? Could it be the school custodian? Someone in the neighborhood? Someone we know?"

He shifted his weight from one foot to the other, uncomfortable with her questions. "The boy at the supermarket did describe the guy . . . generally. But his description won't help much, as I told Mark. Like Katie, the boy spoke of an average joe with dark hair and a mustache who could be anyone."

She clasped her hands to keep them from shaking. "How are we going to stop this?"

"Believe me, Britt, I'm doing everything I can. The nightly patrols have been increased, the trap is still on your phone, and your line is being monitored for taps. We know that the attack dog died from a cyanide-based poison, and we'll check out the nebulizer." He hesitated. "I've scoured the woods behind your house more than once, and I've staked out the area a few times. All we can do is hope for a break."

"Mark wants to buy a gun."

She shuddered at the thought. When Mark had suggested it that morning, she'd been upset. Guns and children weren't a good combination.

"That's not a good idea," he said. "Does Mark know how to use a gun?"

"Only a rifle."

"And you?"

"I hate guns!"

He noted her vehement denial without comment. "Mark would need instruction if he's never handled a pistol—and a gun permit." He scratched his chin, frowning. "And even then, if he shot someone, he'd be arrested."

He noticed her stunned expression and hurried to explain. "If someone comes into your house and endangers you or your family, you can protect yourself. But if you shoot him and he runs outside, you could be in trouble. You can't shoot someone for being in your yard."

"I don't think I can stop Mark from getting a weapon."

"If there's a gun in the house, you'll have to learn how to handle it, too," he said emphatically.

He opened the door and stepped outside. "I'll talk to Mark, see what he's up to." He paused. "And you tell him to take down that trellis."

"He planned to, after you'd looked at it. He also called the burglar alarm company. We're having roof sensors added to the system."

"Good."

"Yeah, good," she repeated, feeling defeated. "What the hell. Everyone should work hard so they can afford high-tech security and live in fear." She leaned closer. "Isn't that the *new* American way?"

"Come on, Britt, don't go cynical on me. It's not becoming and it won't help."

"But it's all I can manage, under the circumstances."

"If it's any consolation, an anti-stalking measure is going up before the state legislature when it convenes in January."

"I know. I've been following its progress."

"If it passes, and I think it will, we'll be able to charge and prosecute this guy, when we catch him."

"This is November, Charlie. What do we do until the law is changed? We could be dead by then."

"You're upset right now." He started toward his car. "Tell Mark I'll call him tonight."

She closed the door and strode toward the den where she'd left Sam in his playpen watching cartoons on television. When the phone rang, she ran the last few steps, grabbing the receiver before the answering machine picked up. It was Dick Burnham, her computer company account. Her heart sank. He'd left a message yesterday, and she'd forgotten to return his call—on top of canceling an appointment with him last week.

The conversation was short and to the point. He no longer needed her services. She hung up, and if Sam hadn't been watching, she would have thrown the phone across the room. Her business had been going so well. She sank onto the sofa, fighting despair, reminding herself that the safety of her family was worth more than any account.

But it didn't help. Every aspect of their lives had been affected by this faceless stalker. Mark was even missing time at work. If he lost his position they could lose their house, their financial security. They had to do something —anything. The stalker had to be stopped.

"He's gone!" Bill Moore was panting when he reached the patio door. "Angie warned me that the weirdo has a great disappearing act. She was right."

"We went deep into the woods," Jim said, his shirt and jeans muddied from the mad dash into the wet undergrowth. "No sign of the bastard."

"Are you sure you saw someone out there, Bill?" Len Holmes asked.

"Positive," Bill replied. "But he was gone by the time we got outside." He handed the night-vision goggles back to Len.

Mark shook his head, disappointed, his eyes burning from fatigue. Hoping to trap the stalker, he and his three friends had staked out the house and yard for the night, using the special goggles Len had brought over. While Bill had been wearing them he'd spotted a figure in the woods beyond the fence. Instantly, the four men had run outside. Mark had stood guard at the door while the others searched the wooded area.

"Next time we'll arm ourselves," Bill said grimly. "I don't know why we didn't think of that before."

"I did," Mark said. "But Charlie reminded me that you can't shoot someone for being on your property."

"We could drag the bastard inside after we shoot him," Jim retorted, "and then swear we shot him in the house."

"I agree with Charlie," Len said. "That could get us into trouble. We don't want to go to jail." He hesitated. "But a gun might help us catch him. Then we'd at least be able to identify him. And maybe that would stop him."

"Don't bet on it," Bill said. "This guy is a two-twenty—a perverted freak. I cover stories about psychos like him all the time for the newspaper. They never change."

"That's it for tonight," Mark said once they were all in the kitchen. "He knows you're here now, that we were waiting for him. I doubt he'll come back tonight."

The men agreed and put on their jackets. Earlier in the evening, after the kids were in bed, Mark had picked them up at Bill's house, according to plan. The three men had ducked low in the car for the drive up the hill, and Mark had driven directly into the garage so that he appeared to be alone. Once inside the darkened house the men had communicated through written notes, which they read in the beam of a penlight. That way their voices wouldn't be picked up by the prowler. Now, as they left in the Honda, Mark watched them go from the dining room window. Bill would bring the car back in the morning.

Mark checked all the safety precautions, then went upstairs, hoping to sleep for a couple of hours before dawn.

For the next week Katie slept in the guest bedroom next to her parents, afraid to stay in her own room. They hadn't told her about the trellis; Mark had quietly taken it down and nailed up the opening in the fence.

"If no one was on my roof, then why did the man put sensors up there?" Katie had asked Britt.

"We thought having them would make us all feel better," Britt had said.

180

"Why didn't you do it before, Mom, when they installed the alarm?"

"We had to wait until we could afford it," Britt had said, improvising.

Katie had become jumpy and aware of every noise. It didn't help that she was isolated from her friends. Britt decided to ask Donny's mother if he could ride with Katie to school, hoping that would give her a sense of normalcy. It was the rainy season and winter was approaching. Other mothers often drove their kids in bad weather. Donny's mother agreed because her son wanted to ride. Britt didn't elaborate and wasn't asked about the stalker. The neighbors still didn't want to believe there was a problem.

On the way home from school on Friday afternoon Britt stopped to pick up some milk. Donny wanted to buy gum, and Katie didn't want to wait alone with Sam, so Britt took all three children into the store. When they came out a few minutes later there was a note on the windshield.

Britt's heart jolted painfully in her chest. She managed to stuff the scrap of paper into her purse while Katie and Donny were getting in the car. She dropped Donny off, then headed home and drove straight into the garage. As soon as Katie went upstairs to change her clothes, Britt pulled out the note and read it.

"Boys are not allowed to ride with Katie."

She dropped onto a chair, her legs too shaky to hold her. He'd sent a similar note about Tippy. *And Tippy was dead.* Like Max.

Later, when they were alone, she showed the note to Mark.

"You'll have to warn Donny's mother," he said, pacing the bedroom. "That bastard is capable of anything."

Britt balled her hands into fists. "I hate him, Mark. I could kill him, and laugh while I'm doing it."

"Shhh," he crooned, pulling her into his arms. "Somehow we'll stop this. We'll get this stalker, and one day soon we'll have our life back. I promise."

Britt tipped her head back so she could meet his eyes. "Or we'll have to move. Has that option crossed your mind?"

He nodded mutely.

"Mrs. Hinson . . . uh, Britt," Ann Gilliam corrected herself. "I find it hard to believe that Donny could be in danger. All this stalker stuff is without substance." Her penciled eyebrows rose into her gray bangs. "Didn't you just say that you've never really seen anyone, that you have no idea who this, um, stalker is?"

"That's right. We don't know who is terrorizing us, but we do know the threat is real."

Britt stood in the entry hall, holding Sam's hand so he couldn't dart into the Gilliams' living room and break a priceless antique. She had to make it quick. Sam was already struggling to free himself. She suspected he was the reason Ann hadn't invited her into the living room.

"I told you about the notes, Ann. You just read the last one and the one about Tippy." She held them up again. "Tippy was taken from our backyard." She hesitated, then decided the woman needed to hear everything. "His ears were cut off and left in the doghouse."

Ann recoiled, backing away from Britt, her eyes wide with horror. "Are you saying that—"

Britt nodded. "Mark brought home an attack dog after that, and it was poisoned."

"And because you are afraid for Katie you're driving her to school?"

"Yes," Britt said, relieved to see that she'd finally gotten through to the woman. "Believe me, we're living through a reign of terror. We're like marionettes without a clue to the identity of the person pulling the strings."

"How could you allow my son to be a part of this? Why did you knowingly place him in this kind of danger?"

"Mark and I are very sorry about that. It didn't occur to us that Donny would be in danger." She hesitated. "And maybe he isn't." Sam fussed louder, and Britt had

182

to raise her voice to be heard above him. "But we wanted to explain, because of what happened to our dogs."

"I should think so. Needless to say, Donny will not ride with you again." Her usually courteous manner was replaced by indignation. Her tone dismissed Britt.

"I hope this won't spoil Katie's friendship with Donny." Britt stopped short of pleading. "This situation isn't Katie's fault."

"We both know their friendship has to end," Ann said crisply. She strode to the door and opened it. "Of course I realize this is not Katie's fault. But it isn't ours, either. Good day, Mrs. Hinson."

Britt moved around her and stepped out onto the porch, feeling humiliated.

The door closed with a final click. Britt half dragged a stubborn, crying Sam down the sidewalk to their house. She could hardly see. Her own tears were blurring her vision.

Now they were losing the goodwill of their neighbors because of *him*. God, she prayed under her breath, make him die.

16

THE AFTERNOON WAS BRIGHT AND CLEAR. THE WEEKS OF FOG and mist and clouds had given way to the incredible vividness of sunshine in a rain-washed sky. The air currents brought fragrances that were reminiscent of the great northwest forests and of the Pacific Ocean to the west. Buddy's hopes soared higher than the snowy peak of Mount Hood off in the distance.

He drove along the winding back road, headed toward the park across the street from Steward's store. He parked his van where he could watch the playground. As he switched off the engine, his eyes were already scanning the groups of children, looking for one. Saturdays brought the kids to the park when the weather was good. He knew Donny would be there today.

A baseball game was in progress in one corner of the park and a touch football match in another. Most of the players were sixteen and under, typical for a neighborhood park. The backdrop of trees and brush had been shorn of maple and alder leaves, but the Douglas firs and the big cedars and the wild English ivy that twisted up every trunk kept the woods green.

He knew Katie wouldn't be there. He didn't want her there, playing with the boys. He knew what boys wanted. It was Donny who interested him today.

Donny was like the boy who'd played with Jenny, his little sister. Jenny was twelve when Buddy caught her with the boy, kissing and petting. That was when he'd realized his innocent little sister, who worshiped him, would grow up to be a slut like their mother. And he'd known he couldn't allow that.

His breath tightened in his chest. He leaned back against the seat, automatically reaching for his nebulizer, a replacement for the one he'd lost.

Don't think about Jenny, he told himself, a warning he'd issued many times. Don't think about her lifeless blue eyes, her curly blond hair matted with her own blood. Or her vaginal blood when she'd been penetrated for the first time—before the others got her.

He breathed deeply, forced his mind away from Jenny —and the other ones. He concentrated on the time when he would be united with his true love. *She* had not succumbed to the sins of the flesh, yet. He would make sure she did not. He, and only he, would be her teacher. She belonged to him.

Then he saw Donny.

His breath quickened again as he leaned forward over the steering wheel to peer through the windshield. The baseball game ended, and Donny left his friends to get his bike. Buddy rolled down his window, letting the din of voices into his van. He heard Donny calling good-bye to his friends.

Buddy started the engine, then waited as it idled. He would give Donny time to leave the park and start up the hill toward the turnoff to his street.

He closed the window and slowly drove away from the park, waiting at the stop sign until Donny entered the stretch of road with the deep ditch. Then Buddy headed up the hill out of sight of the kids in the park. His eyes were riveted on the blue bicycle with the seventy-pound boy who was pumping hard against the grade.

Donny glanced over his shoulder, saw the van coming up behind him, and headed his bike toward the side of the road. He glanced back again and moved over even farther, to the edge of the ditch.

Buddy pressed the gas pedal to the floor and swung the van onto the shoulder. His hands tightened on the wheel and his mouth twisted with resolve.

"Die, you little bastard!" he shouted into the empty cabin of his van.

Fear registered on Donny's round face when he looked back again and saw the van on the shoulder bearing down on him. He pedaled faster, trying to reach a driveway twenty feet ahead of him. In a last furtive glance, his eyes met Buddy's.

The van struck him five feet short of safety. Then he was flying through the air into the ditch. The bicycle landed several feet from where he lay, stunned and bleeding.

Buddy braked, sending up a shower of gravel. As he was about to make sure that he'd killed the kid, another car rounded the curve at the bottom of the hill behind him. He accelerated instantly. He had no intention of being caught.

He pulled in at a gas station farther up the road and stepped into a phone booth, pretending to make a call. When he heard the sirens of the police car, then the ambulance, he was satisfied. He put the receiver back on the hook, got into his van, and headed away from the area.

Buddy opened his window, letting the cool air blow over him. He hoped Donny was dead. He shifted into high gear when the road leveled out. The wind caressed him with affirmation.

Charlie came by that night with the news that Donny had been injured by a hit-and-run driver and was in the hospital. Mark took him into the living room, and Britt joined them after settling the children in the den.

"He's lucky to be alive. Looks like the driver hit him deliberately."

"How do you know that?" Mark asked.

"The vehicle veered six feet off the blacktop. We measured the tire tracks."

"Did anyone see what happened?" Britt gripped the arms of the overstuffed chair.

"There were no witnesses. I was informed about the accident by another detective." He hesitated. "It seems this might be connected to your case."

"You don't think— It wasn't because of the note, was it?" Britt asked.

Charlie nodded. "I think so, yes."

"Oh, dear God, we were afraid of that. Will Donny be okay?"

"He's got a broken arm, a badly bruised leg, and lots of cuts and scrapes, but he'll be all right." He looked down at his shoes. "He was lucky."

"Did his mother tell the police about the note?" Mark leaned forward. "Is that how they knew about us?"

Britt tensed, waiting with Mark for the answer.

"Well, yes, she did, after Donny said he recognized the driver as the man who gave Katie the flowers on the way home from school."

"He meant to kill Donny." Britt's lips trembled. "Just like he killed Tippy and Max."

"Yeah." Charlie's voice sounded hoarse. He cleared his throat and began again. "It looks that way." He seemed nervous, as though he hated to be the bearer of more bad news.

"What else, Charlie?" Britt braced herself.

"We know this guy is obsessed with Katie, that he reacts violently to eliminate anyone who comes between him and her." Charlie paused. "We don't know who'll be his next target."

Britt started to speak and couldn't. She licked her lips and started again, but Mark beat her to it.

"Can we get more police protection?"

"If you mean can I assign around-the-clock surveillance, the answer is no." His features hardened, and for the first time he looked older than his years. "But if we catch him on the hit-and-run we'll arrest him."

"What are the chances of catching him?" Mark asked.

"Good, I hope. Donny said the guy was driving a dark van," Charlie said. "At least we have someone who can identify him now, help us build a case against him."

"You have three someones, Charlie," Britt reminded him. "Aren't you forgetting Katie and the kid in the supermarket at Cannon Beach?"

"I haven't forgotten anything, believe me," Charlie said. "Unfortunately there's a big difference between Katie's situation and Donny's accident. The guy committed a crime by hitting Donny and then leaving the scene."

"And no crime has been committed against Katie?" Britt stood, too jittery to sit.

"Legally, no. Not yet."

"Let's hope you catch this lunatic," Mark said, "before our daughter's the next casualty."

Charlie got to his feet. "I feel just as frustrated as both of you do." His gaze was direct, sweeping them both into its orb. "I can only repeat my warning to be careful."

They walked him to the door, and Charlie was about to head for his car when he hesitated, his eyes glinting under the porch light. "As I've said before, I'm following up on every lead we get, however minute. I mean to catch this bastard."

"Thanks, Charlie," Mark said for both of them. "We appreciate that."

Charlie grinned briefly, then hurried to his car. Britt and Mark closed the door quickly.

The flower man was out there somewhere. They both felt his presence.

Britt picked up the ringing phone the next evening as she and Mark got ready for bed.

Ann Gilliam was on the line. "Britt, I apologize for being insensitive about your fear for Katie. Now I know how scared you are." She paused. "Walt and I are counting our blessings that Donny will be all right."

"We feel terrible about what happened," Britt said, grateful that the woman seemed finally to understand the danger.

"My husband and I have talked about this," Ann went on. "I trust you will understand what I'm compelled to tell you."

There was an awkward silence. Britt stared at the carpet, waiting.

"We've decided that Donny won't be allowed to play with Katie until this, uh, flower man is caught. It would be best if she didn't come over or call Donny on the phone for now."

Before Britt could say anything Ann rushed on. "Walt and I want to make sure this doesn't happen again."

"Ann, I sympathize with your feelings." Britt held the phone with both hands to stop their trembling. "But let's not punish the children. It would be wrong to stop their friendship."

"I'm truly sorry, Britt. But until this stalking business is over, Donny won't be seeing Katie." She took a hurried breath. "Good-bye."

The receiver clicked, and a dial tone sounded in Britt's ear.

Mark came from the bathroom. "Who was that?"

"Donny's mother." She managed to report Ann's conversation. "Oh, Mark, I feel so helpless."

THE FLOWER MAN

He soothed her, and when they finally turned out the lamp she lay in his arms for a long time, listening to the comforting sound of his heart beating under her ear. Somehow he was stronger than she was, less vulnerable. His breathing deepened into a steady rhythm. He was asleep.

Good for you, Mark, she thought. It would be another sleepless night for her. She didn't remember finally drifting off.

The hall was long and narrow, the ceiling obscured by charcoal shadows that moved when she moved, were still when she was still. Britt hesitated, knowing she'd been running, was exhausted. Why was she there? Who was she running from?

The footsteps behind her grew louder. Her heart fluttered. Her mind told her legs to run, but she couldn't move. Then she remembered; she had to find Katie.

The hall was lined with closed doors. Katie was behind one of them. Britt had to find her. They had to flee before he saw them. Fear pressed down on her chest, making it difficult to breathe. She forced her limbs to move, slowly, too slowly. The footsteps were closer, gaining on her.

Terror propelled her from door to door, and as she yanked each one open, a hooded head on a spring popped outward. Her panic rising, she rushed on until all the doors were open and she was at a dead end. Where was Katie?

She whirled around to see her daughter strolling toward her down the hall, unaware of the hooded figure behind her, arms outstretched to grab her.

Britt stood frozen, unable to scream the warning that was trapped behind her lips: *Run, Katie!*

As the man's arms came around her, the child struggled, and from a long distance Britt heard her scream, "Help me, Mom! Make him leave me alone!"

But Britt was helpless, unable to stop what was happening. She struggled against the force that had immobilized her. The pressure in her chest was tremendous, and her heart was beating so fast she felt faint. She tried to shout, but her voice sounded weak, her words falling into the shadows before they reached the struggle in the hall. Her child was being taken away, and she couldn't stop the hooded monster.

A high, shrill scream tore through Britt. It filled her ears and shattered the scene. She lunged up, choking and gulping for air, the blankets falling away from her.

The bedside lamp clicked on. Then Mark was holding her, crooning soothing words against her hair. "It's all right, Britt. It was only a dream. I'm here. You're safe."

Outside, the night was still and black. "I couldn't save her." Her voice was hoarse. "Katie was screaming for help, and I couldn't get to her."

She pulled out of his arms. "I have to look in on Katie and Sam."

He let her go, then got out of bed and followed her from bedroom to bedroom. Sam slept as always, with his legs outside the covers, and Katie was curled up in the fetal position, the covers tucked under her chin, an old Raggedy Ann doll clutched against her chest. Satisfied, Britt allowed Mark to lead her back to their bedroom.

"I couldn't see the face of the person who grabbed Katie."

"That figures," Mark said. "Your nightmare was based on the flower man, and you've never seen his face either."

She felt a chill as she remembered something else about the nightmare: the man in her dream had been wearing a hooded sweatshirt—like the patients at Pinecrest.

"Have you checked on the people at Pinecrest?" Britt asked Charlie the next morning on the phone.

"Yes, I have, Britt. They appear to be harmless." He paused, and she heard him sigh. "I told you that before. We can't arrest someone because he wears a hooded jacket."

"Listen to me, Charlie," she said. "Call it mother's

intuition, a sixth sense, but I had a nightmare about a Pinecrest patient, and it might be prophetic."

"Britt, you're upset right now." His tone was sympathetic. "If it'll make you feel better I'll drop by there again, okay?"

"Thanks, Charlie. It will make me feel better."

"I was going to anyway," he said, and she could hear the smile in his voice. "Pinecrest owns a dark van."

"Like the one that hit Donny?"

"Probably not. But as I said before, I'm looking into every possibility, however remote."

He hesitated, then changed the subject. "Tell me more about this Jay Fisher and the modeling competition."

"I've already told you what little I know about them." She pressed the receiver against her ear. "Why? Have they done something wrong?"

"I'm just going over all of the people you've been in contact with since this started."

"I think I told you our friend Len Holmes was the photographer. You could ask him about Jay Fisher."

"I have. He doesn't know much more than you do. He only got the job when another photographer backed out at the last minute. The competition was his only assignment with Fisher." He hesitated. "You think Holmes could be involved?"

"Absolutely not! Len wouldn't harm a fly, and he loves kids—wants a family of his own one of these days."

"Yeah, that's what he told me, too. And by the way, I've looked into the backgrounds of the people you see on a regular basis—your milkman, the garbageman, the paperboy, the mailman, your neighbors, and all your friends. They're clean as far as I can tell."

"Thanks, Charlie. Mark and I appreciate all you're trying to do. We're just scared, that's all."

"So am I, Britt." His tone was softer. "That's why I'm involved. I want to catch this guy doing something that'll put him away for a long time."

"Doing something? Like what?" Her heart lurched.

"I don't mean I have to catch him hurting Katie." His

voice dropped ominously. "I don't intend that to happen." He paused, then said, "I'll give you a call tomorrow, see how it's going."

She thanked him again and they hung up. She had taken two steps away from the phone when it rang again. She hesitated, then remembered that *he* no longer called. She picked up the handset, still warm from her last conversation.

"Mrs. Hinson? This is Mr. Lotze." The principal went on to say that the flower man had been seen a few minutes ago by Katie and also by the playground supervisor.

Britt hung up and went to find her car keys.

"Mom, he was on the other side of the chain-link fence in the woods, standing against a tree trunk." Katie's eyes glistened like sapphires in the afternoon sunlight. "He was staring at me—and he waved."

"And you ran to the teacher on duty?"

Katie nodded. "She saw him too." She glanced down. "But only for a second. He ran off into the woods."

They were standing on the patio with Sam, and Britt gave her a hug. "Just keep reminding yourself that Detective Simon is going to catch him."

Britt glanced across the fence to the sun-dappled woods. Now that the deciduous trees were bare, she would be able to see anyone who got too close. But she was still jumpy. If Katie hadn't needed a diversion, Britt wouldn't have agreed to let her straighten up the playhouse and bring some of her things into the house for the winter.

Katie toed the edge of the grass. "Donny came back to school today, and . . . he told the other kids that the accident was my fault—that the flower man was mad at him because he was my friend." She looked up. "He told them not to be my friend or the flower man would get them, too."

"Donny's upset about what happened," Britt said gently. "He needs to blame someone, but he's still your friend. Give him time, Katie. Remember how scared he must have been. All of this will pass one day soon."

"I hope so." Katie glanced at the playhouse.

"I've already unlocked the door," Britt said.

"Will you stay in the yard?" Katie's voice betrayed her apprehension. She loved her playhouse, but it had been some time since she'd used it.

"I'll do better than that," Britt said. "I'll give you a hand, just as soon as I take a peek at my poor ruined rosebush. You and Sam go ahead."

Katie crossed the yard to the playhouse, her blond curls caught in the collar of her jacket. Sam ran behind her. She pulled open the door while giving Sam instructions about what he could and could not do.

Britt headed for the climbing rosebush which had collapsed when Mark removed the trellis. She didn't want it to die; it produced great roses—

The scream came from the playhouse.

Britt turned and ran. Katie was clinging to Sam, her face stricken with horror, when Britt reached them.

"My—my dolls." Her voice sounded as though all the air had gone out of her. One of her Barbie dolls lay at her feet.

"What happened?" For a second Britt didn't understand. A glance told her there was no one else in the playhouse.

"He—he hurt my dolls." Katie followed her brother into Britt's arms. "Mom, I'm so scared. He undressed my dolls before he—Before—" She started to cry, a strange choking sound Britt had never heard before.

Over the heads of her children Britt noticed the other naked dolls. They were sitting on little chairs around the doll table that was set for a tea party. Their tiny breasts had been slashed, some almost cut off, their crotches hacked open.

A little bouquet of forget-me-nots sat on the table. Next to it was a note that said, "Whore-dolls."

Britt's terror was instant. If *he* was watching, he'd know they were trapped in the playhouse.

She slung Sam under one arm, grabbed hold of Katie with her other hand, and took them both outside. The back of her neck prickled as she rushed them into the house and locked the door. Then she had another horrible thought.

What if he'd come inside the house while they were in the playhouse?

She took deep breaths, fighting panic. The alarm system hadn't been on. Her glance shifted to the stairway, then to the dining room and hall doors. Her house was suddenly an alien land filled with shadows and places to hide. She decided not to search the house. There were two staircases. She could be cut off from her children.

"We're going out to my car," she whispered, and grabbed her purse from the kitchen table.

"Why, Mom?" Katie's eyes widened. "You don't think—"

"Shhh," Britt whispered. "I just want us all to go to my car."

She murmured reassurances to Katie and Sam as they tiptoed through the laundry room to the garage. Britt turned the knob slowly, quietly, easing the door open. There was no time to set the alarm. She had her key ready when they reached the Volvo. In seconds they were inside, the doors closed and locked. Britt started the engine at the same time she pressed the automatic garage door button.

Once the car was in the driveway, she waited until the garage door slid back down and closed. Then she drove to the nearest phone booth and called Mark. He met them at Steward's store and they drove home together.

"Mark, I locked the patio door when we came in from the backyard."

"It isn't locked now," he said.

Someone *had* been in the house. They called Charlie.

194

17

CHARLIE WAITED DOWN THE STREET IN HIS CAR UNTIL THE school custodian's house had been dark for a half hour. Then he got out, sought the reassuring bulge of the .38 in his shoulder holster, and started down the sidewalk.

He kept to the shadows, and when he reached the opening in the laurel hedge, he hesitated. Maybe he should wait. Give it a few more minutes. Make sure they were asleep. He didn't want to be seen. Cop or no cop, what he was doing was illegal.

But he was so pissed off at the moment that he didn't give a damn. Someone had to start somewhere. When he'd tried to convince Herb, his sergeant, to bootstrap the Gilliam kid's hit-and-run accident to the Hinson case, so that he could beef up his investigation, Herb had laughed him out of the office. Charlie should have expected it. Major Crimes didn't want Traffic's case if they didn't have to take it. They wanted a sure thing; he was bringing them cobwebs.

"I sympathize," Herb had said. "But as far as the legal system is concerned, this case is based entirely on hearsay at this point. We can't do anything for the Hinsons until we have evidence that a crime has been committed. And until the driver who hit the Gilliam kid is arrested, and put in a lineup, we can't assume that the two cases are related."

"Bullshit," Charlie muttered, his eyes on the house.

His leads had boiled down to Graber, the school janitor, and one other. Phil Slater had checked out clean. The residents at Pinecrest were so well monitored that it was impossible for one of them to be a stalker. Furthermore, their IQs were so low that they could not have

195

formulated a plan; they were like children. Milt Graber was his best lead, even though Katie hadn't recognized him and he didn't completely fit the profile.

Charlie shifted his weight from one foot to the other, his senses on full alert. A car approached on the street, and he ducked until it passed. It started to drizzle, and Charlie put his collar up to protect his neck. He'd wait a little longer. Graber and his wife must be in dreamland by now.

The record of Milt Graber's one arrest had alerted Charlie to dig deeper. Some interesting things had come to light: Milt was a liar, and he had cheated the school district; his wife ran a small nursery business without a permit or a business license, on property not zoned for commercial enterprise; and Milt often left his job to deliver flowers for his wife in his dark van.

Straining his eyes, Charlie tried to make out the greenhouse in the shadows behind their house. He wanted to see if they grew lilies, carnations, and hybrid forget-me-nots.

Charlie had already checked the van while it was parked at school. If Graber had hit Donny Gilliam, he hadn't done it with his own van.

But hell, Graber is almost all I've got, he told himself.

Charlie moved forward on the balls of his feet, avoiding the brighter patches of yard. Adrenaline pumped through his veins as he headed down the driveway, past the garage, and into the backyard. He paused, glancing around for an escape route in case he needed it. He was in good shape. He could outrun Milt, whose only exercise probably consisted of shuffling between the television set and the stash of beer in the refrigerator.

Charlie pulled a pair of leather gloves from his pocket and put them on. Just like a real burglar, he thought grimly. If he was caught, he would lose his badge.

Bummer.

The greenhouse loomed ahead, black and silent. He peered through the darkness for the door. Should be on the end closest to the house, he told himself, and grinned when it was. Cautiously he moved forward.

The muscles in his stomach tensed when he stepped out of the shadows. He turned the knob. The door was unlocked. Charlie stepped inside and pulled his penlight from his pocket. The light, small as it was, made him nervous.

The greenhouse was long and narrow, one aisle running down the middle. He quickly walked the length of it, training the beam on one side on the way down, the other side on the way back. The plants all looked alike to him—he was no flower expert—but he was sure there were no carnations, lilies, or forget-me-nots.

He put the penlight away, stepped back outside, and closed the door behind him. A dog barked in the next yard, and Charlie broke into a run. He'd reached the street when a light went on in the Graber house. Seconds later he was climbing into his car. He closed the door gently and tossed his gloves on the seat next to him.

He was still at square one. No evidence, no real suspect.

That left him with one final lead, and a slim one at that. It could be a red herring, but it was at least worth a second glance. You never know what you might find under the next rock, he reminded himself. He started his car and headed home. He would follow up on the other possible suspect tomorrow.

The following week passed without incident. Britt cooked Thanksgiving dinner for both sets of grandparents, but the beginning of the holiday season brought no peace to any of them.

On Monday morning Katie went back to school and Mark to the office. While Sam napped in the afternoon, Britt did some work on one of the two small accounts that hadn't been canceled on her. She'd lost another contract last week because she was unable to attend meetings in the city.

If this is ever over, my credibility will be gone, she thought, making herself a cup of herb tea with calming properties—a blend of chamomile and hibiscus flowers. She was jumpy. Something was going to happen; she could feel it.

Too nervous to sit, she paced the kitchen, sipping her tea. There had been no sign of the stalker for over a week. The uncertainty was almost as bad as the incidents.

When the phone rang she dropped the cup, splashing tea and scattering broken porcelain across the floor.

"Damn!" She stepped over the mess and grabbed the receiver.

"It's Charlie. I need to talk to you and Mark. Can I come over tonight?"

"Of course you can." Her throat constricted. "What's happened? You sound . . . wired."

"We'll talk tonight—I'll know more by then. I'd rather explain in person than on the phone."

She resisted the urge to ask more questions, remembering his warning about sophisticated listening devices.

She was about to hang up when he spoke again. "And, Britt, don't worry. Things might be getting better. See you later."

Charlie's last words stayed with her. Things might be getting better? Did that mean he had a suspect?

By the time Charlie Simon rang the doorbell that evening she and Mark were waiting for him, both anxious. Sam was in bed, and they took Charlie into the living room where Katie wouldn't hear their conversation.

"Sorry about my appearance." Charlie unzipped his jacket and sat down in an overstuffed chair. "I came straight from the gym."

Britt sat on the sofa next to Mark. "You look fine, Charlie."

"I think I have good news," Charlie said. "We've arrested a guy we believe is involved in the stalking."

Britt gaped at him.

"When did this happen?" Mark asked.

"The arrest was coming down when I talked to Britt this morning." He glanced at her. "But I wanted to make sure of the facts before I talked to you." He paused. "As it is, the guy we arrested isn't the actual stalker. We believe he hired someone else to do that. Only trouble is, we'll never know for sure, unless he confesses—and we don't think he's about to do that."

"Let me get this straight," Mark said. "You've arrested the guy, but you can't prove anything?"

"What are you telling us, Charlie?" Britt asked.

Charlie put up two flat silencing hands. "Whoa, I'll explain." He moved forward on the cushion. "We arrested this guy on another charge, and we have proof to back up the bust. He's going to do hard time for quite a few years, even if he hires the best lawyer in Oregon."

Charlie paused and then said, "The D.A.'s office issued a warrant to search Jay Fisher's warehouse. The guys from Vice raided it, and he's been arrested and charged with the exploitation and molestation of children, for starters."

Britt gasped as Charlie went on. "He's been running a child pornography racket. Jay Fisher Productions was a front to scout new talent—for his own use, of course."

Mark reached for Britt's hand. "Just what was he doing?"

"Taking photos, making videos of kids involved in sex acts, various types of perversion that included bondage, bestiality, sadomasochism." Charlie shook his head. "Mostly little girls with men—you don't want to know."

Britt felt numb with shock. Her mind boggled at the mental pictures Charlie's explanation conjured up.

"And Katie?" she said. "How exactly did she fit into Jay Fisher's scheme?"

"He obviously wanted Katie for one of his videos."

"No one ever contacted us about modeling assignments." Her hands were knotted together on her lap. "Wouldn't that have been his way of seducing Katie into working for him? I can't see the reason for stalking her instead."

"Fisher knew Katie had a family to protect her," Mark said. "What he's doing is against the law. If he wanted Katie, he sure as hell wasn't going to ask us for permission."

Charlie nodded. "That's how we have it figured."

Mark rubbed his eyes. "I still can't take it all in." He hesitated. "I'm really disgusted with myself for getting Katie into this. It scares me to think what might have happened, and it would have been my fault, because I insisted on her being in that damned modeling competition."

Charlie explained that he'd discovered the vice unit's investigation of Jay Fisher Productions when he probed deeper into Katie's participation in the modeling competition. "There had been complaints about Fisher, rumors that he was involved in pornography. The vice squad opened a real can of worms. There might be other arrests before it's over."

"You think Jay Fisher hired someone to kidnap Katie?" Britt swallowed hard.

"Yeah, that's what I'm betting on."

"Why would he go to all that trouble?" Britt asked. "It doesn't make sense."

"Look, it isn't necessary to go into all the details. Let it suffice to say she was probably a perfect fit to some weirdo's fantasy."

"But why all the weeks of stalking her? Why the letters, the flowers, and all the rest?" Mark asked.

"To let time pass before they made their move. If you believed there was a stalker, then you wouldn't make the connection to Jay Fisher Productions after Katie disappeared. Also, the person Fisher hired was probably more than a little weird himself. Maybe he enjoyed stretching out his sadistic game." He paused. "As a matter of fact, none of the girls from the competition ever got called for an assignment. I checked the whole list."

"Was Jay Fisher the only one arrested?" Britt had to ask. "What about the people who worked for him?"

"I don't know all the details yet. His assistant—can't remember her name—is involved."

"Was it Pearl—something?"

"Yeah, that's it."

"What about Len Holmes's assistant?" Britt asked. "The girls didn't like him."

Charlie pulled his notebook from the pocket of his jacket and thumbed through it. "Bobby Lee. He checked out. He and Holmes, as I told you before, were only hired for that one event. Seems Fisher never employed outsiders more than once. That way no one caught on to his real occupation." He snapped the notebook shut and put it away. "Don't worry. Vice will check anyone out who is connected to Fisher."

"We're grateful that Fisher, at least, has been caught," Mark said.

"Yeah. We got him on a fluke, but we got him," Charlie said. "We can't prove what he did to you folks, but he's going to jail and that's what counts here."

Britt's voice was hesitant. "Do you think the stalking is over?"

Charlie nodded, his green eyes level and honest. "I do."

"Thank you, Charlie."

She hoped Charlie was right. Maybe he was. It all fit. And thank you, God, she prayed silently.

Their three months of hell were over.

The room was tiny, airless, and dark. It brought back the terror of the closet to Buddy. He would die being locked up again. His breath felt trapped in his chest, and he fumbled in his clothing for the nebulizer.

"It'll be all right. It'll work out." The words were a litany, his hold on sanity. Those words, and the mental vision of his beloved.

She will wait, he reminded himself. Hadn't she waited

for him up until now—throughout all of their lives together?

He changed his chant. "I'll be with her soon. She knows she belongs to me. She will wait until it's safe for me to go to her."

His voice was hoarse when he finally fell asleep.

PART TWO

Spring
1993

18

CHARLIE SIMON HAD BEEN RIGHT. THE STALKER APPEARED TO be gone. At first Britt couldn't believe it and continued to drive Katie to and from school, but she let Katie start walking again after Christmas vacation. By mid-January their lives were almost back to normal. Britt was jogging each day, and Katie no longer had nightmares, although she still slept with a light on and an open bedroom door. And Britt continued to make sure that Katie didn't go anywhere alone.

With Angie's urging, and after talking it over with Mark, Britt accepted the role of Blanche DuBois in a short run of *A Streetcar Named Desire* at City Theater. She'd played the character several years ago and remembered most of the lines, which minimized the time she had to spend memorizing the script.

She had even swallowed her pride and gone to see Dick Burnham, explaining about her family's three months of hell because of a stalker. He'd handed his account back to her. "You handled my employee concerns better than anyone before or since," he'd said with a grin.

In February Jay Fisher had been convicted and sentenced to prison for a minimum of twelve years and six months. There was only one short article about the case buried in the back pages of the *Oregonian*. It stated that Jay Fisher had eleven previous felony charges on his rap sheet. A few days later there was an unrelated article about victims pushing Oregon legislators to pass a law on stalking.

Britt tried to not be bitter. At least their ordeal was over. But she often wondered how many other families had gone through a similar hell because of Jay Fisher.

Britt added gardening to her busy schedule in March. She'd made her herb wreaths, dried flower arrangements, and swags in January, too late for holiday presents, so she'd put them into a boutique on consignment. Next winter she and Katie would have new arrangements done in time for Christmas.

Life is really back to normal, Britt thought, as she drove the winding road into the West Hills. Her play would close on Saturday night, and on Sunday they planned to drive to the beach cabin, their first visit since Halloween.

She tried not to notice that wild forget-me-nots were blooming again. She concentrated on the meeting she'd just attended at Hale Enterprises, reminding herself that she'd probably landed the manufacturing company account. Chalk up another coup, she told herself.

She glimpsed something on the front porch as she drove into the garage, and wondered if her mother and Sam had dropped a letter when they picked up the mail. She smiled as the door closed behind the Volvo. Sam loved going to the mailbox. Since February when valentines had come from both sets of grandparents, he'd been anticipating more cards.

"He was a good boy today," Alice said, opening the back door for her. "Weren't you, Sam?"

Sam nodded, his round face beaming.

Britt kissed her mother's cheek. "I really appreciate all your baby-sitting. Thanks, Mom."

"You're welcome, dear. You know I love spending time with the children."

Britt and Sam stood in the open doorway, watching Alice drive away. Sam was still waving when the car rounded the curve and disappeared. She took him back inside and, a short time later, put him to bed for his nap. Then she changed out of her suit into comfortable jeans and a big shirt.

Time for a little work, she thought, bounding down the front staircase, still energized from her presentation at Hale Enterprises. She paused at the bottom, remembering she'd seen something on the porch.

Without hesitation she swung the front door open, then stopped in her tracks, her eyes fastened on the object at her feet. The air went out of her as if she'd been socked in the stomach.

It was starting again.

The nosegay was edged in white lace. Forget-me-nots, rosemary, and tiny carnations were arranged around one white lily, and the flowers were bound together with a white satin ribbon.

It was . . . a bridal bouquet.

The symbolism of the various flowers was not lost on her: true love, remembrance, first love, purity, and virginity.

Britt waited by the window until Charlie arrived a half hour later. She opened the front door and pointed mutely to the nosegay.

"I didn't touch it." Her voice caught, and she took a deep breath. "I wanted you to see exactly where it was."

His green eyes clouded with concern. The day was blustery and the wind caught the bottom of his raincoat and whipped it against his legs. He looked different. Older. She suddenly realized he'd grown a mustache and it added a few years to his face.

Charlie squatted by the flowers. He glanced up, meeting her eyes. "What did you tell me these flowers meant?"

She told him.

He picked up the bound stems with his forefinger and thumb, and followed her into the kitchen where he dropped the nosegay into the plastic bag she held open for him.

Heaven help us, she thought. It's déjà vu—the same pattern as before. Plastic bags for evidence, relating tales of terror to Charlie in her kitchen. He even sat down on the same chair. Her heart fluttered. Her chest felt heavy. Was this how a panic attack started? she wondered.

He nodded when she offered coffee. In silence, she ground the beans and started the water dripping through the filter. While it dripped, she sat down facing him.

"Did you call Mark?"

She glanced down. "He's coming home early. He was—shocked."

At the moment she wasn't up to relating all of Mark's reaction. He'd been struck dumb at first. Then he'd been angry, and finally she'd heard the tremor in his voice. He'd sounded as defeated as she felt.

"Yeah, aren't we all?" Charlie's gaze shifted to the wall clock. "What time does school let out?"

"Three-ten."

She hesitated, trying to gain some kind of perspective. It was difficult to accept that they were back to square one. Could she handle this? Right now she didn't think so. All she wanted to do was scream and cry . . . and kill that bastard with her bare hands.

"I intend to pick Katie up." Her voice cracked.

"Good. I was going to suggest that." He reached out and patted her clenched hands. "I'm really sorry about this, Britt. It's incredible—if this is really the same stalker."

"It's insane." She got up and poured the coffee.

"The more I think about this, the more puzzling it is," Charlie said. "Jay Fisher is in the slammer, and the stalker disappeared at exactly the same time Jay was arrested." He nodded his thanks as she put the coffee cups on the table and sat down. "Is it possible that someone is playing a sick joke? Someone who knows about what happened before?"

"I seem to remember you asking me that last September, Charlie." She sighed, feeling a ten-ton weight on her shoulders. "The answer is no, same as before."

He pulled at his mustache, digesting her words. "What else is the same, Britt? Think back. What were you doing then that is like now? Is there anything?"

"Well, I was in a play then, and I'm in another play now. *A Streetcar Named Desire*. I have the lead. It's a short run—closes on Saturday night."

He leaned forward. "Are there any people in this play who were in the last one?"

"Yes, but that's not unusual. It's a small company."

His tone was suddenly noncommittal. He glanced up. "It won't hurt to check them out, Britt. We have nothing to lose, and they'll never know they've been investigated. Names?"

"Jeb Walker plays opposite me, Art Sills is directing again, and Angie is working with the costumes and props."

"She's your best friend, isn't she?"

"That's right."

"Isn't she the one who wants kids so bad and can't get pregnant?" He hesitated. "Has she yet?"

Britt shook her head.

"It was her husband Bill who saw the stalker through the night-vision goggles, wasn't it?"

"Yes, the time Mark and his friends staked out the house."

"And none of the other guys saw anything that night, right?"

Britt had lifted her cup, but she put it back down without drinking. "What are you getting at, Charlie? Bill and Angie are our friends. They aren't involved in this. I'd bet my life on that."

"I'm sure you're right. But let's cover everyone, okay?" He blew on his coffee and sipped it, looking at her over the cup. "I'm not dismissing the possibility that someone is playing a bad joke. That nosegay came from a florist."

"Are you sure a florist would use wild forget-me-nots? I don't think so."

"Some of the hybrids look like wild flowers."

"How do you know?"

"I checked—last fall," he said, surprising her.

He finished his coffee and stood up to go. "It's almost time for you to meet Katie." He picked up the bag with the nosegay. "I'll see what I come up with on this."

She walked him to the front hall. "It's a bridal bouquet," she said. "That may give you a place to start."

The wind gusted into the hall when she opened the door. He pulled his collar up and buttoned his coat. After stepping onto the porch he faced her again. "Better go back to all the precautions, just in case."

She nodded. "One more thing, Charlie . . ."

He looked up at her from the bottom of the steps.

"Why would the stalker let this much time pass when he was so—so intense about his intentions?"

"Who can tell? All his waves aren't hitting the beach. Maybe he was in jail, maybe he was sick. Or maybe he gets his rocks off by backing away for a while so he can pounce again later on. One thing is for sure. He's a psycho."

After Britt closed the door, she moved through the house with the old itchy feeling on the back of her neck. Her peace had been destroyed by a nosegay. If it did turn out that someone had played a joke, she would press charges. Her fear was no joke. Like a junkie or an alcoholic, one lapse sent her right back to her addiction.

Terror.

A faint shuffling noise brought Britt to a sitting position.

"Mark, wake up!" She leaped out of bed and headed for the door of their room. "There's somebody on the front porch!"

As she ran down the stairs, Mark right behind her, she noticed that the alarm light glowed red, still armed. No one was in the house. Britt hugged herself, apprehension rippling over her bare arms in goose bumps. Mark peered out the front window from behind the blinds. When he suddenly turned off the alarm and opened the door her heart lurched in her chest.

He bent to pick something up, then backed into the house, shut the door, and rearmed the alarm. When he turned, their eyes met. Even in the shadowy hall his face looked white. But it was his eyes that startled her. Black as his lowered brows, they blazed brighter than the red alarm light. For a second she didn't recognize the face twisted in rage.

"Forget-me-nots." He held them out. "And a note."

"What does it say?" Her whispered words grated in the silence.

He switched on the hall lamp and read aloud.

"'My sweet flower. I know you didn't forget me. I won't disappoint you.'" Mark glanced up. "It's signed 'Forget-Me-Not.'"

"It's not over." Britt was trembling violently. "It'll never be over."

"Mark, I will not have a gun in the house." She'd stepped out of the bathroom after her shower, a towel still wrapped around her wet hair, to see Mark come into the bedroom carrying a shotgun.

Ignoring her protest, he held the gun out toward her. "Here, get used to the feel of it. It's lightweight, automatic, and the barrel is only eighteen inches long. You can handle it easily; I'll show you how. And we'll practice before we load it."

She recoiled from the weapon as if it were a venomous snake. "I hate guns, Mark. You know that. I'm afraid of them. I even circulated a petition to ban the damn things! Kids have been killed because their parents had a gun."

"And someone in this house is liable to get killed if we don't have one."

Perspiration lined his upper lip. She knew he disliked guns almost as much as she did, had never approved of his father's hunting trips. But he was desperate and determined—and a little crazy with fear. He's no more determined than I am, Britt told herself. I will not endanger my babies by exposing them to the dangers of a gun. There has to be another way.

"Take it back *right now,* before my mother brings Katie and Sam home."

"The gun stays. We're just damned lucky that my dad had one we could borrow. This is a state-of-the-art weapon, and we don't need a permit for it."

"I don't care if—"

"Shut up, Britt! The subject is closed."

She made a grab for it. "No!"

He held the gun away from her, furious. "If it wasn't for your acting *friends,* we wouldn't need a gun."

Britt went hot all over. "What's that supposed to mean?"

"I had a talk with Charlie Simon. He told me he was checking on the people in your play."

She glared at him. "Only because it's procedure."

"Kind of coincidental that this shit started up again when you got involved in another play. Huh?" He paused for emphasis. "Especially since it began when you were in the last one."

"Mark, I'd appreciate it if you wouldn't harp on that subject again." She sighed, her anger defused by a stronger sense of defeat. "Are you insinuating that this—this slime ball is after me? I thought—"

"Hell no!" he interrupted. "I'm not stupid. We know who he's after. One of your actor friends wants your daughter."

"That's a hideous thing to say!"

He turned away to put the shotgun in the closet. Her protest hadn't meant anything to him. She couldn't believe it. Mark had never disregarded her feelings on something so important. This was a first. She wondered if it was also the beginning of the end for her and Mark. Would their marriage, like their peace of mind, fall victim to the stalker?

"It's time you recognized that those artsy-fartsy theater types aren't perfect."

His eyes burned into hers. He'd turned into a stranger. Where was the old Mark, the man who loved her? She sank down on the bed. Her robe slipped open, exposing her knees. She quickly covered them, feeling naked under his angry scrutiny.

"It isn't anyone in the company," she said.

"We'll see what Charlie comes up with."

"Yes, we'll see." Her voice was stilted. "And when we do, I'll expect an apology." She stood and, ignoring him, went to find her clothes. She had to do the play tonight, one last time.

"Hey! You can't be leaving. The party only started." Angie caught up with Britt as she headed for the back door of the theater.

"I have to." Britt hoisted the strap of her tote bag higher on her shoulder. She managed a smile. "I already peeked in, shared the toast to a great run."

"You made this play a success, Britt. You were a *great* Blanche DuBois."

"Thanks. I accept the compliment." She hesitated. "It was fun. I loved every minute until—"

She glanced at the empty auditorium. It was so quiet now, but in her mind she heard the thunderous applause after the final curtain. She loved the theater, but would she ever act again? She swallowed hard. She was close to tears—an emotional mess.

Angie scuffed at the floor with the heel of her boot and her calf-length full skirt swirled softly around the leather. She frowned, her dark eyes discerning. "Is something bothering you, Britt?"

Britt shook her head, feeling too fragile to answer.

"Did you have a fight with Mark? Is that why he wasn't here? Bill was asking me why Mark hadn't come to the party."

"No—I mean, yes, we had an argument."

"Whew. That's a relief." She snorted a laugh. "For a second I thought it was serious—like maybe the stalker had come back or something."

"He has, Angie." Her voice was faint and she blinked her lashes over burning eyes. She'd been okay while she was acting. Now a sympathetic word could bring on an emotional collapse.

"Oh, my God!" Angie touched Britt's arm. "Did Jay Fisher get out of jail?"

Britt shook her head. "I can't talk about it right now, Angie." She started walking toward the door, eager to leave the theater before she lost her composure. "Please understand. I've got to get home. I'll call you in the morning."

"No, don't call." Angie looked horrified. "If it's the same guy with the same M.O., he might be listening in on your phone conversations—remember?"

Britt knew her expression crumpled. Hold on, she instructed herself. It won't help to be a crybaby. She'd forgotten about phone taps and sophisticated listening devices.

Angie placed the palms of her hands together, considering options. "I'll come by sometime tomorrow."

Angie walked her to the back door and waited while she crossed the alley to the parking lot. Tears blurred Britt's vision, but she waved in Angie's direction, her signal that everything was all right so Angie would go back inside the theater. Britt had been too embarrassed to admit that Mark suspected someone in the theater company.

After unlocking the car door, Britt slipped behind the wheel and tossed her bag onto the backseat. About to start the engine, she hesitated, noticing that the front right side of the Volvo was too low. She got out of the car to check the tires.

She stooped for a better look and saw that the right front tire was flat.

Her talents didn't run to changing tires. She didn't even know if her spare was any good. She decided to go back to the party and ask someone to help her.

The arm around her middle was sudden and brutal, cutting off her breath. Her scream was stuffed back into her mouth by a gloved hand. Her assailant was behind her, yanking her body upright against him. His breath was hot against her ear as he spoke.

"It's your turn, bitch."

19

SHE WAS BEING DRAGGED BACKWARD OVER THE BLACKTOP TO-ward the alley, the heels of her leather shoes sliding through rain puddles. She twisted her head from side to side, struggling to breathe. His left arm was clamped over her breasts, pinning her arms to her sides and crushing her back against his chest. His raspy breath fanned her hair and filled her nostrils with an odd acrid odor. He had jammed his gloved right hand into her mouth, holding it open, gagging her, and impeding her breathing. She couldn't bite down, and her scream was a muffled squeak trapped in her throat.

She grew faint from lack of oxygen and from the repellent scent of him. He jammed his fist deeper into her mouth until she was close to passing out.

Or dying.

That thought sent a spurt of energy through her.

She had to get away.

Thrashing frantically, Britt tried to break his hold. Her jacket ripped away from her shoulder, and the buttons on her blouse tore off as she struggled. A backward kick caught him in the ankle. She rammed the heel of her shoe into the same bone again and again.

He yelped and jumped backward.

Momentarily he relaxed his hold, and Britt jerked free, propelled forward so fast that she stumbled to her knees. She scarcely felt the pain, her eyes on the alley door to the theater.

Her screams echoed off the buildings bordering the parking lot, a high-pitched sound that vibrated in her head. She scrambled to her feet.

"Fucking bitch!"

He was right on top of her. He grabbed her hair with his left hand and yanked her head backward, pinching off her scream, then swung his right hand out and back, punching her face so hard her upper teeth pierced her lip.

Blood spurted into her mouth, and she tried to pry his right hand out of her hair so she could turn far enough around to see his face.

He pounded her face again, and blood spurted from her nose, dripping onto her chin and chest. When she covered her face, he hit her again from behind, knocking her back onto her knees.

She hardly felt the pain. Her mind was consumed by one thought: getting away from him. She was only a few feet from the stage door—and safety.

He caught her by the elbows, yanked her upright, and slammed her back against his chest, pinning her arms to her sides. Her piercing scream was cut off by his hand over her mouth. She bit down on a leather-covered finger.

"Cunt! Pig!"

In a flash, both his hands were around her throat, brutally cutting off her air. He was ready for her kicks, stopping her foot with his leg, ducking his head as she tried to claw at his eyes. Britt concentrated on the street lamp over the parking lot. It burst into fragments of color as he increased the pressure of his stranglehold on her neck.

It was over. Her strength was gone. She couldn't fight anymore. The gray frame edging her mind moved inward to extinguish the light at the center of her being. Her eyes closed, her hands flopped to her sides, her body went limp.

She was hardly aware that his grip had loosened on her neck. Her chin fell forward onto her chest, and strands of hair stuck to her bloody cheeks.

He hoisted her shoulder against his side, holding her upright as he pulled her deeper into the alley between the theater and the parking lot, the toes of her shoes scraping the blacktop. Her cheek was pressed into his neck, which smelled acrid and strangely familiar.

Britt's eyes popped open. She gulped air into her lungs and let out one final desperate shriek. She felt as though her neck was broken. She was a rag doll. It was like a surrealistic dream.

The theater door opened suddenly, and people started shouting. Her captor's body stiffened. Britt tried to scream again, but her throat went into a spasm.

"Hey! What's going on?"

She recognized Jeb Walker's voice. Then Angie's.

"Oh, my God! It's Britt! Bill, he's got Britt!"

Britt heard feet pounding on the blacktop, running toward them.

"Let her go!" Jeb cried.

The man pushed her away, and she crumpled onto the ground. For a brief second Britt looked straight into his brown eyes, saw the grimace that twisted his angular features. She caught a fleeting glimpse of him: dark hair and brows, black leather jacket and gloves, tight-fitting jeans—like a member of a motorcycle gang in a TV movie.

Then she noticed the bulge in his crotch. *Hurting her had turned him on.*

"Next time, bitch."

His words were a snarl. He spun around and ran down the dark alley. Before Angie and the others could reach her, he'd disappeared into the next street.

"I saw him." Britt felt almost tipsy from the realization. "I finally saw the flower man."

The uniformed police officer who'd answered Angie's 911 call was in his forties, a tall, broad-shouldered man whose expression was softened by concern.

"And you believe this, uh, flower man, as you call him, is the one who assaulted you?" he said. He had already written down her description of the attacker and listened to her saga of the stalker.

"Yes, I do," she whispered. Her voice was still hoarse, and her swollen lips felt as if they were numb with Novocain. "I think he was waiting for me to leave. You said there was a nail in my tire. I believe he put it there, intended my tire to be flat, so he could attack me."

The policeman's ballpoint pen paused on the report form. "There's no way to know for sure when the nail pierced your tire, Mrs. Hinson. You could have picked it up on the road." He hesitated. "But it is possible that your attacker did it."

"I *know* he did it. It's the sort of thing he does."

"But you can't definitely identify the man who attacked you as this—flower guy?"

"No. This is the first time I've seen him."

Britt sat upright on the sofa in the theater's greenroom, feeling stronger, although her neck was hurting and already turning into a mass of purple bruises. Angie had washed the blood from her face; her nose had stopped bleeding, but her bottom lip still oozed. Britt's torn slacks were rolled up to accommodate the cold towels on her skinned knees. Even the flesh on the heels of her hands had been scraped off when she'd scrambled across the pavement.

"I think I've seen him before, though. He's vaguely familiar." She started to shake her head and winced. "I wish I could remember."

Britt looked down at her ruined clothes. She was a wreck. Angie had called Mark, explained she was all right, and reassured him that the officer would bring her home in the patrol car.

"I can only note your suspicions, Mrs. Hinson," he answered patiently, "but my report will record the facts of the incident—assault, possibly with the intent to commit rape." His gaze intensified. "It's possible that this attack isn't connected to the stalking incidents. Maybe some guy saw you in the play, was turned on, and did something about it."

His words were an icy finish to her ordeal. She wondered if he thought she was exaggerating the attack into something more than it was. Was he implying that it was somehow her fault—because she'd played the part of Blanche DuBois in the play?

"I'm not imagining the stalker, Officer." Her throat ached. "Detective Charlie Simon can confirm what I've said."

"Uh-huh," he said, distracted by sudden static from his radio. He listened to the transmission and then stood up. "You sure you don't want to be checked out at the hospital?"

"Positive," she croaked. She just wanted to get home to Mark and the children.

Britt got to her feet, still shaky. She owed that maniac some pain and suffering. At the moment she would have taken great pleasure in killing him with her bare hands for ruining their lives.

As she rode through the streets of Portland with the police officer, reaction set in. Her mind replayed the scene in the parking lot over and over. Fear was a hollow gnawing ache in the pit of her stomach. Had he intended to kill her? Rape her? They knew Katie was the one he wanted, but she'd seen his arousal.

Charlie's words jumped into her mind. "You can't second-guess a sociopath. You have a conscience. He doesn't."

In that instant she understood: her attacker had meant to kill her after he raped her—because she stood between him and Katie.

"I've seen him, Charlie. This time I saw him. And more important, I can identify him."

Britt leaned forward on the sofa. In the time it had taken Charlie to get to the house, she'd taken a bath, washed her hair, bandaged her knees, and gotten into a nightgown and robe. She felt tired and sore, but her lip had stopped oozing blood, helped by the ice pack Mark had made for her. And the trembly sensation was gone, taken away by the jigger of whiskey he'd insisted she drink to relax.

"That's a break." Charlie sat down near the fireplace, crossing his legs as he spoke. "But I'm sorry you got hurt in the process, Britt."

They'd been speaking under the sound of music from the Bang and Olufsen. Charlie had asked that it be turned on when he arrived, explaining that it was cover for their conversation, should anyone be outside with a listening device.

"He has dark hair and eyes—Charles Manson eyes," Britt said. "He's taller than I am, so I guess he's above average height—not as tall as Mark, though. He's lean, but strong, and has angular features. He had a terrible expression on his face, but I suppose in other circumstances he might be considered handsome."

"How was he dressed?"

"Jeans and a black leather jacket." Britt paused, seeing a picture of her attacker in her mind. She shuddered. "He had leather gloves on—also black—and a stocking cap. I think it was to cover his hair and brows, but it slipped back in the scuffle. His shoes didn't make a sound on the pavement. Some kind of running shoes, I think. And . . ."

Charlie glanced up from his notebook. "And what?"

"He had an erection." She didn't look at Mark.

"That fits the profile." Charlie glanced between them. "Dominance, power, and inflicting pain. It turns them on."

"*Is that what he would do to Katie if he got hold of her?*"

"He won't get Katie," Charlie said sharply.

"Damn straight." Mark got up and kicked a smoldering log farther into the fireplace.

"Anything else?" Charlie waited, pen poised.

"He smelled funny, sort of acrid." She glanced down, folding her robe between her thumb and forefinger. "I think I've seen him before. There was something familiar about him."

"What?" Charlie said. "Try to be specific."

Britt shook her head. "Maybe it was how he looked at me just before he ran." She tucked her damp hair behind her ears.

"How did you say he smelled—acrid?" Charlie uncrossed his legs and straightened in his chair.

"And like breath mint, and leather."

"His tone of voice? Accent?"

"Deep—and angry. Local accent."

"Okay, that's enough for tonight." He put his notebook away. "You need some sleep." He stood up and glanced at his watch. "So do I."

When she started to get up, he waved her back down. "Stay put. I can let myself out."

At the doorway he glanced back. "I'd like you to come down to the special assault office on Monday. Look over some mug shots, maybe even try to come up with a composite picture on the computer with the help of one of our artists."

"I'll be glad to do that."

"Good." He fingered his mustache. "I'll pick you up at ten. Figure on a couple of hours."

Mark and Charlie disappeared into the hall, and Britt caught a few words of their conversation before she heard the front door close.

Words like *dangerous, be careful,* and *predators without a conscience.*

She dreaded going upstairs to bed. She was afraid to sleep.

20

CHARLIE DROVE BRITT DOWNTOWN ON MONDAY MORNING, then left her alone to go through mug shots of known sex offenders. She didn't make an identification.

Then she sat next to Matt Shiki, a police artist, as he experimented with facial features on the computer screen. He widened the nose and narrowed it, raised the forehead and then lowered it, enlarged the eyes and made them smaller, punching the keyboard in response to her suggestions. Gradually a face emerged that matched Britt's description.

"That's close," Britt said finally, leaning toward the screen. "Yes, that could be him, except for the hair."

"What about the hair?"

"I didn't see much of it. His stocking cap covered part of his head."

"Okay." Matt tapped the keys, and average-length dark hair slid over the face on the screen. "We'll go with a generic style for now."

She nodded, fascinated.

Britt hadn't realized how advanced police science had become. Charlie had explained that forensic experts could even lift fingerprints off a murder victim if conditions were right. The capability of drawing a face on a computer screen was amazing, as far as she was concerned. That capability allowed Matt to use her description of the attacker to create his likeness on the screen.

"That's it," Matt said, pushing his glasses up on his forehead. He activated the print command.

"Incredible," Britt said. "How many people are apprehended because of this computer program?"

He leaned back in his chair, rubbing his neck. "Not as

many as you think. Sometimes these pictures come out looking just like the suspect, and other times they look nothing like him. And also, the bad-asses move around a lot. They hit one place, then wham! They're hundreds of miles away by the next day."

Britt examined the composite on the screen. The face stared back, mocking her. She knew him, but she didn't know him. "I wish that were true of *him*," she said.

"Yeah, Charlie tells me you've got a real psycho on your hands." He reached for the printout, glanced at it, and passed it over to her. "You can always tell the bad ones. They have *sampa ku* eyes, like this guy."

"Pardon me?"

"A Japanese term. Eyes of death."

She shivered. Evil eyes, she thought. *Killer eyes.*

Matt's chair scraped the wood floor as he stood up. "Let's give this to Charlie. Maybe he can do something with it."

He led her through a clutter of desks to one that was tucked into the corner of the room. Charlie glanced up, tossed his pen down, and tipped back his chair.

"Sit down, Britt." He took the composite drawing from Matt, squinting as he studied it. •

"Good luck, Mrs. Hinson." Matt put out his hand to shake hers. "Let's hope this helps get that wacko off your back."

"Thanks, Matt," she said, taking the chair. "I hope so, too."

After a nod in Charlie's direction, Matt wove his way back through the desks to his computer station. She wondered why Charlie was taking so long to comment. What did he see in the face that was so compelling?

"Well?" He glanced up suddenly. "Is it him?"

"It's close." She chewed on her bottom lip. "As I told you Saturday night, there's something familiar about him."

The front legs of his chair came down on the floor when he tossed the drawing onto his desk. "It's possible that you've seen him and not known who you were seeing. Maybe he's been on the periphery of your life for some time now."

"You mean I saw him in a crowd, like at the grocery store or in some other public place?"

"Uh-huh."

She grabbed the picture. "I can show Katie. Maybe she can identify him."

He frowned. "I'd like to suggest you don't show it to her directly. The best approach would be a lay-down."

"A lay-down?"

"Yeah. I'll print out a couple other computer pictures of guys we know aren't the flower man. You can put them somewhere in your house—like on the kitchen table—where she'll see all of them. Watch her reaction. See if she picks out your drawing from the others. We don't want to plant an image in her mind that might not be accurate. Let her tell you if this guy looks like the flower man."

She clasped her hands tightly in her lap. "What if she gets hysterical when she sees it?"

"Then we'll know."

"Mom, when can we go to the cabin?" Katie asked for the tenth time since Mark and Britt had canceled their weekend trip. She seemed peevish this evening as she set the dinner table.

"I told you, honey," Britt said, thinking fast, trying to dream up an excuse she hadn't used before. "Your father and I are both behind on our work, so we need time to catch up. We'll go soon, though. I promise."

As Katie took cutlery out of a drawer, she paused to glance at the computer drawings Britt had left on the counter. But then she simply began humming as she set the table, showing no sign of recognition.

Britt and Mark exchanged glances.

"Would you put these on the desk in the den?" Britt picked up the drawings and handed them to her.

"Sure, Mom." She thumbed through them. "Who are they? Do we know them?"

"No, I don't think so. Why?"

"This one looks kind of familiar." She indicated Britt's composite. "It's a weird kind of picture, with all those little dots."

"It was made by a computer," Mark told her.

Katie disappeared into the hall without further comment.

"Maybe she's mentally blocking him—because she doesn't want to remember," Mark said. "I've heard of that happening." He glanced out the patio door to the backyard. "When are we going to tell her the stalker is back?" He faced Britt again. "She has to know."

Britt sighed. She'd been putting off the moment of shattering Katie's life again. She'd explained that her cut lip was from a fall backstage, and a turtleneck sweater hid the bruises on her neck.

"Don't you think I know that?" she said, tears welling in her eyes.

"Oh, Britt—sweetheart." He crossed the room and folded her into his arms. "I didn't mean to make you cry. You've been so brave about what he did to you." He dried her eyes with the dish towel, then tipped up her chin and kissed her gently.

"Eat—soon." Sam propelled himself forward from the doorway, grabbing his parents around the legs.

"Sam woke up from his nap so I brought him down," Katie explained.

Britt pulled Katie into the family huddle. She loved them all so much. If only things could stay as safe as they were at that moment.

By Wednesday Katie balked at being driven to school, but Britt explained she didn't want her walking in the rain—her old excuse. I'm being a coward, she thought, hesitant to destroy Katie's peace of mind. Instead she watched her like a hawk.

Maybe the stalker would be caught before Katie had to know, Britt told herself. It hadn't even been a week since they had learned he was back. Charlie had given Mr. Lotze a copy of the composite picture, and the principal had alerted his staff. If the stalker showed his face, they would recognize him and call Charlie so that he could make the arrest.

Each time Britt dropped Katie off at school, she patrolled the nearby streets, looking for a dark van. She took routes past the store, through the park, to all the places Katie frequented. And for the three days she'd bundled Sam into the Volvo to swing around the school at recess and lunchtime, she didn't see anyone who resembled the stalker.

If the police don't find him, I will, she told herself. He will not destroy my family.

Her constant activity kept her from dwelling on the fact that he'd tried to kill her. And could try again.

Toward the end of that week, Mark and Britt got the children dressed up and bundled them into the Honda for a trip to Lake Oswego to hear Britt's mother sing at a church recital.

Apprehensive about being away from the house at night, they left the church immediately after Alice's solo and were home by nine. Mark turned off the alarm system, and Britt took the children upstairs.

"You get ready for bed," she instructed Katie. "I'll tuck you in after Sam's in bed."

"Okay, Mom." Katie kissed Sam good night, then went off to her room, humming her grandmother's song.

Katie's scream was sudden and shrill.

Britt jumped. Sam started to cry. Britt heard Mark's feet pounding up the steps, but she was already running, Sam clutched in her arms, toward Katie's room.

Katie stood just inside the doorway, her arms clasped over her chest, her eyes wide with disbelief.

Mark stepped past Britt into the room.

Britt's jaw sagged. For a moment she was unable to process what her eyes told her. She pulled Katie close, not knowing what to say.

Katie jerked free to wave her arms frantically, tears

streaming down her stricken face. "Everything is gone!
All of it!"

Britt's eyes darted over the bare walls and windows.
Every book, doll, and game was gone. The closet door
stood open—not one hanger had been left behind.
Everything had been removed except the tacked-down
carpeting. Her glance stopped on a tiny bouquet of
forget-me-nots on the floor under the window.

Katie saw the flowers at the same moment. Her eyes
widened as realization hit her. She grabbed Britt, shaking uncontrollably.

Britt's mind boggled. It was impossible. How had he
gotten into their house? The alarm had been on.

Mark turned to her, his face chalky white. "Britt, take
the kids into the bathroom and lock the door."

She hesitated, too stunned to think straight.

"Now, Britt!" His voice reverberated with the command.

He stepped into the hall, glanced around, then motioned her to follow.

"But, Mark—"

"No buts." He had lowered his voice to a whisper.
"We'll talk after I've called the police and checked the
house."

"Don't go back downstairs, Mark." She hardly had
breath to get the words out. Someone had gotten into
their house—could still be there . . . hiding.

"I have to."

She saw him glance toward their bedroom. The shotgun was in the back of the closet. She knew he would go
for it first. If only the stalker hadn't gotten it.

Sam cried louder, and she couldn't calm him. Katie's
lips were compressed, holding back the low keening
animal sound that was stuck in her throat.

Mark nudged them into the bathroom, and Britt
closed and locked the door. She and the children huddled
together on the tile floor next to the tub.

Minutes passed and Britt strained her ears to listen.

What had happened to Mark? She pictured him downstairs, lying bloodied on the floor. Oh, dear God! He could be killed. *They could all be killed.*

The floorboards creaked on the other side of the door. Undiluted terror stopped her breath. Someone was out there.

Frightening images shot through her mind like previews for a horror movie. She got to her feet, pushing the children behind her. The lock wouldn't hold against a strong kick. Her heartbeats flattened into one long flutter as she watched the knob turn. The only weapon she could find was in her hand—her high-heeled pump.

"Britt? Britt!" It was Mark's voice. "Open up. Everything is okay."

The rush of relief was debilitating. Her legs felt like they belonged to a marionette with too much string. She yanked the door open and rushed to him, dragging the children after her. He held them all against him with one arm. The other held the shotgun behind him.

"There's no one in the house," he told them. "I called 911. And Charlie. He's sending a squad car ahead of him."

They went downstairs, and Britt made up a bed in the den for the children. She wanted them close. Sam soon forgot he'd been frightened, excited by the prospect of sleeping downstairs on the sofa-sleeper with his big sister.

Two patrolmen answering the 911 call arrived a few minutes later. Mark took them to the kitchen while Britt stayed with Katie, who was calmer once the police arrived.

She heard Mark showing the patrolmen the alarm system before they walked through the house and went upstairs. A few minutes later they came back down the steps. Sam was already asleep, and Katie sat with her head against Britt's shoulder.

"Why did he come back, Mom? Why did he take all my stuff?"

"We don't know," Britt said, lying. She rubbed Katie's

forehead and tried not to dwell on the obvious answer: *Because he intends to take you next.*

Britt didn't get up when Mark brought the policemen into the den. The officers could not hide their outrage at what had happened.

"I think we've got everything we need," the older of the two officers told Britt. "Unless there's something you'd like to add." The leather holster on his hip creaked when he took his clipboard out from under his arm.

She shook her head. "I'm sure Mark explained."

The red-haired officer stepped forward and patted Katie's shoulder. "I have a little girl about your age." He smiled reassuringly. "I know how she'd feel if this happened to her. I want you to know we'll do everything possible to get all your things back."

"Thank you, sir." Katie's eyes sparkled with fresh tears.

Britt's eyes burned. Her poor little Katie. She was shattered—bewildered. She'd lost her childhood treasures, a part of her roots. Britt dreaded tomorrow. By then the magnitude of the loss would really have sunk in. She wondered if Katie could handle it.

The doorbell rang.

"That'll be Detective Simon," Mark said, glancing at the officers.

They followed Mark into the hall. Britt heard the front door open, then Charlie's voice. A minute later the two patrolmen left.

"Would you like a cup of hot chocolate?" Britt asked Katie.

Katie looked down at her clasped hands. She shook her head.

"It might make you feel better," Britt coaxed. "I'll put marshmallows in it."

She hesitated, finally nodding. "Do you think the police will really find my stuff, Mom?"

"Of course." Britt managed a weak smile. "And what they don't find, Daddy and I will replace. You can pick everything out yourself."

Katie folded the blanket between her fingers. "Even my Raggedy Ann and my old teddy bears?"

Britt's throat constricted, but somehow she found the willpower to keep from crying. "We don't have to think about it now, honey. Let's wait and see what the police find."

Katie nodded again and slid farther under the blanket. "I'll be right back with your hot chocolate."

Britt bent and kissed her, then went to the kitchen. She nodded at Charlie, who'd just stepped in from the backyard.

"Nothing seems to have been disturbed out there." He closed and locked the sliding door.

"I know." Mark's voice cracked, and he got a drink of water. "The officers already checked it out. Even the outside lights were still on."

"He sure as hell has balls, I'll give him that," Charlie said harshly.

Charlie, who was off-duty, was dressed in Levi's and running shoes. They'd taken up a lot of his free time since the advent of the stalker, Britt thought. She hadn't appreciated him at first. She did now. She'd come to depend on him.

"But how did he get in?" Britt had taken the milk carton from the refrigerator, and she stood with it in her hand. "The alarm was on."

"Simple." He squinted at them. "He had a key, and he knew the code to disarm the alarm."

Britt almost dropped the carton. "That's impossible!"

"No one knows the code but us and our parents." A vein beat frantically in Mark's temple. "Unless *he* works for the alarm company and—"

Charlie cut him off. "I doubt it." His eyes intensified. "Are you sure you didn't tell anyone else?"

"Positive," Britt and Mark said in unison.

"How did you tell the grandparents? On the phone?"

Britt shook her head. "We showed them how it worked when they were here."

Mark jerked away from where he leaned on the counter. "But that's how you told me, Britt. Remember? Right after the alarm was installed."

She looked blank.

"You said it was sophisticated—that arming and disarming it was the easiest part of the system. And you repeated the code numbers."

"Oh, my God, I did." Her eyes darted to Charlie. "You think he was listening, is that it?"

"Yeah, that's my guess."

"But how did he get into the house?" Mark asked. "We have a bolt lock."

"But the bolt and the regular lock open simultaneously with one key. I know because I just checked." Charlie glanced at Mark. "You'll have to change the lock. Somehow the bastard got hold of a key that'll open it—or else he has one of yours."

"We have all of our keys, don't we, Britt?" Mark asked.

Her nod was hardly more than a flicker of movement. Goose bumps rippled over her. "He's been in our house—hiding, *watching us*."

Charlie shook his head. "Probably not when you were home. You always put the chain lock on at night. He wouldn't have time to clip it and get inside before the alarm went off."

"And I keep the chain on during the day." Britt suddenly remembered the carton in her hand. She poured milk into a cup and put it in the microwave to heat.

"Damn good thing." Charlie punched his palm. "He'll trip up one of these times. In the meantime I'm bringing someone over from the Identification Division to dust for prints, although I expect he wore gloves."

"Will you dust the whole house?" Mark asked.

"I'm mostly interested in Katie's room, the front door, and the garage."

"Garage?" Britt turned away from the microwave oven.

"Yeah," Charlie said. "I figure he came in the front door, disarmed the alarm, went to the garage, pressed the

231

automatic door opener, drove his vehicle in next to the Volvo, closed the door, and loaded up without being seen."

"That—that piece of shit!" Mark's words sputtered out of his mouth. "I hope I catch that son of a bitch. He's violated our lives. There better be a law that'll take care of him this time." His expression twisted on his next words. "Or I'll take care of him . . . personally."

"I didn't hear that." Charlie frowned. "We've got plenty on him—Donny's accident, the attack on Britt, this burglary—once we nail him." He hesitated. "Don't do anything you'll regret, Mark. You could end up in the slammer instead of him."

Britt moved next to Mark. "We won't, unless we have to protect our family. I can't bear to think about him having Katie's things—that he's touching them, fantasizing about . . . oh, God!"

"Understood." Charlie zipped his jacket, ready to go. "Don't let anyone in Katie's room until my print man gets here. And try not to touch anything in the garage."

Britt stirred the hot chocolate mix and took it to Katie while Mark saw Charlie out. He locked up, set the alarm, and joined them in the den.

"Let's have a slumber party," he said.

Before eight the next morning Mark had already nailed the playhouse door and the crawl-space door closed.

"We aren't having that motherfucker under our house next!" he told Britt.

He called the alarm people at a few minutes after eight, requesting they come out to wire the crawl-space opening and to give them a new code.

"Let the bastard hear the code's being changed," he said, hanging up the phone. "He won't get it this time."

Britt had never seen Mark so out of control. His calm, intellectual manner had been replaced by a dominant need to protect his family.

He grabbed his shotgun and slammed out of the house.

232

She watched him point it toward the woods, daring the stalker.

"C'mon! C'mon!" he shouted. "Show yourself like a man, you fucking coward!" He came back into the house and stomped upstairs.

Charlie arrived a few minutes later with the fingerprint man. Katie was staying home from school, and both children were still asleep. The doorbell woke them up. Mark came downstairs dressed for the office, greeted the men, and saw them get started with their work.

"I've got to go," he said. "I'm late already." He glanced at Britt. "My audit out on Marine Drive shouldn't keep me past four. I'll be home before five." He hurried into the garage, and a couple of minutes later he was headed down the street in the Honda.

Charlie went next door to talk with the Gilliams and came back shaking his head. "They couldn't tell me anything," he said dejectedly.

She wasn't surprised. No one ever saw a trace of the flower man unless he wanted them to. And yet he wanted them to know he'd been in their house.

He was moving in for the kill.

The late afternoon traffic on Marine Drive was sparse for once. There was only the Honda in front of him on the winding road.

Buddy saw the stretch ahead that he was waiting for, where the road edged the bank above the Columbia River. He stepped on the gas, closing the distance between him and the Honda. The driver seemed unaware he was being followed.

"Stupid bastard!" Buddy shouted. "You're all the same! Think you're better than me—that your shit doesn't stink!"

He had only seconds before the road veered away from the bank. He floorboarded the gas pedal and swerved into the oncoming lane. For a moment he was alongside the other car.

"Ha ha!" He laughed and leaned into his horn. "Get your shotgun out now, fucker!"

Buddy twisted the wheel so that his van caught the Honda's front bumper. The driver fought for control and managed to keep the car on the road. The van hit it again. The car wheels hit the edge of the road and slipped onto a narrow strip of gravel.

In his rearview mirror Buddy watched the Honda flip over the embankment and hurtle toward the river. His breath came hard. Mark Hinson was wasted. He wouldn't wave a shotgun at him again.

Buddy glanced at his speedometer. Shit! He was doing seventy. He jerked his foot off the gas pedal. He didn't need a ticket now. He slowed to a sedate forty miles an hour.

Killing Mark Hinson had given him a hard-on. He would save it for *her*.

21

"DAMN THEM!" BRITT SLAMMED THE PHONE BACK ONTO ITS wall mount. "I should have known! Even insurance companies don't recognize stalkers."

"What happened?"

Britt glanced at her mother. "Our agent said they'd send a claims adjuster out, that they'd review the police report, but he wouldn't say for sure if the stolen things are covered."

"Why not, for heaven's sake?" Alice asked. "Aren't you covered for theft?"

"Seems there has to be proof of a burglary."

"You've been robbed. The police were here. Isn't that enough?"

"But there's no evidence of forcible entry—no jimmied lock, no broken window, and we had the burglar alarm on." Britt frowned, fanning her anger so that she wouldn't cry. "He sounded incredulous when I told him the burglar turned it off—because he probably had a listening device on our phone."

"Britt, I'm so sorry about all this. It's unbelievable."

"I know, Mom." Britt bent over the sink, willing a wave of nausea to pass. If only she could wake up and find that the nightmare was gone. She felt her mother's arm go around her shoulders.

"Somehow we'll get past this, Britt. The police will catch him. Maybe soon."

Alice soothed her in the calming voice Britt remembered from childhood. But this time it wasn't a skinned knee or a crush on a boy who'd asked someone else to the prom. This was real life . . . and death.

"I don't know, Mom. I'm beginning to wonder if he'll ever be caught. He's diabolical, and clever. He took everything from Katie's room and didn't leave one fingerprint behind."

"The detective told you that?"

"Uh-huh. They're filing a report, but of course it all comes down to hearsay again."

"What do you mean?"

"Aside from Katie's things being gone, there is no real proof that anyone was in our house." Britt's sigh was ragged. "As far as the law is concerned, we could have staged the whole thing to collect insurance money."

"That's ridiculous," Alice said, indignant. "Someone looking for insurance money wouldn't remove everything from a child's bedroom."

"At least Charlie knows what's happening, and that saves my sanity. But a court of law needs evidence of a crime and so do insurance companies." Britt hesitated. "I have a feeling our insurance won't replace Katie's things. If there's a loophole, the insurance company will take it."

"You mean . . . I won't get my stuff back?" Katie said behind them, her voice breaking.

Alice and Britt exchanged glances. They'd been careful not to discuss anything in front of Katie. Alice had come right over after hearing what had happened, and she planned to stay until Mark got home. Katie had appropriated the den and was using it as her room, and she wanted Sam with her. She refused to go upstairs, and Britt wondered if she'd ever feel safe again.

"Oh, Katie, I was talking about the insurance company, not about your stuff." Britt dropped a kiss on her head. "And don't forget. Daddy and I promised to buy everything new, so you'll have what you need until we get your things back."

"What if—if I don't get them back?"

Katie's face was as white as her blouse, and the fear in her eyes made Britt think of children in a war zone. It isn't fair, Britt thought. What kind of a twisted mind could do this to a child? Katie had been left with only the few pieces of clothing that were in the laundry.

"I know what we'll do," Alice said. "We'll go through the Spiegel catalog and mark everything you need."

Katie glanced down. "I want my own stuff."

"Come on, honey," Alice coaxed. "It'll be fun. We'll go in the den, get a fire going in the fireplace, and then go through the wish book."

"Wish book?"

"Sure—the catalog." Alice took her hand. "When I was your age I sat for hours going through the Sears catalog, wishing for something on every page."

Britt watched them go. Thank goodness for her mother, she thought. Alice had kept the children busy while the door locks were being changed and the alarm system was adjusted for the new code. When Angie had called, Britt had even been able to tell her what happened without Katie overhearing.

"I heard," Angie had said, surprising her. "Bill told Jim and Len about the flower man being back, and Len called Mark at work this morning, offered to stake out your place with the night-vision goggles. Mark said it

236

wasn't necessary, that he had a gun and a plan, and he would take care of the stalker himself."

Talking to Angie had left Britt even more unsettled. What kind of a crazy plan did Mark have? She glanced at the clock, surprised that it was already five. Mark had promised to be home by now. When the phone rang, she picked it up, thinking it was him.

"Mrs. Mark Hinson?" a woman's voice asked.

"Yes."

"This is North Park Hospital. Your husband's been in an automobile accident, Mrs. Hinson . . ."

The wind went out of her chest. She pressed the receiver against her ear. "Please, is he okay?—Is my husband okay?"

"He's in the emergency room." There was a pause. "I'm sorry. That's all I can tell you."

Britt was alone in the waiting room. She thumbed through a magazine, then threw it back on the table. It seemed as if she'd been there all day, but the clock on the wall said it was scarcely two hours since she'd received the call from the hospital.

A nurse had assured Britt that Mark was in capable hands, his vital signs were being monitored, and his neck had been immobilized until neck or spinal injuries could be ruled out. "You'll be able to see him once he's been stabilized," the nurse had said kindly.

When Britt asked about the accident, the young nurse had shaken her head. "The police will answer your questions about the case."

"Case?"

She'd nodded. "I believe they said it was a hit-and-run accident."

Britt had stared in wide-eyed horror. The nurse had excused herself and disappeared into the hall, as though she'd realized she'd said too much. And Britt had gone to call Charlie.

Night had fallen while she waited for word of Mark's

condition. The city lights beyond the windows were fractured prisms of brilliance, caught by the rain on the glass. Restless, she went to the door and glanced into the hall. A voice on the intercom suddenly echoed in the corridor, startling her. She went back to the vinyl sofa and sat down. She was scared. People died in hospitals.

Dr. Peters, where are you? she asked silently. Why haven't you come to tell me Mark is all right and that I can see him? Dear God, she prayed, let Mark recover. Don't let him die.

Their doctor had come to the hospital at once after she'd asked that he be called. He'd sought her out in the waiting room, looked grim as he told her Mark was unconscious and undergoing a neurological examination, which included X-rays. Then he'd disappeared. Her queries to staff members had brought only reassurances that he would get back to her soon.

If only Dr. Peters hadn't looked so serious. Britt's throat ached, she had a sinking sensation in her chest, and her heart was pounding. Lowering her head onto her knees, she took deep breaths. You can't have a panic attack, she instructed herself. You must be strong, for Mark's sake.

"Britt?"

She glanced up.

"How you doing?" Charlie hesitated in the doorway, trying to mask his concern behind a strained grin.

Her throat was tight. She shook her head, unable to answer. The tears she'd been holding back were suddenly rolling down her face.

He sat down and took her hands in his. "He's going to make it, Britt. He's in good hands."

"But he's still unconscious . . . they won't let me see him." Her voice quavered. "The doctors have been working on him for several hours."

He expelled a long breath, as though he was forming his words carefully. "You have to expect that," he said softly. "He was badly banged up from being thrown out of the car."

"I know." She hesitated. "It's just that—Oh, Charlie, someone ran him off the road. A nurse told me it was hit-and-run."

She couldn't go on. Knowing Mark hadn't regained consciousness, was undergoing a neurological workup, overwhelmed her. Maybe he was brain damaged, maybe he was in a coma. Maybe he'd be a vegetable if he did live. She dropped her face into her hands.

Charlie put his arms around her shoulders. "Go ahead and cry, Britt. It'll make you feel better."

"I don't want to cry. Mark isn't dead." She struggled to regain her composure. She lifted her head and reached for a Kleenex in her purse. "It was *him,* Charlie. I know it was." She took a deep breath. "He killed the dogs. He tried to kill Donny, then me, and now Mark."

Charlie stood up and began to pace. "Yeah, I think it's safe to assume it's him." He hesitated. "The bastard has guts, and the luck of the devil. Marine Drive gets its share of traffic, but he got Mark at just the right place and time—between curves, with no other vehicles in sight."

"You know what happened?"

He nodded. "But no details yet."

She bent toward him. "He has to be stopped—before he kills everyone who stands between him and Katie." She clasped her hands together. "I should be home with her, Charlie. She's so traumatized—she needs me."

"Katie's all right for now, Britt. She's in good hands with your parents."

"How did you know that?"

"I went by the house after your call. Your father and mother are there, and they intend to stay as long as they're needed—until Mark is out of the woods. I made sure they knew the safety routine." He stopped pacing. "I've authorized a squad car to patrol your block every hour, and I'm hoping to put a man on stakeout."

"Can you do that now?"

He nodded. "The situation has changed. Oregon may not have a stalking law, but we damn well have laws concerning assault, burglary, and attempted murder. It's obvious now, even to the captain down at Homicide, that someone is out to harm you folks. We just don't know who he is."

"Poor Mark." Britt's lips trembled. "If only he hadn't dared him to come out into the open."

"How so?"

"Mark was so upset this morning that he marched around the yard with the shotgun, pointed it at the woods, and shouted at the stalker. He called him . . . a coward."

"Oh, boy."

"He must have been out there, Charlie—watching."

"We'll catch him, I promise you." About to say more, Charlie hesitated when a uniformed man from the Oregon State Police stepped into the room.

"Mrs. Hinson?" he asked. He was a young man with a serious demeanor.

She nodded.

"I'm Officer Haige. I took the report at the accident scene. I'd like to ask you a few questions, if you're up to it."

Charlie showed his badge and introduced himself. "Mrs. Hinson is pretty upset. Maybe we could keep this brief."

"Shouldn't take long. I just need her to fill in a few gaps."

"I'll help any way I can." Her voice sounded raspy and faint.

"The accident was out on North East Marine Drive," he began. "Do you know why Mr. Hinson was out there?"

"Mark is the chief financial officer of his firm." She cleared her throat and started again. "Their offices are in downtown Portland, but he had an appointment with a client out by the airport. He'd gone to their office and was on his way home."

Officer Haige seated himself on a chair opposite Britt to take down her statements. Charlie folded his arms and watched in silence.

"Please, Officer Haige," she said, "tell me what happened? How did Mark go off the road?"

"The evidence at the scene suggests a hit-and-run accident."

"Weren't there any witnesses at all—a pedestrian? Someone on a boat in the river?" Charlie asked.

"No, none so far." Officer Haige's eyes returned to Britt. "The tire marks indicate your husband slammed on his brakes before veering toward the shoulder, regained control for about thirty feet, and then went off the blacktop entirely. We found some broken glass from a taillight on the highway; that tells us he was hit by another vehicle before he went off the road. He was thrown out of his car, and the Honda rolled down the embankment before it slid into the Columbia."

"His seat belt wasn't buckled?" Charlie asked.

"We assume it wasn't, but we won't know for sure until the car is pulled out of the water. He might have unbuckled it when he realized he was going into the river." The officer shook his head. "It's hard to know for sure, but that could be what saved him. He might have been killed if he'd stayed with the car."

"Mark was a fanatic about seat belts." Britt blew her nose and tried not to break down again. "He wouldn't have driven without his."

"So the evidence indicates that someone ran him off the road?" Charlie asked, leaning forward.

"That's right," the officer said. "The road was dry at the time, visibility was good, and the doc says there was no alcohol in his blood. That, together with the evidence at the scene, gives us a pretty good idea of what happened." He hesitated. "We can't say if it was intentional. We only know the other vehicle left the scene of an accident."

He returned his glance to Britt. "He wasn't epileptic or subject to fainting spells, was he?"

She shook her head. "Mark's in perfect health."

"I guess that's it." He stood up. "Thank you, Mrs.

241

Hinson. Someone will be in touch when we know more."
He put on his cap and stepped into the hall.

Charlie followed. "I'll be back in a few minutes," he
told her.

She stared after them, numbed by what she'd heard.
Where would the stalker strike next? One way or another
he had to be stopped—even if she had to do it herself.

Charlie had nothing more to report after talking with
the state trooper. Britt walked him to the emergency exit,
then called Mark's parents again and finally reached
them at home. She had just returned to the waiting room
when Dr. Peters found her.

"He's been taken upstairs to the operating room," he
told her.

She jumped up. "When? Why wasn't I informed?
What's wrong with him?"

"You signed the release form, don't you remember?"
he reminded her gently.

"But—for surgery?"

"For whatever treatment was needed to save his life."

"Is he going to die?" She could scarcely whisper.

He sat her back down, then seated himself next to her.
His glasses were smudged, his white hospital jacket was
rumpled, and the cowlick at the back of his head stood
up like a gray rooster tail.

"It's serious, Britt. I won't fool you. He's still unconscious, but they know what's causing it now. Surgery is
critical to his recovery, and time is of the essence."

"Surgery for what?" she whispered.

"It's neurological. He has swelling of the brain from
trauma and we suspect there's a blood clot."

"What does that mean?—in layman terms."

"The pressure has to be alleviated and the blood clot
evacuated from the brain."

"How?"

He hesitated. "The procedure requires drilling holes in
the skull—so the swelling has somewhere to go. When
the pressure of the brain against the skull is eased, the

swelling goes down and the patient usually recovers without brain damage." He paused again. "And, Britt, I want you to know that Dr. Elwood is one of the finest neurosurgeons in the Northwest. Mark can come out of this and make a complete recovery if—"

"If what?" she interrupted. "If he makes it through surgery?"

He nodded. "If the clot is successfully evacuated and the swelling subsides, and if there are no other injuries to his neck or spine." He glanced away. "His neck will remain immobilized until he regains consciousness. Then we'll know if he's able to move his limbs."

"How long will that take?"

"Several days. He'll come out of this slowly. They'll insert an instrument tube to measure pressure. When the pressure goes down, they'll remove it."

She lowered her eyes. "What are his chances?"

"The odds are in his favor. When this procedure is done soon after the injury has been sustained, it's usually successful."

He stood, pulling her up with him. "After surgery Mark will be taken to the neurological intensive care unit upstairs. Let's go up there now."

She went with him to the elevator. As they rode up through the floors of the hospital she wondered if she would still have a husband when she came down again.

Charlie gulped the coffee from the convenience store and scalded his throat. His hand jerked and some of it dripped on his slacks.

"Damn it!" That was all his wrinkled pants needed . . . spots. He didn't have time to go home and change. He was expected at the Major Crimes Unit in a half hour.

His eyes felt like sandpaper, and he was asleep on his feet. Usually he could catnap on a stakeout. But not on the Hinsons' street. He sensed the bastard was out there, waiting.

He started the engine, then headed for the I-5 freeway and the morning rush-hour traffic. Shortly after dawn he'd driven out to the accident site, but he hadn't turned up anything new. The Honda was still in the river, and he meant to expedite getting it pulled out. Maybe the crime lab would come up with a paint match.

After leaving the hospital the night before, he'd grabbed a hamburger, then taken the Hinson stakeout himself, because he'd been unsuccessful in getting one authorized. Instinctively he knew the stalker was moving in for the kill.

Charlie concentrated on the traffic, aware of his fatigue. But his mind raced with his options. He still had his eye on Milt Graber. Once Jay Fisher had been arrested, Charlie had informed the school authorities about the custodian's record. Then he'd reported Graber for not having a business permit and license and for violating the zoning regulations.

"Why you hassling this guy?" the captain had demanded after Graber had filed a harassment complaint against Charlie.

"Hassling, hell!" he'd retorted. "The bastard is running a business on school time—on taxpayer money!"

"Okay, okay! Cool it. We got Fisher. Leave Graber alone. Isn't it enough that the school fired him, for Chrissake?"

Now, as Charlie took the city exit, he remembered how relieved he'd been when Graber had dropped his complaint and he was off the hot seat. He wondered what the janitor was doing these days—besides delivering flowers in a dark van. There was something hinky about the guy, something that stuck in Charlie's craw.

He swung into the department parking lot, locked his car, and went inside. He spent the next couple of hours working on an affidavit for probable cause. This time he'd have a search warrant when he knocked on Graber's door.

When he strode into the D.A.'s office, he still had no real evidence, but he hoped it would be enough.

"Your case is too circumstantial," he was told in no uncertain terms by one of the assistant D.A.'s, an Ivy

Leaguer fresh out of law school. "If we prosecute, Milt Graber's rights will be violated—the department will be sued. Graber has already filed one harassment complaint against you. If you think he won't go balls-out, you're wrong."

Charlie wanted to push the kid out of his way, and storm into the boss's office, but he resisted the urge. "I've reported everything. The Hinsons are in grave danger." He brought his fist down on the table. "They have a right to protection after what they've been through."

"And Graber has his constitutional rights, okay? The Hinson girl has never identified him, even though she saw him on a regular basis at school. And he doesn't fit the description of Mrs. Hinson's attacker, either, does he?"

"No, but—"

"But nothing. You don't have a better suspect, so you're grabbing at straws." The lawyer glanced over the paperwork again. "I understand how you feel. But we have to go by the book. That's how we protect innocent citizens. We can't just go off half-cocked."

They stared at each other, neither giving ground. The assistant D.A. was the first to look away.

He stood up, waved the affidavit. "I'll see what I can do, Simon. Maybe I'm wrong. Maybe the judge will sign this."

Charlie went back to his desk. He wasn't surprised when the judge didn't sign. It was par for the course in this case. He paced the floor, high on black coffee. Then he grabbed his jacket and strode out of the office. He'd missed something. He needed to start at the beginning, think everything through again.

"Britt?"

She lifted her head from the padded arm of the sofa. Dr. Peters stepped into the waiting room, followed by a slight, dark-haired man with hawkish features. Because he wore a white coat she assumed he was Dr. Elwood, the surgeon.

She sat up and tried to brace herself. Mark's surgery was over. She'd been waiting for word, and now she wanted to hold it back. What if the news was bad?

"It's all right, Britt, Mark made it through surgery just fine," Dr. Peters said. He introduced the other doctor as the neurosurgeon. "Dr. Elwood will explain everything, and then you can see Mark."

Britt expelled her breath in a rush of air. She got to her feet and quickly introduced Mark's parents, who had come to the hospital to wait with her. Dr. Elwood acknowledged them all with a cool nod.

"Your husband responded well to the procedure, Mrs. Hinson." Dr. Elwood spoke with a precise British accent. "We were successful in evacuating the clot, and now we'll wait and see how he responds."

She licked her lips. "Then he's . . . not okay?"

"He's as okay as can be expected at this point. Now we'll see if the pressure goes down to the normal range. We've inserted an instrument tube to monitor that." He paused. "I understand Dr. Peters explained the process."

"The pressure might not go down?"

"We expect it to, Mrs. Hinson," Dr. Elwood said. "He'll also be given some medication to bring the swelling down. That's all I can say at this time. We'll know more in a few hours."

"Will he regain consciousness soon?" Harriet spoke for the first time. She clung to Paul, her ashen face washed of makeup by her bouts of crying.

"Gradually, over the next couple days," Dr. Elwood replied.

Dr. Peters stepped forward. "I'll take you to Mark," he said, including Harriet and Paul.

They went into the hall where Dr. Elwood left them. "I'll speak with you tomorrow," he told Britt.

"Thank you, Doctor," she said.

For the first time he smiled. "Let's hope for a complete recovery." He continued down the hall.

Britt and her in-laws followed Dr. Peters. She felt better.

Seeing Mark was a shock. A tube was taped into the top of his head, his face was purpled and swollen from bruising, and a fiery line of stitches ran along his jawline. He was completely immobilized so he couldn't move if he woke up unexpectedly, and an intracranial pressure monitor stood next to the bed.

What if he came through brain surgery only to be paralyzed? Britt forced the thought away. It was obvious that the doctors weren't sure about the prognosis, and they weren't hazarding any guesses until they had more information.

Dr. Peters left. Minutes later a shattered Harriet was led out by her husband. Britt sat down next to Mark, afraid to do more than gently touch his hand.

22

AT NIGHT IT WAS HARD TO FIND THE RIGHT HOUSE. SLOWING the van, Buddy looked for the mailbox with the daisy painted on the side. Evergreen trees formed a canopy of branches above the winding lanes through Lake Oswego, south of Portland. He smiled when he finally saw the place. Although the front porch light was on, Buddy knew they weren't at home.

But they'd be home soon, he thought.

He accelerated on past the cottage, heading for the overgrown driveway that led into the woods. At least the retardo had given him good, clear directions to the deserted road—so the stupid bastard had done *something* right. Buddy's anger was instant. But still, the fucker had almost blown everything.

Good thing he hadn't, Buddy thought, as he parked and got out of the van, or the dumb shit would be dead meat right now. As it was, Buddy was only putting off the inevitable. Anyone connected to his past had to be destroyed, so that his rebirth to the new life would be complete, his happiness guaranteed. Once his beloved was with him he wouldn't need anyone else.

He sniffed the air like a dog on the scent. The sweet fragrance of pine needles and fir boughs filled his senses, and the crisp air was reminiscent of spring, of new life about to unfold . . . like his. He was alone in the woods.

His steps were quick and sure, his intent clear in his mind. The tops of the big Douglas firs looked like black etchings against the charcoal sky, and the wild huckleberry and ferns barely rustled as he passed. He had wrapped his sneakers in rags to avoid leaving footprints once he was inside. When he reached the road Buddy kept to the ditch, so he could duck if a car suddenly turned onto the narrow lane.

No dogs barked as he passed the houses that were set back from the street among the trees. It made him laugh. Dogs couldn't protect them from someone who knew the ways of night better than any animal.

He felt like shouting, waking them up from their stupid lives. "Hey! I'm out here! Whether you live or die is up to me!" He resisted the urge. They were not worth his efforts.

The mailbox with the painted daisy brought him out of the ditch to the driveway. He slipped around the attached garage to the backyard, pleased that it was completely secluded by a board fence. No eyes could watch while he broke into the house. And no one was close enough to hear once he was inside.

He moved up the steps to the back door, confident because the little house wasn't wired for an alarm system. His gloved hand grabbed the screen door handle. It was hooked. He snipped the mesh with a wire cutter, then reached in and pushed the hook free of its metal eye.

The door itself was just as easy. The glass cutter scraped faintly as Buddy sliced a circle in the window just above the lock. He placed a suction cup on the cut glass, drew the piece out, and tossed it into the flower bed. Reaching through the hole, careful not to snag his leather glove, he slipped the bolt and opened the door.

He hesitated, listening. Then he stepped inside and gently closed the door. A light had been left on above the kitchen sink, and another shone from the hall. Good, he thought. No need for a flashlight. What he had to do wouldn't take long.

Something brushed against his leg. He jumped, and his foot hit a dish on the floor, tipping dry cat food across the linoleum. The meow at his feet was a relief. He hadn't known about the cat.

"Shoo," he whispered. He pushed it away with his foot. He hated cats, and he despised cat piss. His mother had loved cats. Their house had always reeked of cat piss. She hadn't cared that he was allergic.

His breathing quickened, and he reached for his nebulizer. Cats and his mother . . . he hated them both.

Somewhere in the house a clock gonged the ten o'clock hour. He needed to hurry. His van was hidden from the road, but the longer it was there, the greater the chance someone would see it.

He yanked open the kitchen drawers, dumping the contents on the floor, until he found what he needed—a butcher knife with a sharp-edged blade. He tucked it under his belt, then started emptying the refrigerator, smashing everything on the polished linoleum. Then he went through the cupboards, adding flour and sugar, dishes and pans, to the growing mess on the floor. He tore the pictures from the walls, the plants from the windowsill, and the cloth and centerpiece from the table.

His rag-wrapped feet tracked gunk to the three bedrooms. In each one he yanked the curtains from the windows, smashed mirrors, and slashed the mattresses and pillows. Feathers flew around him like a blizzard. He took cosmetics to the bathroom and dumped them into the toilet, except for one tube of lipstick, which he pocketed. Turning on the water taps in the bathtub, he threw bedding, clothes, and shoes into the filling tub—silk with denim, leather with wool. He left the water running.

In the dining room he tipped over the china closet, gouged the mahogany table surface, and tore strips of wallpaper from the walls. Moving faster now, caught up in the frenzy, he shattered the television screen with a lamp, cut open the chair cushions, and threw the sofa pillows into the sooty fireplace. He sprinkled kerosene from decorative lamps all over the carpet, then broke the lamps against the hearth. The knife seemed to have a life of its own as it sliced the floral drapes.

The cat kept its distance, but followed him from one room to another, meowing. The high-pitched mewing set Buddy's teeth on edge. The water from the bathroom was running down the hall when his destruction was complete, and he returned to the kitchen.

Buddy's breath came in shallow puffs, from exertion and from his allergic reaction to the cat. He watched it from the corner of his eye. When it came close, he grabbed the neck fur and dangled the animal in front of him, the butcher knife poised in his other hand.

The cat clawed air. Buddy grinned at it. "Not so vocal now, are you, kitty cat?" He raised the knife. It would be so simple. He'd done it many times before. One quick slice.

Then he had a better idea. He sloshed across the floor to the refrigerator, slung the cat inside, and slammed the door.

"You stay in there until you learn to mind, until you learn respect," he told the cat in the singsong voice that sounded like that other voice in his head.

Taking the lipstick tube from his pocket he wrote in blood-red letters across the white door he'd just closed: "Mind Your Own Business Or Next Time It'll Be You!"

The lipstick broke off. He tossed it into the slop on the floor, then the butcher knife, and strode to the back door. He stood on one foot and removed the rags from the other foot before allowing it down on the wood porch.

THE FLOWER MAN

He straddled the doorstep and reversed the procedure, freeing his other foot. The rags went into a plastic bag he pulled from his pocket. He left the door open behind him as he melted into the night.

He was exhilarated. The cat was an unexpected bonus.

Britt had been home for an hour when the police called shortly before noon and asked to speak to her father. Wordless with sudden dread, she handed the phone over to him. She watched his expression change from puzzlement to disbelief. He shook his head, as if to deny what phe was hearing. By the time he hung up, she knew something terrible had happened.

"We have to go home, Alice." He wiped a hand over his forehead. The kindly twinkle in his eyes was dulled by a look of defeat. "Someone broke into our house." He paused, cleared his throat, and began again. "One of the neighbors saw some damage and called the police."

Alice grabbed the edge of the table. "How—how much damage did they do?"

"You better sit down, my dear." He glanced at Britt. "You too, Britt."

"Dad, please just tell us what happened." Britt was alarmed. His face had gone white and his hands shook. She put her arm around his shoulders and led him to a chair.

He nodded and sat down. "Alice—honey." Fred took his wife's hands in his. "I want you to remember that we have insurance. Anything that was destroyed can be replaced."

"What things?" Alice's voice was low and faint.

"The cupboards were emptied, dishes broken, bedding shredded—things like that. The water was left on in the tub, and—it flooded the whole house."

"Oh no, the carpets will be ruined. We've got to go home." Alice started to get up, but Fred stopped her.

"No, dear, not yet. There's something else you need to know."

Alice's eyes widened in horror. "Knickers was in the house. Oh, God, Fred, please tell me that he's all right!"

Tears sparkled in Fred's eyes. "Knickers is gone."

"How?" Alice fought for control. A sob tore out of her throat. "I have to know what happened to my little cat." She dropped her face into her hands and cried quietly.

Fred spoke quickly, as though he needed to get the words out while he still could. "He suffocated. The crazy bastard put him in the refrigerator."

"It's *him,*" Britt said. "I think we all know that."

Her dad nodded. "He also issued a threat. He wrote it in lipstick on the refrigerator. The message says we should mind our own business or next time we'll die."

"He's threatening you because you're here," Britt said.

"He knows we're standing between him and Katie," Fred said. "That's my guess. He wants us out of his way."

Britt felt utterly helpless. Her parents were being threatened and terrorized, her daughter was missing school, her husband lay in intensive care—*he* was destroying their lives.

Charlie had listened in silence when she called him. "I'll check on this myself, Britt," he'd told her. "Don't let your parents leave until I get there."

To her surprise, Charlie had driven into the driveway, followed by Mark's parents, Harriet and Paul, in their Mercedes, and a police car. Within minutes of his arrival, Charlie had their lives reorganized, making the change of plans seem like a game to the children. Britt's respect for him was growing stronger all the time. How could she have thought him an immature baby, too young to be a cop? He'll probably end up being the chief of police, she told herself.

She stood in the hall and kissed her parents before they left. "The police car will follow you home, and another officer is at your house now, waiting for you," Charlie told the shaken couple.

Harriet went to pack Sam's things while Paul entertained the children in the den. Harriet had promised Katie they would shop for her by phone, that their purchases would be delivered to the condominium where the two children would be staying for a while. That promise had helped keep Katie's mind off the sudden change of plans, even though Britt had to keep reassuring her that everything was fine.

"The D.A.'s office has finally authorized police protection," Charlie explained once he and Britt were alone. "There will be a guard at the hospital and regular patrols near the condominium while the kids are there. And the hourly patrol of this house will continue."

"I'm impressed, Charlie," she said seriously. "All this time when the police couldn't do anything"—she shook her head—"and now all this."

"The D.A. was impressed by how this guy has accelerated his violence. When we nail him, we'll have a long list of pretty serious charges."

"Do you think you'll really get him?"

"I told you before, Britt. I *will* get him. This guy has to be stopped. He's extremely dangerous. Right now he's terrorizing your family. Next time it'll be someone else." His face muscles tightened. "I intend to end his crime spree—*now.*"

She nodded. If she hadn't been so scared, she would have applauded. The way he'd organized their lives since her call was astounding. He must have kicked ass, as he would say down at headquarters.

"Your in-laws' high-security building will be harder for the wacko to get at," he said. "The kids will be safe there, and I expect you to stay there when you're not at the hospital."

"I intend to." She blew a loose lock of hair out of her eyes. "Do you think he'll trash this house when we're gone?"

"I don't think so. Your security is solid now. And with the patrol he won't dare."

"Then why do you think it necessary for us to leave?"

His eyes wavered. "Well, uh, you never know with an unpredictable guy like this. He could take a bead on—" He broke off, as though he'd said too much.

"You think he might . . . shoot me through the window?"

"Uh, forget I said that, Britt. I don't want you even more scared."

"I couldn't be more scared," she said. Hearing Harriet come downstairs, she stepped closer to Charlie and lowered her voice. "Where do we go from here? What's next?"

"I'm waiting for Mark's account of the accident. If he remembers anything—the color and type of the vehicle, maybe a glimpse of the driver—then I might be able to persuade the D.A. and the frigging judge to give me a search warrant."

"To search where? And who?"

"I'll explain if I get some information from Mark after he wakes up."

"Oh, Charlie, do you think he will?" A tremor ran through her. "What if he doesn't?"

"Hush that talk. Aren't you the lady who didn't give up even back when I thought you might be a hysterical mother?"

"So you *did* think that." For a second she felt like laughing. "I knew it!"

He grinned. "That's better. Try to keep your spirits up, Britt." He sobered. "That's what he's waiting for—to shatter you so you'll be vulnerable."

"Britt?" Harriet interrupted their conversation. "Could I ask a favor?"

She shifted her eyes to her mother-in-law and nodded.

"I was going to buy flowers for Mark so there would be something bright and pretty for him to see when he wakes up." She hesitated. "Since I'm not going to the hospital, would you—"

"I'll get them for you," Britt said, interrupting. She felt Charlie's reaction even though he didn't comment. "But would you mind if I got a nice plant arrangement instead of flowers?"

Harriet's eyes widened with comprehension. "Oh, yes, of course. I didn't think. Flowers might remind Mark of—of *him.*"

Britt busied herself with last-minute preparations and managed to send her children off with a cheerful smile. She was the last one out of the house, exiting through the garage after making sure all safety precautions were in place. She would return to the hospital while Charlie followed Harriet, Paul, and the children to make sure they arrived at the condo safely. Before they left the street, Charlie got out of his car and came back to the Volvo.

"You watch yourself, Britt." He hesitated. "This guy is truly out of control now. You could be his target again, and don't you forget that."

"Believe me, I won't."

"You're going straight to the hospital?"

She nodded.

"I'll radio ahead and have someone watch for you. And make sure you check with me or the officer at Mark's door when you leave. You'll be joining the kids at night, right?"

She nodded. "I packed an overnight bag."

"Good. I'll try to drop by the hospital later, okay?"

"Thanks, Charlie. For everything."

He climbed back into his car. In seconds their little motorcade was moving down the street.

At the bottom of the hill the Mercedes and Charlie's car headed toward the city while Britt waited in the left-turn lane for a traffic light, her thoughts drifting to the plant arrangement she planned to buy. She'd already looked in the hospital florist shop; it was small, and the selection was limited.

Charlie and the Mercedes had disappeared by the time the signal turned green. Instead of driving onto the

255

freeway, Britt made a U-turn and headed back up the hill toward a neighborhood garden shop that had the best selection of plants in the area.

She passed their turnoff and followed the road over the crest of the hill toward Scholls Ferry Road. She kept her eye on the rearview mirror. No one followed her.

Pulling into a parking place, Britt got out of the car and locked it. She hurried past primroses and other early planting flowers on her way to the front entrance of the shop. Once inside, she headed for the section of houseplant arrangements.

Her glance darted among the displays of plants and flowers, coming to rest at the end of the room where wide doors stood open, revealing a greenhouse and a loading zone. A man was placing floral arrangements in a van for delivery. A black van.

Britt stopped in her tracks. Her heartbeat accelerated furiously as her eyes fastened on the man. This has to be a coincidence, she told herself. He only looks like the stalker from a distance. She sucked in deep breaths, suddenly feeling light-headed. What should I do? Confront him? Make sure it's him?

Don't be stupid, she told herself. If it's him, don't let him see you. She mustn't blow it, ruin their chances of locking him up. Would someone restrain him if she announced he was wanted by the police? she wondered, and glanced around at the other shoppers. No, he worked here. He could turn the tables on her, and get away.

She stood in the middle of the store and realized he had only to turn to see her. It was as if her thought triggered his action. He turned away from the van, and she had a full-face view.

It was him!

She ducked behind a giant schefflera and bent her head so he couldn't see her face. She pretended to examine the smaller plants, praying he hadn't seen her. The back of her neck prickled with apprehension.

Was he creeping up on her right now? Or waiting for her outside?

THE FLOWER MAN

She peeked out from behind the foliage of thin waxy leaves. He was intent on his work. He hadn't seen her. Her relief lasted only to the next thought: Maybe he *had* seen her. Maybe he just didn't want her to know he'd spotted her. Perhaps he was playing his usual cat-and-mouse game.

Her first impulse was to get out of there, to be safe. But she stayed put, forcing herself to outthink him. She would watch, make sure. Sooner or later he'd look in her direction if he knew she was there. She waited, pretending to choose a plant, but her eyes were on him. In five minutes he didn't glance at her once. He'd almost completed the loading.

She was jolted into action. If he left before her, he'd see the Volvo in the parking lot. She had to get out of there before he did.

Charlie's warning rang in her head: "You could be his target again, and don't you forget that." She clamped her teeth together to keep them from chattering. Everyone thought she was on her way to the hospital. No one would think to look for her in this garden shop.

Backing away, she kept her eyes on him through the greenery. Once outside, she ran to her car and got inside. She felt strange, filled with fear and elation at the same time. Her lips trembled, her body shook. She was quite sure she got out of the lot without being seen.

The first phone booth was at a gas station several blocks away. She drove in so fast she almost hit it, rocking to a stop only inches from its glass side.

She fumbled for coins in her purse, finally dumping the contents onto the seat. With a quarter in hand, she slipped out of the car and into the booth. She knew the number by heart.

"Please, I need to leave a message—for Charlie Simon." She expelled the words in one whispery breath. "Please, call him on his beeper—this is an emergency. Tell him that Britt found the flower man . . . in a flower shop!"

23

BRITT WAS MET BY A HOSPITAL SECURITY MAN AT THE FRONT door; he'd been sent to escort her upstairs to Mark's room. "We got a call from Detective Simon to watch for you," he told her. "Said he'd gotten your message and would be here as soon as traffic allowed."

She nodded, and managed to keep a lid on her excitement. Her thoughts raced, and her fingertips tingled with each breath.

They got into the elevator, and with each stop the bottom seemed to drop out of her stomach. She'd never been in such a manic state before. She would explode if she didn't talk to Charlie soon.

As she'd driven to the hospital her eyes had been on the rearview mirror as much as on the freeway. The flower man hadn't followed, hadn't realized he'd been discovered. As Britt stepped onto Mark's floor she was certain their terror would soon be over. The stalker would be arrested.

Still, seeing the uniformed policeman beside Mark's door gave her a secure feeling. It was a relief to know that they were being protected now. She went into the room and sat down next to Mark's bed. He was connected to an intravenous drip, and he looked the same as when she'd left him. If Dr. Elwood hadn't told her that morning that the brain pressure was subsiding, she would have been alarmed.

"It'll take time for him to regain consciousness," he'd reminded her again. "Maybe another day or two before he's completely awake."

"Oh, Mark," she whispered, "I love you so much. Please come back to me."

THE FLOWER MAN

She bent to brush her lips over his, mindful that he was still immobilized. She had to believe he would make a full recovery. The alternative was too awful to contemplate. She dropped her head onto the bedcover, emotionally spent.

The door opened and a "pssst" brought her upright. Charlie stood in the doorway and motioned her into the hall. After a final glance at the still figure on the bed, she left the room.

"Whew! I'm relieved to see you," he said. "Your message scared the shit out of me. I couldn't figure out what happened. A flower shop? I thought you were coming directly to the hospital."

"I was, but I found him, Charlie! I found the flower man!"

"Where? Did he see you?"

She started to answer, but he put a finger over his lips, silencing her. "Wait. Let's find a place where we can talk privately."

He led her down the hall to the waiting room. A glance told them it was empty, and they sat down. Charlie looked worried as he waited for her to explain.

"Do you remember Harriet asking me to buy a plant arrangement for Mark?"

He nodded.

"I decided to take a little detour to a garden shop near our house—and I saw him." She spoke faster, her story spilling out in rapid-fire bursts of words. Charlie listened without interruption, a habit she'd come to appreciate in him.

"And his delivery van is black, Charlie."

"You're sure he's the guy?"

"Positive. The resemblance to my composite drawing is remarkable. You'll see."

"And you're certain he didn't see you?"

"Uh-huh. I waited and watched to make sure. And no one followed me to the phone booth or to the hospital."

He'd taken out his notebook to jot down the name and location of the garden store. When his pen stilled, he stared at the page, as though contemplating his next move.

"You can arrest him now, can't you?" she asked, when he didn't voice his thoughts.

"I want to get this guy as bad as you do, Britt." He tossed his head to flip back his hair. "But we have to handle this carefully. All we've really got on him at this point is attempted rape."

She slid forward on the vinyl seat. "But, Charlie, he tried to kill Mark."

"I know, I know. But as I've been saying all along, we need hard evidence to pin everything on him."

She started to interrupt, but he waved her to silence and continued. "Yeah, I could arrest him now on the attempted rape charge." His facial muscles tightened. "But what if he can make bail and some dime-store lawyer springs him? Have you thought of that? He'd vanish into the woodwork."

"But he's guilty as hell."

"You know that. I know that. But the D.A. goes by the book, which says we can't violate a citizen's constitutional rights. In other words, we can't charge someone without evidence sufficient for probable cause."

"What about my rights, the rights of my daughter? Katie will identify him. I'll drive her by so she can see him, too."

"No, Britt. Please don't do that." Now he leaned forward on his seat. "Katie could contaminate the case by seeing him before I can arrange a lineup."

"Can you arrange the lineup right away?"

He shook his head. "I need to get this guy's name and Social Security number. That way I can run him through the state computers, and the NCIC computers at Quantico, and if we're lucky, we'll learn that he's wanted somewhere else."

Britt clenched her hands, frustrated by this additional delay.

"Hey, don't get me wrong," Charlie said, noticing her

dejection. "I have no intention of letting this nut slip away. I want my case to be solid, that's all."

"What if he comes up clean on the computer scan?"

"That's another reason I need to get all my ducks in a row before we move in on him. For example, what if I put him in a lineup and Katie doesn't make him?" He leaned even closer. "You just told me he looked like your composite of him. And Katie didn't recognize that drawing. Remember?"

"But he drives a black van." Desperation clawed at Britt.

"So does Milt Graber, and Pinecrest has one as well. And we don't know yet if it was a van that ran Mark off the road."

"What about Donny? He saw the man who ran him off the road."

"We'll bring Donny in for the lineup, too. When we're ready."

"And what am I supposed to do in the meantime?" she said. "Pretend that everything is just hunky-dory, while *he* goes on about his life, free as a bird?"

"Look, Britt, I understand your frustration, and I sympathize. I promise I'll arrest him immediately if my other leads don't work out."

"Leads?"

He nodded. "We have some other leads, and now we have a solid suspect to check out. We'll find out where he lives, who his friends are, if he has family. And each area of his life will tell us more about the guy."

"Mark might be able to identify him." She glanced away. "When he wakes up."

"I'm counting on that. And we have the flower shop van, which might have the Honda's paint on it. We might be able to get him for attempted murder if we can make a paint match. That, on top of his attack on you, would suggest premeditation, and give credence to our suspicion that he's responsible for all the other incidents. On the basis of that, the D.A. would authorize a search warrant of his premises, and who knows? We might find Katie's things, a tablet to match the notes, a listening device, a prescription to match the nebulizer, or even the poison that killed Max."

She stood up. "So you're saying we have to wait while you build a case."

Nodding again, he got to his feet. "But not for long. In the meantime this loony will think he's free. I'll put a tail on him."

"Right away?"

"As soon as the D.A. will authorize it."

She bit back a retort. She didn't have much hope that the D.A.'s office would do anything.

Charlie walked her back to Mark's room, stopping her as she was about to leave him. "Carry on with all the safety precautions, Britt. And be careful. This guy means business. It'll only be for a short time, I promise."

She managed a smile, but her euphoria had collapsed, leaving her dejected and fearful.

"Don't forget, we know who he is now. We'll be on him like spray paint if he tries anything."

"Aren't you Detective Simon?" a woman asked, as Charlie passed the nurses' station after leaving Britt at Mark's door.

He paused, nodding.

"You sure got here quick," she said.

"What do you mean?"

"You just called." She glanced at her watch. "Not ten minutes ago."

"I didn't call." Charlie stepped closer. "What exactly did this caller say?"

She stood up, concern washing over her features. "He said he was Detective Simon, and he asked about Mr. Hinson."

He glanced at her name tag. "Mrs. Bader, just what did you tell him?"

"That Mr. Hinson had come out of surgery and was holding his own, but that he was still unconscious."

THE FLOWER MAN

Charlie tried to conceal his annoyance. She had done precisely what he'd instructed the hospital staff not to do: she'd given out information over the telephone.

The nurse was clearly uncomfortable now. "I did think it odd that he asked for the room number," she said.

"Did you tell him?"

"No. I thought it was you, so I said, 'You know which room—the one with the police guard you authorized.' He laughed and said, 'That's right, just checking,' and hung up."

"After this, Mrs. Bader, don't give out any information to anyone, including me, okay?" He hesitated. "And would you reinforce that with the other nurses on this floor?"

She nodded and he turned back to Mark's room. He needed to warn the cop on duty.

Charlie was in the hall talking with Dr. Elwood when Britt arrived at the hospital the next morning.

"Good news, Britt," Charlie said. "Mark is conscious."

"He's still foggy about what happened," the doctor added quickly, "but at least we know he's not paralyzed, and he no longer needs to be immobilized."

"Thank God." Britt expelled her breath in relief. "Does this mean he'll make a complete recovery?"

"I have every hope of that happening, Mrs. Hinson." A brief smile cracked his serious demeanor.

"When can I talk to him?"

"You can go in now. But don't expect too much. He'll be in and out of awareness for a while."

From the moment Britt entered the room Mark's eyes were on her. She went to the bed, took his hand, and kissed him gently on the mouth. "I love you, Mark," she whispered. "Welcome back."

"Love—you," he whispered hoarsely.

He closed his eyes abruptly, alarming her. "Mark," she murmured, "I'm here. It's me—Britt."

"I know," he said without lifting his lashes, his voice

so low that it was hard to distinguish his words. "Be careful. You and the kids . . . he's—"

A hand on her shoulder startled her. "It's okay, Britt," Charlie said behind her. "The doc says this is typical. He'll be back, and pretty soon he won't drift off at all."

She nodded, grateful for his calming presence.

Charlie hung around for another half hour, and finally had to leave.

By afternoon Mark seemed more alert. Charlie returned around three, and Mark was able to tell him a little of what happened, although he still seemed confused.

"He came out of nowhere . . . kept trying to—to run me off the road," Mark said faintly. "Could have been a van . . . can't remember."

"That's all right, Mark," Britt said soothingly. "You just rest. It'll come back to you."

He closed his eyes again, and Charlie and Britt went out to the hall. Charlie looked grim, and Britt wondered if something else had happened that she didn't know about.

"It'll take time to check out the vans," he told her over coffee in the hospital cafeteria.

"Vans? More than one?"

He looked at her over the rim of his cup. "I'm not taking any chances. I want authorization to examine Milt Graber's van, the one from Pinecrest, and the one you saw at the flower shop." He put his cup down. "The guy who works at the garden shop—the man who assaulted you—is our prime suspect, but I want to make sure no one else is involved. The vans should clear the owners of suspicion once and for all—if they're clean. Especially Graber. There wasn't even a dent on his van after Donny was hit."

"How do you know that? I thought the D.A.'s office refused to give you a search warrant."

"That's right," he replied quickly, looking guilty.

She didn't question his methods. Her respect for him grew. He was on their side.

THE FLOWER MAN

"The Honda is a different matter," he said. "Whatever hit it will have evidence of the incident—paint, dents, whatever."

"Will that be enough to stand up in court?"

"You bet. It would be considered solid physical evidence. No smart-ass lawyer can argue away the evidence of a high-tech laser-equipped spectrometer with a scanning electron microscope match."

"It sounds impressive."

"It is. But first we have to get Mark's car out of the river."

"It wasn't pulled out already?"

"I'm working on it. As we speak it's probably drying off in the police garage. We're also working on collecting information on the guy in the garden shop." He finished his coffee and stood up. "Which reminds me, I need to get going."

He walked her back to Mark's room and left her with his usual warning to be careful, and a request to call him if Mark remembered anything else.

"I'll be in touch, Britt. Be patient and *be careful.*" His grin was crooked. "Tell Mark we'll celebrate when this is over, okay?"

She nodded, watched him talk to his officer, and then disappear down the hall. She wished they were celebrating tonight.

The following afternoon, when she hadn't heard from Charlie for more than twenty-four hours, Britt called his office. He did not call her back. When she was unable to reach him that night, she left another message. By the next afternoon she was frazzled from lack of sleep and from not knowing what Charlie was up to.

She tried to figure out why he had been out of touch, telling herself that perhaps he hadn't called because he had nothing new to report. But still, she thought, it was unlike him to keep her in suspense. As time passed, she began to feel annoyed, then angry, and eventually outraged.

265

She left Mark's hospital room and headed for the cafeteria. By now she was ready to scream, throw things, get the attention of someone who could help. A low-life piece of slime was destroying their lives. And no one was stopping him.

"*I'll* stop him," she muttered furiously, and ignored the startled glances of others in the hall. She'd found the stalker, and she would come up with a way to beat him at his own game. An idea came to her suddenly.

Turning on her heel, she headed for the exit. She had to do something before he buried them all.

24

BRITT PULLED INTO THE PARKING LOT OF A SUPERMARKET, GOT out of the Volvo, and locked it. Then she headed down the street toward the garden shop, staying close to storefronts in case she needed to beat a fast retreat.

If Charlie wouldn't tell her what was going on, she'd find out for herself. What do I have to lose? she asked herself. My life? She gave a wry laugh. That was almost a certainty anyway if someone didn't put the lunatic away for good.

As she neared the shop, she stopped to make sure her hair was still concealed under her beret and her coat collar up to hide the curve of her face. Then, with her head lowered, her walking pattern altered to short quick steps, she strode to the door and stepped inside.

No one paid any attention to her, and the stalker was nowhere in sight. As before, she browsed among the houseplants, but her eyes scanned every corner and alcove of the store. Most of the customers were in line, anticipating closing time.

Charlie must have arrested him, she thought.

Britt moved toward the attached greenhouse. She had to make sure. She was about to step through the doorway when she saw him, not ten feet away.

Again his back was turned and he didn't see her. Britt retraced her steps to the front door and left the shop. She jogged back to her car and got inside.

Britt glanced at her watch. It was a minute to five, closing time. From where she sat behind the wheel, she had a perfect view of anyone leaving the shop on foot or by car.

He was the first one to drive out of the parking lot to the street. His left turn signal blinked furiously as he waited to cross over a lane of traffic.

It figures, Britt thought, starting her car. He left on the dot of closing time because he has another job . . . stalking a little girl. She put on her sunglasses, watched as he passed, then swung out into the traffic, keeping several cars between them so he wouldn't notice the Volvo.

He took the route up the back of the West Hills and down the other side, passing the turnoff to her street. His left turn signal went on again as he approached Steward's. He drove into a parking place and she went on by, turned around at the next street, and headed back up the hill. Again she parked and waited, this time across from the store by the park where her kids played—used to play, she corrected herself.

Anger was a bitter taste in her mouth. The bastard worked close to their neighborhood, drove their road every day to and from his job, even shopped at their neighborhood store.

After a few minutes he came out with a half case of beer under his arm and got back into his van. She hung back, fearful of being seen.

Once he was on the road, she got stuck at the stop sign waiting for an opening in the line of cars coming down the hill. He had disappeared around a curve before she accelerated into the street amid honking horns and squealing brakes. She didn't look back; her one thought was to catch up, before she lost him. She wondered if Charlie had managed to put a tail on him. She hadn't noticed anyone else watching him.

He'd stopped for a red light at the bottom of the hill and she pulled in four cars behind him. She intended to follow him home, confident he wouldn't spot her in the rush-hour traffic. Her mind whirled with thoughts of how she intended to trap him. The police *had* to arrest him if they caught him in the act.

Tailing him was hectic. She had to stay far enough back to avoid being seen, then run caution lights to catch up. She followed him across the Burnside Bridge to the eastern half of the city, then north into a section of run-down houses and overgrown empty lots.

The traffic thinned, and she dropped back even farther and was glad she had when he suddenly turned into a trailer park. She pulled into an abandoned gas station to watch him from behind a billboard. He got out of the van, grabbed his beer, and went inside a trailer with sides so weathered she couldn't distinguish its color. Dirty blinds were closed over the windows.

As the engine idled, she dug in her purse for her daybook and wrote down his address and license plate number. Then she wheeled the car onto the street and headed south. Before she went back to the hospital, she wanted to check the house, now while the stalker was in his trailer.

She felt exhilarated. It was a strange twist for her to be stalking the stalker.

The exterior lights were on, and Britt drove into the garage, feeling safe for the moment. When the automatic doors closed behind her, she went into the house, disarmed the alarm system, and walked quickly through the rooms to make sure nothing had been disturbed. Upstairs, she paused at Katie's empty bedroom, fueling her resolve.

She took the shotgun and a carton of shells from the bedroom closet, picked up another change of clothes, and went downstairs. She tossed her clothes into the car and hid the gun behind a piece of plywood in the garage. Then she went back to the kitchen and picked up the phone to call Angie. About to punch in the numbers, she hesitated, remembering Charlie's warning about listening devices. She replaced the receiver.

The silence of the house pressed down on her. Already it felt unlived in . . . abandoned. It's your state of mind, Britt Hinson, she reminded herself sternly. But her apprehension grew, and when she heard a faint rustling sound from the backyard, she froze, all the terror of the past few months sweeping over her.

It's the wind, she told herself. You know where the stalker is. He couldn't be in the backyard. Stop being a scaredy-cat.

She peeked outside, taking care to stay out of sight. Her yard, illuminated by the exterior lights, looked undisturbed.

But then a thought came unbidden, and it frightened her: the yard always looked undisturbed—even when the stalker had been there. She ran to the alarm pad by the door to the garage and armed it. Her skin prickled, as if someone was watching her. The eerie sensation wouldn't go away.

Once in the car, she pushed the automatic door button and backed out quickly. She passed a patrol car as she left her street. Even knowing Charlie had kept that promise didn't ease her apprehension.

There was a pay phone at Steward's, and she pulled in and parked. Angie answered on the second ring.

Britt blurted out her plan nonstop. "Will you do it?" she ended, breathless.

"Britt, uh, I don't know if this is a wise idea. It could be dangerous." Angie was hedging. "And I don't know if you can use the theater. A traveling company has booked it—they could be there already. There will be

269

rehearsals—I don't know their schedule. I understand they have a huge truck arriving at any time with a load of sets and special lighting apparatus."

"I'll check on that part." Impatiently, Britt switched the receiver to her other ear, her glance sweeping over the woods across the street. "Will you or won't you fix up a child mannequin to look like Katie?"

"Britt, I always believed you had good sense, but this harebrained scheme of yours could get you killed!"

"It's not that dangerous." She wiped her free hand over her forehead, willing the first twinges of a headache away. "I'll have protection." She paused, thinking fast. Angie had to agree; the plan wouldn't work without her help. "And don't forget, Katie won't be in any danger. The mannequin will be there in her place. But *he'll* think it's Katie."

"How will you get the mannequin into the theater without him seeing it and knowing it's a doll?"

"I'll take it to the condo in the car trunk, right into the garage, and when I leave, it'll be sitting on the front seat with me, a Katie clone."

Britt paused, her gaze darting over the parking lot, her nervous system on full alert. "And I'll park by the back entrance of the theater—I still have a key to that door. I can sneak the doll in fast before he gets there."

"Presuming he does follow you."

"He will."

"This is crazy, Britt. How can I make you change your mind?"

"You can't, Angie. I'm desperate. I've got to stop him once and for all." Her tone lowered into a plea. "You've got to help me, Angie. You're an expert on makeup and props, and you're the only one I can trust to do this. You can make the mannequin look just like Katie. Once it's on the stage, with the lights low, he'll think it's her—and I'll nail him."

"Britt, listen to me. It won't work."

"Are you refusing to help me?"

270

"I didn't say that."

Britt drew in a deep breath, and tried another tack. "Would you do it if you knew that Charlie Simon is in on this plan?"

"You wouldn't lie about something this serious, would you, Britt?"

"Of course not," she replied at once. Her hand tightened into a white-knuckled fist on the receiver. "I, uh, didn't mention Charlie before because—uh, this operation is off the record, so to speak. You know our hands, and Charlie's, have been tied because Oregon doesn't have a stalking law."

There was a silence. Then a sigh came over the lines. "All right, Britt. As long as Charlie is in on this, I'll help in any way I can."

"I appreciate that, Angie."

"So when do you need this clone?"

"By noon tomorrow."

"Britt, I don't know if that's possible."

"Could you do your best?"

"Yeah, I guess so. Noon it is."

"I'll pick it up." Her hand relaxed on the receiver. "Thanks, Angie. After I've, uh, we've scared that creep into a confession I'll take you out to celebrate."

"It's a deal." Angie's voice lacked conviction. "Please be careful, Britt. This guy isn't stupid."

Britt hung up and ran back to her car, Angie's final warning circling her thoughts like a vulture. She wished she didn't feel so damned uneasy, but the feeling lasted all the way to the hospital and all through her evening visit with Mark. It grew even stronger as she drove to the condominium. Even though she stayed on busy streets and was met by Paul on her arrival, she could not shake the feeling that *he* was lurking just beyond her range of vision.

The next afternoon Britt drove right up to the garden shop and parked by the front door. She'd already picked up the mannequin, and it was safe in the trunk of the Volvo. Angie had done a good job on it. At a glance, it could even have fooled Britt.

After stepping out of the car, she casually took off her jacket and tossed it on the backseat. She smoothed her bright red sweater over its matching wool skirt, grabbed her shoulder bag, and then swung the car door shut. Her long hair, which she'd clipped loosely off her face, moved freely on her back as she strode into the shop. She would stand out in a crowd. A slender blonde in brilliant red was always a showstopper. She'd planned her outfit with care; she wanted to be seen.

At first she browsed to get her bearings. She didn't want to play her part only to discover that her audience wasn't present. When she saw him stacking crates at the other end of the room, she made sure that her browsing took her toward him, but not so close that she seemed obvious. She didn't even glance in his direction, careful to keep several aisles of plants between them. A perfect performance, Britt told herself, too absorbed in her role to be scared.

She knew when he saw her. Out of the corner of her eye she watched him straighten, saw his head turn in her direction. She moved away then, picked up a container holding an ivy starter, and took it to the cashier.

"I'd also like one of your nosegays—the pink roses, I think," she told the clerk, a stout woman in her fifties. Britt smiled brightly and pointed to the glass-enclosed cooler behind the clerk. "It's for my daughter."

"How nice," the woman said. "A special occasion?"

Britt noticed that the man had moved within listening distance, although he was playing it cool. He pretended to rearrange the shelves of primroses, careful to keep his face turned away from her.

That's it, you sneaky shit. Come closer so you can hear everything.

"Actually it's a dry run," Britt began as she casually opened her purse and took out her checkbook. "Our little girl has been going through a bad time lately, so her daddy and I let her do something she's had her heart set on. Only trouble is, she's terribly nervous about it, hence the flowers."

The woman was stapling film around the bouquet. "What is she doing?"

Britt leaned over the counter, pen poised over her check. "She's practicing to audition for a modeling competition."

"Oh, that sounds exciting. She must be very pretty."

"She is, but unfortunately she's also very scared. Don't get me wrong, she wants to do this." Britt gave a laugh. "Believe me, I'm not a stage mother by any means. We didn't go after this; she was approached."

"Approached?"

Britt nodded. "She was in another competition last year. It seems a scout from a New York agency saw her and was so impressed that he recently contacted us. We weren't going to let her do it, but"—Britt shrugged—"she needed something to take her mind off, uh, things, so we relented. If Katie does well, they'll offer her a contract."

Sobering, Britt injected a somber note into her voice. "Her father was in an accident. He's in the hospital, but he wants her to go on with this nevertheless. He said it would guarantee her college education if we couldn't afford—" She broke off to dab at her eyes with a Kleenex. "He almost died."

"Oh, I'm so sorry," the woman said. She quickly rang up the flowers and the ivy and told Britt the price.

Britt's story was beginning to sound corny, and she reminded herself not to overact and spoil the scene. But at least the part about the college education wasn't a complete lie.

"I'm sorry," she went on with a timid smile. "It's just that my husband's condition is serious and we're trying to make him feel better about, uh, the situation. And this competition is so important to both him and Katie."

The clerk handed her the flowers. Britt thanked her and picked up the ivy with her free hand.

"Tell your daughter good luck."

"Thanks, I will." She smiled. "We're having a little practice at City Theater this evening. I'm hoping the flowers will help her feel she really did well, so she'll be over her nervousness for the real audition this weekend."

"I hope so too, dear."

Britt managed to walk at a sedate pace all the way out to the car, even though every nerve in her body screamed for her to run. She felt his eyes even after she'd driven a mile down the road. He'd heard every word; she was sure of it.

Oh, my God! What have I done?

She straightened on the seat, told herself to get a grip. But she'd started to shake and couldn't stop. Like Scarlett O'Hara, she wouldn't think about it now.

25

BUDDY STEPPED FROM BEHIND THE TUBBED SHRUBS AT THE back of the plant store. The other man looked up, startled, then frightened. Before he could cry out, the knife flashed in a downward arc, striking him in the chest. With a yank, Buddy pulled the blade free. The man crumpled onto the soft earth, his cry fading to a long gurgling sigh. Blood gushed from the wound.

Bending over, Buddy grabbed the man's hair, jerking his head off the ground. "You betrayed me," he said, his voice thick with rage. "You tried to take her away—make her a whore."

"No—please." The man's voice was a weak plea. "I didn't do it—after I knew—you wanted her."

Buddy raised the knife again, his fury too intense to be

contained. He was about to finish what he had come to do when a scream behind him froze his hand in the air.

"Someone help!" a woman cried. "A man is being stabbed!"

Buddy let go of the man's hair, and the head flopped back down. The man's eyes closed. The sound of people approaching propelled Buddy into motion.

He wiped the blade clean on the man's clothing, then straightened and slipped the knife under his jacket. For a moment longer he stared down at the bleeding form, satisfied that the man was dying.

He kicked the body viciously, his own flesh tingling with exhilaration.

His breath came in shallow puffs as he ran from the scene.

"Britt . . . you've got to be careful. The kids—" Mark's face twisted with worry as he struggled to sit up.

Gently she pushed him back. "Shhh," she whispered. "Everything is fine. The kids are with your parents." She kissed his forehead and glanced away.

He grabbed her hand. "Britt, look at me." His voice was hoarse and lacked volume, but his fingers tightened on her hand. "You won't do anything foolish, will you?"

"What do you mean?" She played dumb. Damn, she thought. He always knew when she didn't tell him everything.

"Don't goad him, try to trick him into the open—like I did."

"I won't," she lied.

He expelled a sharp breath. "I hope not, Britt. Because it won't work . . . he's a killer . . . doesn't think like us." His voice faded. "Let Charlie handle it. You take care of yourself . . . and Katie and Sam."

"I will," she said soothingly. "Charlie knows who he is now." Her tone hardened. "He won't get away with terrorizing us for much longer."

Britt hoped her words came true. She'd arrived at the hospital to find Mark more alert—and she'd missed

Charlie again. It was obvious that he was still trying to put his case together. She wondered if he would succeed —before it was too late.

She stiffened her resolve. She couldn't weaken now, even though Mark's warning had struck a nerve. The traveling theater company would arrive soon. If she didn't go ahead with her plan tonight it would be weeks before she would have another chance.

After leaving the hospital Britt took the freeway into the city, presuming the stalker knew Katie was with her grandparents. Reaching the condominium, she punched the security code and drove into the garage. She waited fifteen minutes, the time it would have taken to go upstairs for Katie and return to the car. Then she took the mannequin out of the trunk and arranged it on the passenger seat.

No one was on the street when Britt left the garage. She headed toward home, just in case the stalker was watching their house instead of the condo.

All the way into the West Hills Britt pretended to be having a conversation with the mannequin. "What kind of a man is sexually attracted to a child? I'm going to get you, pervert. I'm going to stop your obsession . . . permanently."

It was almost dark when Britt drove into her own garage and waited again. She went into the house only to change into jeans and to make the stalker think she had a real purpose for being there.

Returning to the garage, she took the loaded shotgun from behind the plywood and placed it next to the nosegay on the floor in the backseat. She stuffed extra shells into her pockets, then got behind the wheel.

For a second she hesitated, suddenly afraid of the unknown. What if he was waiting to leap inside the garage when she opened the door? Stop imagining things, she told herself. Remember what's at stake. Taking a deep breath, she hit the automatic button, her eyes glued to the slowly rising door, then backed out fast.

THE FLOWER MAN

"Come on, you bastard," she told him, talking to the mannequin. "It's your turn to step onto center stage."

Britt drove down the winding road to the city, careful to avoid the well-lighted streets this time. Pulling into the alley behind City Theater brought back frightening images of the attack. She forced her fears aside and got out of the car. A quick glance told her no one watched. He would park down the street, she reminded herself. He was never obvious.

She had to hurry. Her handbag swung on its shoulder strap as she juggled the shotgun and nosegay in one hand and the mannequin in the other one. She ran to the stage door, the key in hand, and remembered she hadn't locked the car. There was no time to go back. He might see her. She unlocked the stage door and slipped inside the theater. Silence settled with the blackness around her.

Her fear was instant. I should have called Charlie, she thought as goose bumps rippled over her flesh. I should have told him what I was doing . . . just in case.

Britt felt along the wall for the light switch. When the light came on, her gaze went directly to the coin-operated phone on the opposite wall. She was running toward it before she'd consciously made the decision to call Charlie. Dropping her purse and keys on a chair, she propped the gun and the mannequin against the wall and rummaged for a quarter, still holding the nosegay. She doubted the stalker was in the theater yet, but he would be soon.

In seconds the phone in Charlie's office was ringing. He's probably left for the day, she thought, and was surprised when he said hello. Whispering into the mouthpiece, she quickly told him where she was and what she was doing.

"Have you lost your mind, Britt? Get out of there. Right now!"

"I intend to trap him, Charlie, before it's too late. You *have* to arrest him if he tries to kill me."

"For God's sake, Britt, you've never used a shotgun."

"Mark showed me how."

"I want you to get out of there, Britt," he repeated. *Right now.* There are some things you don't know—"

"I'm hanging up, Charlie," she interrupted. "Just get here."

"No, Britt. Wait—"

She replaced the receiver, cutting him off. But she was even more apprehensive as she picked up her props. Before stepping onstage, she peered around the curtain into the auditorium. A light shone down the center aisle from the lobby, providing enough illumination for her to see that no one was there.

After concealing the shotgun behind the curtain she crossed the stage and propped the mannequin up against a wall set. Then she switched on an overhead light in the rigging to give the stage a pale glow, enough to see the child but not enough to know the child was a doll.

Moving to the piano, Britt dropped the nosegay on the bench. A sound, like pressure on a loose floorboard, made her whirl around.

Seconds stretched away from her. The sound had come from backstage, she decided, and suppressed an impulse to run . . . while she still could. It helped to know the loaded shotgun was just an arm's length away. She sat down on the piano bench facing the wings and talked aloud to the mannequin.

"You just stand there for a minute, honey. Don't talk. Concentrate on how you want to project yourself to the audience."

She ran her hands over the piano keys, as though looking for the right note. The stalker's face was a ghostly presence, superimposed over all the good times she'd had in City Theater. Her fingers froze on the keyboard.

She remembered where she'd seen the stalker.

Here, in this very theater. Oh, my God! she thought. The stalker was Len's assistant at the modeling competition. The pungent, somewhat acrid odor she'd smelled on him was developing solution. She hadn't recognized him because he'd shaved off his beard.

"Mom! We're here!" a voice called.

Katie's voice struck her like a jolt of electricity. Britt flew off the bench and ran to the apron of the stage, her eyes on Katie, who was coming down the center aisle from the front door. Angie was behind her.

"Stop! Don't come up here!" Britt hollered.

Angie grabbed Katie's arm, pulling her up short. "Charlie Simon called and told me to pick up Katie and bring her here. He said it was urgent."

"When did he call you?"

"About an hour ago."

Britt's eyes darted around the theater. "Angie, that wasn't Charlie. I only told him I was here five minutes ago."

"But you told me that Charlie was in on your plan."

"I lied, so you'd help me."

"Then who called?" Angie's eyes widened as realization hit her. "It was *him?*"

"It must have been." Britt's skin prickled a warning. "We've got to get out of here."

"Look out, Britt!" Angie screamed.

She whirled around to see a tall man in black lunge toward her from backstage, a long-bladed knife raised to strike. She jumped backward, stumbled against the piano bench, and sat down hard.

He didn't break stride, leaping from the stage into the orchestra pit next to Katie and Angie, moving so fast that Britt only glimpsed his slitted eyes behind a ski mask. She hadn't fooled him. He'd seen through her ruse and turned the tables on her.

"Run, Katie!" Britt scrambled to her feet and went for the shotgun, pulling it out from behind the curtain. "Get out of here!"

Katie stood mesmerized by fear. Her hesitation cost vital seconds. He grabbed Katie and lunged at Angie with the knife.

"Let her go!" Angie cried. Ignoring the knife, she tried to pull Katie away from him.

"Out of my way, bitch!" His voice was high-pitched—and vaguely familiar. The knife caught the light as he stabbed at Angie, slicing her wool jacket open from shoulder to hip.

Angie screamed. Blood was a brilliant patch of red on her white blouse. She managed to throw her handbag at him before slumping to the floor.

He ducked, losing his balance as the contents of Angie's purse rained down on him. As he relaxed his grip momentarily, Katie pulled free.

"Run, Katie!" Britt shrieked. "Now! Don't stop for anything!" She stood on the apron of the stage, the shotgun aimed at the stalker. But she couldn't fire. Katie was in the way.

Propelled by panic, Katie ran up the steps and behind Britt rather than out of the theater. But at least she was clear of the stalker.

Britt braced herself and fired. She was knocked backward by the recoil.

Most of the shot missed him, but the outer circle of pellets grazed his foot. He yelped, dropped the knife, and collapsed on the floor.

"You whore!" he screamed. "You're dead!"

Britt hesitated, uncertain about firing again. If she missed and was jolted off her feet, he could be on top of her before she regained her footing. She lowered the gun.

Britt's glance darted to Angie. She'd gotten to her feet and was weaving up the aisle toward the exit. The stalker was on his knees, trying to stand. The eyes behind the mask were fixed on Britt. There was no mistaking his intent. He meant to kill her and reclaim Katie.

Grabbing Katie's hand, Britt pulled her across the stage toward the alley entrance. She held the shotgun by the stock, barrel down, so it wouldn't accidentally discharge. God, help Angie get away, she prayed silently.

The light went off suddenly, plunging them into darkness. Katie screamed, the sound echoing in the rigging high above them.

"Shhh," Britt whispered, trying to calm Katie's terror. She forced herself to think rationally. There were two switches for the light. One by the alley entrance, the other by the door that connected the auditorium to the backstage area.

Her heart thumped against her rib cage. He was between them and the back door. He'd cut them off—because he knew the layout of the building. He'd been in the theater before, she reminded herself.

Britt moved slowly to the wall. Katie's sobbing gave the stalker an edge. He knew where they were, but she had no idea where he was. When her fingers found a switch, she flipped on a light above the costume lockers.

She glanced at the alley door, thirty feet away. The stalker was standing there . . . waiting for them.

"She's mine now. You know that." His eyes glinted at Britt, and his voice rasped through the still air. He started toward them, dragging his injured foot.

Silenced by fear, Katie clung to her mother.

Britt fought panic. There was no time to aim the shotgun, and if they ran back to the stage he could retrace his route and reach the auditorium when they did. She and Katie were cornered.

Her glance darted upward.

The catwalk. They could go up. There were two ladders that provided access to the rigging, and at the highest level there was a door to the roof. She'd been up there once. Don't think about the catwalk being old and dangerous, she told herself. Once you're up there, you can shoot him if he follows.

Britt started running, yanking Katie toward the nearest ladder. She pushed her onto the wooden rungs ahead of her. Katie froze on the first rung.

"No! I'm scared. I'll fall."

"I won't let you fall," Britt said sharply. There was no time to coax her. "Get going. *Now!*"

Katie scrambled up the ladder, with Britt close behind her. When Katie missed a rung, nearly falling, Britt grabbed her, letting the shotgun slip from her grasp. It dropped to the pine floor and slid into the shadows.

By the time they made it to the narrow catwalk, he was already at the bottom of the ladder. High above the stage, Britt struggled to balance herself and Katie on the shaky walkway, which hung from ropes and cables, inching toward the place where it intersected the route to the roof.

"You can't escape," the stalker taunted, his monotone echoing in the hollow space above them. "There's no one to help you now. Angie is dead."

Britt's breath came in shallow gasps; her limbs trembled from exertion. She glanced behind her and was horrified to see that he had reached the catwalk. But for his injured foot, he would have been on top of them by now.

Stupid! Why hadn't she shot him when she had the chance? She tried to move faster, but the movement made the catwalk bounce and roll dangerously under her feet.

"Mom—"

"Don't talk, Katie. Just keep going." Britt tried sliding her feet to counteract the roll. When it helped, she told Katie to do the same. Her adrenaline—and the fact that she was in top physical shape—kept her going.

They reached the end of the catwalk that hung high above the stage. She either had to head for the back wall, where steps led to the roof, or get to the second ladder that led back down to the stage.

Was the roof door locked? Britt wondered suddenly. And if they gained the roof, was there a way off it? She glanced behind her. In the seconds she'd hesitated, he'd gained on them. She went to the right. The ladder down was her only choice.

A strange grating sound, like chalk against a blackboard, drew her glance back to him. Her heart almost stopped. He'd cut the cross-ropes holding the floor slats to the frame, dislodging a section of the catwalk between himself and them. Only the two double cables still swung across the chasm. Already he was backtracking to the ladder they'd climbed up on. He intended to approach them from the opposite direction by coming up the second ladder, so that he could trap them on the ruined walkway.

She tried to move faster. Their only chance was to beat him back to the stage, but when he dropped onto the floor she had reached only the top of the second ladder.

"You're trapped."

He was wheezing. She suddenly thought of the nebulizer that Mark had found under the rosebush. Charlie, Charlie, please get here in time! We finally have our evidence.

"Katie is mine, and you're going to die," he chanted.

"Charlie Simon will be here any second," Britt shouted back.

"Not in time to help you, cunt!"

Desperate, but unwilling to give up, Britt turned back toward the first ladder. When she reached the broken section, she kicked off her shoes.

"Katie, sweetheart, you must do exactly what I tell you, even if you're scared." She hesitated. "Do you hear me?"

Katie nodded mutely.

"I'm going to carry you. I want you to put your arms around my neck and wrap your legs around my waist. Can you do that?"

Katie swallowed, her eyes fixed on the abyss at their feet. She nodded again.

With one hand on the cable that had served as a railing, and the other arm around Katie, she hoisted her into position. Immediately Katie's arms locked around Britt's neck, and her legs circled Britt's middle.

"Hang on tight." Britt stepped onto the lower cable that had held the slat flooring. It swung under her feet like a power line in the wind. She stood motionless until it subsided.

Slowly she inched her way across the chasm, sliding her feet over the lower cable, holding the upper cable in both hands. She didn't dare look down. Her muscles went into spasms but she kept on, knowing he had almost reached the dislodged section.

We're going to make it, she chanted to herself over and over. Her feet touched the firm slats of the intact end of the catwalk just as he reached the other side. Their eyes met over the six feet of space separating them. Once again they were on opposite sides of the chasm.

"I'm coming, bitch," he snarled.

He stepped onto the cable, but his injured foot wouldn't hold his weight. He slipped, almost fell, and for seconds hung by one hand from the railing cable. While he struggled to make his way back onto the walkway, Britt set Katie on her feet and pushed her forward as fast as she dared. They had to get down the ladder and out of the theater.

Britt swung onto the ladder first so she could steady Katie above her. She kept up a steady chatter, encouraging Katie to keep going. A glance told her the stalker was backtracking to the other ladder.

Too slow, Britt thought. Still fifteen feet above the floor, she remembered the shotgun.

"Hang on, Katie," she ordered. "Don't move and don't look down. I'll come back for you."

Britt let go, hoping for the best. She scrambled down to the stage, found the shotgun, and ran to the other ladder. She pointed the barrel upward, braced herself, and fired. The first shot shattered the top ladder rungs. The reverberation was deafening.

It was as though she'd disconnected herself from the person with the shotgun. Her hands didn't shake when she took aim again. She was reacting from gut instinct, from some visceral need to protect her child. Only one thought was cemented in her brain: she had to stop him.

She emptied the gun on the scaffolding and ladder, and

284

they exploded into slivers of dry wood that hailed down onto the stage. The stalker stopped in his tracks.

The sounds reverberated off the upper walls of the theater.

"You bitch!" the stalker shouted.

Lowering the shotgun, she calmly pulled eight shotgun shells from her pockets and reloaded, working carefully so the gun wouldn't jam when she fired again. From somewhere in her mind she remembered Mark telling her about that.

She went through the process again, only this time she aimed at the section of catwalk above the ladder, blasting it to bits. Trapped like a rat in a maze, he turned and moved back toward the missing section of catwalk.

Britt loaded her last three shot shells. She was under the ruined catwalk before he could reach the missing section. Two shots brought down more floor slats and broadened the chasm. He was trapped with no way down.

There was one shot left in the chamber. Carefully, and with cool precision, she took a bead on him. At that range she couldn't miss; she realized that the greater the distance, the broader the range of the shot pellets. Her finger trembled on the trigger. She hesitated, and reason reasserted itself. The shot would blow him to pieces—in front of Katie.

There was no need to shoot him. He was the monster without a conscience, not her. He couldn't escape. She would leave him for the police.

She altered her aim and sent the last shell into the catwalk. Then, flinging the gun aside, she ran to help Katie down. They started across the stage.

"You—you whore!" the stalker shouted. "I'm going to cut off your tits. I'll make you wish you'd never been born." He shuffled along the section of catwalk that was still intact, blood dripping from his foot, until he was almost above them.

"I love you, Katie." His voice altered into a silky caress. "You belong to me." His tone intensified. "If we can't be together in this life"—he broke off, and there was a slight scraping sound—"we'll be together in the next one."

Something—a shift of air currents, the crazy cadence of his voice—drew Britt's glance upward. Her reaction was instant. She yanked Katie out of the way.

A second later he flew out of the rigging, his arms outspread like a sky diver's, to land with a sickening thud on a stack of canvas sets several feet away. Bile rose up in Britt's throat. He'd aimed to land on Katie, to kill her, too.

She and Katie ran down the center aisle to the front entrance and burst through the doors to the street. Britt kept them running, headed for the car in the alley. She saw Angie in a lighted phone booth down the street.

Thank God! she thought. Angie was alive. She was calling 911. She'd pick Angie up on the way out of there.

Britt didn't remember the car keys until she found the doors unlocked. She glanced around wildly, disoriented. Katie was already huddled down on the front seat, as though she wanted to hide. Quickly Britt explained that she had to go back for the keys, that Katie was to keep the doors locked.

"No, Mom," she pleaded. "Don't leave me."

"Shhh, honey. You're safe now. The flower man is dead. He'll never harm you again."

Before she lost her nerve, Britt ran back inside, using the alley door. The stalker was dead, she told herself. No one could survive a forty-foot fall.

She felt her way around the theater, not quite brave enough to turn on the lights. It took a couple of minutes to find her purse and keys and return to the door. Her hand was on the knob when she remembered that a light had been on backstage. She'd switched it on herself.

Her terror rushed back. She flung the door open and ran to the car. Sliding under the wheel, Britt jammed the key in the ignition. Katie was still hunched on the seat.

Britt backed to the street so fast her tires screeched on the blacktop. From out of nowhere Angie suddenly staggered in front of the Volvo's headlights. Britt's foot came down hard on the brake. The car rocked to a stop.

She unwound her window. "Get in, Angie!"

Angie stared back, dazed. Slowly she lifted a bloody hand and pointed at Katie.

Britt glanced at her daughter. The mannequin stared back.

26

SHOCK SUSPENDED REALITY. BRITT WAS UNABLE TO ACCEPT what her eyes told her. A gray mist thickened over her vision, a high-pitched buzzing sounded in her ears. Ordinary perceptions—a siren wailing somewhere in the distance, a horn honking a street away, the light spring rain—all faded. Angie's cry sounded far away.

"Britt! You can't faint. Wake up!"

Britt wiped her hair back with leaden fingers, forced her mind up through a vortex of swirling fog and needle points of light. Katie was gone. She had to find her.

The flower man was alive. He hadn't died in the fall. The canvas sets had broken his fall. *And he had Katie.*

Angie steadied herself against the car. Her jacket was in tatters, and she was covered with blood. But her eyes glowed with feverish determination.

"Angie," Britt managed weakly, "you're badly hurt. You're—"

Angie shook her head. "I'm shaky . . . dizzy . . . but I'll be okay." She hesitated. "He came out of the theater right after you and Katie, saw you go back in, and went back himself. When he came out with the mannequin, I thought he'd . . . killed you, Britt."

"Was he still wearing a mask?"

"I was too far away to see, and the alley was dark. I

tried to get to her, but I couldn't move fast enough . . . couldn't even make her hear me. Katie went with him, Britt, like she trusted him. Then Charlie got here."

"Charlie—where is he?" Britt hardly had wind to speak.

A movement farther down the street drew her eyes away from Angie. A huge truck stood at the curb, the back doors flung wide open. Long double ramps ran from the truck bed to the street. The visiting theater company had arrived.

Then she saw the black van parked a few car lengths behind the truck—and Charlie's car blocking it. Two men struggled in the street beside it, then one of them fell and lay still. The other man took off running, headed for the cab of the truck. He turned briefly toward her headlights.

She recognized him. She knew who he was. *The flower man wasn't Bobby Lee.*

Angie's eyes followed her glance. "That's him," she cried. "Oh, my God! It can't be!"

"Get out of the way, Angie!"

Britt revved the engine, and the Volvo shot forward with a squeal of spinning tires. The stalker had backed his van out of the truck. He'd intended to leave the truck and drive away with Katie, but Charlie's car had blocked the van and ruined his plan.

"Get help for Charlie!" Britt shouted at Angie.

As the Volvo sped along the shiny street, her realization hammered at her brain. How could they have been so thoroughly fooled? Why hadn't they known it was him all the time? No wonder Katie had gone willingly. Katie had trusted him—just as she and Mark had.

The sick bastard! She'd die before letting him take Katie.

He heard her coming, whirled around, and tried to kick the long double ramps away from the truck. Not clamped down, they jumped but didn't fall to the ground. He gave up, ran to the cab, and climbed in. He'd started the engine and was letting out the clutch when the Volvo's wheels caught the split-board ramp and hurtled up the narrow boards toward the bed of the truck.

Britt braced herself, eyes narrowed, jaw set. There had been no time to consider if her tires were properly spaced, or if the ramp would hold. She could crash into the back of the truck. But that would stop him, she told herself grimly.

The front wheels hit the truck bed, and the car high-centered as it bounced into the empty storage area. Metal scraped metal in a thunderous sound that reverberated in the confined space. The pan, the driveshaft, the exhaust system—everything under the car sounded as if it had been destroyed by the grinding contact that slowed her speed.

Once the back wheels cleared the lip of the ramp she slammed on the brakes, but there wasn't enough space to stop. The bumper and grille crashed into the back wall. The headlights shattered in a shower of flying glass that spilled like buckshot onto the hood. The last thing she remembered was switching off the ignition and hearing the back doors of the truck slam shut behind her.

Britt opened her eyes to absolute blackness. For a moment she was disoriented. Where was she? How long had she been out? Gingerly she touched her forehead, feeling the lump where she'd hit the windshield. Realization filled her with dread. The stalker—their friend— had Katie.

She grabbed the handle and pushed open the car door. The dome light came on, illuminating her surroundings. She was still trapped inside the truck, which wasn't moving.

He would come for her and she'd have to defend herself. "Don't panic—don't panic," she chanted, reaching for the four-cell flashlight in the glove box, the only weapon available. Slipping out of the car, she closed the door and the dome light flickered out. Blackness settled around her. She felt her way around the car to the side wall of the truck. She squeezed down into the narrow space to wait.

The sound of the bar being lifted from the truck doors startled her. She hadn't heard him get out of the truck. He must have gotten out while she was unconscious.

Britt crouched lower as the doors clanked open and a flashlight beam flickered over the Volvo. She heard his rapid breathing, sensed his eyes probing the shadows. If he moved in her direction she'd be cornered. She gripped the flashlight in her right hand, ready to defend herself.

When he climbed into one side of the truck she sprang forward and jumped out the other side to land on a wooden floor. Surprised, she hesitated, her glance darting everywhere. He'd driven into a warehouse of some sort. Oh, God! She'd escaped from the truck only to find herself in a larger black box.

A light shone through an open doorway from a room at the back of the building. She started running, thinking that he must have taken Katie into that room. Then she heard him behind her.

"Britt! Britt, it's okay! It's me—Charlie!"

Britt burst through the doorway and came to a skidding stop in what must have once been an office. It was empty. She whirled around to face Charlie, who now stood in the doorway. His trousers and jacket were streaked with dirt, his lip was bleeding, and a huge bruise had darkened his right cheek.

"What happened to you?" she asked breathless.

"I tangled with the flower man." He gulped in air. "You don't know how glad I am to know you're okay, Britt."

She licked dry lips, desperate for answers. "Where is he?"

"The creep's out back, unconscious. He tried to climb the bridge to get away, but he fell. I've radioed for an ambulance—and for more manpower."

"How did you get here, Charlie? I thought you were hurt."

"I was just stunned." He shook his head as if to clear it. "After you drove into the van I managed to follow, but the truck had a good head start and I lost it on the way to the Steel Street Bridge. Then I got lucky and spotted it pulling into this warehouse. But I was still on the bridge and it took me ten minutes to get off it and circle back to this building."

"Where's Katie?"

"I don't know, Britt. I'd hoped she was with you in the truck."

"I was knocked out, Charlie. I came to just minutes before you found me." Fear clawed at her stomach. "Katie has to be here, if he only arrived ten minutes ahead of you. He must have hidden her somewhere in this building."

"Unless he dropped her off someplace near here. Do you remember the truck stopping?"

"I don't remember anything until I woke up." Her voice sounded shrill. "Didn't you ask him where he took her?"

His own frustration was apparent. "He fell before I could reach him."

"I'll make him tell me!" She started past him, but he grabbed her arm. "It's no use, Britt. We have to wait for the medics to revive him."

She jerked away and ran back into the warehouse. She had to do something—now! The sound of approaching sirens, of Charlie running to meet the police, hardly registered. The vision of Katie being trapped in a dark place overpowered everything else, taking her breath away.

Her eyes fell on a wooden staircase set against the back wall. Her hope soared. Katie could be up there.

Her foot was on the first step when she hesitated. Goose bumps rippled over her skin. An image of Katie, hurt like the Barbie dolls, surfaced in her mind. She could almost hear her child calling for her, screaming for help.

With a burst of energy, Britt rushed up the steps into

the murky darkness. At the top she paused, feeling the wall until she found a light switch. Two dusty bulbs hanging on long cords from the open rafters came on, illuminating the whole upper floor.

The second floor was one big room. Cobwebs dangled in the dead air, like frayed gray threads. There was no furniture, no sign that anyone had occupied the place in a long time.

Katie wasn't there.

Britt circled the room like a wild animal, sniffing the air, scratching the grooves between the wall boards for a possible opening, a place where someone could hide a child. There was nothing.

Running again, she stumbled down the steps, trying to keep ahead of her rising hysteria. At the bottom she turned on more lights, then went from wall to wall, corner to corner, hoping to find another door. Was there a basement? She saw no sign of one.

She'd searched everywhere. There wasn't a place left to look. Her eyes circled the cavernous room again, slid over the truck, then back. *The truck cab*—she hadn't looked there.

The passenger door was ajar, and a quick yank jerked it wide open. The leather seat was cracked and peeling . . . and empty.

She fell on all fours, pounding the floor with her fists, each blow sending puffs of dust into her face. Her sobs were dry-retching, wild sounds. She didn't know where else to look.

Him! She would make the stalker tell her . . . make him wake up.

She got to her feet and burst through the front doors of the warehouse just as Charlie was coming toward them, two uniformed policemen behind him. She flung herself into his arms and broke down, crying against his leather jacket.

"I . . . I can't find . . . Katie." Her words were almost indistinguishable.

"We'll find her," he replied grimly, and motioned for

the officers to search the place. More patrol cars, sirens screaming and lights flashing, pulled up in a squeal of rubber on blacktop. "Wait in my car while I take the officers out back," Charlie told her firmly. "I'll be right with you."

Britt nodded mutely and slumped onto the front seat of his car. She wanted to go with the police but her legs felt like Jell-O. She dropped her face into her hands and willed a bout of dizziness to pass.

"He's still out cold," Charlie said when he returned and leaned on the open car door. "The medics should be here any minute."

She lifted her head and focused her eyes on Charlie's battered face. "Were you surprised that the flower man wasn't Bobby Lee?"

He shook his head. "I'd discovered who the guy really was shortly before you called from the theater."

"How?"

"I went to the nursery to take Bobby Lee into custody. I got there just as he was being taken away in an ambulance. He'd been stabbed—by the real flower man, a guy I'd begun to suspect wasn't who he said he was."

"Len Holmes." Her whispered words reflected the shock and disbelief that still circled her reality.

"Yeah. Mark's football buddy. Your friend."

Britt swallowed hard. "He wasn't anyone's friend. Len even tried to kill Angie—and Angie and Bill were the first ones to befriend him when he moved to Portland several years ago."

"Yeah, he fooled all of us," Charlie said. "Fortunately, Bobby Lee talked before he died. I went to Holmes's place to arrest him, but he wasn't there. I left the guys from the crime lab in his trailer to do their work while I went down to Homicide to run my information through the computers. That's when you called." His gaze intensified. "You can imagine my shock when I found out what you'd done."

She looked down, torn by guilt. "I really believed it was Bobby Lee . . . that I was in control . . . could stop him once and for all." Her body shuddered on a deep breath. "Instead I gave him Katie."

Charlie shuffled his feet, giving her a minute. "Did you know that Len Holmes and Bobby Lee live in the same trailer park?"

She shook her head.

"The two of them met a couple of years ago, in a court-ordered program for sexual deviates up in Washington State. Holmes was there for pedophilia, Lee for serial rape."

"They're ex-convicts?" Her voice squeaked with shock.

"That's right, on probation. Both are dangerous sexual predators."

"Why are they free? In the name of God, why would they be released?"

"Ask the judge." His tone reflected frustration with the judicial system. "I haven't been sitting on my thumbs for the past few days, Britt. But I should have kept you informed. If I had, this wouldn't have happened." He hesitated. "I didn't want to call you at the condo because of the kids hearing, and I kept thinking I'd run into you at the hospital. I'm sorry."

She hung her head. Hearing that he too felt guilty didn't help.

"It took time to get the evidence together." He thumped the car roof with the palm of his hand. "I thought I'd go nuts before I got the results from the state crime lab—once they finally pulled Mark's Honda out of the Columbia." He stepped back to lean on the open door again. "Then the paint wasn't a match to Bobby Lee's van—or to the vans belonging to Milt Graber or Pinecrest."

"Because neither of them was the stalker," she said.

"Yeah, that was when I realized I might be concentrating on the wrong man. I'd had my sights on Bobby Lee. Then, because of his association with Len Holmes, who also owns a black van, and because of their earlier connection with Jay Fisher, I shifted my focus to Holmes." He grinned wryly. "Even though he was a friend of the family. But I was about a day late. You already had your own plan in place."

"Mark and I never saw Len's black van."

"You wouldn't have. It was part of his secret life."

"Why didn't the police find all this out when Jay Fisher was arrested?"

"Holmes and Lee checked out clean—because their names, birth dates, and Social Security numbers were fake. They'd gone back in the records of children who'd died and used their identities. Once they had the birth certificates of the dead children, little boys who would have been about their age now, they were able to get a Social Security number, a driver's license with their own photo, and other documents in each of those names."

A vision of Katie flashed before her eyes. She'd been at the mercy of Len Holmes, a man who'd been in their own home, a friend who'd professed concern. A convicted pedophile. He'd even been there when Bill saw someone in their backyard—Bobby Lee. Len had planned that to fool them all.

Britt glanced at the building. The first two officers were still inside, searching. She forced her panic back, for the moment.

"How do you know all this?"

"Holmes had a drawer full of fake I.D. in his trailer." He hesitated. "His probation papers were also there—with the correct information. Once I had his real name and numbers, the police computers did the rest. Trouble is, it all takes time . . . and patience."

"Which I didn't have," she said faintly, and wondered if Charlie was trying to keep her mind occupied with Len's background until the property search was completed.

"Holmes hired Lee to monitor your phone when he couldn't," he went on. "We found a high-tech listening device in Len's van at the theater. And Holmes got his flowers at Lee's garden shop, except the forget-me-nots, which he picked himself. Bobby Lee confessed to assaulting you, said it turned him on to watch you."

"It's so sick."

"Bobby Lee said Holmes went crazy when he heard about his attack on you, threatened to kill him for interfering with his plan. Holmes feared Bobby being arrested would lead back to him. Which it did. He probably planned to kill him anyway, but when you discovered Bobby, he moved in quick." He paused. "And there was another reason he went after Bobby."

She waited, dazed by it all.

His eyes wavered again. "He'd found out that Bobby Lee had been hired by Jay Fisher to kidnap Katie last fall."

"You mean they were both stalking Katie—for different reasons?"

He nodded. "Only at first. In a crazy way Len's obsession with Katie probably saved her from Fisher. When Bobby Lee realized what Len was up to, he backed off, terrified that Len would find out. In a manner typical of these sociopathic perverts who have no loyalty to anyone, Bobby Lee strung Jay Fisher along for the money, and still helped Len when he asked, because he was afraid not to. Fisher's arrest scared both Len and Bobby Lee. That's why the stalking stopped—until things cooled off. Neither wanted to go back to prison."

"And that's why we thought the stalker was gone. But he really wasn't. He was in our lives, pretending to be our friend." She paused. "Why didn't Katie recognize him, Charlie? He gave her forget-me-nots in person that first time, and she saw him on other occasions."

"We found disguises—beards, mustaches, wigs, contact lenses—in his trailer."

"He even offered to come over with his night-vision goggles again, but Mark refused." Her voice broke. "That was the day he tried to kill Mark."

"If Mark had agreed and he'd come over . . ." Charlie shrugged.

"He planned to kill us then."

"It's a good possibility."

In the distance she heard the ambulance siren. She climbed out of the car, too upset to sit. Len Holmes was a monster behind his mask of niceness. And he'd fooled everyone.

"Hey, Detective Simon," the patrolman called from the car behind them. "The dispatcher says this building belongs to Jay Fisher. It's where he made his porno flicks. The truck is also registered in his name."

"No shit!"

Before Charlie could say anything more, the ambulance pulled up in the street, and two uniformed medics jumped out. Charlie pointed the way to Len, and they took off around the building. They came back a few minutes later with Len on the stretcher. Before they could place him in the ambulance Britt rushed forward.

"Wait!" she cried. "I need to talk to him."

Charlie restrained her when she would have taken hold of Len's shoulders to shake him. "They need to get him to the hospital. He's pretty broken up, inside and out."

"But his eyes are open! Maybe he can talk!"

"I . . . won," he whispered, his lips twisting into a grimace. "I was on to you, Britt—from the beginning."

"Where's Katie?" she demanded.

"I followed you following Bobby. I knew all about your silly mannequin game," he said, ignoring her question. "When you called Angie, I listened in on my pencil microphone from across the street."

"And you called Angie pretending to be Charlie, told her to bring Katie to the theater," Britt said.

"I even brought the big truck . . ." His voice faltered. "My own prop, Britt. It almost . . . worked."

"Tell me where you've taken Katie!"

"I won," he said again. "Katie and I will be together . . . soon." His lashes closed and he was still.

As the significance of his words sank in, Britt lunged toward the stretcher. Charlie's hold on her tightened, restraining her. Somehow she managed to keep her screams in her throat, but she couldn't stop the tremors tearing through her.

Mutely she watched the medics load him into the ambulance. In seconds it started down the street, the red bubble lights flashing over the dingy waterfront. Then it was gone, leaving her alone with Charlie and the other police officers, who'd come out of the warehouse . . . without Katie.

"Get back in the car, Britt. I'll have the men turn out the lights and lock up here," Charlie told her. His voice sounded far away.

Britt shook her head back and forth, trying to focus her thoughts. "Lock up? I'm not leaving—not until I've found Katie."

"Britt, she's not here." He spoke softly, as a father would speak to a terrified child. "The men have scoured every inch of this place."

"She has to be here." Britt backed away from him. "I'm not giving up, Charlie. We've missed something. *I know it.*"

Her glance darted over the red brick building, a turn-of-the-century firehouse that had been converted into a warehouse, she'd overheard one of the officers say. It was perfectly square but for a huge chimney on one side.

"Britt—"

"Charlie, Len Holmes was already injured when he got here. He could hardly walk." She waved her arms wildly. "He couldn't have taken her far."

"I've authorized an immediate door-to-door canvass of the area."

"My child might be dying," she cried. "I have to find her now!"

When he moved to take her arm again, she darted back into the warehouse, her glance flickering to the open doorway of the small room.

"Action cures fear." She chanted her mother's saying over and over. Somehow it helped. She heard Charlie

behind her as she ran into the office. Good, she told herself. She had work for him and the officers. She was down on all fours examining the floorboards when he reached the room.

"This is crazy, Britt. Let me take you home so you—"

She looked up at him from behind tangles of hair. "I told you, I'm not leaving here without my child!" She crawled around the edge of the room, through the dust and spiderwebs.

After a minute she glanced at him. He stared back, as if he thought she'd lost her mind. Well, maybe I have, she thought. And if Katie isn't found, I'll never be normal again.

"You heard what the dispatcher said. Jay Fisher made his child pornography flicks here," she said. "I think someone like that would have a secret place to hide the children if the place was raided."

"The crime lab guys went over this place with a microscope after Fisher was arrested. Don't you think they would have found it?"

"I don't assume anything. Not anymore." She looked up at him. "Are you going to help me?"

He sucked air. "To do what, Britt?"

"I want the boards taken off the walls and floor, even the ceiling." She stood facing him. "We'll need more help, and some tools—a crowbar and hammer."

He clapped a hand over his forehead. "I know how you feel—what you've been through, but—"

"Charlie, please, either help me or get the hell out of here!"

"Okay. I'll make a deal with you." His voice was a blend of annoyance and concern. "I'll have this room taken apart. But that's all. If we come up with nothing, then you leave."

"No promises." She turned her back on him and started searching again.

After he went outside, she pried a loose nail out of the

windowsill and used it to scratch between the boards. If there was a secret room, she meant to find it.

After a while she sat back against the wall, exhausted, her legs splayed out in front of her. Where was Charlie? Had he left, after all?

Please God, help me find my precious child, she prayed. Don't let that evil person win.

Britt knew she was irrational, unhinged by the endless images in her mind, all too terrible to endure.

Closing her eyes didn't help. The old two-story firehouse superimposed itself over every thought in her mind. It was like a child's drawing of a house—straight walls, a window, and a front door.

Her eyes popped open. One side of the building's exterior wasn't straight. There was a big chimney on that wall. *But there was no furnace or fireplace.*

She scrambled to her knees. That chimney was on the outside of the office wall, beside the window. Why was the window boarded up? Crawling toward the corner, she ran her fingers over the beveled baseboard, probing it with the point of the nail. It moved. The reality of what that could mean jolted her with a burst of energy. She jumped to her feet.

"Charlie!" she screamed. She ran to the doorway, almost colliding with him as he came toward her, several patrolmen right behind him, carrying hammers and crowbars.

"The baseboard—it's loose!" she cried.

Charlie went to where she pointed, going down on his knees to test it himself.

In short bursts of words, Britt explained about the jog in the outside wall. Then Charlie pulled a piece of baseboard free from the wall.

"It wasn't nailed down, only fitted into the corner to look as if it was," he said, catching her excitement. The other officers moved to help, soon prying up a two-foot square of flooring to expose an iron ring on a trapdoor.

"Son of a bitch!" Charlie muttered.

"I was right." Britt dropped to her knees next to the men as they swung the trap open.

"There's a concrete block under it," Charlie said.

"But that has an iron ring, too!" Britt cried. "Pull it up!"

Charlie already had hold of it and was slowly lifting the slab. "It's not as heavy as it looks," he said. "Only an inch thick."

They stared into what appeared to be a black concrete well. A ladder clung to one side. The air smelled of sour earth and decayed vegetation, so putrid that Britt gagged.

"I'm going down," Charlie said tersely. He fished in his pocket for his penlight, thumbed it on, and aimed the beam downward. "Looks maybe ten feet deep." He lowered himself through the opening onto the top rung.

Britt pushed her way in front of the other men. "I'm going with you."

"No, Britt. Wait here." He hesitated. "We don't know what's down there."

Their eyes locked, neither giving ground.

"My daughter is down there. I'm coming." Her voice caught. He was trying to protect her in case—*No!* She fought back a floating sensation. Katie was alive. She was waiting for her at the bottom of the ladder.

Charlie gave a short nod, as though he knew it was hopeless to argue with her. He started down. She was right behind him, pacing herself to his descent. The concrete sides of the well were slimy, and the rungs were cold and dirty under her hands. She instructed herself to stay focused. Think one rung at a time, she told herself. Don't lose it now.

"Wait." The word was a hollow sound below her. "I'm at the bottom, and there's not enough room for both of us. Wait a minute." He hesitated and she saw his light flickering around him. "There's another door."

She heard him push it inward. A faint glow of light shot into the well. When he stepped through the doorway, she scrambled down the remaining rungs, pausing at the opening which was no more than four feet high. Bending, she stepped into a room surrounded by crumbling brick walls.

"I'll be damned." Charlie expelled his breath in a rush. "This is the bottom of that jog in the building. It's wired for electricity and plumbed to generate fresh air." He shook his head in disbelief. "They used to hang the fire hoses here to dry when this was a firehouse."

Horror hit her like a physical blow as the penlight beam swept over the shadowy ten-foot chamber. Katie's stolen pink curtains hung over a window that had been painted on the bricks, and her furniture, teddy bears, dolls, and books were placed exactly as they had been in her bedroom. Even the carpet over the brick floor matched the carpet in Katie's room.

"How did he get it all down here?" she whispered, her words flat in the dead space.

"He must have taken the furniture apart and put it back together."

Her eyes were drawn to the little night-light by the bed. A small figure swathed in blankets, its head covered, lay motionless on the spread.

"Oh, my God!"

Britt's knees nearly buckled. She crumpled to the floor. *They were too late.*

Charlie saw the child at the same moment. He moved quickly to the bed, his body deliberately blocking Britt's view as he pulled back the blankets.

"No! Please—no!"

Britt stretched out her hands in supplication, trying to hold back the truth. Great racking sobs tore through her body. Her beautiful little Katie had died alone in this hole. Her reality receded into a vortex of black swirling mist.

At first Britt thought she was hallucinating, hearing

302

voices. *Katie's voice.* She lifted her head. Charlie was calling to her.

Unable to stand, she managed to crawl to the bed. She forced herself to look. Katie was swaddled and pinned to the bed like a mummy. Charlie quickly freed her, pulling the gag from her mouth so that it hung beneath her chin. Large blue eyes found Britt's.

"Mom!" Katie whispered faintly, fresh tears washing over the dried salt lines on her face. "I knew you'd find me, Mom. I knew he hadn't killed you . . . like he told me. I love you, Mom. I want to go home."

Britt's throat constricted. She couldn't speak. She wrapped her child in her arms and they cried together.

Thank you, God, for giving her back to me.

"He didn't have a chance to touch her," Charlie whispered near her ear. "She's been here the whole time."

There was only one thought in Britt's mind: Katie was safe. Her family was safe.

They went home to what had once been Britt's dream house. It wasn't any longer. It never would be again.

Angie spent three days in the hospital. She was lucky. Aside from losing a lot of blood, her wounds hadn't been serious. Katie returned to school a week later, but Britt drove her back and forth in their new Honda. Both the old Honda and the Volvo had been totaled.

Charlie kept her informed about Len Holmes, who clung to life in the hospital. After it was all over, Charlie told her the whole story. Len had never known a father. His mother had abused him, ridiculed him, and flaunted her endless stream of men in his face. At thirteen he'd been suspected of killing his younger sister, and at fourteen he was convicted of murdering his mother. He'd been institutionalized until he was twenty-five.

After he was arrested a few years later for abducting and molesting another little girl, the judge had ordered him into a therapy program for sexual deviates. Upon completion, he'd been released on probation. He'd used his Len Holmes alias to live in Portland and his real name to maintain a residence in Washington, where he reported to his parole officer.

"If he lives, he'll spend the rest of his life in prison," Charlie assured her. "Our case is solid, from probable cause to physical evidence. We've matched the paint on his van to that of the Honda. We've got all the people he tried to hurt, the poison he used on Max, even the nebulizer Mark found in your yard. And a murder charge for killing Bobby Lee."

Within days of finding Katie, the police reopened the Jay Fisher case. The concrete room brought back an earlier suspicion that he'd been producing snuff flicks, underground movies depicting sexual exploitation and murder of children. They suspected that Len had been the cinematographer and that Bobby Lee had assisted.

Mark was released from the hospital, and the next day Len Holmes died without regaining consciousness. The day after that Mark and Britt put the house on the market and started making plans to move out to Lake Oswego, to a new school, new neighbors, a new life.

Once Britt had valued all of life. Once she had been opposed to the death penalty. She no longer was. People like Len Holmes didn't have a conscience, did not care that their obsessive lust would destroy another human being. As long as the manipulative psychopath lived, the pedophile who stalked an innocent child, he would destroy everything in his path to attain what he believed he deserved.

Death had stopped Len Holmes. But he had taken away her family's innocence, their belief that one person could not terrorize another and get away with it. And he'd stolen Britt's integrity. She would never forget that she had taken the law into her own hands, that she would have killed to save her child.

Britt was glad that Len Holmes had died, and relieved

that his blood wasn't on her hands. Nevertheless, the residue of his evil presence would linger for a long time, perhaps forever.

Because there had been no law to stop him.

On July 27, 1993, the Oregon House passed Senate Bill 833, voting 59–0 to establish an anti-stalking law. On August 12, 1993, Governor Barbara Roberts signed it into law. The new law took effect on September 1, 1993.

Printed in the United States
By Bookmasters